HARNESS THE STORM

HARNESS THE STORM

Sharon Lee Villone

This is a work of fiction. Names, characters, and incidents are the product of the author's imagination, except in the case of certain historical events and locales, which are used fictitiously.

HARNESS THE STORM

DEDICATION

To Samantha and Nicholas. You are my pride and joy,
my heart and soul, and my
greatest source of inspiration.

ACKNOWLEDGMENTS

I would like to thank my children, Samantha and Nicholas, for always believing in me. Your unwavering love and support kept me motivated throughout the years of writing this book. Thank you to my sister, Cheryl, for taking my calls no matter what time of day or night, for always listening and for showing such enthusiasm for this project. A special thanks to my mom, Della, whose subtle strength and unconditional love built an indestructible foundation for which to stand. You've shown me that small shoulders can indeed carry heavy weights. Thank you for your patience, for being my biggest cheerleader and for always reminding me to "Finish the book!" Most of all, I want to thank God for his bountiful blessings.

Proverbs 3:5-6 (NKJV)
Trust in the Lord with all your heart,
And lean not on your own understanding;
In all your ways acknowledge Him,
And He shall direct your paths.

EPIGRAPH

There will be storms, child
There will be storms
And with each tempest
You will seem to stand alone
Against cruel winds
But with time, the rage and fury
Shall subside
And when the sky clears
You will find yourself
Clinging to someone
You would have never known
But for storms

~Margie DeMerrell, "Storms"

PREFACE

It wasn't my mother's fault entirely. The noise alone in that goddamned city was enough to drive anyone mad. Bethlehem, Pennsylvania, my hometown, founded by the Moravians in 1741 and once home to the second-largest steel producing plants in the country. For many who lived there, it represented the heart of America, a melting pot of hardworking immigrants who came together to build a strong, flourishing community. And for the most part, they did. But there were secrets in that town that hovered beneath the relentless crashing and thundering of the steel, dirty secrets that should have brought the town to its knees long before the demise of the plant. Perhaps that's why ghosts still haunt the city to this day, refusing to leave.

Perhaps they know, as I do, the shameful secrets that dwell there.

I've carried those secrets with me for too long...far too long.

1

It's my turn.

All eyes rest on me as I look up from the shredded tissue scattered across my lap.

It's my turn to tell the others in the room about myself.

I hesitate.

Clear my throat.

Swallow hard.

And begin…

> "My name is Danielle Hoffman Pane.
> I was born here, in the small industrial town of Bethlehem, Pennsylvania.
> Not far from the old steel plant.

I never had a father.
And my mother went crazy.
Oh…
one more thing…

I'm a murderer."

2

There is a breeze now, here, in the midst of the woods, a gentle breeze. Suddenly I feel it. I don't think it was here a moment ago when it happened. There was a stillness then, eerie and deliberate. Everything was still then, especially her. But now, as I kneel over her limp, bloodied body, I feel the air brushing over me, painfully forcing the hairs standing up on the surface of my skin in the opposite direction. I cross my arms and pull them close to my chest to protect myself from the irritating shift in the air. It's getting colder as the sun sets in the distance. The last fiery rays of daylight dart through the trees, stabbing my corneas, leaving me temporarily blinded, and yet I can't help but feel a certain amount of delight in the momentary reprieve from the horrific sight that lay before me. The branches sway as the breeze transforms into a gusty, biting wind that tosses about leaves and twigs, firing particles of dirt and debris at my flesh. Up above the trees, the sky has deepened to a darker shade of blue as the fierce wind violently flings my hair from side to side, incessantly slapping and stinging my face.

A storm is coming.

Even the geese know it, as they squawk overhead, making their way in the opposite direction of the ominous clouds.

Everything is moving.

Everything but her.

She's still.

So goddamned still, it's pathetic.

She could have at least put up more of a fight, but fear can be paralyzing I guess...like betrayal.

Paralyzing.

The storm looms and rumbles in the distance like a lion waiting to pounce, and the air is growing colder by the minute. Night is almost here, and I manage to feel comforted by the impending darkness.

I am still now, just like her.

Drops of rain hit the leaves above me and trickle down, wetting me and diluting her bloodstained skirt from a crimson red to a vile, putrid pink. As the wind grows more intense, I can barely hear the cars passing along the interstate, not far away. The traffic has lessened with the coming of the night. How bothersome, that the occasional glare of headlights cuts through the trees and casts light on such a gruesome reality. I should get up and head out to the highway, thumb a ride with a big truck heading out of town, and simply disappear like the sun into the horizon. Once again, headlights slice through the trees, hitting me dead in the eye and blinding me. I close my eyes, run my tongue across my lips, and taste the rain that pours down my face, drenching and soaking me through and through. I open my eyes and lift my hand to shield them from the intensity of the piercing brightness that is moving about in the trees.

Side to side.

Up and down.

My heart is beating, and I am suddenly completely and totally aware of myself, like waking from a dream. The light is getting brighter and closer. I close my eyes, hoping to feel numb again, unaware and unaffected.

The storm is upon me.

The pounding and crashing of Mother Nature is all around, and yet in the midst of such a splendid storm, I hear something that seems even louder and more deafening than any noise nature could create. It's very distinct: the sound of leaves crunching beneath footsteps. I bow my head and rest my face in my hands as the noise grows louder and the light comes closer, narrowing in on the two of us. Bathed in the radiant light that has brightened the night into day, I part my fingers and peek through, resting my eyes upon her beautiful face one more time. Only now, as the rain washes her clean, do I see the faint scar that she meticulously hid so well, extending from the center of her top lip to the bottom of her nose. As I reach down and gently trace the scar with my finger, I am reminded of the cross that weighed so heavily upon her shoulders, burdening her with such anguish and despair, which ultimately sealed her fate.

And with the revolting taste of bile in my mouth…I say her name.

Before the vomit erupts from my gut…I say her name.

Over and over again, as I am helped to my feet by the officer holding the flashlight…

I say her name.

Hindsight is twenty-twenty.

That couldn't be truer or more fucking unfortunate. But looking back I knew something wasn't right. I could feel it in the relentless, irritating voices that echoed in the hollows of my brain. They were there—the demons, I mean—lurking and lingering in the depths of my soul, calling out my name.

Warning me.

Cautioning me.

Flagging me down as I raced passed at record speed. They begged me to stop and listen, and they dared me to grow some balls. If I had stopped, just for a moment, to catch my breath and listen, really listen, maybe this wouldn't have happened. Maybe I wouldn't be sitting here in this goddamned hospital waiting room with bloodstained hands trembling uncontrollably while she fights for her life.

Maybe.

Just maybe.

"Mrs. Pane? Excuse me, are you Mrs. Danielle Pane?"

A man stands in front of me. His pants are a deep navy blue, ironed and creased to perfection. His shoes have been buffed to a mirrorlike glow. He smells freshly showered, and I wonder, just for a moment, what his life is like. I wonder if he is happy and if he has made wise decisions and been fortunate enough to live a life without regrets. I peer down at his shoes and catch the reflection of a haggard woman I don't recognize. She is staring at me, hard, with long, stringy hair that drapes down the sides of her face. Her eyes are deeply troubled, and she looks tired as though she hasn't slept in a very long time.

"Mrs. Pane, I'm Officer Cooper."

A masculine hand reaches out and rests on my forearm. His fingers are long and slender. He wears a simple gold band on his wedding finger, and I wonder if he is a good man, if he tells his wife he loves her, and more importantly if he means it. I wonder if his wife has blessed him with children, and if so, how many…and if the sound of their innocent laughter echoing through the house brings them much happiness.

"Mrs. Pane, I need to speak with you for a moment."

He speaks in a quiet manner with a voice that is gentle and kind.

"I won't take but a moment of your time, I need to ask you a few questions."

I sit still, unable to respond to his simple request. I don't know how long I've been sitting here, but I am suddenly aware that my neck hurts from the weight of my hanging head. My elbows press deep into the soft spot above my knees, causing a tingly, numbing sensation in my legs, and my hands, tightly clasped in front of me, look foreign, almost unrecognizable. They won't stop shaking, and the blood that seeped into the pores and crevices has dried crusty and stiff. The color has changed from bright red to a foul shade of brown. The sight of it makes my stomach uneasy and causes my jaw to tighten and constrict in response to the burning substance that has shot up into my mouth.

"Mrs. Pane, do you hear me?"

My head is pounding, throbbing with every beat of my heart that reverberates in my ears. I want to stand up and scream at the top of my lungs: *Of course, I fucking hear you! You're standing right in front of me!*

But I can't. Doesn't he know that I can't say a word? My thoughts, filled with years of regret, have welled up in my throat, filling it completely, choking and suffocating me until I can hardly breathe. My body aches from incessant shaking and convulsing. I am cold, and a chill has taken over, causing every muscle to painfully contract, almost in a rhythmical pattern. My jaw hurts, and I am grateful for the thunderous sound of my teeth clattering against one another, silencing the deafening voices of the demon that is very much present—no longer lurking but blatantly revealing itself.

"Mrs. Pane? I know this is difficult. Please, I promise to make it short."

I slowly lift my head and focus my weary eyes upon the gentleman for the first time. He is a handsome man, probably around my age, with kind blue eyes and neatly groomed brown hair that is graying at the temples. The lines around his eyes and mouth gently mark the joyous times in his life, and the furrow between his brows is an obvious reminder of the bad. He lowers himself and kneels before me with a pad and pencil in his hand.

"Can I get you anything? Perhaps a glass of water or a cup of coffee?"

I look into his eyes and wonder if he is a good, caring man, as he appears to be, or if he is just eager to get the job done so he can hop in his car and head to the nearest doughnut shop to have a good laugh with all of his buddies about the mute bitch at the hospital. I want to grab him by his neatly starched shirt, pull him close, and look him dead in the eye: *Fuck the water—do you really want to know what I want or what I need? How about another chance, huh? How about you find a way to get me the last thirty years of my life back? Can you do that, Officer Cooper?*

"Mrs. Pane, are you OK?"

He looks at me, patiently waiting for my response, when suddenly, in the silence of the waiting room, I hear a woman screaming. The sound is gut-wrenching, and I quickly look around, frantically searching for her so that I can curl up beside her and share in her agony. I want to tell her that I understand and that the pain in my gut is clawing its way out too, ripping through every last inch of sanity. I want to tell her that she is not alone.

Officer Cooper is still kneeling in front of me. He pulls a tissue from his shirt pocket that proudly displays a large, shiny silver badge. The fluorescent lights of the waiting room reflect off the badge and shoot directly into my eyes, momentarily blinding me like the light in the woods. My sight returns, and through the badge I see her again, the tired woman with the long, stringy hair I saw in Officer Cooper's shoe. She looks different now. She's not staring at me anymore. Her mouth is open wide. Tears are streaming down her face. She is grasping and clawing at her clothing, pulling at her hair, and rocking back and forth.

She's the one screaming.

She's here.

Close to me.

I can feel her.

I quickly turn around and reach out, hoping to hold her, hoping to grab onto someone who is brave enough to release the demon inside. I turn side to side and suddenly realize that the only other person in the waiting room is Officer Cooper, who is still kneeling before me with wide eyes and a broadened stance...

ready to catch the screaming woman who is collapsing to her knees...

ready to catch the screaming woman whose face is now bloodied and streaked with tears...

ready to catch...

me.

_

"I need help out here!" Officer Cooper yells out from the waiting room. "Nurse! Nurse! Somebody...please!"

I collapse like a rag doll onto him. He wraps his arms tightly around me and rises to his feet. A sharp pain stabs my groin, forcing me to double over, and suddenly there is a rush of warm fluid spilling out from between my legs. It saturates my pants and leaks out onto the floor until a puddle of blood forms beneath me.

"I need help out here, quick! I need help!"

Several people in white uniforms huddle around me, firing questions one after another.

But I don't answer.

I can't.

The pain is too great.

I feel dizzy, light-headed, and faint as the blood on the floor splashes against their stark white shoes.

"Grab her legs."

Two men lift me onto a gurney and rush me through the hospital halls, poking and prodding every step of the way. A woman with kind eyes leans over me.

"You're going to be OK, Mrs. Pane. Don't worry, you're going to be just fine."

She places a mask over my face and holds it firmly against my mouth.

I want to tell her that it doesn't matter.

Really.

Because I've never been OK.

I never will be.

My eyelids grow heavy as I part my lips to speak. Gently, she rests her hand on my forehead and looks down at me with a warm smile. Up ahead, at the end of the hallway, is a set of large double doors. The gurney wheels screech to a sudden halt, resulting in a shrill sound that sends chills down my spine, reminding me of something I wish I could forget.

My childhood.

All of it.

And everything that reminds me of it, like the chilling noises of the steel plant, the goddamned steel plant that never slept.

I suppose I'll be forever haunted by its unforgettable sounds, crashing and thundering through the air like a continuous storm.

Twenty-four hours a day.

Seven days a week.

But it was the offensive, high-pitched noise of the metal slag cars grinding along the tracks that bothered me the most. The doors open in front of me as I close my eyes and drift in and out of consciousness, remembering the day I turned ten. The day the metal cars squealed and screamed louder than ever before.

Or so it seemed. They screamed.

3

THE GARRITY HOUSE, 1981, TEN YEARS OLD

"**D**anni, can I thing to you firtht thith year? Pleathe, Danni? Pleathe?"

My little sister, Becca, sits before me wide-eyed, struggling to correctly pronounce every "s."

"Sure, Becca, go ahead. You sing first."

"Happy birthday to you…"

She softly sings to me as we sit across from each other, Indian-style, on the floor of our bedroom at the Garritys' twin house on 8th Street.

"Happy birthday to you…"

She's doing well with her speech, in spite of the large separation in her top lip that runs up into her left nostril.

"Happy birthday, dear Danni…"

I read to her every night, slowly pronouncing every syllable of every word. She mimics each word the best she can, repeating them over and over again.

"Happy birthday to you…"

I extend my arms out toward her, hands open, palms up, as I do each year on our birthday and wait for my younger sister to place her delicate hands in mine. I hold them tight, cross my eyes, and stick out my tongue until she giggles with delight. We sit for a moment, in silence, peering down at the two flickering candles that Becca carefully squished into the top of a Hostess Twinkie.

One for each of us.

I am ten years old today.

It has been five years since Mom made them take us away.

Five years since she gave birth to Becca in the back bedroom of our old house on Liberty Street. Five years since she screamed in horror when she saw Becca's face.

Her beautifully deformed face.

Five years and two foster homes.

She couldn't handle it, I guess: a single mom giving birth to a child with a birth defect. I'll never forget the big white truck that pulled up outside of our house on my fifth birthday. It had flashing red lights on top and a loud irritating siren. Three men jumped out and rushed into the house straight past me to the back bedroom where she lay drenched from sweat and in a pool of blood. Two men worked feverishly at her side while the other one closed the door. They must have been in there for hours because I watched countless cartoons and ate half my birthday cake before one man emerged from the back room with a small bundle in his arms.

Becca.

She sure was the best birthday present I ever got. I thought babies were supposed to cry when they are born, but Becca was as quiet as a mouse peering out from the sheet like she was looking straight at me. She didn't cry at all, not once.

It was our mother who cried hard from the back bedroom as the men tried to explain what was wrong with Becca's mouth. A birth defect, known as cleft lip. They tried to calm her by telling her that although Becca's eating and speech would be affected, she could, with the proper treatment, lead a normal life. Her screams echoed through the house and reverberated off the walls.

"Get her away from me!" she yelled, "I don't want to look at her! He's never coming back now! He's never coming back now!"

From the living room where I stood by the man holding Becca, I could see down the hallway into the back bedroom where I watched her thrashing about on the bed. She repeated the same thing over and over again.

"He's never coming back! Oh God! He's never coming back!"

I didn't recognize the woman back there. I had never seen her before. I held my hands over my ears and pressed as hard as I could so as not to hear her shrill screams. Slowly, I walked to the edge of the living room where the hallway began and stood watching her, waiting for her to stop.

Praying for her to stop.

The hallway seemed longer, foreign and distorted, like gazing into one of the funny mirrors at a carnival. I ached for something familiar to comfort me and assure me that everything would be OK. In the midst of the chaos that surrounded me, I rested my eyes on my bedroom door a few feet away. I wanted to see the notches that Mom had scratched into the doorframe each year on my birthday to chart my growth. I wanted to remember how I'd stand in sock feet, heels flat on the floor, back pressed firmly against the wall while she held a pencil on the top of my head to mark my height. I wanted to know that she was going to be OK.

She'll be all right, I said to myself over and over again. *She's gonna be all right. I'll bring her some birthday cake and a pencil so she can mark my spot. Then she'll feel better. I know she will. I can't wait to see how much I've grown this year.*

But I couldn't see the notches through the stupid tears that welled up in my eyes. I fought to keep my eyes wide open so those silly tears would go away. I drew in a deep breath and bit down on my bottom lip until it hurt. I wanted it to hurt so I wouldn't feel the pain in my heart so much. And then, like an erupting volcano, as the men dressed in white lifted Mom onto a rolling bed and rushed her up the hallway right passed me, the tears came fast, streaming down my cheeks. I dropped my hands from my ears and ran to her bedside, wrapping both hands tightly around the cold metal frame. Her screaming was too much to bear.

Bloodcurdling.

My mouth filled with the salty taste of tears and mucus that leaked from my nose, but I held on in spite of her shrieks that grew louder.

"Mommy, stop!" I yelled. "Get off the bed! Tell them to go away! It's my birthday! It's my birthday!"

I kicked as hard as I could as one man pulled me away and pried my fingers from the bed. He held me against him as they rolled her out the front door, across the front yard, and into the big white truck with the red flashing lights on top. She never stopped screaming, and she never looked back. It was as though something inside her broke into a million pieces and either she didn't know how to put them back together or she was too afraid to try.

I hated her for that.

I still do.

For being so fucking afraid.

As I watched the truck drive away, I grabbed the bottom of my shirt, wiped my face dry, and promised myself that I would never be like her: afraid, pathetic, and weak. With a wink and a smile, the man put me down, swaddled Becca tightly in a sheet, and wrapped me in Mom's sweater that hung over the kitchen chair—the sweater she often wore, the sweater that smelled like her. He grabbed my hand and took Becca and me outside to the police car in front of our house. As we exited, a faint voice called out to me from somewhere within the vacant house. "Close your eyes," it said as the sun started to set on that crisp, clear September day. "Don't look back."

The taunting clamor of the steel plant sounded in the distance, tormenting me for the first time with its menacing noises.

Banging.

Booming.

Screeching.

Overhead, a flock of geese in a splendid *V* formation flew by, loudly chattering and momentarily hushing the revolting cacophony of steel. I stopped for a moment and watched as the large birds feverishly made their way across the azure sky.

I wondered if they were watching me, too.

I wondered if they knew where we were going.

I was five years old.

"Go ahead, Danni, make the wish. You know, the thpecial wish we talk about all the time, for a mommy and daddy, a real mommy and daddy."

Becca looks up at me through thick-lens glasses that she has worn since she was a toddler to correct a stigma in her right eye. Her eyes are as wide and blue as the sky on a midsummer day. The blond curls that softly frame her heart-shaped face are boldly streaked with silvery highlights from hours of play in the summer sun. I can't help but smile at the handful of freckles that God sprinkled across her nose on the day she was born, like chocolate sprinkles on a vanilla ice cream cone. At least that's what Erma said, our last foster mom. She said that sometimes they looked so yummy they made her hungry. Erma wasn't a bad person. She taught me a lot, like how some women can lose their minds after childbirth. No telling why it happens.

It just does.

And it's a crying shame.

She taught me that there's no sense crying over spilt milk and that when life hands you lemons you make lemonade. I've never figured out why, but a lot of Erma's lessons involved some sort of beverage. Like I said, she wasn't a bad person, she just wasn't good enough for Becca. So as soon as Becca was old enough to understand, I promised her that I would wish us the best mommy and daddy ever, a mommy and daddy who would make us eat spinach, take long bubble baths, and tuck us into bed at night with a good book and a warm hug... a mommy and daddy who would love her beautiful smile as much as I do. I told her that birthday wishes are magical, and since everyone gets only one a year, I would use mine for our special wish and she could save hers for fun stuff like dolls and puppy dogs.

Erma didn't like dolls or puppy dogs. She treated us pretty well, for the most part. She made sure we had food in our stomachs and clothes on our backs, but there was something about that bottle in the little brown paper bag that she couldn't leave alone. She took it wherever she went. It seemed like whatever was in it made her really happy one day and really sad the next. Then one day, after three years of living with Erma and her brown paper bag, Mrs. Rogers from child services showed up at the door, took us just like that, and brought us here, to the Garritys' house on 8th Street.

It's been a year and seven months since Mrs. Rogers brought Becca and me here...one year, seven months, and eight days since we drove along 8th Street looking for house number 5515. I had a bad feeling about that number. Too many fives. I hate the number five. I was five when the men in the truck took us away, and it has been five years since I last saw Mom. I draw in a deep breath and hold it until my lungs feel ready to burst. The disturbing sounds of the steel plant slice through the air as the metal cars scream and howl along the tracks. It makes my skin crawl, the sound of metal on metal, steel on steel. Like rubbing foil on a silver filling. I hold Becca's hands tighter than ever before and blow the candle out with every ounce of air I have. And with the power of a ten-year-old's birthday wish, I change our lives.

Forever.

4

I wake to voices, a hushed conversation above me, between a man and a woman I don't recognize. I'm awake, I think, lying on my back with my arms by my side. I struggle to open my eyes, fighting against a seemingly insurmountable force. My lids are heavy, and my eyes cross and shift side to side beneath them. Others are with me, and their voices sound slow and muffled like when Becca and I were little and talked to each other with our heads submerged in a bathtub filled with water. We laughed then…in spite of everything, we laughed. Suddenly, I am completely aware of my body. A dull pain in my lower abdomen aches and throbs. I need to open my eyes. They mention my name once or twice, but I can't make out what they are saying. *God, if you're there, help me, please!*

I try to lift my hands, which seem bound to my sides. I try harder, lifting and pulling, lifting and pulling. I wiggle side to side, trying to get the voices' attention, and still they continue talking as though unaware of my struggle. A glimmer of light slices through the darkness as I manage to lift my eyelids to a space that is foggy and blurred. I open my mouth and call out to them. *Where am I? What happened?* But they don't respond. The ache in my abdomen intensifies, sending sharp pains into my lower back and thighs. I kick my legs against the footboard, thrashing about in a desperate attempt to get their attention, and yet the hushed voices above me continue on.

I call out again. Louder this time, I think. *Help me! Please!* I am horrified and stunned by the realization that, in spite of my efforts, I am as she was in the woods: silent and still. I can't move or speak. My body is far too weak, practically lifeless. What is happening? Where the hell am I? I observe a young man as he comes closer and places his hand on my wrist to check my pulse. He whispers to the woman by his side: "I heard she freaked out in the waiting room while some cop was questioning her."

He picks up a clipboard, flips through a couple of pages, and jots something down. I strain to listen as his voice softens even more. "They said she started screaming and yelling like she was crazy, and then started hemorrhaging right then and there. Turns out she was pregnant, about four months. They rushed her to the ER but couldn't save the baby. A little boy. Weird thing is, they don't think she even knew she was pregnant."

His words hit me like a fierce wave in a tempestuous ocean, first crashing up against me, knocking me off balance and sucking the air out of me, then swallowing me and tumbling me about in a vast and infinite abyss before spitting me out motionless and still. But I don't want to be still. The stillness is where the demons thrive, the voices that began years ago as a faint, irritating whisper. Taunting. Teasing. Provoking. Refusing to be ignored. Swelling into maddening screams when dismissed and now triumphantly celebrating in the materialization of my worst nightmare. *Close your eyes! Don't look back! Close your eyes! Don't look back!* I try not to listen to the incessant voices that stir up thoughts of Michael, my husband, the man whose love I've never deserved, who tirelessly fought for a life I could never give him. How can I ever forgive myself for what I've done to our baby? Michael's son. The child he prayed for again and again, the child who would have made everything right again, the child the doctor said we could never have.

I'll never forget the look on Michael's face when, after years of trying to conceive, the doctor diagnosed me with a severe case of endometriosis and told us that I would not be able to get pregnant. It was like someone turned off a switch. Michael's face fell, his shoulders dropped, and his eyes grew dim and narrow when Dr. Radner spoke in a solemn voice as he rested his hand on mine and looked Michael directly in the eye.

"I'm sorry. I know how much this means to both of you, but I would be creating a false hope if I were to tell you that it would take anything less than a miracle."

And with that statement, that statement alone, the switch turned back on. Michael's eyes lit up and sparkled the way they did on the day that I officially became Mrs. Reverend Michael Pane.

"Miracle?"

Michael raised his eyebrows, clasped his hands in front of him, and rapidly rubbed them together as though creating friction to spark a fire.

"Did you say miracle, Dr. Radner? Well, it just so happens that I am a strong believer." He turned to me, grabbed my hand and pulled me to him. "Come on, baby, we've got work to do."

Michael was no stranger to miracles. He had witnessed several during his years of ministering at the Evangelical Lutheran Church on the Upper East Side of Manhattan.

It was there that we first met in the summer of 1993.

I had just moved to the city after accepting an internship at the *New York Times*. At the age of twenty-two, I was ready to start a new life and eager to forget the old. I threw myself into my job and worked long hours, as many as I could, so I wouldn't have time to think about my past and the guilt that festered inside of me.

It was the story of a young boy's miraculous recovery that first brought me to Michael. After being dragged alongside a school bus for almost a mile when his sweatshirt hood got caught in the bus door, eight-year-old Kevin McKneely was rushed to the hospital where doctors told his parents that his internal injuries were far too extensive for him to survive. A young reverend by the name of Michael Pane had contacted the *Times* to cover the story of how community members from mixed denominations were pulling together in honor of the boy, holding a nonstop, 'round-the-clock, prayer service at his church. I visited the church and interviewed Reverend Pane, whose soulful eyes and calm voice quickly captivated me. I found myself fascinated by his unwavering faith and asked him how, in the face of such a horrific and senseless tragedy, his beliefs could remain undaunted.

"Ah, but tragedies such as this make me believe all the more," he said as he guided me through the historic church, pointing out it's unique architectural design dating back to the late 1800s and praising the dedication and commitment of its parishioners. He spoke of little Kevin McKneely's courageous struggle for life and how he believed that, through divine intervention, this young soul was being used as a tool to cultivate a sense of oneness among people of varying races and religions.

"Nothing is an accident, Miss Hoffman. We will continue to pray for Kevin, for God to bless him with a full recovery. But if it is his time to go home, I assure you that many good things will come from his loss. Most often the greatest lessons are learned during times of hardship."

He then escorted me to the large doors at the front of the church.

"Miss Hoffman," he said, as he reached out his hand. "Thank you for your time. I hope your readers will find this story as heartwarming and inspirational as I do."

With the soft sound of whispered prayers in the background, I lifted my hand and rested it in his. I didn't want to leave. I wanted to hear more of what he had to say.

"You're very welcome, Reverend." I smiled. "And please, call me Danni."

His hand felt warm and steady beneath mine. I became immersed in the tenderness of his touch, glancing down at my hand in his before looking up into his warm, brown eyes that seemed to overflow with the hope and promise of a million dreams. I wanted to stay with this man who exuded an internal strength that I craved. There was a familiarity in him—in his voice, his eyes, his touch—that I knew would be difficult to ignore. He placed his other hand on top of mine and sandwiched it in between his, harnessing the warmth that seemed to rapidly generate.

"Danni," he said. "It's a beautiful name. Short for Danielle?"

"Yes." I nodded and then glanced away from his penetrating stare.

"God is my judge," he said, drawing my eyes back to his.

"Excuse me?"

He pressed his hands firmer into mine. "I'm sorry, I have a bit of a fascination for names. The meaning or origin of Danielle, for instance, is the French variant of the male name *Daniel*, which in Hebrew means, 'God is my judge.'"

He paused as if waiting for a response.

"I see," I said, excited by the rising intensity of his stare.

"In the scriptures," he continued, "Daniel was thrown into the lions' den where he faced certain death had it not been for his unwavering faith, which sustained and protected him."

In the moment that followed, I felt an overwhelming urge to apologize. "I'm sorry, Reverend. I'm not familiar with the story. I'm afraid I haven't had much religion in my life."

He wrapped his arm around my shoulders and guided me to the exit. "I don't judge, Danielle." He released my hand. "Have a nice day. I hope to see you again soon."

I left the church intrigued by such an attractive and interesting man, and eager to become one of the newest members of the Evangelical Church on the Upper East Side of Manhattan.

Once more I fight to lift my head, barely opening my eyes, trying everything and anything to let them know that I'm awake, listening to everything they're saying about me and my baby, our son, Michael's son. But they continue their discussion, fidgeting with the machines at my bedside.

How could they be so stupid? *I'm awake! Look at me! I'm awake!*

Through blurred vision, I notice the outline of a woman standing in the doorway. She is quiet and still, shoddily dressed in a garment that seems much too large for her frame. Her arms hang loosely by her side as she gazes in at me. In a futile attempt to clear my vision, I blink several times, desperately trying to focus on the disturbing woman whose abrupt appearance has commanded my attention. Perhaps she is a patient roaming the hallways, sticking her nose into my business where it doesn't belong. Or maybe she is just a figment of my imagination, a self-fabricated illusion that I've conjured up in my troubled mind. She begins rocking back and forth, tapping her shoes against the floor as though growing seemingly restless. She covers her mouth to stifle a fit of weeping that has crept up inside of her, erupting quietly at first, then louder until it penetrates the room in a shrill vibrato that bounces off the walls and echoes in my ears like the sharp ting of metal on metal.

Steel on steel.

Fucking steel on steel.

The nurse hangs the chart at the end of the bed, picks up a syringe, and pierces the needle into a tiny bottle filled with clear fluid.

"The story I got is that they found her and another woman last night in the woods under the hill-to-hill bridge. The other woman is pretty bad off, in ICU with some pretty serious injuries."

He draws back on the syringe, holds it out in front of him, and gently pushes until a tiny drop of liquid erupts from the top.

"I was talking with an EMT on the scene; he said it was a real mess. Something about a suicide or homicide attempt, they're not sure which. They don't know if she's gonna make it. Crazy thing is, she's pregnant, too. Both she and her baby have a real struggle ahead of them. That's all I know."

Slowly, the strange woman turns and retreats down the long hallway. I am still now, deliberately so, like a frightened rabbit whose heart pounds recklessly within. I hang on his every hushed word. "They're in the process of trying to contact relatives, but so far they haven't had much luck."

Suddenly, I can't breathe. I did this…to all of them. My chest is heavy and tight. I want to rip the IV from my arm and run far away so I can't hurt anyone anymore. I want to never look back. He inserts the needle into the tube taped to my wrist and slowly pushes on the end of the syringe. I feel a slow, cool rush through my veins as a calm settles over me. The calm is welcome. I want to sleep and stop my racing thoughts. I want to sleep and never wake up.

Never.

5

THE GARRITY HOUSE, 1979,
EIGHT YEARS OLD

I'll never forget the day we met Mr. and Mrs. Garrity. It seemed like we drove up and down that street for hours. Becca and I sat in the back seat of Mrs. Rogers's maroon Cutlass. We squished tightly up against each other, held hands, and quietly sang the song that Erma used to sing to us.

> *Just what makes that little old ant...*
> *think he can move that rubber tree plant...*
> *Anyone knows an ant...can't...*
> *move a rubber tree plant...*

Erma said that happy songs were like medicine for the heart and that singing them would make a sad heart glad again, even if just for a while.

Cause he's got...high hopes,
he's got...high hopes,
he's got...high apple pie in the sky hopes...

Becca lifts her head and turns toward me. I rest my fore-head against hers and look into her hope-filled eyes.

So anytime you're gettin' low...
'stead of lettin' go...
just remember that ant...

Becca laughs in anticipation of her favorite part of the song. I release my hand from her sweaty grip and put my index finger on her belly button, poking it gently with every "*Oops.*"

Oops, there goes another rubber tree...
Oops, there goes another rubber tree...
Oops, there goes another rubber tree plant.

We giggle as Mrs. Rogers parks the car at 5515 8th Street. Mr. and Mrs. Garrity are standing on the front porch. Waiting. Mrs. Garrity looks tired. She has dirty-blond hair that hangs to her shoulders. It's stringy and messy, and looks like it hasn't been washed in a while. One thing Erma taught us well is good hygiene. She said a hot shower and a clean head of hair was the closest she'd ever been to heaven. Erma let Becca and I take baths three times a week, sometimes four if we were behaving real well, just so long as we only filled the tub halfway.

Mrs. Garrity looks like she needs a long hot bath and some new clothes. Her housecoat falls slightly above her knees, has a few buttons missing from the top, and drapes off her right shoulder exposing a tattered bra strap. Her shoes are worn and scuffed, and I can't help but wonder if she knows about Sally's downtown, where Erma took us to shop for clothes. "Sally's" was Erma's code name for the Salvation Army. She said that one person's trash is another person's treasure, so we went treasure hunting a lot. Erma was fun…sometimes.

I feel bad for Mrs. Garrity and sorry for Becca because Mrs. Garrity looks too messy to be a good mommy. But Erma always said, "You can't judge a book by its cover," so I decide not to rule her out as a mommy just yet.

Becca and I step out of the car and follow Mrs. Rogers around to the back of her car. She opens the trunk, pulls out our backpacks, and hands them to us. I've never been in this part of town before. There are many row homes that line 8th Street. In spite of the various colors, most of the homes look the same: small yards and small porches with a glass Moravian star that hangs above each entryway. Next door, a large fluffy dog paces back and forth inside a chain-link fence. He jumps up and down, whines and whimpers numerous times, before sitting down on the dirt path that has worn into the grass from hours of restless boredom. Mrs. Rogers closes the trunk of her car, places one arm around each of our shoulders, and leads us toward the Garritys' porch.

The steel plant is closer than it has ever been before, louder and more persistent, pounding and shaking the ground beneath me. I grab Becca's hand as we approach the Garritys' house. The dog jumps to his feet and wildly barks, turning his attention to a woman standing in the distance, at the end of the street, next to a stop sign. He lowers his tail, raises the hair on his back, and growls. The woman, average in stature, is wearing a large brown-hooded coat that drapes loosely to her knees. The hood is pulled up over her head and hangs down on her face, covering it completely. She buries one hand deep in her pocket, holds a shopping bag in the other, and faces in our direction, as though looking straight at us.

Becca and I have seen the woman before, several times, although never up close. Each time she emerges in the distance, out of nowhere, for no apparent reason, lingering and hovering behind trees and fences, vanishing as mysteriously as she appears. She never shows her face, and she never comes too close. Erma scoffed when I told her about the creepy coat lady on my eighth birthday when Becca and I were making mud pies in Erma's backyard.

"You have quite an imagination, Danni," she said, forcing her eyebrows down toward her nose.

"But it's not my imagination," I insisted. "Becca saw her, too! On the other side of the fence! Peeking in at us! Right, Becca?"

Becca shrugged her shoulders and wiped the hair out of her eyes with muddy fingers that left a dirt smudge across her forehead.

"And you say she appeared and disappeared, just like that?" Erma asked, snapping her red, gnarled fingers.

"Yes! Just like that!" I said, raising my voice with confidence. "Missy Lacintosh says that there are ghosts in Bethlehem! Maybe that's what she is—a ghost!"

Becca's eyes widened beneath her eyeglasses that sat tilted to one side of her malformed nose.

"A ghotht?" Becca asked.

Erma chuckled, wiped the dirt from Becca's forehead with a spit-dampened dishtowel, and snarled at me with an unnerving smile still on her face. "And do you believe everything that Missy Lacintosh tells you, Danni?"

"No…but…"

"No…but what?" she asked.

I looked down at the old wooden floor beneath Erma's feet and visually followed the worn path that ran from the kitchen cupboard where she kept her bottles to the kitchen table where she drank them. Erma's bracelets jingled around her wrist as she lifted the brown paper bag to her lips, tilted back her head, and gulped down the last drop of what she liked to call "grown-up juice." She slammed the bottle down on the counter, held her arms out in front of her, and walked like a zombie across the kitchen floor. "OOOOHHHH! I am a ghost of Bethlehem! I like to tickle little girls before I gobble them up for dinner!" She grabbed Becca's tiny waist and tickled her until she laughed out loud.

"Erma?" Becca said, still laughing. "Are ghotht real?"

"What do *you* think, darlin'?" Erma said in a raspy voice. She coughed to clear the phlegm from her throat as she squinted one eye and held a lighter up to the cigarette that dangled from her lips. Becca tilted her head and waited for Erma's response.

"There's no such thing as ghosts," Erma said with a wink, drawing her wrinkled cheeks inward until a long tube of ashes dangled from the end of her cigarette. "Now go play."

Becca ran outside, letting the screen door slam shut behind her, as Erma leaned down, looked me in the eye, and pointed her crooked finger at me. "And you better not scare your sister anymore or tell anyone your foolish story about a ghost," she said in a stern, gruff voice, swirling her warped finger in circles next to her head. "People will think you're crazy."

I thought long and hard about what Erma said. I sure didn't want anyone thinking I was crazy like Mom, so I didn't talk about ghosts anymore to anyone. I hoped the woman in the long coat would never appear again, but sure enough she did several months later as Becca and I walked home from a neighbor's house. I nudged Becca when I saw the woman peering out from behind a tree. Becca looked up at me but didn't say a word. Neither of us said a word as we increased our pace from a steady walk to a quick sprint. That was the last time I saw the odd woman.

Until now.

Becca tugs on my arm, leans in close, and softly speaks. "Danni, are you thcared?"

I squeeze Becca's hand and continue walking straight ahead. "Of course not. There's nothing to be scared of, Becca, I promise."

We trail closely alongside Mrs. Rogers, up the steps, and onto the Garritys' porch. Mrs. Garrity greets us with a weak handshake and a modest grin. Mr. Garrity nods and stares at us hard. He looks freshly showered. His hair is medium brown, graying at the temples, buzzed up the sides, and flat like a table on top. Mrs. Rogers said he had been in the military years ago, served in Vietnam for a while, but was sent home because of an injury. He never made it to sergeant as he had hoped. And most of his friends never made it home. Mr. Garrity wears neatly pressed khaki pants, a starched white undershirt, and a pair of black shoes that shine so bright they hurt my eyes.

With his hands in his pockets, he walks to the edge of the porch, leans over, and spits out a thick stream of brown fluid. The sun glimmers and dances on the shiny buckle around his waist as he meanders back to where we are standing. While Mrs. Rogers and Mrs. Garrity discuss Becca's medical background, he removes a small, crumpled bag from his right pocket, opens it, reaches in with his thumb and index finger, and pulls out a dark wad of something that resembles dirt. With his heavy gaze still upon us, he opens his mouth and stuffs it up into the side of his cheek. The strong scent of aftershave pierces my nostrils as he walks past us to an old wooden rocking chair positioned in the corner of the porch that faces the steel plant.

I don't like the way he looks at us. I especially don't like the way he looks at Becca, like a lion upon its prey. There's something about Mr. Garrity—Sergeant, as he insists on being called—that makes the hair on the back of my neck stand straight up. He begins rocking back and forth, back and forth, without ever speaking a word. Even when Mrs. Rogers hands him the check to cover our first month of care, he doesn't speak but neatly folds it and slides it into his back pocket. Mrs. Rogers leans in toward Mrs. Garrity, holds her hand over her mouth to hide her words, and softly speaks: "I hope everything works out. These two little girls deserve some good to come their way."

"No worries, ma'am," Mrs. Garrity says, as she massages the back of her neck. "When Sergeant saw their names on the church registry for children in crisis, he insisted that we help. He said it was the right thing to do, being Christian and all."

"Well, we sure do appreciate all of our foster parents. More than you know."

Mrs. Rogers lowers her hand and forces a smile. We must look pretty scared because she leans down, looks us in the eye, and rubs her hands up and down our arms in a soothing manner. "Don't worry, girls. The Garritys are going to take real good care of you. They're nice people. I'll be back from time to time to check up on you and make sure everything is going all right. If you need anything, anything at all, you call me."

She slips a small white card into the side pocket of my backpack and gives us a quick hug before she walks down the steps, gets into her Cutlass, and drives away. I like Mrs. Rogers. She's tall and thin with smooth brown hair that she keeps softly pulled back away from her face with an assortment of colorful ribbons that match her outfits. She has a kind smile and soft brown eyes, and smells of rose petals. I wonder if she has children of her own. And if she doesn't, why she doesn't want Becca and me?

The neighbor's dog stops barking and sits in the corner of the yard gazing over at us with soulful eyes. As Mrs. Garrity removes the backpacks from our shoulders, I glance down the street at the stop sign that teeters back and forth with a sudden gust of wind. The woman is gone, and the street is as empty and desolate as it was when we first arrived. Mrs. Garrity opens the screen door and motions for us to go inside, while Sergeant continues rocking. Becca tightens her grip on my hand and quietly hums the ant song. Dozens of geese fly above us. Their obnoxious banter grows louder, silencing Becca's tiny voice and the ominous roar of the steel plant as they did the day that Mom went crazy. Perhaps they knew we were coming here, to the Garritys' house on 8th Street. I gaze up at the sky and step into our next home. I wonder if they know something we don't.

I wonder.

Mrs. Garrity leads us through the kitchen and into the living room to meet Alfred, who is almost twelve years old. He is sitting up tall at one end of the sofa with his feet planted firmly on the floor in front of him, reading a book that is thicker than any book I have ever seen before. Mrs. Garrity speaks with a strong Southern accent, drawing out every syllable like a sad song.

"Alfred, this here is Danni and Becca. These youngin's gonna be stayin' with us for a while. I want you to make 'em feel right at home now, ya hear?"

He looks up only after Mrs. Garrity repeats his name to introduce us. "Nice to meet you," he says.

It's Alfred's eyes that I notice first. I have never seen pink eyes before. Becca tugs at my arm, steps behind me, and peers out from my left side. Alfred's skin and hair are as white as snow. I stare at him long and hard before Mrs. Garrity breaks the silence.

"Has the cat got your tongue, child?"

Alfred is the strangest creature I have ever seen. The only time I ever saw pink eyes was in the second grade when Richy Hartman brought in his pet rat, Ernie, for show-and-tell. Alfred returns my stare and waits for my response. I look down, suddenly feeling uneasy, and twist the rubber band that Erma placed around my wrist before Mrs. Rogers took us away from her. She told me that whenever I get upset about something, I should snap the rubber band. She said that the pain in my wrist would help the pain in my heart not hurt as much. But the truth is, I never have any real pain in my heart, just an empty kind of feeling, like something should be in there that isn't. I stare at the floor and answer: "Nice to meet you, too."

Mrs. Garrity sets our backpacks down beside us. "Alfred, why don't you take the girls on up to their room while I get supper started."

Alfred places his book down on the sofa beside him, stands up, grabs our backpacks, and throws them over his shoulder. Like Sergeant, he is immaculately groomed from the top of his flat, white head to the bottom of his perfectly polished shoes. He is rather small for his age, thin and narrow, with long scrawny arms that awkwardly swing by his side. He leads the way up the stairs and down the hallway. I follow behind him and Becca behind me. He stops at the first door on the right, opens the door, and stands in the hallway while Becca and I enter.

The room is dreary and bland. The walls are plain and flat white, and the blinds on the window are old and yellowed, with several missing slats. An old white dresser stands at one side of the room directly facing a black wrought-iron double bed at the other. The bed-spread is the only thing that is pretty in the entire room: white with small purple flowers. A large clock hangs on the wall directly over the bed. It looks the same as the clock in the living room where we met Alfred, big and round with a white face and black numbers, like the one that hangs in the school cafeteria. The clocks tick loudly in perfect synchronicity, so loud that it makes my head ache. Or maybe it's the unsettling silence in the Garrity house that is too loud, the silence that comes between every second on the clock and between the incessant booming of the steel plant in the distance. Alfred sets our backpacks on the floor.

"Dinner will be served at exactly eighteen hundred hours. Today's Thursday. Meatloaf. Oh, and by the way, I'm not a freak." Alfred looks down at Becca who is standing by my side. A small stream of saliva drips out from the corner of her deformed mouth. Alfred reaches into his pocket, removes a handful of sunflower seeds, toss-es a couple in his mouth, and holds the others out for Becca. "I might look a little different than everyone else, but that's what makes me so special," he says, smiling at Becca who follows his lead by throwing several seeds into her mouth.

"They're thalty," she giggles.

Alfred holds his hand out to me. "Want some?" he asks, looking down at the floor as his white cheeks turn a pale shade of red.

"Sure," I say, scooping a couple off his palm, "Thanks." Alfred is the most curious boy I have ever met. "I'll save them for later," I say, shoving the seeds into my pocket, unable to take my eyes off him as he bashfully lifts his gaze to a safe place beneath mine.

"You have pretty hair," he says, speaking barely above a whisper as he sharply turns to go. "Remember, eighteen-hundred hours."

Alfred closes the door behind him leaving Becca and I standing in the middle of the dull room that the Garritys have been kind enough to let us stay in for a while. I don't know how long we'll live here. Weeks. Months. Maybe years. That's the thing about foster care, we never know how long we'll be staying, when we'll be leaving, or where we'll be going. So we never really have a home. Becca places her backpack on the bed, unzips it, and pulls out the small blanket that she has carried around with her since she was a baby. The same blanket that I used to carry around when I was small, when I still lived with Mom, when I still had a home.

The pale pink-and-yellow sheep that cover the blanket are barely recognizable anymore, faded from countless washings. Becca unfolds the blanket and spreads it out as best she can at the foot of the bed. With her small hands, she pats it down and smooths it out.

"Ith this our home now, Danni?" she asks. Her tousled curls dangle in front of her face as she pushes up her glasses and continues straightening out her blanket.

"Ith Mithter and Mitheth Garrity gonna be our mommy and daddy?"

I put my backpack down by the dresser, take my sweater off, and neatly fold it in the top drawer. "The three bottom drawers are yours, Becca."

Becca's soft voice, filled with uncertainty and excitement, carries through the air. "Ith Mithter and Mitheth Garrity gonna be our mommy and daddy?" She sits on the floor, takes her sneakers off, and places them beneath her side of the bed.

"Becca, bring your backpack over here and I'll help you unpack."

Becca walks over and hands me her backpack. "Danni?"

"What Becca…what?" I look down at my sister, whose disfigured mouth makes it impossible for her to properly pronounce the letter *S*. Once again, she repeats the same question that I don't have an answer for.

"I said, ith Mithter and Mitheth Garrity gonna be our mommy and daddy?"

I change the subject to focus on her speech and hope that she won't insist on an answer. "*Sssssss*, Becca. Say *sssssssssss*nake."

Becca raises her eyebrows and presses her tongue against the back of her teeth. "*Sssssssthhhhhh*nake…"

I smile and fill the drawers with her clothes. "Now say 'Sally sells seashells by the seashore' five times real fast."

Becca giggles, grabs my waist, and hugs me tight. "I love you, Danni."

"I love you too, Becca."

When Becca and I are finished unpacking, we sit on the bed, side by side, paging through the library book that I brought home from school for her: Dr. Seuss's *Green Eggs and Ham*, one of Becca's favorites. Dinner is at eighteen hundred hours…at least that's what Alfred said before he closed the door behind him several hours ago. But I don't know what eighteen hundred hours means, so I am grateful to Alfred when he knocks on our door at precisely 6:00 in the evening. We follow him downstairs, one behind the other.

Alfred.

Me.

Becca.

Alfred doesn't say a word as he leads us into the kitchen where Mr. and Mrs. Garrity are already positioned at the table. Waiting. Sergeant sits at the head of the table, Mrs. Garrity to his left. Alfred takes his place to the right of Sergeant. I sit in the chair next to Alfred, and Becca sits directly across from me next to Mrs. Garrity. Alfred unfolds his napkin, tucks it into his shirt, and places his folded hands on his lap. He turns to me, looks down at his hands, and looks at me again. Mr. and Mrs. Garrity wait. I smile at Becca, kick her gently under the table, and pray that she mimics me as I unfold my napkin and tuck it into my blouse. When we are all settled and still,

Sergeant turns to Mrs. Garrity and nods as though giving her permission. She bows her head.

"Thank you, Lord, for these gifts we are about to receive from thy bounty, in Christ's name, Amen."

And with nothing but the sound of forks clattering against our plates, the ticking of the clock on the wall, and the sharp, offensive noises of the steel plant, we eat Mrs. Garrity's meatloaf precisely five minutes after the eighteen hundredth hour on Thursday night.

Becca and I have a lot to learn about how things work at the Garrity house. After dinner, Mrs. Garrity knocks on our bedroom door. She enters, sits us down on the bed, and stands before us with her arms crossed in front of her. Her eyes are bloodshot and puffy. Her left cheek is swollen and tearstained. I watch in amazement at how, right before my eyes, it turns shades of red and purple. Her voice quivers as she speaks.

"Sergeant likes things done in a certain way around here," she says, nodding her head at me, then Becca. "There are chores that need tendin' to and rules that have to be followed. He says that every child needs responsibilities and guidance. You girls do as you're told, and you'll be just fine. If you don't, well, Sergeant says if you spare the rod, you spoil the child. Sergeant doesn't like spoiled children. Never did. He says every child needs to learn a good work ethic and the value of a dollar. Just like he did workin' on his cousin's farm. He worked all day for a penny and a meal. Times were tough back then, but Sergeant says that the hardship made him a better man. Sergeant is a good man and kind enough to take y'all in. So you girls just do as you're told, ya hear? Just do as you're told, and you'll be better off for it. We'll all be better off for it."

Her body trembles as she touches her cheek, winces, and sucks air between her teeth while reaching out to hand me a folded piece of paper.

"Here are your chores," she says. "Sergeant prepares a new list every week."

We sit silent and still for a moment until a sudden pounding on the wall startles us. Mrs. Garrity gasps with a look in her eyes that I have never seen before on anyone. She unravels a wad of tissue from her tight grip, wipes her eyes, blows her nose, and forces half a smile while walking over to the small mirror that sits on top of the dresser. She pulls a tube of lipstick from her house-coat pocket and with shaking hands applies several coats until her lips are as red as a cherry on top of an ice cream sundae. She fluffs her hair, walks to the door, and opens it. Before turning off the light, she speaks again, soft as a whisper, clear as a bell: "You girls get a good night's sleep. And remember what I told you."

She pulls the door closed behind her and disappears into the night, leaving the room black and motionless. I lift my hand and strain to see my fingers wiggling inches from my face. My heart is pounding in my throat, and I can feel Becca's hot breath on my arm as she sits frozen on the bed beside me, afraid to speak or move.

"It's OK, Becca," I whisper. "Everything is going to be OK."

I kneel down, sweep my hands across the floor, and search for the pair of purple fuzzy slippers that Erma bought me on our last trip to Sally's. I tuck the piece of paper deep into the toe and place them by the bed. I'll read it first thing in the morning when I wake. Becca and I crawl into bed and pull the covers up over our heads. We turn toward each other, hold hands, and sing "High Hopes" to drown out the sound of the ticking clocks, and the muffled grunts and moans that come from the other side of the wall.

Mrs. Winthrop, my third grade science teacher, taught us about reproduction. She talked about males and females in the animal kingdom. We learned about how males produce sperm and females produce eggs, and about how a baby begins to grow when the sperm fertilizes the egg. Conception. The miracle of life. I didn't need Mrs. Winthrop to tell me about babies; I learned everything I needed to know from Erma. I was seven years old when she sat me down at the kitchen table and told me to listen up. She told me that there were some things I needed to know about boys and girls, and that I should know how to protect myself so that I wouldn't get myself into any trouble, like she did. I wondered what she meant by that, but I didn't ask. A cigarette dangled from Erma's lips as I watched her move about the kitchen in a cloud of smoke that formed around her head. She wore a bright yellow sweat suit, red sneakers, and a stack of bracelets around both wrists that clinked with every move. Her hair, shoddily wrapped in rollers, was an odd shade of orange that she said came straight from the supermarket. She took two flowered teacups from the cabinet, placed each on a mismatched saucer, and removed the whistling kettle from the stove.

I liked Erma. Most of the time. Except around the fifth day of every month when she got her check in the mail. Her first stop after the bank was always the liquor store downtown. She'd come out of the store, wrap the brown paper bag tightly around the neck of the bottle, and drink all day until she passed out on the couch in front of the television. She'd stay on that sofa for days sometimes, drifting in and out of a deep sleep, getting up occasionally to stumble to the bathroom. Becca and I learned how to take care of ourselves when Erma slept like that, and I learned how to be pretty handy in the kitchen. My specialties were SpaghettiOs and peanut-butter-and-banana sandwiches, Becca's favorite. I prayed that Erma would get rid of whatever was in that bottle, and I prayed even harder that Mom would get well and come for us.

Erma placed a cup of tea in front of me and sat down at the table. She told me how bodies grow and change, and how feelings can start churning and bubbling up out of nowhere, making boys all nervous and girls all giddy. I wanted to know more because I sure felt giddy whenever I was around Tommy Snyder. It seemed to me that whenever I was near him, all I could do was giggle, no matter what he said or did. So I listened to what Erma had to tell me, and I listened good. She brought out a book that had pictures in it like I had never seen before. She told me about private parts and said there was no shame in calling them by name.

"Boys have a penis, and girls have a vagina," she said. "I just don't understand why people make up such silly names."

Erma taught me about menstruation, sexual intercourse, and how a baby grows inside of a woman. She said that one day I would meet the right man, fall in love, and get married. And that until then, no one, but no one, should ever touch my private parts. She said that a proper young gentleman would be perfectly happy holding my hand and that if he wasn't, then he was definitely not the boy for me. She said that sex between a man and a woman is beautiful and is something that should be shared between two people who are committed and devoted to each other.

Then she told me a story about cows getting milk for free. I didn't understand the cow story, and I wasn't about to ask her to explain it. I was too busy wondering if Tommy Snyder would hold my hand. Besides, Tommy didn't even drink milk. I knew that for sure because he sat three seats down from me at the lunch table and every day he ate the same thing: tuna on rye, chocolate cupcakes, and apple juice. Erma said that I would never regret making the right choices and that one day I would see that it was well worth the wait. I often think about what Erma told me. It makes me wonder if Mrs. Garrity has made the right choices, because what goes on in her bedroom every night between her and Sergeant doesn't sound beautiful at all.

At the Garrity house, each of us is assigned specific duties. Mrs. Garrity makes it clear that we are not to stray from the carefully planned schedule.

"Sergeant works hard all day," she says, "so that he can provide for us, and the only thing he expects in return is a little hard work and respect. Nothing less will do."

So we work hard. All of us. But it's Alfred who works the hardest. Aside from the chores around the house, he has two jobs, one before school and one after. It seems like his day is never done. Every morning at o-five hundred hours, Alfred gets up before the sun, goes downstairs, and prepares the newspapers for his paper route. At first I find his subtle movement about the house disturbing as I wake each morning to the same sound of creaking floorboards beneath his feet. I hear his every move as he walks to the bathroom,

closes the door behind him,
urinates,
flushes the toilet,
runs the water,
brushes his teeth,
spits three times,
turns off the water,

opens the door, and creeps down the hallway, by our bedroom, where one floorboard squeaks louder than the others. I know when he is there, on the other side of our door, only feet away. It's as though he pauses each day as he passes. Sometimes, in the silence of the morning, if I lay still enough, I can hear his gentle breath as he briefly hovers nearby. And I wonder if he hears mine, too.

When he continues down the hall, I lay in bed listening to the ticking of the clock, timing his every move and tracing his footsteps in my head. I wait patiently, counting every moment until the front door closes behind him. So as not to wake Becca, I carefully slip out of bed, position myself by our bedroom window, and watch Alfred leave into the early darkness. His thin, white physique grows smaller and smaller as he pedals down the street until he becomes a speck in the road that disappears into the dawn. In some ways I am comforted by his routine, eagerly awaiting his return and joyfully anticipating the stability he brings to each new day.

Alfred and I hardly know each other. We barely speak. And yet I grow increasingly troubled at the thought of his absence and fearful that one morning he will leave on his bike filled with papers and never return. I can't bear the thought of living at the Garritys' house without him. I'm not sure why, but I feel safer with him around. So I do something terrible. Something unforgivable. Erma always told me to pray on things that were troubling me and to never be afraid to ask God for anything. She said that prayers are always answered, maybe not as quickly as we would like or in the way we would like, but in good time, when the Lord sees fit. So I pray every night that Alfred won't find a mommy and daddy to adopt him. It's a horrible thing to pray for. But I do it anyway.

Sergeant works at the steel plant, where he spends long hours in the blast furnace inches away from three-thousand-degree liquid molten steel. He hates his job, or at least it seems that way, although I never hear him complain about it. It's the way he behaves that makes it seem like that, I guess. Sergeant is bothered and agitated all the time. He doesn't holler much or even raise his voice but I can tell by the way he drops his feet hard on the floor and fires sharp glares at us when he thinks we are even close to misbehaving. So I try to act the way he wants me to, and I tell Becca to do the same.

"Remember your manners, Becca," I say each day before school. "And if you have any crying or whining to do, wait until we're alone in our room. OK?"

Becca moves her head up and down, and pats her curls down in the mirror. "OK."

But sometimes I think Becca isn't old enough to understand or to be as afraid of Sergeant as I am. I suppose it's Sergeant's silence that scares me the most. Erma was loud. When we did something wrong, she'd let us have it by pointing her long, bent finger directly at us and yelling so hard that I thought she would explode. I hated when Erma yelled, but she was predictable and would always wear herself out in ten minutes or so. Sergeant is different. It's as though he has something cooped up deep inside of him that's just waiting to erupt, maybe some sort of shame or secret that he doesn't want the world to know about, like the shame I feel whenever someone at school asks me why I don't have a mother or father and why Becca and I move around so much.

Sometimes I get so mad that I want to hit something or someone, like the day I punched Missy Lacintosh in the arm for calling me "Little Orphan Danni." She had been calling me that stupid name every day for months. "Little Orphan Danni…Little Orphan Danni," she'd say over and over again until she had every kid on the playground laughing and pointing at me. Then one day I couldn't bear it anymore. I curled up my fist as tight as I could, drew my arm back, and punched her with all my might. Missy ran crying to the teacher and lifted up her sleeve to reveal the red, swollen print of my fist on her arm. It felt good at first, seeing her cry like that, but I was sent to the principal's office and suspended for three days. The principal had a long talk with Erma, who explained to me that if I couldn't control my anger, I could be sent away to a special school where I would never see Becca again. That scared me enough to realize that I can't fight fire with fire without paying a price. Becca needed me, so I made a promise to myself that I would take whatever Missy Lacintosh could dish out for Becca's sake.

Funny thing was, Missy never bothered me again. As a matter of fact, she started acting nicer than ever, greeting me each day and offering to sharpen my pencils before class. She said that she wanted to be friends. But I didn't want to be friends with Missy Lacintosh. She was nothing but a big, fat bully. Sergeant isn't a bully. I think he is something much worse. Maybe he's one of the people Erma told me about.

"Some people have the devil in them," she had said as she rested her hand on mine in a moment of random affection that came far too seldom to feel genuine. "There's no telling why, and there's no understanding it."

I don't want to understand Sergeant. I don't even want to be near him. So I avoid him as much as possible and I tell Becca to do the same, which isn't too difficult most of the time since he leaves for work before sunrise and doesn't return home until six o'clock each evening. Becca and I like when he is gone. We enjoy spending time alone with Mrs. Garrity, especially after school when we gather in the kitchen to prepare dinner. She seems almost happy when it's just the three of us, smiling effortlessly as she moves about, gathering ingredients and utensils for dinner. She teaches Becca and me a lot about cooking, like how to peel potatoes, shuck corn, and knead dough.

"Ya'll gonna be real Southern cooks by the time I'm done with you," she says.

Becca beams and presses her tiny fingers deep into the floured dough that Mrs. Garrity has piled on the table in front of her. She takes a rolling pin from the drawer and puts it in Becca's tiny hands, then places her hands over Becca's to guide her through the motion, rolling back and forth, flattening the dough with every stroke. I stand at the end of the table, a peach in one hand and a paring knife in the other, and carefully begin peeling and slicing the way I have been taught.

"Ya'll remind me of myself when I was a little girl helping my mamma bake and still darin' to dream. Told myself I'd open up my very own bakery one day where folks would come from miles around just to get a taste of Sarah Cunningham's famous cobblers."

She smiles as she speaks, and for the first time I see a beauty in Mrs. Garrity that I hadn't noticed before. It's as though the lines that have been carved into her face from years of sorrow suddenly melt away, giving light to a youthfulness and exposing Sarah, a brilliantly alive girl filled with ambition and drive. She is quite beautiful, actually, with eyes as green and clear as Caribbean water and skin as creamy and beige as the beaches it washes over.

"I see real potential in ya'll, a fire in your eyes like I used to have," she says, pushing the rolling pin slightly faster and harder. "That fire only burns when you're doing something you love, something you're passionate about. Don't let anyone put out that fire, girls." She lifts her head to look straight at me as though warning me of an impending danger. "Because once it's gone," she insists, "it's gone. Seems impossible to get back."

Becca's arms move faster beneath Mrs. Garrity's, back and forth, each time stretching slightly farther, beyond her reach.

"Who knows, maybe one day y'all can open up your own Southern-style restaurant and let all these northern folks have a taste of some real down-home cookin'." Mrs. Garrity stops, releases the rolling pin, and pushes the hair off her face with the back of her hand. Her smile fades into a fixed gaze. "If I had it to do over again, that's what I'd do—sure as shootin, that's what I'd do 'stead of believing in some sweet-talking military man. Ain't no such thing as a knight in shining armor, girls. I don't want y'all believin' in some fairy-tale ending like I did." She swats the flour from her apron, sniffs a couple of times, and blinks hard to fight back tears. "There ain't nothin' worse than livin' with a lifetime of regrets, day after day after day."

Becca rolls the dough. Her curls swing in unison with the sweeping motion as I watch and wait for Mrs.

Garrity's next move. I've seen this look before...on Mom, right after she gave birth to Becca as she stared vacantly down the hallway, moments before her screams began...on Erma, toward the end of every month when money was running low and there was nothing left in the little bottle in the brown paper bag. It's easy to recognize the look of someone teetering on the fence between insanity and mere survival. I feel sorry for Sarah, the young girl who let go of her dream. And I fear for Mrs. Garrity, that she may collapse and shatter into pieces like fine china thrown to the floor. It's the shrill sound of Bandit, the neighbor's dog, barking next door that jars Mrs. Garrity into the moment. She looks up at the clock: 5:55 p.m. She rushes to the window, pushes the curtain aside, and turns toward us in a panic. "You girls go on upstairs now, ya hear?" She unties her apron, rolls it up, and shoves it into one of the kitchen drawers. The dog continues barking louder as though being taunted.

Yelping.

Squealing.

Mrs. Garrity lifts Becca off her seat, grabs me by the arm, and hurries us along. "Go on now, quick, up to your room. Dinner is gonna be a little late. I'll call y'all down when it's done." As Becca climbs the stairs, she looks back at Mrs. Garrity and says, "I wanna woll the dough... I wanna woll the dough!" But Mrs. Garrity has already returned to the kitchen, where she is frantically cleaning up the table.

Becca looks up at me with tears in her eyes. "Danni, I wanna woll the dough...when can I woll the dough?" I lean over the stair rail and peer into the kitchen, where I see Sergeant walk through the door, dirty and sweaty from a long day at the plant. I grab Becca's hand, run up the stairs into our bedroom, and lock the door behind us. The ticking of the clock pounds in perfect cadence with the thunder of the steel.

I pull Becca close,
sit on the floor by our bed,
and wait for the storm.

Mumbling.

Hushed voices.

The oven door opens and slams shut.

A gasp.

Glass crashes to the floor.

A chair slides out from the table, screeches across the floor, and bangs against the wall.

With Becca's hand still in mine, I lean down and put my ear to the cold, wood floor.

I hold my breath, close my eyes, and listen.

I can hear her breathing, hard and quick.

"Please, sir, don't," Mrs. Garrity pleads. "Just give me a few minutes to get dinner on the table. I'm sorry...I...I was making dessert. I know how much you like my cobbler. I must have lost track of time."

Another gasp.

And the low, eerie rumble of his voice. "You lost track of time?" Sergeant exhales in a snide huff. "You say that like it's some sort of acceptable excuse. Do you think I'd still have a job if I lost track of time?"

Scuffling.

"Every job has a description, baby. Part of yours is to have a hot meal on the table every day at precisely eighteen hundred hours. We've been over this."

A drawer opens.

"I don't see a hot meal on the table."

"Please," she begs. "All I need is ten minutes."

Pots and pans clatter against one another.

"You know that everything I do is for your own good."

The drawer slams shut.

Whimpering.

"Please don't do this."

"Do you know what this is?"

Stifled crying.

"I said, do you know what this is!"

More scuffling.

"All I need is ten minutes."

"That's *not* the answer I was looking for!"

The crisp slap of an open hand on bare flesh.

A suppressed shriek.

Stumbling.

A thud on the floor.

Hushed crying.

"Don't make me repeat myself."

Silence.

She speaks, trembling.

"It's a pot."

Sergeant's words shoot off his tongue, cold, deliberate, and precise.

"It's a pot, *what?*"

Silence.

"It's a pot, sir."

"And what do you do with a pot?"

Feet shuffle about on the floor.

"Answer the fucking question!"

She stutters and stammers over her words.

"Y…you c…cook…wi…with it."

"You cook with it, *what?*"

"You cook with it…S…sir."

"Where do you cook with it?"

She sobs.

"Please, Sergeant, the children are upstairs."

"Answer the question!"

"On the…st…stove, sir."

"Very good…maybe you're not as stupid as you look."

She's breathless now.

Sobbing.

"I have one more question for you…see if that little brain is smart enough to get it right. Do you know what the question is?"

She repeatedly sucks in air.

"Do you?"

Her voice quivers. "I don't know, I don't know, I don't know!"

Crying.

"Of course you don't know. You're too much of an idiot to know anything except how to make some stupid fucking pie."

He chuckles, then speaks slowly, exaggerating the pronunciation of every syllable in every word. "Now pay attention. I'm going to tell you what the question is. Listen carefully, and think long and hard before you answer because I'm only going to ask you once. What...do...you...cook...in...it?"

Sergeant's voice deepens and tightens through clenched teeth.

She whimpers.

Sobs.

"Don't make me hurt you right here in the kitchen... the children might see. You wouldn't want that now, would you?"

She pauses before answering, flattening her voice to a cold, unvaried pitch.

"You cook dinner...in the pot...on the stove...sir."

Sniffling.

Sergeant claps his hands together.

"Good answer! I suggest you get to it. I'm going upstairs to shower. I'll be down for dinner at nineteen hundred hours. Not a minute later."

Kissing.

"I love you, baby, you know that, right? God, I hate to see you cry like this. You better clean yourself up a bit before dinner. You wouldn't want the kids to see you like this. Put some lipstick on—you look like shit."

Footsteps.

I sit up.

My back presses against the side of the bed.

I grab Becca's hand.

"Don't move, Becca."

"OK," Becca answers in a tiny, hushed voice. "Danni?"

"Shh, Becca, be quiet."

The footsteps grow louder.

Harder.

Up the stairs.

Climbing.

His hand slides along the rail.

With each step, the military ring he wears on his right finger taps and skims up against the wall.

I know the steps.

Sixteen in all.

I count them every morning when Alfred leaves.

He climbs.

His feet are slow and heavy.

I count.

Five.

Six.

Tapping.

Seven.

Eight.

Skimming.

Nine.

Ten.

Each step grows louder.

Thirteen.

Heavier.

Fourteen.

Closer.

Fifteen.

Tapping.

Sixteen.

Skimming.

He's at the top.

On the landing.

Footsteps.

Down the hallway.

His ring scrapes louder against the wall.

Closer.

Louder.

Heavier.

The floorboard creaks.

Just outside our room.

Then silence.

He is still.

I strain to listen for his movement, but my heart pounds so hard that it impairs my senses.

I am still.

Except for my chest that rises and falls rapidly.

I hear him now.

His breath.
Heavy against the door.
I close my eyes.
Tapping.
Skimming.
I draw in a deep breath and hold it.
Tapping.
Skimming.
This time against the door.
Scraping.
Skimming.
Our door.
I squeeze Becca's hand, hard.
I pray she doesn't move.
Or speak.
Or breathe.
I pray the only prayer I know, the bedtime prayer that Mom and I used to say every night, one of the few things I remember about her.

> *Now I lay me down to sleep,*
> *I pray the Lord my soul to keep.*
> *If I should die before I wake,*
> *I pray the Lord my soul to take.*

My lungs ache.
My heart pounds.
My hands sweat.
We won't move.

We won't breathe.
We won't let him know we're here.
We won't.
Silence.
The ticking clock.
Silence.
Then footsteps.
Down the hallway.
Tapping.
Farther away.
Skimming.
Fainter.
A door opens and closes.
Silence.
Silence.
I exhale and release Becca's hand.
"Danni?" Becca whispers.

I turn to Becca, who is peering up at me with trusting eyes. Her hair is tousled, her glasses rest low on the tip of her nose, and a curl dangles over her left eye. Her cheeks and forehead are smudged with flour.

"Danni," she whispers again as she pushes her glasses up the bridge of her nose with her small index finger, still covered in dough. I notice her deformed mouth. The mouth that drove Mom mad. The mouth that forced us here. Into foster care. Into the Garritys' twin on 8th Street.

"What, Becca?" I lean toward her, give her an Eskimo kiss, nose to nose, and rest my forehead against hers.

Her innocent voice floats through the air as soft and light as a feather.

"When can I finith wolling the dough?"

With our foreheads pressed firmly together, I look into her eyes, which appear to have merged into one. Her breath is sweet and warm.

"Soon, Becca, soon."

6

THE GARRITY HOUSE, 1980,
NINE YEARS OLD

I know that Becca and I have to get out of this house. And I wonder if Alfred feels the same way. I want to talk to Alfred. I want to know why he lives with the Garritys. I want to know what happened to his mother and father. I want to know if his mother went crazy after childbirth when she saw the way he looked, just like our mother had on the day Becca was born. But most of all, I want to know if he is as afraid as I am. Afraid of never having a real home. Afraid of what the future holds. Afraid of Sergeant. And afraid of how I've watched every second pass by at a turtle's pace in this house but hours seem to disappear, turning days into weeks, weeks into months.

Every morning, when Alfred returns home from his paper route, he gathers up his books and walks Becca and me to school. On sunny days, he covers his delicate face and arms with sunblock and wears a baseball cap to shield his fragile eyes from the bright rays of the sun. Alfred hardly speaks a word and always remains a couple of steps behind. He is fascinating to me, his mere existence hopelessly intriguing and bewildering, diligently moving about in such a manner that can easily go unnoticed. I am curious to know if his behavior is intentional, and if so, I want to know why. Why he is so quiet and secretive, and why sometimes I catch him staring at me when he thinks I don't notice. But I notice everything about Alfred.

It's Friday morning. Alfred is outside on the front porch waiting to walk Becca and me to school. I finish brushing Becca's hair, gather our books, grab her hand, and run downstairs. It's my favorite day of the week. Every Friday, our teacher, Miss Jenkins, brings us into Mr. Grasso's sixth grade class, where we get to play with the animals he has scattered on the shelves of his room: fish, snakes, mice, hermit crabs, and a big tarantula named Harry. Some girls are afraid of Harry, but not me. I pick him up and let him walk up my arm like the boys do. I once asked Alfred if he'd ever held Harry when he was in Miss Jenkins class. He shrugged his shoulders and made an icky face. I took that as a no.

The screen door slams shut behind us as we rush out onto the porch where Alfred is patiently waiting on the steps. He pulls some sunflower seeds from his pocket and chews on them, one at a time, until nothing but a mound of tasteless mush remains in his mouth. Using the same technique as Sergeant, he turns his head and spits the brown mass to the ground before starting again. Several times I look back at Alfred, who sucks and chews while quietly trailing behind Becca and me. As we approach the school grounds, three boys around Alfred's age step out from a thick patch of trees across the street. They cross the road and in a fast pace, walk behind Alfred. The largest boy, taller and broader than the rest, yells out. "Hey, Snow White! Wait up! I want to talk to you!"

Becca and I stop as the boys move closer to Alfred, who never looks back.

"Don't ignore me, you milky-white pussy!" the boy shouts and cracks his knuckles.

But Alfred does ignore him, walking faster, steadily increasing his pace to a slow jog, then a swift sprint, as he moves in front of Becca and me. We follow, trying our hardest to keep up with Alfred, who runs as fast as his skinny legs will carry him. But that big boy is so fast that he runs right up behind Alfred and pushes him hard until he trips and stumbles, drops his books, tumbles, and falls to the ground. The boys surround Alfred, who jumps to his feet, shaking and panting with fear, the way Mrs. Garrity does right before Sergeant teaches her a lesson. The biggest boy stands in front of Alfred, grins, and knocks Alfred's hat off his head onto the ground. Alfred's mouth is quivering as he bends down to pick up his hat, which is held firmly beneath the boy's shoe.

"May I have my hat back?"

The boy laughs and nudges his friend. "What's the magic word?"

Alfred looks up at him. His face is blotchy and red. "Please."

The boy picks up the hat and examines the team logo on the front. "I'm afraid I can't do that. You see, baseball is my favorite sport and the Phils are my favorite team, so what kind of fan would I be if I let a queer like you walk around in one of their hats? It just wouldn't be right. Baseball is for guys, not faggots." He pokes his finger into Alfred's frail chest. "Don't ever wear it again."

Alfred's voice trembles. "I...can wear whatever I want."

"What did you say?"

"I...I can wear whatever I want."

The boy laughs again and gestures to his friend beside him. "Did you hear that? This faggot doesn't know who he's talking to. I'll give you one chance to apologize for being the pussy you are."

Alfred drops his head, shoves his hands into his pockets, and clenches his teeth until his jawbone waves beneath his mottled skin.

"Well, faggot? I'm waiting," the boy says before drawing his arm back and sinking his tightened fist deep into Alfred's gut. "How's that feel, pussy?" Alfred drops to his knees and gasps for air. "Now get the fuck out of here before I really kick your ass."

Alfred stands, squeezes through the wall of boys that surrounds him, and runs as fast as he can down the street in the opposite direction of school. He disappears into the distance, leaving nothing but a scattered trail of sunflower seeds behind him. Becca and I pick Alfred's books up off the ground while the boys continue on to school. I don't know where Alfred went. He never makes it to school but shows up at precisely 3:15 p.m. by the bike rack, as he does every day, to walk us home. Becca runs up to him, holding out the pencil that she picked up off the ground that morning.

"Alfred, why were the boyth mean to you? And what does 'faggot' mean?"

Alfred takes the pencil from her grip and walks toward home. I motion for Becca to be quiet by holding my finger against my pursed lips. Sometimes I wish Becca wouldn't ask so many questions. I don't know why those boys don't like Alfred. Maybe it's the paleness of his skin or the pink hue of his eyes. I suppose some people refuse to accept someone who looks a little different. Shame on them, and shame on Mom for never giving Becca a chance. It seems to me that those who stand out in a crowd because of their differences are the most interesting people of all. Alfred stands out in a crowd…just like Becca. I wish he would talk to me more. I don't know if Alfred is a faggot, I don't even know what the word means, but after what happened this morning, I intend to find out.

Bethlehem.

The wretched city I call home.

Where moms go crazy, husbands hit their wives, and bullies beat up faggots. Becca and I will get out of here one day, far away from the blaring clashes of the steel plant and far away from the ghosts that haunt this historic town, refusing to leave. At least that's what townspeople say who claim to witness sightings throughout the city, appearing and disappearing, hovering and lingering, like the strange lady in the long brown coat.

Ghosts exist. I know they do. Erma didn't believe me when I told her about the coat lady, so I decided not to talk about her anymore to anyone except Becca. We pinky swore that the only time we would discuss her was late at night in bed under the covers where no one could hear. And we promised to never be afraid of her because Erma once said that fear can be your worst enemy and we definitely didn't need any enemies, not in this town anyway.

Bethlehem. I loved it once, when I lived with Mom, a lifetime ago. Before I turned five. Before the sounds of steel kept me up at night. Before Becca made Mom go crazy. I especially loved it around the holidays, when Mom and I would stroll along Main Street hand in hand, marveling at the Christmas lights as we shopped and listened to the joyous sounds of the season. Erma never took us to Main Street, but Mrs. Garrity takes us there once a week, on Friday afternoons, while Sergeant is at the pub on the other side of town. Occasionally we'll go into the five and dime where Mrs. Garrity buys her cosmetics, but most of the time we stand outside the stores peering into the windows at the beautiful mannequins dressed in fine clothes.

Just once I wish Becca and I could get a new dress or a pair of shiny new shoes out of one of those pretty windows instead of out of the big green garbage bags in the church basement. Just once. But Sergeant's the only one in the Garrity family who gets anything new because he's "the only one in this goddamn house who deserves it." But Mrs. Garrity still goes every week and stares into the store windows at things she can't have. Seems kind of stupid to me. Every Friday, like clockwork, when Alfred, Becca, and I get home from school, we sit on the edge of Mrs. Garrity's bed and watch at she gets ready to go. As she is doing now. Because it's Friday. But today is different. Today is our birthday. Mine and Becca's.

Becca really liked the gum-wrapper bracelet I gave to her moments ago, when we quietly celebrated in our room with a Hostess Twinkie and a birthday wish, just the two of us sitting hand in hand the way we have for the past five years.

"Today is our special day, Becca. Make a wish, any wish, the bigger the better."

Becca closed her eyes and squeezed my hands. I tried to imagine what was going on inside her head while she made her wish. It must have been something pretty special to put a smile on her face that big.

Mrs. Garrity is putting on her only pair of heels and her finest dress, the blue one that she wears to church on Sunday, the one with the hole in the pocket and the broken zipper in the back that she keeps fastened with a safety pin. She removes a small black tube of lipstick from her top drawer, swipes the cherry red stick across her mouth, and rubs her lips together numerous times. I turn to Becca and hold my hand out and thumb up. "I declare a thumb war."

Becca giggles, clasps her hand in mine, lifts her thumb, and struggles to pin mine. Alfred moves closer to the edge of the bed, sits up straight, folds his hands in his lap, and closely watches Mrs. Garrity's every move.

"You look very pretty," he says.

"Why, thank you, Alfred."

Becca and I continue battling and laughing as Mrs. Garrity opens a shiny gold compact, presses her fingers into cream-colored makeup, and gently dabs it onto the purplish bruise on the side of her face. The bruise she got last week when she put a double crease in one of Sergeant's dress shirts. She should have known better, at least that's what Sergeant told her when he made that "worthless bitch" wash, dry, and correctly iron that shirt five times before teaching her a final lesson with the back side of his hand. But Sergeant isn't here now. He's at the pub with his friends, so Mrs. Garrity doesn't have to worry about the back of his hand or the sting of his sharp tongue, not right now anyway.

It's a short drive to Main Street. Becca sits beside me in the backseat of Mrs. Garrity's old Dodge with her feet dangling off the edge of the seat.

"Danni?"

"Yeah?"

"Tell me about Mom again."

"What do you want to know?"

"Everything."

"I don't know everything, Becca."

"What wuth her name?"

"Amy."

"That's a pretty name."

"Yes, it is."

"Wuth she nice?"

"Yes."

"Wuth she pretty?"

"Very."

"Like you?"

"No…like you."

"I'm not pretty."

"Of course you are, Becca. You're beautiful on the outside and on the inside where it counts."

"What did Mom look like, Danni?"

"She had wavy brown hair and big blue eyes, just like yours."

"Wuth her mouth like mine, too?"

"No."

"Why?"

"Because you're special."

"Like Alfred?"

"Yes, you're special like Alfred."

Becca grabs my hand and interlocks her fingers in mine.

"Danni, where doeth Mom live?"

"I don't know."

"Why doethn't she want to live with uth?"

"I don't know, Becca! I don't know! Maybe she just got too tired to be a mommy."

Becca looks down in deep thought before softly speaking again.

"When I get too tired, I take a nap."

I smile. "I know. That's because you're a good girl."

As we turn onto Main Street, a faint voice calls out to me: *Close your eyes.* A chill runs up the back of my neck as I turn toward Becca, who sits next to me fiddling with a small stone she found in the Garritys' front yard. *Don't look back!* The voice is louder than before but not loud enough to distract Alfred, who is sitting in the front passenger seat telling Mrs. Garrity about a fascinating book he is reading about a boy named Huck. I look out the window as Mrs. Garrity parks the car on the corner of Broad and Main. How dare someone taunt me like this and not have the guts to show his or her face! *Close your eyes! Don't look back!* I hold Becca's hand tighter in my grasp and try to ignore the relentless banter of the cowardly voice that gradually fades into the distance.

Becca draws her knees to her chest. "Ouch! Danni, you're hurting me!"

Startled, I release Becca's hand from my grip. "I'm sorry, Becca, are you OK?"

She nods and rubs her hand with the other. "Danni?"

"Yeah?"

"Maybe when Amy ithn't too tired anymore she'll want to be our mommy again."

Becca's words sting sometimes like rubbing alcohol on an open cut. It's been five years. I thought Mom would have come for us by now. I thought she would have missed me as much as I miss her. I lift Becca's foot up onto my lap and tie the tattered shoelace that has come undone. I place my hand on Becca's back and rub in small circles, patting several times the way that Mom used to when I sat next to her on the sofa, watching cartoons while she read the newspaper. Mrs. Garrity and Alfred get out of the car and head toward the five and dime, immersed in conversation. I draw in a deep breath, shove my hands into my jacket pockets, and force the tips of my nails into the soft flesh in the center of my palms.

"Yeah," I say. "Maybe."

It's early evening. Mrs. Garrity and I are finishing the dinner dishes. She washes while I dry and neatly stack them on the counter next to the sink. Mrs. Garrity then places each dish in the cabinet, according to size, the way Sergeant likes them. She calculates every move, avoiding any sound that may disrupt Sergeant, who is in the living room reading the newspaper. Becca is upstairs playing in our room, and Alfred is taking out the garbage. I dry the last dish and neatly fold the dish towel and lay it beside the sink. It's almost seven o'clock, and I am eager to get upstairs and read to Becca. I told her that, because it's our birthday, I would finish reading *Charlotte's Web* tonight. Becca cried a bit when Charlotte died, but I told her not to be sad because it has a happy ending that I promised would make her smile. Before I can exit the kitchen, Mrs. Garrity grabs my arm and pulls me aside. She bends down, eye level, holds her hand out, palm up, and whispers. "Danni, don't you have something for me?"

I look at her, bewildered. "Excuse me, ma'am?"

Mrs. Garrity peers over my shoulder into the living room where Sergeant is still engrossed in his reading. "Please don't play games with me. Just give it back, and we'll pretend this never happened."

I look around the kitchen and out the window where Alfred is piling trash bags into the garbage can.

"I'm sorry, ma'am, but I don't understand."

Mrs. Garrity stands up straight and rubs her eyes and the back of her neck with both hands in an obvious display of frustration and exhaustion. She unties her apron, lifts it up over her head, and hangs it on the back of the kitchen door as Alfred enters from outside. He walks to the sink, turns on the faucet, grabs the bar of soap from the counter, and rolls it around in his hands.

With her back to Alfred, Mrs. Garrity bends down again and looks at me harshly. Her whisper is sharp and stern. "I know that you took my lipstick, Danni, the new lipstick I bought on Main Street today. Please give it back...now!"

Alfred continues washing his hands, glancing over his shoulder while straining to listen to every hushed word.

"But I didn't take your lipstick, ma'am."

Mrs. Garrity grabs me by the shoulders with both hands. "Danni, this is very important. Don't make me punish you. Where is it?"

There is a reckless desperation in Mrs. Garrity's voice that I recognize all too well, and my heart begins to race with the dreaded anticipation of what's to come. I look around the room at Alfred, then at Mrs. Garrity, whose face has now contorted into an angry glare.

"I don't know, ma'am. Honestly, I don't know. I didn't take it, I swear."

Mrs. Garrity straightens out her faded flowered housecoat and clears her throat. "OK, then, you leave me no choice. One thing I will not tolerate in this house is a liar."

She grabs my hand and leads me out of the kitchen, through the living room, right past Sergeant, who never once looks up from his paper as he reaches into his shirt pocket and removes a small pouch. He pulls out a clump of brown chew and shoves it high up into his cheek. The smell lingers in the air as I pull back from Mrs. Garrity, trying to break the grip she has on my wrist that begins to sting. On the far side of the living room, beneath the staircase, there is a small door, stark white, like every other door in the house. It has a round, black doorknob with a key protruding out from the keyhole. We stop and stand before it.

There are no chips in the paint, no smudges, no marks anywhere on any door or on any wall in the house. Sergeant won't allow it. He keeps gallons of flat white paint neatly stacked in the basement, and every Saturday morning, at o-seven hundred hours, Alfred enters the basement and scurries about for a bit before emerging with a cup of paint in one hand and a small paintbrush in the other. He methodically walks around the house, thoroughly inspecting every inch for nicks and marks that need touching up. When he is finished, he retreats again into the basement, sometimes for hours. I often wonder what he does down there for such long periods of time. I'll ask him one day, when I get the courage.

My face begins to burn as I stare at the door in front of me. I don't know what's behind it. I've never opened it. We're not allowed to. Mrs. Garrity releases my arm and leans down. "I'll give you one more chance to tell me the truth."

I lean in close to Mrs. Garrity, so close that I can smell the subtle scent of laundry detergent on her clothes, and I tell her again, quiet enough so as not to attract any attention from Sergeant. "I'm telling you the truth, ma'am. Honest I am. I didn't take anything."

Mrs. Garrity places her hand on my back, opens the door, and guides me in. "OK, young lady...you stay in there and think about what you've done. I don't want to hear a peep out of you."

She closes the door behind me. It's dark in here. Very dark. I turn to face the door, feeling my way through the black air the way we did at school weeks ago when we studied the five senses with Miss Jenkins, who blindfolded us and had us find our way around the classroom using our sense of touch and hearing. I press my ear against the door and listen to Mrs. Garrity on the other side, who fidgets with the key in the doorknob before removing it, allowing a small beam of light to stream through. With one eye to the small opening, I watch as she places the key in her pocket, turns, and walks away. I can hear perfectly now. Everything. The house and those within it. Sergeant, ruffling the newspaper to turn a page. Alfred, discreetly scrambling around in the basement. Becca, stepping lightly across our bedroom floor, waiting for me. Mrs. Garrity, rummaging through her bedroom, frantically opening and closing drawers, searching for her lipstick. And the clock...the goddamned clock.

Erma told me to always tell the truth, no matter what. She said, "The truth will set you free." But that's not always true. Not this time anyway. Sergeant folds the newspaper and places it on the sofa beside him, picks up the empty coffee can on the end table, and spits a thick stream of tarlike fluid into it. He stands, stretches, and climbs the stairs above me. His ring scrapes against the wall as he whistles an eerie tune that, in some way, resembles the shrill sound of the rusty old swing on the school playground when it sways in a gust of wind. I don't know how much trouble I'm in, but I have a sick feeling inside that Mrs. Garrity is in for far more. I crouch down by the door, hug my knees, and rest my head in my arms, welcoming the small, dark space that envelops me. Upstairs, Mrs. Garrity's bedroom door opens. The hinge squeals just like the sound the metal cars at the steel plant make when they come to a screeching halt along the tracks.

His voice.

Then hers.

A sharp slap.

A heavy thud on the floor.

Whimpering.

I press my hands against my ears to block out the vile sounds of their bedroom. It's our birthday. I wish birthday wishes really did come true. And I wish something bad would happen to Sergeant that would make him go away. Forever.

By the time Mrs. Garrity tiptoes down the stairs and opens the door to the closet, it feels like I've used up every bit of oxygen it contained. With one hand, she holds her robe closed in front of her while wiping her swollen, tearful eyes with the other. She won't look at me as she turns her face and motions for me to exit.

"Go on upstairs now, Danni," she says. "It's well past your bedtime."

As I climb the stairs, Mrs. Garrity walks over to the refrigerator, removes a package of peas from the freezer, and sits down at the kitchen table with her head resting into the makeshift ice pack. According to Sergeant, she's nothing but a "stupid bitch," a "useless cunt," and a "good-for-nothing, white-trash whore." And according to the boys at school, Alfred is nothing but a "snow-white faggot." Erma taught us to say, "Sticks and stones may break my bones, but names will never hurt me." But I never say that. I know better. Because being called "little orphan Danni" hurt a lot, and it seems to me that being called those names hurt Mrs. Garrity and Alfred a whole lot, too. Sometimes the tongue can be stronger than the fist, more destructive and more detrimental. Maybe I'll tell Erma that one day, if I ever get the chance, because that's all I could think about while I was locked in the closet listening to Mrs. Garrity. She didn't fight back when Sergeant threw her to the floor, held her head against the hard wood, and took what he wanted from her.

"You're only good for one thing," he told her before exhaling, rolling off her, and climbing into bed. The walls in the Garrity house are thin, too thin, because I heard everything from where I sat, huddled up in the corner of the dark closet. I lifted my shirt and tightly gripped a portion of skin on my lower abdomen. But I still heard everything, regardless of how hard I pinched and squeezed. I heard it all.

"My head hurts," Mrs. Garrity murmured. I imagined her, remaining as he left her, on her hands and knees with her buttocks exposed. The floorboards creaked under Sergeant's heavy feet as he got up, walked across the room and removed something from his top dresser drawer.

"Here baby," he said, dropping what sounded like a pill bottle by her side. He waited as it rolled to a stop. "Take a couple…you'll feel better." He smacked her bare bottom, belched a couple of times and climbed into bed. "Now get up off the floor and go wash up. You look like a fucking dog." She stood, took a labored breath that filtered through the floor between us, and walked to the door. "And don't make any noise," he added. "I need to get some sleep."

Mrs. Garrity closed the door behind her and paused outside Alfred's room before coming for me. I couldn't help but notice the similarities between the two of them. Alfred didn't fight back either when that boy called him a "faggot" and followed it up with a swift punch to the gut. If I were Alfred, I would have hit him first, like I hit Missy Lacintosh. I would have made him sorry he called me that name. I didn't even know what the word "faggot" meant. But I do now.

I am glad to get back to my bedroom, where I find Becca curled up at the end of the bed, sound asleep, with *Charlotte's Web* still held between her hands at the precise page where I was supposed to continue reading. I remove the book from her grasp, pull the covers up over her, and climb in on the other side. I must have fallen asleep for a short time, but I am awake now, listening to Alfred cry in his room. I can faintly hear his muffled sobs as I lie here counting the second hand that slowly ticks away every minute of every hour. His high-pitched weeping penetrates the night air, somewhere between the unnerving ticking and the reckless clatter of the steel. Hours seem to pass before I sneak out of bed, creep down the hallway to his door, and press my ear against the cool wood, listening as Alfred struggles to catch his breath. I had never stepped foot in Alfred's room before. Not once. His room, like Alfred, is a mystery to me, until tonight, when an uncontrollable sense of curiosity leads me to him. I turn the doorknob, enter, and close the door behind me. Sensing my presence, he holds his breath.

Silence. I stand by the door, blinded by darkness, and wait for him to exhale.

"Alfred?" I make my way through his bedroom, shuffling my sock feet across the cold, bare floor. "Alfred," I say, extending my arms out to explore my surroundings. I listen carefully for the delicate sounds of his suppressed breathing. "I know you're here. I heard you crying. Are you OK?" A few seconds pass before a small beam of light flashes on from beneath Alfred's bedcovers, subtly illuminating the room where he lies trembling under his sheets. He releases his breath, coughs, and sucks in short bursts of air between each quivering word.

"What do you want?"

"Are you OK?"

"I'm fine."

"You don't sound fine."

"So."

"So…why are you crying?"

"Why do you care?"

"Because I do."

"It doesn't matter."

"Of course it does."

"Nothing matters."

"Are you upset about what happened with those boys from school?"

He pauses. "Nope."

I take a seat at the end of Alfred's bed, draw my knees to my chest, and pull my nightgown down over them. There are so many questions I want to ask Alfred, and there is so much I want to tell him about Becca and me, and what happened to our mother when Becca was born.

"I know how it feels ya know…to be made fun of."

Alfred sniffs. "You don't know anything." In the soft light that shines through Alfred's sheets, I can see that his room is bare and plain. There is a tall stack of books beside his bed and a large map of the United States that hangs on the wall beneath his clock. Small, red tacks trail across the entire country, from Bethlehem to Los Angeles. Outside, the wind kicks up, brushing a tree branch against the window as the clock strikes the midnight hour. I hug my legs tighter and rest my chin on top of my knees.

"I know that I'll never fit in anywhere because I don't have parents and a real home. I know that I hate being called names and laughed at. And I know that sometimes I want to run away, far away, where no one knows who I am or where I'm from."

Alfred lifts his head out from beneath the covers, sits up, and secures the flashlight between his legs so that the light shines up under his chin, spotlighting his face, red and blotchy, his eyes, puffy and bloodshot. He stares down into the light as his scrawny white chest rises and falls, outlining every rib with each irrepressible breath.

"I want to run away, too," he says. With the heels of his hands, he wipes the tears from his eyes and looks up at me, waiting for more.

Calmly I speak to Alfred, whose attention I have somehow managed to attract. "And sometimes…I hurt real bad." I point to my heart. "In here."

Alfred nods. "Me, too."

I hug my knees and gently rock back and forth. "But no matter how hard I try, I can't stop the hurt, or my thoughts. Especially late at night when it's so quiet and still, and all I can hear is the ticking and the banging and the irritating voice that hardly ever shuts up." I cup my hands over my ears to soften the sound of the clock over Alfred's bed that seems to grow louder with each passing second. "Don't you hear it, Alfred…don't you hear any of it?" Alfred wipes his nose with the back of his hand and shrugs his shoulders. "Alfred?"

"What?"

"Can you keep a secret?"

"Yes."

"If I show you something, do you promise not to tell anyone?"

"I promise."

I take the flashlight from Alfred, lay it on the bed beside me, and lift my shirt up just above my navel. Alfred wipes his eyes again, leans in closer, and stares at the welts and bruises that cover my lower abdomen and upper thighs. I point to the newest one, larger than the others, just above my right pelvic bone, black and blue from minutes of pinching and twisting. Alfred's eyes grow wide as I gently run my fingers over my latest infliction, the one that took my breath away just hours ago when I sat in the closet with several inches of flesh tightly gripped between my thumb and index finger, the one that causes me to wince with the slightest touch, the one that makes the noises go away and my thoughts stop.

Alfred's face contorts. He sucks in his breath and holds it for a moment before speaking. "Did he do that to you?"

"Who?"

Alfred looks down and shakes his head side to side. "Never mind." He lifts one hand to his mouth and bites nails that have already been chewed down into the quick so that the tips of his fleshy fingers curl up over them.

I pause for a moment. "The bruises help me," I say.

"What do you mean?" he asks.

"The pain makes me stop thinking so much about everything."

He looks at me with shock and disgust. "You do that to yourself?"

I pull down my shirt and draw my knees back to my chest.

"Yeah...well...I knew you wouldn't understand...forget about it."

Alfred moves closer to me.

"I'm sorry, Danni. I won't tell anyone. I promise." He pulls the covers close to his chin, tightly clenching them between both hands. "Danni?"

"Yeah?"

"I have a secret, too." Alfred pauses before he continues. "You know what those guys were calling me this morning?"

"Yeah?"

"Do you know what it means?" I nod my head. Alfred takes a deep breath and another while looking side to side several times as though making sure no one else is around who could possibly hear what he is about to reveal. He parts his lips to speak, when suddenly we hear a noise.

A door.

Opening and closing.

Heavy footsteps.

Up and down the hallway.

Outside Alfred's room.

Sergeant.

Pacing...belching...and rubbing his stomach...trying to soothe the ulcers that often keep him up in the middle of the night. Alfred tenses, raises his hand to his mouth, and firmly presses his index finger against his puckered lips just before turning off the flashlight. We sit motionless, barely breathing, with Sergeant milling about only feet away. Sergeant's presence is unsettling to me, but it is obvious that to Alfred his presence is something far more as he succumbs to an immobilizing fear that leaves him rigid and stiff. The moon is bright tonight as the clouds pass. It casts shadows throughout the room that look like monsters creeping across the walls. I stare at the doorknob, hoping and praying that it won't turn, when suddenly I am startled by something that I never would have expected. Alfred's skin is soft and smooth as he tenderly rests his palm in mine, touching me for the first time, on his bed, in the dark, awakening something within me. Something different. Something exciting.

I hope that Sergeant can't hear my wildly racing heart because I don't want Alfred to get mad at me and I don't want him to take his hand away. The only time I ever held a boy's hand before was in the third grade when Eddie Keiser and I reached into a small bag filled with our classmates' names to pick out a Pollyanna for our school Christmas party. We laughed when we grabbed each other's hands as we rummaged through the mound of paper. I had hardly even noticed Eddie before that, but for some reason after that day I couldn't take my eyes off him, just as I can't take my eyes off Alfred, whose stoic facial expression is now subtly highlighted in the blue hue of the moon. Alfred's brilliant eyes have dried with the sound of Sergeant so near. He barely blinks, staring ahead into the night air as he sits up, straight and tall, in perfect posture, like a soldier called to duty, listening and waiting with baited breath. He is much different now than he was moments ago when he quivered beneath his sheets like a timid little bunny prematurely extracted from his nest. He juts out his chin, takes a deep breath, fully expands his chest, and sits at attention as he has been so stringently taught, ready to obey or ready to act, I'm not sure which. I sit with Alfred on his bed, hand in hand, until well past the midnight hour when Sergeant returns to his room and closes the door. Alfred exhales, pulls his hand from my sweaty grip, and falls to a slouched position.

"Alfred?" I speak in a hushed voice that blankets the air calmly and quietly like the early morning dew.

"Yeah?"

"You OK?"

"Yep...you OK?"

"Yep."

"The sun's gonna be coming up soon, Danni...you should go."

I look away from Alfred, perhaps for the first time since I entered the room hours ago. I don't want to leave his side, and I don't want to ignore the unforgettable sense of excitement that erupted when he touched me.

"Alfred?"

"Yeah?"

"Was there something you wanted to tell me?" Alfred lays back down and pulls the covers up over his head.

"Nope."

"Are you sure?"

"Yep."

I stand and walk to the door, place my hand on the doorknob, and look back at Alfred, who has once again retreated, wrapping himself up completely like a carefully spun cocoon. Fear has a strange way of masking itself. Anger. Sorrow. Betrayal. Denial. Each one has the ability to single-handedly destroy. I don't know what Alfred was going to tell me and I don't know if he felt the same way I did when he held my hand. But it doesn't matter now. Because I'm smiling.

Here in the Garrity house.

I'm actually smiling.

7

THE GARRITY HOUSE, 1981,
TEN YEARS OLD

On Saturday mornings, if we have been good all week and have completed all of our chores, Mr. and Mrs. Garrity allow us to sleep in until o-nine hundred hours. So I am startled when I wake to a knocking on our door an hour earlier. It's Mrs. Garrity.

"Danni, get dressed quickly and come downstairs, ya hear?"

I sit up in bed and look at Becca, who is lying beside me rubbing her eyes.

Again Mrs. Garrity raps on the door, this time a little bit harder. "Danni, do you hear me?"

"Yes, ma'am." My voice is deep and groggy from the night's sleep. "I'll be right down."

I throw off the covers and sit at the edge of the bed for a moment before stepping down onto the cold wood-en floor where the crumb-filled plate from our birthday celebration yesterday still sits. I pick it up and hide it in a drawer until later, when I will sneak it back downstairs and into the cabinet before Mrs. Garrity misses it. And she will miss it.

She has exactly eight plates. Eight saucers. Eight cups. And eight glasses. All perfectly stacked in the cabinet. They are all white, nothing else is allowed. No colors. No prints. If one breaks, it is replaced by another exactly like it. Everything at the Garrity house is in perfect order. Always. Sergeant will have it no other way. Even the canned goods in the cupboard are perfectly aligned alphabetically, labels facing out. I once saw him punish Mrs. Garrity for having the green beans before the corn. He squeezed her arm so tight that it was a week or more before the purplish imprints of his fingers disappeared from her flesh. Sergeant didn't know that I was outside watching him through the window as he grabbed her arm and dragged her to the pantry, forcing the weight of her body into the neatly organized cans that tumbled and crashed to the floor. But Mrs. Garrity knew. Her eyes met mine as he shoved one side of her face up against the wooden pantry shelf.

I hate them both: Mr. Garrity for treating everyone like nothing and Mrs. Garrity for allowing it. Erma said it's a sin to hate anyone. She said that hate is a dangerous thing to hold in your heart because it can fill up so fast that there's no room for anything else. She said it can destroy you if you let it, that when you spend so much time hating someone else, there's no time left for loving yourself. And that loving yourself is what's most important because you have to love yourself in order to love anyone else. I wonder if Erma loved herself. It seems to me that she loved what was in that little brown bag a whole lot more. So I decide that it doesn't matter so much if I love myself or not as long as I love Becca. She needs it the most. So I give her all that I have. And I hate Mom even more.

I dress and pull my hair back into a high ponytail with the rubber bands from around my wrist.

"Becca," I say in a hushed voice, wincing as I grab my ponytail with both hands and tighten it until the skin around the sides of my face is taut. "Go back to sleep. I'll be right back."

At the top of the steps, I pause to listen to the familiar voice of Mrs. Rogers coming from the kitchen.

"So what part of Alabama are you from?"

It takes Mrs. Garrity a moment to answer. "Fort Rucker," she says.

"Is that where you met your husband?"

"That's right," she replies.

"It must have been quite a transition moving up here. How do you like it?"

Mrs. Garrity fills a teapot with water, places it on top of the stove, and turns the knob until a hissing sound shoots out from beneath it.

"I reckon I'm still adjusting," she says, pulling a book of matches from her housecoat to ignite the flammable gas.

Straining to hear the conversation, I step lightly down each step, intrigued by the voice of a woman I do not recognize. Her voice is precise and deliberate.

"Mrs. Garrity, how long has Danni been staying with you?"

"It's been about a year and a half."

"And have there been any problems, social or otherwise?"

I enter the kitchen before Mrs. Garrity can respond. The teapot whistles and all eyes rest on me.

"Danni!" Mrs. Rogers says, throwing her arms out. "You look beautiful. How have you been?" Mrs. Rogers is wearing an ivory-colored dress that is belted and swings loosely below the knee. Her chestnut hair is pulled back into a soft twist, and she smells sweet like a garden of honeysuckles. I wrap my arms around her waist and breathe her in, comforted by the way she pulls me into the supple cushioning of her abdomen. I want to tell her about Sergeant. I want to tell her that the faint yellow bruise on the side of Mrs. Garrity's face is from his forearm. I want to tell her about the noises I hear coming from their bedroom late at night, and I want to beg her to take Becca and me with her.

Mrs. Rogers looks down at me and sweeps her hand across my forehead to brush the hair from my eyes.

"So tell me...how are you?"

"Fine, thanks."

"And school?"

"Good."

"Do you have a nice teacher this year?"

"Yes, Miss Jenkins is very nice. And funny."

"The Garritys are a wonderful family, aren't they?" she says. "We were very fortunate to have them open up their home for fostering. How's everything going? Have they been treating you well?"

Mrs. Garrity lifts the teapot from the fire and glances at me out of the corner of her eye. Her look speaks a thousand words that silently beg for my secrecy. I look around the kitchen that echoes a multitude of Sergeant's sins. I see all of them. The cabinet door that sits cockeyed on its hinges. The dents and scrapes in the linoleum floor. And the strategically placed pictures that hang on the walls to hide the holes from his right fist. I want to tell Mrs. Rogers that there is a secret here. That within these walls there is a dirty and shameful secret, and that as disgraceful as the secret is, I am terrified that I only know a small part of it. I want to tell her that I can't sleep at night and that the ticking clock above my bed is like a time bomb waiting to go off. I look at Mrs. Garrity, whose widened eyes plead for my silence. He'll kill her if the secret gets out. I know he will.

"Yes, Mrs. Rogers. The Garritys have been treating Becca and me very well."

Mrs. Garrity exhales, blinks hard, and wipes her eyes with a crumpled napkin she's been clutching in her left hand.

"Good, good, I'm glad to hear that." Mrs. Rogers places her hands on my shoulders and turns me toward the refined woman who is sitting at the table with her legs crossed and her hands clasped in her lap. "Danni, I want you to meet Mrs. Suzanne Whiteker. Her husband, Dr. Tom Whiteker, is a physician downtown. I told her a little bit about you, and she has been eager to meet you."

Mrs. Whiteker stands up and reaches her hand out toward mine. "Hello, Danni. I've heard so much about you. Mrs. Rogers speaks very highly of you."

Mrs. Whiteker is perfect, like a brand-new doll, perfect. I've never met anyone like her before. Flawless. Like the porcelain doll that Mom bought me when I was three years old. I named her Cindy. She was the most beautiful doll I had ever seen. I wanted to take her everywhere I went, but Mom told me I had to be very careful with her and couldn't play with her too much because she was fragile and would break easily. It seemed kind of silly to have a doll that I could hardly play with, but I didn't want to break her, so I didn't play with her at all. As a matter of fact, I rarely even touched her. I just left her there, standing on top of my dresser in her blue velvet dress and patent-leather shoes, looking as pretty and perfect as the day Mom gave her to me. The only time I touched her was at night, right before bed, when I would gently lay her down to make her eyes close so she wouldn't watch me while I slept. And then again in the morning, when I would stand her back up again, taking extra care not to soil or damage her.

Mrs. Whiteker looks a lot like Cindy. Perfect, polished, and new. Her flaxen hair is silky smooth and curls under at the base of her neck. It doesn't move at all, even when a breeze blows through the open kitchen window. She is wearing a tailored blue suit that accents her slim figure, and a single strand of brilliant white pearls drapes around her neck against her creamy complexion. She is absolutely impeccable, right down to her perfectly pink fingernails. She seems far too colorful to be sitting here in the Garrity house where everything is so drab. I reach my hand out to hers, and the diamond-faced watch dangling on her wrist catches a beam of sun that shines through the window. It casts an array of dazzling colors around the room that sparkle and shimmer as she does. Her perfume scents the air with vanilla and spice, which weighs as heavily in the air as her presence weighs heavily on my mind.

"Hello, Mrs. Whiteker. It's nice to meet you, too," I say.

Mrs. Rogers motions for me to take a seat at the table next to her, directly across from Mrs. Whiteker, who won't take her eyes off me. She lifts and drops a tea bag in and out of a steaming cup of water that Mrs. Garrity has placed in front of her.

"Tell me, Danni, how do you like fifth grade? Mrs. Rogers tells me that you are a very smart girl, with straight As. You must be very proud of yourself."

Mrs. Garrity pours a glass of milk and hands it to me, along with a neatly folded white napkin. I take a sip, use the napkin to wipe my lips, and clear my throat before robotically spewing the same general information that I tell every new grown-up I meet.

"I like school. My teacher's name is Miss Jenkins, and she is very nice. My favorite subject is Science, and I like holding Harry, Mr. Grasso's pet tarantula." I grin, shrug my shoulders, take another sip of milk, and wipe my mouth again. "Oh…I like jumping rope and playing hopscotch, and my favorite color is pink."

I look around the room, fidget in my seat, and wait to be dismissed. I wonder if Becca is awake, and if so, what she is doing upstairs all by herself. I wonder why Mrs. Rogers hasn't asked to see her, too.

"Danni?" Mrs. Whiteker stirs her tea, clanking the metal spoon against the inside of the small white cup. "Dr. Tom and I are going to the zoo next week. I hear they have a wonderful new monkey exhibit." I stare at the clock on the kitchen wall and time the rhythmical ticking with Suzanne Whiteker's clanking spoon. I wonder if anyone else feels it like I do, pounding in my chest. "We would love for you to join us," she says and sips her tea. She folds her hands, places them properly in her lap, and raises one beautifully arched eyebrow in anticipation of my response.

"Well, Danni?" Mrs. Rogers rests her hand on my shoulder. "Doesn't that sound exciting? The zoo is a great place to visit this time of year, and I hear the monkey exhibit is incredible." She nods and winks. "You'll have a great time."

My eyes dart back and forth between Mrs. Rogers and Mrs. Whiteker, and for the first time it dawns on me that Mrs. Whiteker isn't just a guest at the Garrity house. She has come here looking for something or someone. Maybe she has come to take Becca and me away from here. Away from the eternal hammering that continually interrupts the morbid silence of the Garrity house, away from Mrs. Garrity's frail and feeble whimpers, and most importantly, away from Sergeant's escalating fury.

"I've never been to the zoo before, ma'am. I'd love to! I mean…we'd love to!" I pick up the glass of milk, drink it as fast as I can, every last drop, and then place it down on the table in front of me. "May I be excused from the table now?"

Mrs. Rogers glances at Mrs. Whiteker before looking at me. "Sure, Danni, but…"

I don't hear anything else that Mrs. Rogers says as I get up, push my chair in, and run upstairs as fast as I can, skipping every other step and disobeying at least two or three of Sergeant's house rules along the way. I fling open our bedroom door and find Becca still asleep, sprawled out on top of the covers, snoring with her mouth wide open.

"Becca, wake up." I sit beside her and give her a nudge. "Becca, wake up. I have something to tell you." Becca stops snoring, opens her eyes for a moment, and rolls over. "Get up," I say. "We're going to the zoo next week…to see the monkeys!" Becca rolls back, faces me, and opens her eyes.

"The thoo?" She yawns and stretches before sitting up in bed. "Did you thay we're goin' to the thoo, Danni?"

I brush the curls off her face. "That's exactly what I said. Dr. and Mrs. Whiteker are going to take us."

"Dr. and Mrs. who?" she asks.

"That doesn't matter now, Becca. We're going to see the monkeys!" I rush to the dresser and pull open the drawers. "Let's see…what should we wear? We want to make a very good impression."

As I sort through our clothes, I think about Alfred and wonder if he has ever been to the zoo. Becca gets up and jumps on the bed. Her loose, yellow curls bounce around her head as she claps her hands and sings. "We're goin' to the thoo…we're goin' to the thoo…we're goin' to the thoo."

I pick out two of our nicest outfits and neatly fold them on top of the dresser, along with the pink hair ribbon that Mrs. Rogers gave to me. I stand in front of the mirror and hold the ribbon up against my hair the way that she did as she said, "This will look beautiful with your auburn hair, Danni. Pink is definitely your color."

I never knew I had a color. But Mrs. Rogers was right. The ribbon looks pretty in my hair, which has grown long and wavy down the center of my back. I tie it back and lean in toward the mirror, looking at my face as though for the first time, studying every feature, running my fingers over my nose, lips, and eyes that are shades of brown or hazel, depending on how the light hits them. My skin is lightly tanned from the summer sun, and I look different suddenly. My face is thinner, my nose tips up at the end, and my lips are fuller and pinker. I think I'm pretty, but I'm not sure. Johnny Bittner thinks I'm pretty. At least that's what he wrote in the letter that he slipped in my desk last week at school. Maybe Alfred thinks I'm pretty, too. Maybe that's why he held my hand last night.

Mom was pretty. Before she started screaming like she did. I wonder if I will look like her. I wonder where she is and why she never came for us. I wonder how someone so hard to remember can be so hard to forget. And I wonder if I will ever see her again. I hope not. I hate her.

Becca's sweet voice swirls through the air like a falling leaf on a breezy autumn day, drowning out the ominous pounding of the steel plant and momentarily silencing the ticking of the big, round clock on the plain white wall above our bed.

Sergeant never misses Sunday mass. Neither does Mrs. Garrity, unless her face is bruised real bad, in which case Sergeant forbids her to attend. On occasion, like today, Sergeant orders the entire family to go—if we can clean up good enough, that is. Becca gets dressed, brushes her teeth, rushes downstairs, and sits by the window, gazing out at Bandit, the neighbor's dog, sitting by the fence staring back at her, playfully wagging his tail. She calls out to Mrs. Garrity, who scrambles around the kitchen putting dishes away and wiping down countertops.

"Can I go outhide to pet Bandit? Pleathe?"

"Sure Becca...but don't get yourself all dirty now...ya hear? We'll be fixin' to leave real soon."

"Yeth ma'am." Becca runs outside, slamming the screen door behind her, in spite of how many times I've told her not to. I cringe at the jolt that shakes the house, and I keep my fingers crossed that, just once, Sergeant won't notice. But Sergeant notices everything. He once made Alfred stand for eight hours, nose to the wall, for accidentally dropping a few cake crumbs on the kitchen floor after Mrs. Garrity had swept. I told Becca to always be quiet when Sergeant is around, as quiet as a mouse. But she didn't listen because I hear her now, yelling and laughing. From my bedroom window, I watch her run to the fence, poke her fingers through the chain links, and giggle as the fluffy canine sniffs her hand with his cold, black nose. "That tickleth, Bandit! Ha-ha! That tickleth!" She runs the length of the fence, coaxing the dog to follow her. "Come on, Bandit...come here, boy!"

Sergeant is moving about in his bedroom, stepping hard across the wooden floor. The sound of hinges seeps down the hall as he opens and closes his door, walks past my room, and descends down the stairs, pounding his shiny black shoes against each step until he enters the kitchen where Mrs. Garrity is rushing to finish her morning cleaning.

I'm wearing a dress today, the yellow one that I got out of the used clothes bin in the church basement a few weeks ago. The one that looks a lot like the dress that

Jenny Kingston, the most popular girl in school, wore last year for our class pictures, when we were in the fourth grade. I must have stared at her for hours that day as she strutted around school with a confidence I couldn't dare to have. Maybe the dress I'm wearing is Jenny's old dress that she crumpled up and threw in a big green garbage bag for the church clothing drive. Maybe it is, but I don't care, because I look pretty—perhaps not as pretty as Jenny did that day, but pretty all the same.

Outside, Becca's laugh penetrates the morning air, harshly breaking the silence of the new day as Bandit barks in response to her gleeful voice. I stand in front of the mirror brushing the long amber locks that flow down my back, listening to Sergeant's voice as it begins to rumble downstairs, quiet enough to stay within the walls of this house yet loud enough to command the attention of everyone within it. Becca and Bandit race up and down the yard, and it frightens me that, in the midst of their commotion, I can clearly hear every word that Sergeant spews from his toxic mouth. I close my eyes and brush through my hair from top to bottom, again and again, raking through every strand, keenly focused on every word and every sound that takes place on the floor below me.

"Did you tell that child she could go outside and play with that dog?" Sergeant asks.

The distinct sound of dishes being stacked on top of one another clatters in the kitchen below, and a cabinet door thuds to a close before she reluctantly answers.

"Yes, sir, I did, but I told her not to dirty herself because I know how important it is that we all look acceptable," she answers, carefully choosing her words. I press the brush harder against the top of my head and drag the plastic bristles across my scalp as Sergeant's heavy feet step across the linoleum floor. I feel uneasy in the moments of silence that follow. I place the hairbrush down in precise coordination with the ticking clock to ensure the tapping sound of the wooden handle on the dresser surface gets lost in it's rhythm. I crack open the bedroom door and peer down the stairs into the kitchen. He stops behind her. Close enough for her to feel his breath on her neck. "Acceptable?" he asks.

She nods.

"Is that so?"

Mrs. Garrity turns the faucet handle and allows the warm water to rush over her trembling hands. As usual, she seems to rehearse her response in her head before speaking. "Yes sir, we all want to look acceptable so that we can make you proud in your place of worship."

Sergeant grabs her buttocks, leans in against her, and breathes heavy with rising anger and excitement. He drags his hands over her hips, around the subtle curve of her waist, and up her back until both hands rest on her shoulders, above her delicate collarbone. "Acceptable is a mark of mediocrity, baby. You should know that," he says, wrapping both hands around her neck until she gasps. "And mediocrity is never acceptable."

Outside Becca yells out, "Get the stick, Bandit! Good boy!"

I listen to the joyous sounds of my little sister outside overlapping the daunting sounds of Sergeant inside.

"I suppose you think it's acceptable for a child to be carrying on like that on a holy day?"

It's quite predictable, the change in Mrs. Garrity's voice right before Sergeant teaches her a lesson. I watch and listen closely, disgusted by the weak way she answers her husband, the man she wakes up with every morning and goes to sleep with every night, the man she says she loves, the man she vowed her life to, for better or for worse, 'til death do they part.

"I...I didn't think that..." she begins.

Sergeant covers her mouth with his hands. "Sshhhh." He presses his body into hers, grinding her pelvic bones into the rigid edge of the porcelain sink. "That's the problem, baby...you didn't think...you never think...because you're too stupid to think." He releases his hands from her neck, slides them over her shoulders and down both arms, wrapping himself completely around her, immobilizing her while securing her dainty wrists in his hands. "That's why I have to do all the thinking for you," he adds, gripping both of her wrists in one hand and the cold water knob in the other. "Isn't that right?" The water rushes over Mrs. Garrity's hands as Sergeant increases the temperature by turning the knob slightly closer to the off position. "I said...isn't that right?" She whimpers and struggles to pull away, widening her eyes to the increasing heat of the water that turns her skin red. "I don't want to hurt you baby...I love you! Now answer the goddamned question! Isn't it true that I have to do all the thinking for you because you're too fucking stupid to think for yourself?"

Bandit barks louder. I rush to the window, shuffling my sock feet across the hardwood floor so as not to attract any attention. Outside, Becca climbs the fence and laughs in response to Bandit's tongue that swipes her face. I wish she would be quiet. She needs to be quiet! I open the window to her high-pitched voice that carries into the bedroom along with Bandit's relentless barking and the grating clanking of the steel plant in full operation.

Clanking!

Booming!

Screeching!

I lean out the window and wave my arms, hoping to get Becca's attention.

Downstairs, Sergeant repeats himself one more time, demanding an answer from the "stupid bitch" he calls his wife, the one who promised to honor and obey him. "You need me because you're too stupid...isn't that right?" I shuffle back to the door. He clenches his teeth together and forces out every word until spit foams up on either side of his mouth like a rabid animal. "How dare you disrespect me in my own house! Answer me!"

But Mrs. Garrity doesn't answer the goddamned question fast enough for that son of a bitch because he turns the cold water knob off and lets the scalding hot water scorch her hands until she screams out the answer to his question.

"Yes, sir!" she cries, falling to the floor as Sergeant releases her hands. "You're right, I'm too stupid." She buries her wrists into her chest and sobs over the blistering pain and torturous sting of a broken spirit.

Sergeant stands above her, shaking his head. "You never learn, do you?"

Once again, I drag my feet across the floor and wave my arms out the window to get Becca's attention when a subtle knock on the door startles me.

"Danni?" A small voice calls out. "Are you in there? It's me, Alfred."

I can barely hear Alfred calling out to me from the other side of the slightly open door. His voice is soft and sweet, unlike any other boy I know.

"Just a minute, Alfred. I'll be right there."

I put my shoes on and swipe a tiny bit of Vaseline across my lips before opening the door. Alfred is neatly dressed in a blue suit, white shirt, and red tie. He looks very handsome today, in spite of his lanky, white arms that awkwardly extend out beyond the bottom of his sleeves. He looks down the hallway before discretely speaking again. "Can I come in?"

I stand back and gesture for him to enter. "Sure."

Alfred leaves a scented trail of ivory soap behind him as he walks to the center of my room, turns, and faces me. "Your dress is very pretty," he says, ignoring the situation downstairs that continues with another round of yelling and whimpering.

It's hard to look at Alfred without feeling a sudden burst of heat in my face. I close the door. "Thanks."

Downstairs the kitchen door opens and shuts. Only this time it's not Becca because she is still outside teaching Bandit to roll over. I fidget with the rubber band around my wrist, twisting, pulling, and snapping. "Is there something you want, Alfred?"

Alfred shakes his head side to side and pushes his pale, thin hands into his suit pockets. He is restless and uneasy, obviously so. "No, nothing."

I take Mom's sweater out of my drawer, wrap it around my shoulders, and place one arm in at a time. It fits me better than it did five years ago when it hung down past my shins. Outside, Bandit barks louder. Alfred moves closer toward me, scanning me up and down with his pink eyes. "Is it new?" he asks, lifting his white eyebrows.

"Is what new?"

"Your dress."

I look down and run my hands along the rich yellow fabric that stops several inches above my knees. "Um... yeah...I guess you could say that...why?"

Alfred reaches out, wraps his hands around the back of my hair, gathers it together, and pulls it out from beneath my sweater. My stomach feels different when Alfred touches me. I felt it the other night when he held my hand on his bed, and I feel it now as he strokes my hair. Alfred's brilliant eyes dart from the top of my sore, well-brushed head to the bottom of my worn shoes as he tenderly tucks my hair behind my ears.

"You look very pretty," he says, looking down at the floor before our eyes meet.

"No, I don't."

"Yes, you do," he insists.

"Really?"

Alfred can't look me in the eye without his face turning red, so he looks away. "Yes, really," he says.

It's strange how the more time I spend with Alfred, the more baffling he becomes. Aside from his appearance, there's something so unique about him that I can't put my finger on and yet feel an overwhelming urge to try. He moves and talks differently than any boy I have ever known. Never before have I felt this way.

Fascinated.

Captivated.

Infatuated.

I could watch him all day, the way he tilts his head to one side when he talks and the way small lines form around the outer corners of his eyes when he smiles, as he's doing now. Alfred clasps his hands behind his back and shifts his weight to one side as he speaks. "Can I ask you something, Danni?"

"Sure." In mere seconds, Alfred's cheeks change to a color that reminds me of strawberry milk.

"Do you have a boyfriend?" he asks.

I laugh at his silly question, twirl my hair between my fingers, and enjoy the sudden rush of giddiness that I get when Alfred is around. Outside, Bandit's bark turns from gleeful to aggressive with the sudden sound of Sergeant's voice, which startles us as he calls out Becca's name. I don't want to walk away from Alfred. I want to answer his question. I want to stay close to him, close enough to feel his warmth and close enough to smell his scent. But Becca's outside with Bandit and Sergeant, who exited the house after ordering Mrs. Garrity upstairs to get herself together.

Without answering Alfred, I rush to the window and watch Sergeant approach Becca, pick her up, wrap her legs around his waist, and hold her tight against his chest. Bandit snarls, lifts one lip to expose his impressive incisors, and aggressively jumps up and down. Alfred joins me by the window, and together we stand, side by side, watching Sergeant reach down and grab the dog by the scruff of his neck. Bandit growls, snaps at his hand, and rips into his flesh until drops of blood fall to the ground. I can feel Alfred's leg shaking alongside mine as he grabs my hand and squeezes until my fingers tingle. Sergeant leans against the fence, adjusts his grip, and with the strength of evil, single handedly lifts a 100-pound golden retriever clear off his feet until his fluffy body freezes with fear. He stares him dead in the eye before dropping Bandit, who runs squealing and yelping to the back door of the neighbor's house. Sergeant draws Becca closer and bounces her up and down against his stomach until a bulge erupts in the front of his pants. Alfred moves closer and leans against me to steady the tremors that consume his narrow body.

"I'm not allowed to be in here," he whispers. "I'll get in trouble if Sergeant finds out."

"I won't tell," I say.

"Promise?"

I make an *X* over my heart with my finger. "Promise."

Alfred and I stand in front of the window peering out over Bethlehem. Smoke billows up from the steel stacks and forms small clouds that drift slowly across the sky.

"Alfred?"

"Yeah?"

"The answer to your question is no...I don't have a boyfriend."

Alfred smiles and we watch the clouds grow smaller in the distance, escaping to somewhere far, far away.

Mrs. Rogers called Sergeant a "Good Christian man who had served and protected our country." But what I want to know, as Sergeant storms into the house, is who will protect us from him?

Huh?

Who will protect us from him?

It was Mrs. Garrity's fault that we didn't go to church yesterday.

"You have your mother to blame," Sergeant said, directing his words at Alfred who stood by Mrs. Garrity, shouldering her pain and the tears that dripped down the sides of her face onto his blue suit. "I was planning on taking all of you to the candy store after mass," he said, "It would have been a nice day for the entire family had she not acted up." Sergeant has a way of diminishing his victims by deliberately speaking about them as if they weren't standing right there listening to every word. "If I said it once," he continued, "I've said it a thousand times. There will be no tolerance for disobedience, not in this man's house."

Sergeant then grabbed Becca by the hand and pulled her toward the front door. "Come on, baby girl, you're going with me."

He took Becca along to receive the Lord's blessing and to sit with him in the back pew, on his lap, in her dress. She got three pieces of candy in the hour they were gone, and they both returned home with a smile on their face.

Sergeant's smile lasts well into the next morning when he insists on a "family" breakfast before he leaves for work, something he has never done before. "I'm a lucky man," he says, devouring Mrs. Garrity's homemade blueberry pancakes and maple syrup. He wraps his arm around her waist while she stands to top off his coffee. "Listen up, kids," he announces. "This woman right here is the finest cook in the Northeast." He pulls her close. "The best looking, too." (Mrs. Garrity lights up when Sergeant compliments her, and he knows it. I've seen it time and time again.)

"Stop it, you're makin' me blush," she says, and she runs her hand through the side of her hair still flattened by her pillow. "I look an awful sight today."

Every once in a while Sergeant will say or do something nice. It's as though he has a tiny bit of decency somewhere deep inside that seeps out when we least expect it, just long enough to throw us off our game so that we let our guards down and relax for a minute. But it never lasts long.

"I own this," he says, belching into his napkin while administering a crisp slap on her buttocks. "Tell 'em, baby."

"Tell them?" Mrs. Garrity asks, and she places the pot of coffee back onto the stove. "Tell them what?"

"Tell the kids that I own you." Sergeant pulls a bag of chew from his pocket, stuffs a pinch up into his cheek, and leans back in his chair to wait for her answer.

Mrs. Garrity hesitates. "I…uh…I don't think we have time for all that. These youngin's best be gettin' on to school, or they're gonna be late. Go on, Alfred," she says. "Finish up right quick so ya'll don't miss the first bell."

Alfred wipes a napkin across his mouth, neatly folds it along the side of his plate, and looks to Sergeant. "May I be excused, sir?"

Sergeant places his hands behind his head and tips back on two legs of his chair, something he would never tolerate from any of us. He nods to Alfred, raises a brow, and sets a bullying smile on Mrs. Garrity as we rush out the door. I think about that smile all day at school, from the time Suzy Carlson reads the daily announcements over the loud speaker until Ronald Smith and I swipe dampened sponges across the large green chalkboard in the front of our classroom.

Sergeant isn't smiling now as he commands the attention of everyone in the house with the penetrating rumble of his voice. It takes nothing more to make us scramble, because we know that it's better for all of us if we do. Sergeant is waiting in the living room when he orders Becca, Alfred, and me to have a seat on the sofa next to Mrs. Garrity, who is sitting up tall at the far end with red, blistered hands clasped in her lap. She flinches as we huddle close together, hip-to-hip, shoulder-to-shoulder, on a sofa barely large enough to accommodate all of us.

"Like pigs in a pen," Sergeant sneers, and he spits a long stream of brown chew into the tin coffee can on the end table. He takes a stance in the middle of the living room with his feet shoulder-width apart and his hands firmly fixed on the leather belt around his waist.

Out of the corner of my eye, I watch Mrs. Garrity straighten out her ragged housecoat, the one with the faded flowers that she washes and irons every morning, the one covered with cooking stains that hangs slightly above her red, swollen knees. I feel a little sick inside when Sergeant's eyes look dark and glassy as they do now, and it seems that Alfred's legs always begin to tremble for the same reason.

"This house looks like shit," Sergeant says. He lifts his nose into the air. "Smells like it, too." From his pocket, he pulls out a small white bundle, lifts his upper lip in disgust, and holds the bundle inches from Alfred's nose. "Smell it," he says.

"Yes, sir." Alfred leans forward and does as he is told. As he always does. No matter what. Becca grabs my hand and looks at me, confused by Alfred's reaction as he snaps his head back and pinches his nostrils closed with his white, dainty fingers.

"What ith it?" Becca asks. "Are we in trouble?"

Sergeant is quick to respond to her question as he lifts the bundle to his nose. "Smells to me like a dirty little pig," he says and unravels it to divulge something that I immediately recognize. I don't know how he found them. I thought I had hidden them well when I wrapped them in toilet paper and shoved them deep into the bathroom-trashcan. Heat surges to my cheeks as he reveals what I thought I had properly disposed of last week when I entered the bathroom, pulled down my pants, and gasped at the sight of blood that had soaked through my underwear. Erma warned me that this would happen. She said that menstruating would make me a woman one day, but I'm not ready to be a woman. Not yet. And I'm not ready for what Sergeant does next as he holds my bloody underwear up for everyone to see.

"If you're gonna treat my house like a pigpen, then I'm gonna treat you like a bunch of pigs. Now I want the pig who left this mess in the bathroom to stand up." His eyes are narrow and red, and a strand of white spit extends from his upper to lower lip as he speaks. He nods at Mrs. Garrity, who hurries into the kitchen and returns with an open bottle of beer.

It rained earlier this evening, and if it weren't for the width of Sergeant's shoulders, I could see out the window across the room where a setting sun has emerged. I could look for the rainbow that Dorothy followed to the Land of Oz when she ran far away from home. But none of that was real. And this is. Maybe if I pull the clock off the wall, throw it on the ground, and stomp on it, the ticking will stop. And maybe my real father, whoever he is, will love me enough to come back, because he's probably a good man who doesn't smoke or drink or curse. Sergeant gulps down half the bottle, looks me straight in the eye, and threatens to teach all of us a lesson if the "pig" doesn't confess. So for the sake of Alfred, who is sitting beside me quivering over something he didn't even do, and for the sake of Becca, my little sister, the one I promised to protect, and for the sake of Sarah, whose face is still bruised from her last lesson, I shamefully apologize.

"I'm sorry, sir. I did it," I say, standing up before Sergeant as the woman that I have now become, like it or not.

"Put them on," he says, holding them out to me.

"Sir?"

"You heard me." His teeth clench and grind behind tightened lips. "I said put them on." This could have been a good day. I won the spelling bee at school, and Jenny Kingston complimented me on my denim skirt.

"But I don't want to, sir. They're dirty."

"And so are pigs," he says. "They're dirty, and they stink. Now put them on."

Mrs. Garrity stares down at the floor. "Go on," she says beneath her breath. "Do as he says."

If I were Dorothy, I would click my heels three times and wish to be anywhere but home. I lift my blue denim skirt, the one that Erma bought me at Sally's several years ago with the cool rhinestone studs on the pockets. It was too big then, but Erma said it was one of the cutest things she had ever seen and that I would grow into it one day, so she bought it for me anyway. I looked pretty wearing it to school today for the first time, and I had hoped that Alfred would notice the way the rhinestones sparkle when I walk. I lift my skirt higher, pull my clean underwear down past my knees to my ankles, and step out of them one foot at a time. Sergeant bends down, picks them up, puts them in his pocket, and hands me the soiled pair. He is breathing faster, and a light sweat emerges on the surface of his skin. I've never exposed myself in this way before. Erma told me that private parts were to remain private. Nighttime is approaching as I step into the bloody underwear that reeks with the foul stench of womanhood.

"Look at the pig," Sergeant says, and he guzzles down the remainder of his beer. "Oink, oink."

I can see out the window now. The sky has faded to sapphire over the city streets of Bethlehem as I pull the stained garment up past my knees and over my buttocks until Sergeant grins with delight at the hard, crusty cloth between my legs. I lower my skirt and stand to face Sergeant, looking him directly in his eyes for the first time since I came here because I hate him as much as he hates me and I want him to know it.

"Is there anything else, sir?" I ask, boldly confronting the man who calls himself a servant of God. My mouth fills with the distinct taste of copper as I sink my teeth into the tip of my tongue and wait for Sergeant's response. But I won't shake and tremble the way the others do. And I won't look at Alfred. I don't want him to see me like this. Because I'm not a "dirty fucking pig."

Sergeant is.

"I thee it! I thee it!" Becca says, pointing her index finger into the night sky.

"You're right, Becca, that's the Big Dipper," Alfred says. "And right up there," he adds, aiming his finger farther north, "is the Little Dipper."

"Wow," she says, squinting. "That'th cool!" She removes her glasses, cleans them with the sleeve of her shirt, and places them back on the bridge of her nose.

It was nice of Alfred to invite Becca and me into his room tonight to stargaze. It was even nicer that he never mentioned what Sergeant made me do the other night in front of them…or what he made me do yesterday to complete my punishment. He made Mrs. Garrity finish his dirty work by ordering her to check inside my pants before school. Like a good wife, she obeyed and did as she was told.

"Don't you ever back talk Sergeant again, ya hear?" she warned, turning her nose away from the pungent odor that floated up from the dirty panties I was forced to leave on. "You're causin' us all a lot of trouble." Mrs. Garrity handed me a small pink box of feminine napkins. "Don't let this happen again," she said.

"Yes, ma'am," I answered, staring at the fresh new cut on her right cheekbone, below her eye, the size of Sergeant's military ring. "Why do you let him do it?" I asked.

Mrs. Garrity held her hand over her cheek. "Like I said, Danni, you're causing us a lot of trouble round here. You mind your own business now."

It crossed my mind that standing up to bullies might not be such a smart idea after all, although it sure did work with Missy Lacintosh. For the first time ever, I received an invitation to her birthday party. She handed it to me at school yesterday where she found me sitting alone on a bench with my legs crossed, hoping that my womanly sins would go undetected by my peers.

"I'm having a birthday party next week," she said. "Wanna come?" I clenched my legs together so that

Missy wouldn't smell the offensive stench that occasionally wafted up from the inside of my pants.

"Sorry, but I can't," I said, noticing the pretty flowers imprinted on the front of the invitation, pink and purple, exactly what I would choose if it were my party. "I'm busy that day," I lied, because who would want to go to Missy's stupid party anyway? Not me, that's for sure. Erma once said that a leopard never changes its spots. She spent all afternoon explaining to me what she meant. So even though Missy was acting real nice, I knew better. People don't change unless they have to. Missy treats me nice because she's afraid that I'll punch her again if she doesn't. Sergeant, on the other hand, is a different story. He doesn't have to treat anyone nice at all.

Becca directs her finger to the biggest and brightest star in the sky.

"Look at that one," she says. Alfred and I look up at the star that stands out among the others.

"That's the North Star," I say, reminding her of the story we learned in church about Jesus and how the Mother Mary followed the star to Bethlehem where he was born.

Becca's eyes widen. "Jesus wath born here?"

"Not this Bethlehem, Becca," Alfred says, tossing a handful of sunflower seeds into his mouth. "He was born in the town of Bethlehem that's far, far away, remember?"

"Oh yeah," she says, tilting her head farther back. "Maybe one day we can all go somewhere far away."

Alfred spits a lump of chewed seeds from his mouth, draws his knees to his chest, and folds his arms on top of them. "Yep," he says, looking into the night sky. "Someday we can go wherever we want."

Becca reaches out and grabs my hand, then Alfred's. "Let'th make a wish," she says.

Alfred rolls his eyes. "Nah, that's girl stuff."

Missy Lacintosh told me that it's bad luck to make more than one wish in a week. She said that bad things happen if you do. But the North Star is brighter than usual tonight so I do it anyway.

"Star light, star bright, first star I see tonight...I wish I may... I wish I might...have the wish I wish tonight." Becca and I close our eyes as we did when we made our birthday wishes. I wished for a mommy and daddy that day because it was the one thing I wanted more than anything else in the world. But now, peeking over at Alfred, whose eyes twitch with enthusiasm beneath shiny, white lids as he gives into the irresistible temptation of a wish, I think otherwise. Right now, the one thing I want the most in this world...is him.

Becca springs out of bed, opens the nightstand drawer, and puts on her glasses. She reaches up to the calendar hanging on our bedroom wall and runs a black magic marker through the day's designated box, blacking it out completely, as she has done every day this week. Slowly, she drags her finger across each day. "One...two...three."

She turns to me, wipes her malformed mouth on her sleeve, and rubs her eyes. "Three more dayth, Danni," she says, holding her pinky down with her thumb so her first three fingers stand straight up in the air. She clasps her hands in front of her and jumps up and down, unable to contain her excitement. "I'm tho happy," she whispers. "I'm gonna thee the monkeyth."

The sun is bright this morning. It shines through the window and warms my face. The weatherman on television last night talked about an Indian summer and how some of the hottest days of the year are still to come. Sergeant scowled when he heard that, wiped the sweat from his forehead with his handkerchief, and mumbled something about how that "pussy son of a bitch doesn't know what heat is" and how "he should try working in hell for a couple of days," referring to the steel plant where "real men work": real men like his grandfather, his father, himself, and one day the "little bitch" he calls his son. But Alfred has other plans for his future, none of which include steel. That's what he told me late last night in his bedroom when we lay side by side on his bed staring up at the ceiling, as we've done every night this week.

"No one's gonna tell me what to do with my life," he said. "I mean it, Danni. I'd rather die than stay in this town and work at that plant." Alfred thought for a moment before continuing on. "Danni?" he asked.

"Yeah?"

"Do you ever feel like no matter what you do or how you do it, you'll never be who you're supposed to be?" He crossed his arms on his chest. "Or who everyone wants you to be?"

"Yeah, I guess," I said, not wanting to disappoint him with my answer.

He turned on his side, bent his arm, and rested his head in his hand, surprised and excited by my answer. "You do?" he asked, bravely facing me in the shelter of the night.

I could barely see Alfred in the darkness of his room as I turned toward him, leaving only inches between us, face to face, chest to chest, as I inhaled the sweet smell of mint-flavored toothpaste on his breath.

"Sure I do."

Outside, the headlights of a passing car shot through the window and streamed across the walls, washing over Alfred, revealing a delighted expression on his face as he probed on. "You mean you feel trapped, too?"

I nodded. "Sure," I replied, pretending to fully understand what he meant.

Alfred smiled from ear to ear, exposing white teeth that penetrated the dark night. His front tooth jutted out farther than the rest, almost deliberately so, standing apart from the others, begging to be seen and noticed, unlike Alfred.

But I notice everything about Alfred.

I always have.

Like a fanatic spectator, I carefully observe him, studying his every move, captured by the unsettled look in his eyes and the way his mouth tilts slightly upward on one side when he speaks.

"Your hair is very long," he said, lifting his slender hand to brush it off my shoulder. "And soft."

I looked away, embarrassed and thrilled once again by his touch. Missy Lacintosh says that when a boy touches you a lot, it means that he likes you. Missy is normally a big, fat liar. But just this one time, I'd like to think she's telling the truth.

"One day," Alfred said, interrupting my thoughts, "I'm getting out of here. I'm gonna run far away where no one knows who I am or where I'm from...just like you said. I'm gonna make my own rules and lead my own life, like Huck Finn."

"Huck Finn?" I asked.

"He's the boy in my favorite book. I've read it six times already." He reached under his pillow, pulled out a tattered soft-covered book, and held it to his chest. "Huck didn't let anyone tell him what he was gonna do, especially that son-of-a-bitch father of his, so he ran away."

I nodded, struggling to show enthusiasm. The thought of Alfred running away frightened me. I rolled onto my back and placed my hands on my lower stomach, rubbing back and forth, searching for the self-inflicted bruises that were starting to heal from last week's binge. "That sounds great, Alfred."

Alfred opened the book to a turned-down page and read out loud: "It was kind of solemn, drifting down the big, still river, laying on our backs looking up at the stars, and we didn't ever feel like talking loud, and it warn't often that we laughed...only a little kind of a low chuckle." He closed the book and held it again to his chest. "That's one of my favorite parts," he said.

I pressed hard on the tender areas, hoping to ease the panic as Alfred and I lay still on his bed in a moment of silence that felt like an eternity. Alfred cleared his throat and rolled onto his back. "You can come with me if you want," he said, staring up at the ceiling.

I turned to Alfred. "Really? You mean it?"

Alfred didn't hesitate in his response. "Yep."

I removed my hands from my abdomen and relished in the thought of somewhere new, somewhere different. "Becca, too?"

Once again, there was no hesitation in Alfred's answer. "Sure."

"Wow, Alfred, I'd really like that." I smiled for real this time with a sense of elation that I hadn't felt before.

"Danni?" Alfred said.

"Yeah?"

"What happened to your mother and father?"

His question caught me off guard as I thought about the future for once, instead of the past. Since the day I'd moved in, I had waited for this, when I could find out more about Alfred and tell him more about myself. Without so much as a second thought, the answer erupted from my mouth with no pause or reluctance. It was the only answer I had for him in that precise moment.

"I don't know," I said, wrapping a clump of hair around my finger and twisting until it tugged at my scalp. "And I don't care—I hate them both."

Alfred grabbed my hand. "I know what you mean," he said. "I hate my parents, too."

It would have been the perfect time to ask Alfred all the questions that had plagued me since the day we first met: about his mom and dad, and about how long he's been here in the Garritys' house. I should have asked him everything, right then and there. But I didn't want to disrupt the warm feeling that filled me up as I lay next to him. So I kept my mouth shut, closed my eyes, and fell fast asleep next to Alfred, who quietly read *Huck Finn* until well into the early morning hours when I snuck out of his bedroom and back into mine. I crawled in bed next to Becca, who was curled up tightly beneath the covers with a grin on her face, dreaming sweet dreams. I couldn't remember the last time I had dreamed of anything sweet because I couldn't remember the last time I had a reason to. But last night was different.

No ticking. No voices. No banging. Just sweet dreams of something better.

"Danni!" Becca's shrill voice disrupts my early morning daydream. "Did you hear me? We're going to thee the monkeyth in three days!" She jumps on the bed and giggles.

"Get up, thleepyhead, we're gonna be late for thchool."

She throws the covers back, grabs my hands, and pulls me to my feet. The Whitekers are taking us to the zoo in a couple of days. And I have a friend. A boyfriend. Maybe, for the first time in a long time, things are looking up.

Becca and I are excited about our trip to the zoo tomorrow. I promise her that if we finish our Saturday morning chores early enough, we'll have time to play hopscotch while Sergeant is at his church youth group meeting—as long as we make sure to scrub all the chalk off the sidewalk when we're done. Becca finishes her chores first and rushes outside to see Bandit, who excitedly barks at the sight of her.

Sergeant is acting especially peculiar this morning as he prepares to leave, walking in and out of the house, back and forth to the small shed in the backyard where he keeps his tools. He's in the kitchen now, rummaging through the freezer, as I spray a light stream of furniture polish on the coffee table and wipe it down with a soft cloth until the wood shines to perfection: no smudges, no streaks, as Sergeant ordered. With his head still buried in the freezer, he mumbles something about "that fucking dog," removes one of the white packages he gets from the butcher, and closes the freezer door with a swift punch. Out of the corner of my eye, I see Sergeant move from drawer to drawer, explosively opening and closing each one until he finally removes a large butcher knife. With the knife in one hand and the package in the other, he exits the house, slams the kitchen door shut behind him, and rambles on about "teaching her a lesson once and for all."

I don't want him to teach me a lesson, so I take my time, dusting every inch of wood in the house so that Sergeant's white glove will remain white when he swipes his fingers across every table later this afternoon.

Mrs. Garrity is upstairs taking a shower. The water flows through the pipes that lead to the basement where Alfred is preparing for his chores of the day. It's comforting to know that he's so near because I can't stop thinking about him and what he said about getting out of this town one day, together. From the window, I watch Sergeant exit the toolshed. With a slab of raw meat in one hand, he marches directly toward Becca, who sits by the fence, close to Bandit, stroking his nose with her small fingers. It's the smirk on Sergeant's face that I don't like. Something doesn't feel right about the unusual grin that extends from one cheek to the other as he approaches Becca with a thawed cut of steak that is dripping wet with a bright green liquid that trails on the walkway behind him. He kneels over Becca and speaks to her in a low voice. "I bet Bandit would love a treat."

Becca looks up and answers, "Yeth he would!" She leans into the fence. "Do you wanna treat, boy?" she asks.

Bandit stands, tucks his tail between his legs, and salivates as Sergeant hands the meat to Becca, who dangles it over the fence for several seconds before dropping it to the ground. "Good boy," Becca says, watching Bandit lick the steak dry before devouring it with a few swift bites. "He ate the whole thing," she chuckles. "He sure does love thteak."

Sergeant nods, pulls a rag from his pocket, and wipes his and Becca's hands clean. Bandit wags his tail. "Stupid animal," Sergeant mumbles, shoving the dirtied rag back into his pocket.

Becca squeezes her petite hand through the fence. "We're gonna be best friends forever."

"Nothing lasts forever," Sergeant says with a wink. "And some lessons are best learned while you're young. You'll see." He walks to his truck, gets in, and drives away.

Mrs. Garrity is finished with her shower. She comes down the stairs in her worn-out bathrobe with her hair wrapped in a towel piled on top of her head.

"Did you get all the dustin' done, Danni?" she asks, standing with her hands on her hips.

"Yes, ma'am. Can I go outside to play with Becca now?"

She examines each table before answering. "I reckon that'll be all right."

It's a warm autumn day. The sky is as blue as the crayon in the big craft box at school. An occasional breeze brushes across my skin and tosses my hair back. Becca and I draw a hopscotch board on the sidewalk with a brand new piece of yellow chalk that I took from school last week when I was on chalkboard duty. I slipped the smooth yellow stick into my pocket when no one was looking. I suppose it wasn't right to take it like I did, but I did it for Becca, to see her eyes light up from holding something new.

We each choose a pebble from the street and place it outside the box numbered "one."

"Can I go firtht?" Becca asks. "You went first last time."

"Sure, Becca." Becca picks up her stone and drops it on the number one. With one foot held behind her, she hops into the square, bends down, and picks it up.

"OK...your turn!" she yells.

From where I stand, I can see the small basement window of the Garrity house where Alfred retreats every Saturday for hours. Today is no different.

Alfred briefly came up from the basement this morning with a cup of paint in one hand and a paintbrush in the other. He touched up a couple of spots on the walls before returning to the basement with a smile on his face and a mound of sunflower seeds nestled in his cheek like a hamster.

"Danni! It'th your turn!" Becca yells, snapping her fingers in front of my face. I drop my stone in the first square and hop to pick it up. "Now we're both on number two," she says as she leans to toss her stone into the second square before taking two small hops to retrieve it. Bandit watches from the yard next door. He whimpers and staggers to the far side of the fence, where he hangs his head low and expands his jaw until a mound of vomit erupts from his gut.

"Your turn!"

With the vile sound of Bandit coughing and gagging in the background, I toss my stone onto the number two. His body contorts, and another mound of mush bursts from his mouth.

"Uh oh...Bandit's sick!" Becca says, running over to the fence. She grips the cold, metal links and watches as Bandit's legs begin to wobble. He sways to one side, takes a step toward Becca, and collapses.

"Danni!" Becca yells. "Something's wrong with Bandit!"

I wrap my arm around her shoulder. "He'll be OK, Becca," I say, trying to convince myself, as much as my little sister, that Bandit's twisting and writhing is nothing to be concerned about.

Within minutes, our neighbor, Mr. Harrison, comes running out from his house. He kneels by Bandit's side and strokes his head. "You OK, boy?" he asks, trying to comfort the panting dog struggling for each shallow breath.

But Bandit isn't OK. His eyes roll back into his head, and his tongue drops to the ground. He isn't OK at all. Mr. Harrison picks up Bandit's limp body, carries him to the porch, and drapes himself over his loving pet until the sun lifts higher in the sky. He wipes his eyes, walks into the house, and returns with a large white sheet that he throws over Bandit to cover him completely.

"Ith Bandit cold, Danni? Maybe I should get him my blanket."

I walk Becca into the house, sit her down on our bed, and try to explain to her what "death" is. Erma once said that when good people die, they earn a pair of wings and fly to heaven where they live in paradise forever, and that when bad people die, they fall into an endless fiery pit where they burn for all eternity. She never said anything about animals. But Bandit was a good boy, so I tell Becca that he earned his wings and is flying to doggy heaven where he can run and jump with all the other animals just like he did when he played with her, only faster and higher. I make it sound fun, really fun, because I don't want Becca to feel sad.

"I want wingth, too," Becca says, "so I can fly to heaven and play with Bandit."

"Becca, you won't get your wings for a long time."

"But I want them now!" she says, kicking her feet against the side of the bed.

"You can't have them now."

"Why?" she asks as her eyes fill up.

"Because Bandit was sick and you're not."

"I wanna be sick, too!"

"Don't say that!"

"I wanna play with Bandit!" she yells. "When can I play with him, Danni?" Becca hops down from the bed and runs to the bedroom window. She presses her hands against the glass and watches Mr. Harrison carry the lifeless bundle to his car. She sucks in short bursts of air. "I want my wings, Danni," she says, falling to the floor in a fit of tears. "I want my wings!"

I sit next to Becca and listen to the clock that hangs above our bed, perfectly centered on the dull white wall. Blocks from here, large metal slag cars carrying molten steel waste screech to a halt before spilling massive amounts of glowing, liquid fire out onto the ground. I close my eyes and wait for the cars to fully empty so I won't see the blazing inferno of sparks that shoot up into the sky…

turning day into night…

heaven into hell.

Becca's breathing has calmed as she drifts off to sleep. I hope the sudden clattering that echoes through the floor vents won't wake her.

Alfred.

He should be here with us instead of downstairs in that goddamned basement where he's been all day, finding some sort of pleasure in a house full of pain. But it won't be long until the sky clears and the slag cars begin to move again, rumbling and squealing down the tracks. Not long at all. And when they do, I'm going to open my eyes and go downstairs to the basement…

to Alfred…

to find out what I should have found out a long time ago.

The basement is cool and damp as I enter, close the door behind me, and position myself at the top of the old wooden stairs. My nostrils sting with the potent smell of mildew and paint as I listen for Alfred who has been down here for hours, somewhere beneath the kitchen floor where I sometimes lie flat on my stomach, driving my ear into the cold linoleum, listening to him scampering about. I hear him now, within these dingy cement walls...

his soft voice...

joyfully humming.

I tiptoe down the steps and pause for a moment, gazing into the far corner that echoes the subtle sporadic tapping of small objects being set down on a countertop.

But I can't see him anywhere.

The sun streams in from the basement window and casts a light upon a wall of paint cans stacked high on the other side of the room. I wait and listen to the sounds that come from behind it.

His sounds.

The sounds he makes every Saturday afternoon as he fidgets and tinkers around down here right before emerging with an uneasy smile on his face as though trying to suppress some incredible secret that he is dying to share. How dare he find something enjoyable in this dreadful house and not have the decency to share it with me. The basement floor is cold and coarse against my sock feet as I shuffle toward him until the only thing between us is the barrier of cans that have been strategically positioned in a way that intentionally partitions off a small corner of the basement.

A dent in one of the cans creates a thin space barely wide enough for me to see through to Alfred, who is completely undressed except for a pair of white brief underwear that snugly fit his petite boyish build and thin black socks that are rolled down to his ankles. His back is facing me as he gleefully struts about in direct opposition with his typical state of existence. I have never seen Alfred move like this before, with such poise, grace, and elegance.

He is beautiful, actually, with skin as flawless, smooth, and white as freshly fallen snow. He moves brazenly, posing and posturing with a fevered excitement that further peeks my curiosity and makes me yearn to discover whatever it is that brings him such pleasure. He squats down before a small makeshift table formed by several paint cans stacked in front of him. A broken mirror is sitting on top, propped against the concrete wall. It looks like the mirror that Mrs. Garrity threw into the trash last month, the mirror that used to hang on the kitchen wall so that Mrs. Garrity could check her makeup every day right before dinner, for Sergeant. Until one day, several weeks ago, when Sergeant wasn't pleased with Mrs. Garrity's appearance at the dinner table, and he told Alfred, Becca and I to go upstairs to our rooms.

But I didn't go to my room.

I stood at the top of the stairs and listened to the poisonous venom that spewed from his mouth and watched as he unleashed the devil on her.

Again.

"How dare you sit across from me at this table looking like a piece of white trash? I work hard all day to provide a good home for you and those goddamned kids, and this is the thanks I get? You look like you just rolled out of bed." He sneered and shook his head in disgust. "You don't appreciate a fucking thing."

He grabbed her by her hair, dragged her over to the mirror, and held her head in front of it like a ventriloquist holds a puppet. "Take a good look at yourself," he said, and he forced her face against the mirror. "I couldn't fuck you looking like that, let alone eat." He held his teeth tightly together as he spoke.

"Just another good-for-nothin' bitch livin' off the back of a hard workin' man. I'll tell you one thing: maybe my father was stupid enough to put up with a worthless, back-talkin' woman, but not me. As long as I'm footin' the bill, you'll do as you're told, and that includes looking the way I tell you to look. If not, well…"

With the tip of his finger, Sergeant drew an imaginary line across the base of Mrs. Garrity's neck, from one side to the other. "My KA-BAR knife would cut through your skin like warm butter," he said, pressing his head against hers until his lips lay heavy on her ear. "How's a man's supposed to eat with shit at his table?" He wiped his thumb over her bare lips. "My mother always told me that if you want something done, you have to do it yourself."

He reached his hand into her dress pocket, removed a small black tube, and twisted it until a full stick of red lipstick erupted from the top. Touching it to her lips, he traced every curve, over and over again, until her entire mouth was coated in a shiny, thick red paste. His breathing intensified as his hand traveled from the back of her head, down the gentle curve of her back, and over her buttocks to the bottom of her dress. "Now that's what a woman's mouth should look like."

She closed her eyes, took a deep breath, and held it as Sergeant slipped his hand beneath her dress and ran it up in between her legs. He moved his arm up and down until Mrs. Garrity let out a lingering moan as a result of either intense pain or extreme pleasure. I wasn't sure which, but the sound made me feel sick inside. He removed his hand, stood directly in front of her, and wiped his wet fingers across her lips before grabbing her head from behind and vulgarly pressing his mouth against hers, tasting and inhaling her female scent.

"Remember…"

He released her.

"I own you."

He lifted the mirror off the wall, opened the door, and heaved it outside onto the back porch where it broke into pieces on the ground. "Now make yourself useful and clean that shit up."

And Mrs. Garrity did just that. Without a single word, she made herself useful by cleaning up the mess that Sergeant had made, sweeping up every last fragment of glass before throwing the mirror into the garbage.

Alfred takes a seat on the floor, still humming and tinkering with something that I can't see. On top of the paint cans, there is an assortment of small items neatly positioned. I lean in closer as the sun shifts higher in the sky, brightening his secret space and exposing a collection of various cosmetics, like Mom used to keep in her bathroom drawer, like Mrs. Garrity keeps in her dress pockets. They are lined up perfectly, according to size, with the smallest item, a small black tube of lipstick, at the end, just like the one that Mrs. Garrity uses every day before dinner. I don't understand Alfred, the way he looks or the way he behaves. I don't understand why he has her makeup, why he didn't give the lipstick back to her when she was frantically looking for it, and why he would allow me to get into trouble for something I didn't do.

Alfred stands, lifts up a large piece of white material that looks like an old sheet, and holds it out in front of him to display the meticulously cut strips that drape down from one end. He wraps it around the top of his head, tucks it behind his ears and lets the strips flow down his back, flinging it from side to side like long locks of hair. He bends down again and picks up a dress, pink with a yellow daisy print, the most colorful thing in the entire Garrity house. I've seen the dress before, in one of the big green garbage bags in the church basement. He unzips the back, holds it open, and steps in, one foot at a time, pulling it up past his waist, shimmying his milky white arms into each sleeve. He places his hands on his hips and strikes various poses in front of the mirror, when suddenly there are footsteps upstairs.

Hard and heavy.

Loud and strong.

Sergeant is home early from the pub down the street where he goes for drinks every Saturday after his church meeting. In a panic, Alfred rips the sheet off his head and removes the dress, taking extra care not to trip and make any noise that may bring attention to himself. He puts the dress and sheet into a white plastic bag, along with the cosmetics, and shoves everything into an empty paint can before turning around toward me, exposing his beautifully decorated face. Dark shades of blue shadow cover his pale pink eyes that are boldly outlined with thick black lashes. His cheeks are deep pink, in stark contrast with his pale white skin, and his lips are red...

bright red...

like Mrs. Garrity's.

Startled by his appearance, I turn to escape where I know I shouldn't be. With one swift movement, I knock into the paint cans that come crashing down. They roll and clank across the basement floor in an explosive revelation of Alfred…

who stands before me now…

adorned in color…

silent and still.

For the first time in broad daylight, he looks me directly in the eye, timid and frightened, like a deer stunned by the blinding glare of headlights. There's a secret in Alfred's pink eyes, full of pain and shame. Something that only he knows about.

Until now.

I don't know why Alfred plays dress up down here in the corner of the basement. And I don't know if it's right or wrong. But by the look in his eyes and the feeling in my stomach, I know that no one else can find out. Especially Sergeant. Erma always told me to mind my own business.

This time I wish I had.

A tear slides down Alfred's cheek, and his shoulders drop, relieved to finally unload the weight of such a tremendous burden and terrified of the backlash that my discovery may bring.

There are footsteps again.

Upstairs.

Across the kitchen floor.

Sergeant.

We don't move.

Or breathe.

Perhaps he didn't hear us down here, only several feet beneath him.

The refrigerator door opens and slams shut.

Followed by the snap and hiss of a beer can opening.

More footsteps.

We look up at the ceiling.

Tracing the sound of his footsteps across the floor.

His noises are amplified.

Reverberating through the pipes and vents.

Rumbling within these hollow walls.

He is pacing.

Back and forth.

An empty can clanks on the table.

He belches.

Loudly.

His feet are heavy moving across the floor.

Toward the edge of the kitchen.

Where the basement door is.

He hovers.

On the other side.

Waiting to pounce.

Like a predator seeking its kill.

I close my eyes.

To listen.

The doorknob jiggles.

And turns.

The hinges squeal and the door opens.

Slowly.

He steps down onto the top step.

Closes the door behind him.

And waits for a moment.

At the top.

In his perfectly polished shoes.

My eyes dart back and forth between Sergeant and Alfred.

As usual, in his presence, my heart races and my breath quickens.

He knows we're here and yet he remains motionless at the top of the steps.

Relishing in his ability to intimidate.

Feeding off our mounting horror.

He's coming.

One step at a time, he descends down the stairs.

I run to the far side of the basement, lie down on my stomach, and slide under an old, worn sofa that is pushed up against the wall.

I wait and watch.

Hoping Alfred will do the same.

But he's still running around, crazed, recklessly trying to put his pants on.

I want to yell out to him, *Quick Alfred...hide!*

I want to grab him, pull him under the sofa with me, and protect him.

With one leg in his pants, Alfred scampers about like a mouse in a maze, dashing back and forth, knocking into paint cans, searching for a place to disappear. I reach my arm out from beneath the sofa and hold my hand open, hoping he'll see me. Hoping he'll grab on.

But it's too late.

Sergeant is standing at the bottom of the stairs with his arms crossed, swaying side to side in his Saturday afternoon stupor. His eyes are glassy and bloodshot as he watches Alfred scurry around the basement, whimpering like a wounded animal, harshly wiping the makeup from his face with the back of his hand. Streaks of color stream down his cheeks onto his bare ivory chest and over his stomach until each colorful tear is absorbed into his small white underwear. Sergeant waits for Alfred to slow down, exhausted and fatigued, as the last paint can rolls and clanks to a subtle stop. He stands in the middle of the floor, panting like a dog in the hot sun, flaring his nostrils in and out with the rise and fall of his scrawny chest.

Sergeant rests his hands on the black leather belt around his waist and staggers to one side before unbuckling it. With one swift move, he pulls the belt from his pants, wraps it around his hand, and fixes his eyes on Alfred, whose thin white legs seem ready to give.

"I always knew you were a faggot," Sergeant says, and he takes a step toward Alfred, who is standing with his pants around one ankle in a yellow puddle that slowly forms by his feet. Several sunflower seeds fall from Alfred's pocket into the odorous liquid. I never saw anyone pee themselves before. But Alfred did.

"Look at you. You're a fucking freak." Sergeant stumbles. "Did you think I wouldn't find out about this?" he asks, and he slaps the tail end of his leather belt against his outer thigh. "You must be as stupid as your mother. I did you both a favor when I adopted you, and this is how you repay me? Do you have any idea how hard it is to hold my head high in this community with a pussy white queer like you for a son?" He looks around the room and adjusts the irritating bulge between his legs. "I've tried everything to teach you how to be a man." Sergeant unravels the belt from his hand and dangles it by his side. He leans in close to Alfred and sniffs like a dog on a scented trail. "You smell like a girl," he says and rubs his fingers over Alfred's red lips, smearing the red stain across his already streaked face. "You wanna be a girl? Huh? Is that what you want? You wanna be a pretty little girl?" Alfred drops his head. "Answer me boy!"

Alfred squeezes his eyes shut and cups his hands over his ears.

"I said answer me!"

In a moment of deliberate hesitation, Alfred takes a breath deep enough to distinctly outline every rib. And then finally, after years of sleepless nights and extreme anguish, he surrenders, spilling out the shameful torment that has gradually built up inside of him like single drops of water in a teetering bucket ready to overflow.

"Yes, sir," he says with the courage of an entire army. "I do."

He drops to his knees, buries his face in his hands, and sobs for every minute of every day since the day he was born that he harbored the secret he wanted so desperately to share but fought so tirelessly to hide. Sergeant spits a stream of saliva onto the basement floor, nods, and circles his frail victim. Alfred's eyes are smudged in black and blue as he peeks out between his fingers to follow the path of Sergeant's shiny shoes. I want to scream out to him. *Run, Alfred, run!* But I'm afraid it's too late. Alfred knows it as much as I do as he widens his eyes to the sound of Sergeant's zipper.

"Well, then," Sergeant says, stalking Alfred before stopping directly behind him. "I guess I'll have to show you what it's like to be somebody's bitch."

He opens his pants, drops them to the floor, pulls his penis out through the opening of his boxers, and strokes himself until he grows hard and erect. He squats down, holds his belt out in front of him with both hands, and wraps it around Alfred's face, shoving the leather between his lipstick-stained teeth. Alfred chokes as spit foams up in the corners of his mouth. Using one firm hand, Sergeant presses on Alfred's upper back, forcing his head to the floor until his chin sits in his own pool of urine. With his other hand, he exposes Alfred. All of him. Ripping his underwear down over his buttocks, to his knees, until they rest on the hard cement and absorb the wetness on the floor.

I close my eyes, squeeze them shut as hard as I can, drive my nails deep into my palms, and scream Erma's happy song in my head to try and drown out the noises that come from the center of the basement floor. The vile, repulsive noises that will haunt me for the rest of my life. The sound of Sergeant's slow rhythmical grunting that steadily increases into a rapid, breathless pant as he forces himself deep into Alfred, tearing him open, again and again. And Alfred's incessant squeal, bloodcurdling, shrill and muffled, crying out from somewhere deep within his gut, howling through the stagnant air in wretched agony, ending as horrifically as it began.

And now an eerie silence.

I crack open my eyes. Sergeant stands, pulls up his pants, and removes the belt from Alfred's mouth. He slides it through his belt loops and tucks in his shirt, leaving Alfred in the center of the floor, curled up on his side like a newborn baby, violently shivering.

Sergeant's footsteps drag across the floor.

Up the stairs.

The door creaks open.

And slams shut.

Mrs. Garrity shuffles around upstairs preparing lunch. Cabinets open and close, dishes clatter and slide along the kitchen table. Becca should be waking from her nap soon. Any minute now she'll wonder where I am. I squeeze out from beneath the sofa, dust myself off, and step lightly across the floor, carefully avoiding the scattered paint cans.

I don't want to look at him.

I won't look at him and shame him more with such a coward's eyes. And it dawns on me for the first time that Alfred is Sarah's biological son. Unlike Becca and me, Alfred has no hope of ever finding a better home, because this *is* his home. Mrs. Rogers will never come to take him away as I prayed she wouldn't.

I creep past him, gagging on the pungent odor of ammonia, feces, and semen that permeates the air. I stop for a moment at the bottom of the steps and stare up at the basement door, paralyzed by his agonizing moans that beg me to respond.

If I could turn back time, I would.

For Alfred's sake.

I look back at Alfred, who is hugging his knees, shuddering and staring vacantly into the afternoon sun that streams through the basement window. The orange rays shine brilliantly onto his once pure and flawless body, tainted and soiled by human excrement.

Exhausted...

weakened...

and depleted.

In a matter of minutes, Sergeant had robbed him of everything and reduced him to nothing.

Because of me.

Because I couldn't let him be happy in the basement, alone. I force my nails into my palms and rip at the soft tissue.

I hate myself for what I've done.

I hate Sergeant.

I hate Mom.

But most of all, I hate God for answering the one prayer I wish he hadn't. I shove my bloodied hands into my pants pockets and run up the stairs and back to my bedroom to get Becca ready for lunch.

It's Saturday.

Quiche.

Except for the few nights I spent with Alfred, I've never slept well in the Garrity house. Evil is imminent here. Bandit died yesterday. So did a piece of Alfred. Sergeant made sure of it. Mr. Harrison came over after dinner to let us know of the unfortunate incident. He walked in as we were finishing our Saturday stroganoff, sat down at the kitchen table, and shook his head.

"I don't understand how it could have happened," he said, scratching his forehead. "The vet said it looked like some kind of poisoning, maybe antifreeze. I suppose he could have licked it off the ground when I took him for his morning walk, but I'm not sure."

Sergeant finished his beer, wiped his mouth with a napkin, crumpled it up, and dropped it into his empty plate. "It's unfortunate, Joe. Bandit was a good dog. Becca's really gonna miss him," he said and gave Becca a wink. "Aren't ya?"

Becca's tears had dried by dinnertime, but the skin around her cool blue eyes remained red and puffy. "Yeth, thir," she managed, looking up at Sergeant while sucking in an involuntary burst of air from her afternoon cry.

Mr. Harrison got up from the table and rubbed his hand through Becca's tousled curls. "Well, he sure loved you a lot, sweetie. He'd bark like crazy every time he heard you outside. We're all gonna miss him," he said and patted her back before exiting.

Becca folded her hands in her lap and waited quietly to be dismissed. But Becca wasn't the only quiet one at the dinner table. Alfred was the quietest of all.

Quiet and still.

He didn't eat any of Mrs. Garrity's beef stroganoff, not one bite. He sat clenching his jaw together, repeatedly shifting in his seat.

"Is everything all right, Alfred?" Mrs. Garrity asked.

Alfred stared into his plate and answered, "Yes, ma'am. I'm not very hungry tonight, that's all."

But that wasn't a good enough excuse for Sergeant, who dismissed everyone but Alfred from the table. For hours, Sergeant sat across from the beautiful boy he was ashamed to call "son" and demanded that he eat every last bite of food that he had worked so hard to provide...

every bite...

before midnight...

or else.

Alfred stayed strong, defiantly drawing on any shred of manliness he could summon up from within a body that yearned to be a woman. Until finally, as I lay in bed and listened to the minute hand on the Garrity clocks palpably tick toward the number twelve, as my eyelids grew too heavy to hold open for one more second, I heard the ghastly sounds of a fork clattering and scraping against the dish as Alfred, barely taking the time to chew, scrambled to shovel in every ounce of food on his plate. I held my breath and crossed my fingers until he finished, merely seconds before the new day, just in time to save him from Sergeant's wrath.

"That a boy," Sergeant laughed. "I'm gonna make a man out of you yet." Sergeant slid his chair out from the table. "Now get to bed, soldier. You're done," he said, slapping Alfred square on the back before walking toward the stairs. But Alfred wasn't done, not by a long shot and I shuddered at the gut wrenching sounds that followed. It all came up, seconds later, right back into his plate. Sergeant stormed the table and slammed his hands down on the surface. I squeezed my eyes shut and envisioned Alfred, hanging his weakened head over the regurgitated pile while he coughed and spit out the last strands of saliva that dangled from his mouth.

"Eat it," Sergeant ordered. "You won't make a fool of me in my own house, soldier. You'll crawl, not walk, away from this table unless you do as I say." Sergeant lowered the pitch of his voice as he often does when he teaches someone a lesson. "Listen, you little bitch, I'll make what happened in the basement seem like a walk in the park if you disobey me." I couldn't bear to listen to Alfred choking down his own vomit, so I pushed my fingers into my ears and hummed the ant song until half past midnight when I heard Alfred's door open and close. I thought about sneaking into his room as I'd done every night this week.

But it wouldn't have been right.

Not last night.

After what happened, I'm afraid it will never be right again.

I woke early this morning, soon after sunrise, to the sound of someone stirring in the hallway. A piece of paper, folded in half, then in half again, came sliding across the floor from beneath the door. I crept out of bed, picked up the note, and opened it. A subtle amber light streamed through the window highlighting Alfred's words and a heart he drew next to his name.

> Danni,
> I'm running away tonight, at midnight. I've saved up enough money to get out of this town. You can come with me if you want...Becca, too. Meet me in my bedroom at midnight, not a minute later.
> Alfred

The Whitekers are coming to take us to the zoo today, but it doesn't matter anymore because we're leaving tonight with Alfred. I'll explain everything to Becca when we get back, after we see the monkeys. In the meantime, we sit on the edge of our bed and wave our hands in front of us to dry our fingernails that I painted with the last amount of polish from Erma. Light pink, the color of good little girls…at least that's what she said.

Downstairs, the doorbell rings and Mrs. Garrity calls out, "Danni! The Whitekers are here!"

Becca gasps and raises her eyebrows. I've never seen her eyes this big or this blue. "We're gonna see the monkeyth," she whispers, covering her mouth to contain her excitement. I hold Becca's hand and hop down from the bed.

"Becca, remember to use your manners, OK?"

"I promithe," she says, delicately crossing her heart so as not to smudge her nails.

Sergeant is waiting at the bottom of the stairs with Alfred, who stands at attention, his chest out, arms by his side, staring straight ahead. Each step draws me closer to him, to the stunning boy whose tortured soul has seeped into mine. I want him to look at me so that I can let him know with a subtle wink or nod that we'll be there tonight, in his room, at midnight. I reach the bottom step, inches from him, and stare at his delicate face, scraped on one side from the cement floor that Sergeant forced him into.

But Alfred doesn't look at me.

Not once.

He stands perfectly pressed and polished in khaki pants, white shirt, and shiny black shoes. He doesn't notice me at all, not the ribbon in my hair or the way the gloss on my lips sparkles in the sunlight. Mrs. Whiteker looks as clean and new as the day we met.

"Good morning, Danni."

"Good morning, ma'am."

"Are you ready to go?"

"Yes, ma'am, we're ready."

"Well, let's go. The animals are waiting."

She reaches her hand out for mine while grasping a fully stuffed backpack in the other.

My backpack.

The one I keep in the closet.

The one I pack my clothes in when I move to a new home.

Her friendly smile melts away as Becca pushes her glasses up on her nose, tugs on my hand, and waits for an introduction. But I can't speak. I can barely move with the wave of heat that suddenly consumes me, starting in my feet and rapidly rushing up my body until my face burns with my worst fear. Mrs. Garrity wraps her arm around Becca's shoulder and begins pulling her away. I want to scream at all of them, and I want to stop Becca's small fingers from slipping through mine. Sergeant wraps his hand around my upper arm, lifts me onto my toes, and forces me out the front door to the porch where Dr. Whiteker is waiting.

"Hello, Danni," he says. "I'm Tom, but you can call me Doc. It's nice to finally meet you."

Doc is a rather short man with gray hair that is thin enough on top for me to see through to his scalp. I had pictured him much differently, polished like Suzanne and groomed to perfection. But he is far more casual, dressed in blue jeans and a striped polo shirt that hugs his bulging stomach. Mrs. Whiteker exits the house, throws her handbag over her shoulder, and pretends not to notice Becca running up behind her.

"Danni!" Becca yells, hitting into the screen door that slams shut in front of her. "Wait for me! I'm coming!" she says, grabbing on to the handle. Sergeant presses his glossy shoe against the bottom of the door and pulls a clump of chew from the small bag in his pocket. With their hands pressed against my back, Dr. and Mrs. Whiteker usher me to a car parked out front with the engine still running. At the end of the street, the coat lady appears, standing by the stop sign with her shoulders hung low, watching. If Missy Lacintosh is right, she's a ghost of Bethlehem, a useless unsettled soul of a Moravian settler that has roamed the city streets for hundreds of years. But if she's real, she can hear Becca's screams. If she's real, she can do something to stop this. If I were a bad girl like Missy, I would raise my middle finger to her and tell her to go to hell where she belongs for doing absolutely nothing. Becca's mouth presses against the screen creating a trail of saliva that smears into the small mesh holes.

"Danni, wait!" she cries. "I wanna go to the zoo! I wanna go to the zoo!"

Mrs. Garrity picks her up and wraps her arms around Becca's flailing limbs. But restraining someone's panic is near impossible. I want to beg Dr. and Mrs. Whiteker to bring Becca with us because she's never been to the zoo before either. And I want to tell them how Becca and I do everything together, and how I promised her that I would never leave her alone, and how Alfred, Becca, and I are getting out of this horrendous town tonight. I want to, but the lump in my throat is much too large. I snap the rubber bands around my wrist, pinch my stomach, and drive my nails deep into my palms until a burning pressure builds up behind my eyes. But I won't let myself cry, not on the outside anyway. I wouldn't give any of them the satisfaction. I'm much too strong for that.

Mr. and Mrs. Whiteker's car is newer than anything I've ever seen before. It smells new too, like a combination of fine leather and fresh carpet. As I climb into the backseat, the coat lady gazes out from beneath her hood and Becca's voice becomes distant and muffled. I grip the arm of the car door with both hands and dig my nails into the soft, supple upholstery, hoping to destroy a small part of the Whitekers' perfect world. Becca is still fighting Mrs. Garrity.

"Danni! Wait! I wanna go to the zoo! You promithed! You promithed!"

I lean my forehead against the window and breathe heavy so the moist heat fogs the glass into a cloudy haze. With my index finger, I write my name in the steamed window. Erma hollered at me for drawing on her window. She said it streaked the glass and made more work for her, so I never did it again. But I don't care what the

Whitekers say because I'm not the good little girl they think I am and I intend to prove it. Sergeant rocks on the front porch as we pull away from the curb, and the curtain in Alfred's bedroom window moves aside, exposing his stunning white face that leans against the glass, steaming it into a fog. Alfred glares at me while tracing a large heart in the misty pane.

I'd like to stop this.

Right here.

Right now.

The Garrity home grows smaller in the distance as the Whitekers' car accelerates. The coat lady walks in the opposite direction until completely disappearing from sight. A bothersome voice whispers in my ear, taunting me the way it has before. *Close your eyes! Don't look back! Close your eyes! Don't look back!* I shouldn't have been so nice to Mrs. Whiteker the day she came to visit. I should have shown her what trouble I could be. I draw my knees to my chest and curl up in the corner of the Whitekers' Cadillac.

I didn't have a chance to say good-bye to Becca.

Or Alfred.

Dr. and Mrs. Whiteker say that it's all for the best.

But I don't believe them.

Not for a minute.

8

Several people in light blue scrubs surround me as I am once again rolled down a long corridor toward a large set of double doors.

"Everything's going to be OK, I promise," Michael says, resting his hand on mine as he leans over and kisses my forehead. "I'll be waiting right here when you come out." Michael doesn't look well. His skin is ashen and his face unshaved. "I never meant to hurt you," he says, staring at me with bloodshot eyes. "I love you, Danielle. You know that, right?"

But I don't know anything right now. None of this makes sense. The doors open in front of me as I try to recall the events that led me here, to this sterile, brightly lit room where hospital staff scurry about preparing for me. They roll me into the center of the room, slide me onto the operating table, and place an oxygen mask over my mouth and nose. A woman in a surgical mask inserts a thin needle into a long intravenous tube that runs alongside the table and is taped and secured to my wrist. I can tell by the wrinkles that crease at the outer edges of her eyes that she is smiling as she adjusts the mask over my mouth and asks me to breathe normally.

"OK, Danielle, I need you to count backward from one hundred."

I look up at the large clock on the wall, white with big black numbers.

"One hundred."

Life can change in an instant, from bad to good, good to bad.

"Ninety-nine."

I concentrate on the second hand that ticks toward the number five.

"Ninety-eight."

I think about what Michael said to me minutes ago.

"Ninety-seven."

And what the nurses said about an accident when they thought I couldn't hear them.

"Ninety-six."

About a baby.

"Ninety-five."

And Becca.

The second hand positions itself over the number five as my eyelids close. Michael always told me to trust him. He said that trust is a fundamental part of any successful relationship and that without it we would lose everything.

I agreed.

But the truth is, the only person I've ever trusted.

With all my heart.

Is Alfred.

10

BETHLEHEM, PENNSYLVANIA, 1981, TEN YEARS OLD

The Whitekers never planned on taking Becca to the zoo today.

They came for me.

Just me.

The pretty one.

The smart one.

The one with no complications.

But complications aren't always visible. There are a whole lot of problems that can ferment on the inside, beneath a beautiful face. Adults should know that, but the Whitekers sure don't. I haven't spoken a word to them all night, in spite of their tireless attempts to please me, the beautiful bedroom they prepared for me at their home on Market Street, the large closet filled with new clothes, the forced smiles and strained hugs. Choosing me over my sister was a terrible mistake, and I'll show them, one way or another, that a worthless mound of broken glass can be easily wrapped up in a pretty package. Shame on them, and shame on me for lying to Becca. I should have told her as soon as she was old enough to understand that she shouldn't trust anyone. Not even me. If I had told her the truth, she wouldn't have cried so hard when I left. She would have hated me so much that she would have wanted me to go. It would have been better that way.

For both of us.

My bed at the Whitekers house is soft and cushiony. If I were to jump on it just once, I bet I could touch the ceiling. The sheets are adorned with small pink rosebuds. They smell like summer air and feel cool against my freshly bathed skin. I didn't smile once when Suzanne (Mrs. Whiteker) drew me a rose milk bubble bath. Not once. And I'm not smiling now as I stroke the plush teddy bear that is laying his head on the pillow beside me. If Becca were here, I'd smile from ear to ear. And if Alfred were here, I'd tell him not to run away because it's safe here. But it's half past midnight, and Alfred should be on his way out of town, without me. He probably bought a bus ticket or hitched a ride with someone heading out to the highway.

The sounds of the Whiteker house are much different than the Garritys. The heater kicks on and off every twenty minutes, and the refrigerator hums in the kitchen downstairs. If I sleep, maybe I'll wake up next to Becca. Maybe this is just a dream. A horrible, wonderful dream. Outside, an occasional car passes, and the branches on the maple tree out front gently brush against the house. My eyes will soon be too heavy to hold open. I could sleep if it weren't for the sudden *tings* against my window. I step lightly across the room and open the curtains to find Alfred on the sidewalk below tossing pebbles. His milky face shines through the night as he gazes up at me from beneath a baseball cap pulled down low on his head.

"Alfred, what are you doing? How did you get here?"

"It doesn't matter," he says. "We have to go, Danni. We don't have much time." He turns his head to the side, then jerks it to the other, scouring the street in both directions. It's easy to recognize Alfred's sense of urgency by the way his shallow breathing forces his shoulders to rise and fall. "You're coming, right?" he asks, lifting his platinum brows.

Sometimes all we have is a split second to make a decision that can change our lives forever. And sometimes, in that split second, our heart speaks the loudest. It takes me only minutes to dress, pack, and sneak out the back door of the Whitekers' house toward Alfred who is waiting by the old maple tree. The yard seems larger than it did earlier today and more difficult to navigate as I step through bushes and over plants to get to the petite boy who leans against the tree with his hands deep in his pockets.

I have to get to him.

Nothing else matters.

As I draw nearer, the moon shines down and lights up all that is white: my T-shirt, the turtle-shaped lawn ornament in the Whitekers' front yard, and Alfred, who keeps a vigilant watch on the street's activities. I know exactly what he's doing and exactly who he's looking for. My gut tells me so. As I reach the end of the yard, Alfred's face illuminates brighter than it had before with the onset of lights that creep around the corner. I recognize, all too well, the old red pickup truck that is headed in our direction and the petrified look in Alfred's eyes as his dream is about to be shattered. Alfred pulls off his baseball cap.

"It was kind of solemn," he says, reciting Huck again, "drifting down the big, still river, laying on our backs looking up at the stars, and we didn't ever feel like talking loud, and it warn't often that we laughed, only a little kind of a low chuckle." Alfred smiles and shoves his hat into his back pocket. "I won't let him do it, Danni," he says, shaking his head while staring into the oncoming lights. "That son of a bitch will never lay his hands on me again."

If we had more time, I would touch Alfred the way we touched on his bed. I would tell him everything is going to be all right and that it doesn't matter what I saw in the basement because I've loved him since the moment I saw him.

Alfred pulls a book from his jacket and trembles as he tosses it to my feet. "Take this," he says. "I have to go."

I stuff the book under my shirt and step back into the shadows so that Sergeant won't see me when he passes. Alfred turns and darts up the street.

"Are you coming back, Alfred?" I call out as his thin legs quickly carry him away from me. "Are you coming back?" I yell out again, louder, hoping for a response because I know that I'll wait here forever if the answer is yes. Sergeant's truck rumbles past. The headlights reflect off the bottom of Alfred's sneakers as they pound up the street and onto the sidewalk before disappearing into the nearby parking garage. Outside the entrance, Sergeant's truck screeches to a stop. He throws open the door and marches inside, gripping the baseball bat he used on the back of Mrs. Garrity's thighs a few weeks ago when he needed to teach her another lesson.

"I want you at attention, soldier!" he orders. "Or else!"

I should wake the Whitekers, tell them everything, and beg them for help because I owe it to Alfred. I slip the book out from beneath my shirt and flip through the tattered pages that contain the thousands of words that Alfred read over the years while planning for the day he would escape. The truth is, no one can help him. Alfred decided a long time ago that he was going to help himself. And that's exactly what he's doing.

There are only a few vehicles left in the parking garage as I enter and crouch down behind a large

Dumpster positioned in the far corner. The plastic soles on Alfred's sneakers tap against the cement floor.

"I know you're in here, you little faggot," Sergeant's voice thunders. "The longer you make me wait, the worse you're gonna hurt when I get a hold of you." Sergeant stuffs a clump of chew up into the corner of his mouth, gnaws on it for a minute, and spews a stream of tarry fluid onto the ground. "Don't make me come lookin' for you, soldier," he growls, and he wipes the thick black liquid off his lips with the back of his hand. Alfred doesn't make him wait long before he steps out from behind a car and walks toward him with a steady gait, stopping only several feet away to look Sergeant in the eye with the rage and fury of countless humiliations. Alfred is standing tall, military style, arms by his side, chest out, chin up, as he has done so many times before. Only this time is different. This time he stands against Sergeant instead of with him, at the young age of thirteen, before puberty graces him with the strength of the man that Mother Nature has mistaken him for. But there is so much more to Alfred than a mere adolescent boy. He is different. I knew it from the time I first laid eyes on him: such a divine and unique creature, arduously struggling for individuality with the resilience and internal fortitude that could only come from someone who possesses such rare traits.

The body of a boy.

The heart of a man.

The soul of a woman.

Sergeant chuckles at Alfred's newfound confidence as he dares to stand in opposition of him. "I taught you well, soldier," he says, taking a swig from his flask. "But once a pussy, always a pussy," he sneers, and he staggers toward Alfred who stiffens his legs, presses his sneakers into the floor, and prepares to confront the man determined to ruin him. Sergeant throws his head back in a fit of laughter while Alfred draws his right hand up to salute the man who vowed to be his father.

"Yes, sir," Alfred says. "I learned from the best." His sweet voice cracks as he speaks, drops to a lower octave, then back again. "Like father like son, right?"

Sergeant narrows his eyes. "No real son of mine would ever be a pussy like you," he says. Alfred clenches his teeth.

"Why don't you go back to hell where you came from?" Sergeant lunges toward Alfred, who steps aside to allow him to stumble and fall to the ground. "You little prick," Sergeant mumbles while rising to his feet. He throws the flask to the ground and rolls up his sleeves. "You're gonna wish you hadn't done that." He spits, wipes his mouth, and charges toward Alfred, who lifts his jacket and, without hesitation, draws a small black pistol from his waist—Sergeant's pistol, the one he keeps in his nightstand drawer, the one he waved at Mrs. Garrity's head on the day that she took too long at the post office, where, according to the guilty look on her face, she had obviously been "fucking the mailman." Alfred clutches the gun with both hands and extends his arms out toward Sergeant, who freezes at the sight of his own gun pointed back at him.

"You don't have the balls, boy," he says, raising his hands above his head.

Up until now, I would have thought that Sergeant was right. I would have agreed that Alfred didn't have the guts to shoot anyone. But I don't know the glassy-eyed boy standing in the center of the parking garage. I don't recognize his confident stance or the way his jawbone waves and trembles beneath his flushed face. And I certainly don't recognize his voice, which cracks and deepens again as he challenges the man who has abused him his entire life.

"Stop calling me boy!"

The garage is silent. And the steel plant is quieter than normal. Stillness settles over the city as the slag cars squeal along the tracks and halt to a sudden stop. Perhaps the only thing moving is Alfred's scrawny arms. Shaking.

"You wanna be called bitch instead?" Sergeant reaches down and grabs between his legs. He wraps his hands around his belt and takes another step toward Alfred. "Don't worry, soldier. I'll make it quick."

I squeeze my eyes shut and shove my fingers deep into my ears, but nothing can block out the sound of Alfred's new voice as he screams and pulls the trigger to shoot Sergeant point-blank in the chest. The strident echo of gunfire resounds through the garage as he wobbles, falls straight back, and crashes to the floor like a mighty oak. Spattered in blood, Alfred kneels down beside him.

"Forgive me, sir," he says, and he wipes the gun clean before returning it to its owner. Sirens sound in the distance, and the steel plant comes alive again. I'm not sure which screams louder, the slag cars or Alfred as he runs out the back entrance, minutes before a team of police officers storm inside to where Sergeant soaks in a pool of blood, still alive, gasping for air. They lift him onto a stretcher, rush him out to an ambulance, and speed off down Market Street. A crowd is gathering as I sneak out the back where Alfred escaped. He is gone forever. I can feel it somewhere deep within the unoccupied space in my heart that only he can fill.

I love Alfred.

Perhaps not in the same way that he loves me.

But I don't care.

Because it's love.

Regardless of the circumstances.

It's actually love.

11

There's a fine line between life and death.
One thought.
One blink.
One breath.

Suddenly I am falling.

Faster and faster through a black hole.

My eyes are open yet I see nothing but darkness.

My heart pounds and my arms and legs whirl out of control.

I've heard of this tunnel.

But there is no light at the end.

Not for me.

My failure to grab hold of anything sends me spiraling faster through the endless vacuum. Perhaps my life is over and the demons are calling on me to serve my penance.

I knew this day would come.

I close my eyes and succumb to my inevitable fate.

And suddenly I see myself, age sixteen, the day the devil took hold of me.

12

S weet sixteen.

Bittersweet, actually.

I wake early to the sound of wind gusting outside my window. It's been six years since the Whitekers adopted me. They wanted a child who would fit into their lifestyle and complete their idea of a perfect family. They had an image to uphold in this community, and I was the right fit, or so they thought. But they weren't prepared for all that I was. Not by a long shot. They've spent six years on therapists who have tried to help me work out my "issues," and I'm proud to say that I'm still in the same place.

Socially connected.

Emotionally unavailable.

The Whitekers and I live downtown in a lovely historic home on Market Street. Dr. Tom keeps busy running his practice out of a few rooms on the main floor. Suzanne spends most of her time restoring the house to its original grandeur and attending local charity events. I attend a local private school where I have many friends and an active social life, and receive the finest education that money can buy. It all looks good on the outside. With years of practice, we have managed to paint a pretty picture, a splendid manifestation of a wholesome nuclear family.

But there's a whole lot more to life than outward appearances. I learned this at an early age from Becca and Alfred, the most beautiful people I have ever known: on the inside, where it counts. There's not a day that passes that I don't think about both of them. Over the years, I have asked the Whitekers to arrange for me to see Becca. But the Garritys are adamant that it is not in her best interest.

Not then.

Not now.

They say that Becca is doing well, thriving as a matter of fact, both in school and at home. But I'm not buying it. No one in that house can do well as long as Sergeant is around.

Not Becca.

Not Mrs. Garrity.

Not Alfred.

They would have all been better off if that son of a bitch had died. But Sergeant recovered from the nearly fatal gunshot wound and, oddly enough, never revealed the truth about what happened. Rumor has it, he told authorities that he had been mugged and shot with his own gun when the attacker wrestled it away from him. I don't know why he let Alfred go. Maybe, in some odd way, Sergeant finally found something in him to be proud of. Alfred never went home. Word around town is that he's been down south for the past five years, attending a military academy to learn some discipline so that he can make his father proud by following in his footsteps.

But I think otherwise.

I think Alfred ran far away to the West Coast, just like he said he would, because Alfred had enough discipline. He just didn't have enough love.

I'm sixteen today.

The Whitekers threw me a party last night, even though I asked them not to. Like everything else they do, it was an attempt to make everything seem normal in a home that never will be, not with this child anyway. Suzanne baked me a cake and wrote "Happy Birthday" on the top in purple icing. But a good parent would know that pink is my favorite color, not purple. And a good parent would know why I hate birthdays and why I never want candles on my cake. Ever. A good parent would care enough to ask.

The phone rings.

It's my best friend Andrea.

"Morning, sunshine."

"Hey Andrea, what's going on?"

"A bunch of us are going to the movies tonight, wanna go? She teasingly draws out her voice. "Errrrric's gonna be there."

I sit up and hold the phone closer to my ear. "What time?"

"Seven thirty."

"Sure, can you pick me up?"

"Yep, be there at seven."

"Cool. See ya."

"Ciao!"

ॐ

Becca is eleven years old today. The thought of her always makes my stomach churn until even the smallest amount of food left in it comes up and out. I grab the rubber bands around my wrist.

One for Mom.

One for Becca.

I draw them back as far as they will go and release, as Erma told me to do. The swift snap sends a sharp pain through my wrist and into my gut where the churning begins, rumbling like the subtle warning of an impending earthquake. But the rubber bands don't always hurt enough. I learned a long time ago that sometimes it takes a whole lot more. Maybe if Erma had taken her own advice she could have tamed whatever was eating away at her insides. Maybe then, she'd still be alive.

Erma died when I was twelve. Liver failure. Suzanne insisted we go to the funeral to pay our respects. But she wasn't fooling me. Our attendance had nothing to do with respect. It was an event like all the others that Suzanne spent days preparing for. She bought us new dresses and had our hair and nails done so that we would look our best when she placed her arm around my shoulder to console me as we approached the coffin. Erma didn't look anything like I remembered, lying on a bed of ivory white satin. She looked much smaller in death than she had in life and much less colorful. As we knelt by her side, Suzanne bowed her head to pray, and I kept my fingers crossed that her prayer would be enough to get Erma to heaven. I snapped the rubber bands around my wrist and giggled at the sound it made amid the unsettling silence of the room. I giggled all the way out to the car and all the way home.

I don't know why.

But I did.

Dr. Tom is sitting at the kitchen table when I enter.

"I thought we'd take a trip into the city, see a show, and grab a bite to eat. How's that sound, kid?" He sets his coffee cup on the table and peers over his morning paper. "We might as well keep this birthday celebration going," he says, waiting for my response.

I drop two pieces of bread into the toaster and pour myself a glass of orange juice. "Sounds like fun, Doc, really, but can we make it another time? I promised some friends we'd hang out later."

He gives me a half smile and bobs his head up and down, like he always does when he's disappointed but doesn't want to show it. "Sure, another time," he says, licking his index finger to turn the page as he drops his head back into the paper.

"Tom, darling," Suzanne says, entering the kitchen. She looks divine as always, perfectly prepared for the day in creased jeans and white cotton shirt that she has unbuttoned to the top of her cleavage where the large diamond necklace that Doc bought her rests. "Be a dear," she says, "and pick up some wine this afternoon. I invited a few friends over tonight for cocktails."

Dr. Tom folds the paper, places it on the table in front of him, and sneers. "Again? Can't we ever enjoy a quiet night at home alone?"

"Sure we can," she answers, scooping up his half-filled coffee cup and dumping it into the sink. "But not tonight. Some of the biggest charity events of the year are coming up, and if we want an invite, we need to stay connected to the more prominent members of our community. You know that."

Dr. Tom scratches the bald spot on the top of his head. "Who said we want to get invited? They're all a bunch of pompous snobs anyway. Why don't we send our donations in the mail and skip the parties?"

"Don't be ridiculous," Suzanne says, leaning down to kiss the same shiny spot. "And don't forget about the wine. I have some errands to run—I'll be back later. Oh, Danielle, sweetheart," she adds before walking out the door, "it's adults only tonight, so I'd appreciate it if you could make some plans for a couple of hours, OK?"

I set my toast and juice on the table. "Done," I say, shoving half a piece of toast into my mouth, then the other, until both cheeks are filled like a chipmunk.

Suzanne rolls her eyes. "You're a lady, Danielle," she says, tossing her hair back. "I expect you to act like one."

Her stern glares have never had much of an effect on me, but Doc, on the other hand, would move a mountain to avoid them.

"Do as you're told, kid," he says, and he raises an eyebrow to show me he means business.

"Fine." It takes an entire glass of juice to wash down the lump of dough that has formed in my mouth. I wrap a linen napkin around my finger, delicately dab the corners of my lips the way Suzanne taught me, and wait for a victorious smile to cross her lips.

"Much better," she says and grins the way I knew she would. "Now you may be excused."

As I climb the stairs to my room, I belch out loud, hoping that Suzanne will hear it before she leaves. I'm sick of being part of this pretentious little world where Suzanne gets her way, I get excused, and Doc gets the wine.

The movie theater is crowded tonight, as well as the surrounding stores. Andrea and I are standing outside waiting for her boyfriend Rob to arrive with Eric, the most popular boy in school, the boy I've had a crush on since the beginning of the school year. People hurry in and out of stores, heading in all directions. Behind every face there is a different story of personal joy and heartache. With some it's like a flashing neon sign, while others disguise it well. I could spend hours here trying to determine which hearts are full and which are empty. Andrea throws up her hand to Rob and Eric, who approach holding their stomachs with laughter.

"What's so funny?" she asks.

"You gotta see this," Rob says. "I've never seen anything like it before."

Eric grabs my hand and leads me through a crowd that has gathered outside the theater. I had hoped he would hold my hand tonight in a way that would finally make me stop thinking of Alfred. But his cold, rigid grip only makes me long for Alfred more.

"Wait 'til you see this," he says, pulling me behind him. "You're gonna laugh your ass off." Eric points through the people who pass in front of us. "Over there!"

"No way," Andrea says, breaking into laughter.

"Where?" I ask, rising to my toes, "What are you looking at?"

Eric points again. "Over there, in the green sweatshirt."

The air is crisp tonight. I feel it in my lungs and on my skin as summer gracefully bows its head to the coming of fall. Eric points again. "In front of the grocery store!"

A haggard woman in an old blue dress exits the supermarket, reaches into her cleavage, removes a tube of lipstick, and repeatedly glides it over her colorless lips until they're stained with a vibrant red paste.

Andrea nudges me with her elbow. "Over there, Danni! In the green!"

"Where? What's so funny?" I ask, and I follow the path of her finger to a young girl in a hooded sweatshirt kicking stones along the sidewalk. She extends her arms and dances in a sudden gust of wind that swirls around and throws her hood back.

September winds can be cunning.

Devious and deliberate.

Unpredictable and unsettling.

Her long, blond curls whip into the blustery air and slap against her beautifully deformed face.

"Becca," I say, quietly enough so no one will hear. I've never told anyone about her before, the girl in the green sweatshirt who has everyone laughing out loud. A hot, tingly sensation begins in my feet and rushes up my legs, through my stomach, into my chest, and onto my face.

Becca is a young lady now. The baby fat that once filled her cheeks has diminished, and the gaping hole between her nose and mouth is accentuated with a row of large protruding teeth. She picks up a handful of stones, examines each one, and places them in her pocket before glancing out into the sea of strange faces that surround her. Few others would be able to disregard the stares and sneers of passersby. Even fewer would sense my presence. Becca removes her glasses, wipes them clean with the bottom of her sweatshirt, and places them back on her nose. Her eyes sparkle like a pool of blue water as they scan the crowd for mine.

"What a fucking freak, right?" Eric says, bumping his shoulder against mine.

Becca adjusts her glasses, swipes her sleeve across her mouth, and smiles. I want to run to her and tell her that I'm sorry, wrap my arms around her and make everything all right.

"Now that's a face only a mother could love," Eric says, stirring up a new round of laughter.

But he's wrong. Her mother didn't love her at all. She didn't love either one of us. Their laughter grows louder, escalating like a fire siren that gradually heightens into an excruciating roar. I stare into Becca's eyes and press my hands against my ears.

"Hey, you OK?" Eric asks as a haunting voice rises above theirs, screaming out to me as it has done in the past. *Close your eyes! Don't look back! Close your eyes! Don't look back!* The woman with the red lips approaches Becca with a bag of groceries and a bruise on the side of her face about the size of a grown man's fist. In any other situation, I would not recognize Mrs. Garrity—the years have not been kind.

Eric throws his arm around me and waves his hand in front of my face. "Well? You gonna answer me or what?" he says, tickling my side. "Come on, we're gonna be late for the show."

Mrs. Garrity takes Becca by the hand and pulls her through the thickening crowd toward an old red pick-up truck parked by the curb. Becca peers back over her shoulder, still smiling at the sister who abandoned her.

"You don't know that freak, do you?" Eric asks. If I told him the truth, he wouldn't understand. None of them would.

"Danni, we have to go!" Andrea says, tugging on my arm. Through the crowd, I can barely see Becca as she climbs into the old red truck. Sergeant is behind the wheel. Looking this way. The last time I saw him he was lying in a pool of blood in a vacant parking garage. Alfred tried to kill him for all that he had done. But that son of a bitch didn't die. Mrs. Garrity climbs into the front seat behind Becca and pulls the door shut. They are heading in this direction.

Andrea snaps her fingers in front of my eyes. "Danni, what's wrong with you?"

Sergeant's truck inches toward me until he is close enough for me to see the ring on his hand that grips the steering wheel, the same ring that left a welt the size of a golf ball on Mrs. Garrity's arm the day she served him a cup of lukewarm coffee. I wished him dead that day, but wishes don't always come true because he's here now, glaring at me as he crawls past with Becca. He wraps his arm around her, pulls her close, and breathes her in.

"Do you know those losers?" Andrea asks, planting her hands on her hips.

The lenses on Becca's glasses make her eyes appear even larger than they are. I should act now. Right now. Before her eyes swell with desperation. Before she passes me by. Before Sergeant touches her again. But I'm a Whiteker now, and Eric Seton likes me. Andrea tilts her head, raises her brows, and cracks her gum. A bitter tasting bile shoots up into my mouth and stings my tongue

"Of course not," I say, forcing it back down and securing my place in hell. "I never saw those losers before in my life."

"Well, c'mon then, let's go!" Andrea says, running toward the theater with Rob and Eric.

Sergeant's tires are turning, time is running out, and Becca should know better than to expect anything more from this coward. Perhaps this time she'll learn that I'm so much less than she thought. Her smile drops from her face as she lifts her hood up over her tousled curls. Disappointment looks much different on her today than it did six years ago.

Calm and peaceful.

Tranquil and still.

As they pass, Sergeant's truck accelerates, and they race through the parking lot until the taillights fade into the night. I pull the rubber bands off my wrist, toss them to the ground, and reach into my handbag, running my hand back and forth along the bottom like a junkie in need of a fix. The simplest of tools can become weapons with the right mind-set. I unravel a paper clip, press it firmly into the underside of my wrist, and slowly drag it up my arm until a warm rush of blood flows down beneath my sleeve, into my hand. The pain is agonizing, and the stars are out tonight. They dance and twinkle in the blackened sky as I push my bloodied hand deep into my jacket pocket.

"Hey Andrea...wait for me!"

Life is full of missed chances and failed opportunities. I think that sometimes, if we're fortunate, God gives us a second chance to turn a wrong into a right. He'll never forgive me for what I did tonight. I'll never forgive myself. My arm stings and throbs as I repeatedly rub it against the inside of my sleeve, aggravating and irritating it until it swells into an excruciating ache.

I want it to hurt.

I deserve it.

For Becca.

The Whitekers' house is located farther away from the steel plant than the Garritys' house but not far enough to keep its repugnant noises from waking me in the night. Tonight is no different. I can't sleep. And I can't stop thinking about Becca now that the sweet buzz of Eric's cheap beer has worn off. Only loathsome people can deny their own family. Mom taught me well.

With the foul aftertaste of alcohol lingering on my breath, I replay the night, the movie, the beer, and what happened in Eric's car in the vacant lot next to the steel plant. I always thought sex would be different, something worth remembering. I suppose I "asked for it" the way Eric said I did, kissing and rubbing against him all night. But the beer made it easy, like doing something for him would ease the guilt of doing nothing for Becca. Bursts of hot breath erupted from Eric's mouth as he panted in the cold night air that seeped into the car. He "gave me what I wanted" when he pinned me against the leather car seat, held my arms up over my head, and spread my legs. With no thought of consequence, I gave him my virginity as carelessly as he took it. The windows barely even fogged as I stared out and focused on the fiery sparks that shot up into the black sky from somewhere within the plant, like fireworks on the Fourth of July.

But it's not July.

It's September.

It's fucking September.

Doc was barely awake on the sofa when I returned home.

"How was your night?" he asked, yawning.

"Fine, thanks," I said. The crotch of my pants felt cold and damp as I took off my shoes and placed them on the mat by the door, side by side, next to the umbrella stand, the way Suzanne likes them. Doc turned off the television and roared with a stretch that extended from his head to his toes.

"You hungry?" he asked, sitting up. "There's some apple pie left in there with our names all over it, and I know you don't want me to eat it all by myself. It might ruin my figure." He rubbed his hand over his stomach and forced it out until it protruded over his pants. I would have liked to join Doc in the kitchen because he makes me laugh and he's the only person who actually listens when I talk, but the cut on my arm ached for attention.

"Thanks, but not tonight. I'm super tired," I said, forcing a yawn.

"Are you sure? We can share what's left: two forks, one plate, no napkins." Doc raised an eyebrow and tipped his head toward the kitchen.

I shook my head.

"Is everything all right, kid?"

I smiled and started up the stairs, knowing it wasn't Doc's style to press for more. "OK, get some sleep," he said and winked. "I'll save you a piece for tomorrow."

For ten minutes straight I scrubbed my underwear with a bar of soap in the bathroom sink until every last trace of semen was gone. I hopped in the shower, rinsed Eric's sticky fluid from my inner thighs, and let the warm water wash the remainder of him down the drain. With the shower control adjusted completely in the red, it didn't take long for my skin to turn the same shade as the inflamed cut on my forearm. It was one of my finest wounds: eight inches long and an eighth of an inch wide. It would take weeks to heal and leave a scar that would forever serve as a reminder of the day I failed to save Becca and the night I refused to save myself.

After I showered, I wrapped Mom's sweater around my dampened body. It had lost her smell years ago but finally fits me the way I remember it fitting her. I climbed into bed and took Alfred's book out from beneath my pillow where I safely hide it the way he did. I opened it to the neatly creased page that contained his favorite quote and read it to myself like a bedtime prayer: "… and we didn't ever feel like talking loud, it warn't often that we laughed, only a little kind of a low chuckle." I tucked the book back under my pillow, pushed a pair of headphones into my ears, and fell asleep to my favorite U2 song.

But sleep never lasts long in this town. I press rewind and play the U2 song again, relishing the fusion of the band's instruments that create a rhythm that steadily rises and drowns out the foreboding sounds of this toxic town.

Bono sings…as if directly to me.

"I want to run…"

I sit up and remove the fine-leather journal that Doc gave me from my nightstand.

"I want to hide…"

I open to the first page and stare at the blank, crisp white paper thirsting for ink. I should write about Mom, Becca, the Garritys, and what happened with Eric tonight. I should write about every hurt and heartache, as Bono does.

"I want to tear down the walls that hold me inside…I want to reach out and touch the flame…"

I pull the ballpoint pen out from the spine of the book and click down on the end several times before placing the tip on the empty sheet.

"Where the streets have no name…"

I turn up the volume and allow the pen to feverishly rush over the page as Bono continues to belt out lyrics.

"I want to feel sunlight on my face…"

For the first time I write whatever comes to mind, no matter how twisted or sick.

"I see the dust cloud disappear without a trace…"

I don't care about penmanship or grammar or the lingering aching that Eric caused between my legs.

"I want to take shelter from the poison rain…"

I just write.

"Where the streets have no name…"

One page after another.

"Where the streets have no name..."

I write with the help of Bono and the screaming voice that even the eight-inch cut on my arm won't silence. It rises above Bono, hushing his soulful vocals, as it demands to be acknowledged.

"We're still building then burning down love..."

Bono croons in the distance.

"Burning down love..."

I close my eyes as the voice instructs me to.

"And when I go there..."

But this time is different.

"I go there with you..."

Because this time I listen.

"I go there with you..."

And write down every revolting word.

"It's all I can do..."

No one ever knew what happened between Eric Seton and me. It was my fault, drinking and flirting the way that I did. Not since Alfred had I liked a boy so much. But Alfred was different, a perfect gentleman, unforgettable, like Becca, Mom, and the tiny fetus that Dr. Cressman cut up and suctioned out of me two months after Eric and I both got what we wanted. Suzanne didn't say a word when I sat down on the bed next to her holding a white stick from a home pregnancy test that I had picked up at the local pharmacy. I couldn't stop looking at the bold blue line that appeared in the small window minutes after I urinated onto the stick as directed. Suzanne grabbed the stick from my hand, walked to the bathroom, dropped it into the toilet, and flushed my problem away. I bit and tore at every fingernail as she sat back down on the bed, picked the phone up off the nightstand, and dialed a number she obviously knew by heart.

Suzanne rested her hand on my leg. "Don't you worry, we're going to take care of this," she said, and she covered the mouthpiece of the phone. "No one ever needs to know, Danielle, do you understand? It was a mistake and it's no one's business. This," she added, pointing in the direction of my stomach, "will be our little secret. Promise me that."

I bit deeper into the cuticle around my thumbnail, clenched down on a small piece of flesh, and pulled until it tore so far back that a drop of blood trickled down my hand. The foul taste of metal filled my mouth as I muttered the words that would fix my "mistake."

"I promise."

Suzanne nodded.

"Hello, this is Suzanne Whiteker. I have a bit of a problem, and I need to speak with Dr. Cressman immediately."

And with a wink and a nod, we took care of it. With the help of Dr. Cressman, we took care of "It." As Suzanne said we would. In only a few days. It was done. "Problem" solved. Like plucking the stem of a divinely formed bud from a rich bed of soil before it ever had the chance to blossom. Just like that. Just that simple. No one ever knew. I returned to school with a note from Suzanne.

Please excuse Danielle's absence from school.
She was home with an upset stomach.

Thank you,
Dr. and Mrs. Suzanne Whiteker

I suppose it wasn't really a lie. I was sick to my stomach. Still am. After all, I can't think of anything more nauseating than murdering my own child.

Damn Bethlehem.

"Truth or dare," Andrea says, pointing her finger directly at me as she pulls her car into the parking lot of a vacant building on the far side of the steel plant. School let out hours ago, and the sun has fallen beneath the Blue Mountains in the distance.

"Of course she has to pick me first," I say, rolling my eyes at Jenny and Nicole, two of our friends sitting in the backseat. "I really don't want to play this game." I rummage through a shoebox filled with cassette tapes.

"Why," she asks. "Are you a chicken?"

"Of course not. It's a really stupid game, that's all."

Andrea holds her hands beneath her underarms and flaps them back and forth. "Bawk, bawk, bawk!"

"That's real mature, Andrea."

"We're sixteen!" she says. "We don't have to be mature, so lighten up and have some fun, Danni!"

"But we're not even supposed to be here," I say, pointing to the sign posted outside the plant that reads RESTRICTED AREA KEEP OUT. "If anyone sees us, we'll get into trouble."

Andrea inches her car closer to the back gate. "What are they gonna do? Trust me, we'll be fine. So what's it gonna be, truth or dare?"

Andrea and I have played this game before. I choose the dare every time because I don't want to talk about my truths, not to her. Not to anyone. But with the towering steel stacks looming in front of us, the dare seems just as frightening.

"OK, fine, I'll take the dare."

"Cool," Andrea says, squinting her eyes. "I dare you to squeeze through the fence, climb into that building through one of the broken windows, and not come out until we count to one hundred and I beep the horn."

"All right, whatever," I say, sliding the tapes back under the passenger seat. I open the car door, quietly close it behind me, and cringe at the weight of my feet crushing into the gravel-covered ground. The grass is growing high on the other side of the fence. It brushes against my legs as I creep toward a large broken window and hoist myself up onto the ledge. If it weren't for the light of the moon, I wouldn't be able to see my hand in front of my face or the chair that seems intentionally placed beneath the window as I step down onto it and look back at Andrea, who flashes her lights to begin the count.

One-thousand one, one-thousand two, one-thousand three. As I stare into the darkness, the room feels large and vacant. It faintly echoes the continuous banging that still exists on the other side of the plant. *Twenty-one, twenty-two, twenty-three.* With my back against the wall, I close my eyes and wait. *Thirty-five, thirty-six, thirty-seven.* If I didn't know better, I would think that I wasn't alone. I would think that I heard the sound of feet lightly stepping across the concrete floor and the erratic, trembling breath of another. But I do know better, and if I open my eyes right now, I'll prove to myself that this is nothing more than my mind playing tricks on me and that the subtle noises I hear are merely a reverberation of the not-so-distant workers.

Outside, Andrea revs her car engine as the dare reaches the halfway mark. I've lost count with the eager anticipation of her horn. But it doesn't come. Not yet. Not before I lift one eye to a shadowed figure standing on the opposite side of the room. I blink hard to clear my eyes of the bizarre illusion. The air has turned colder. It rushes in and out of my nostrils, stinging and burning with each inhalation. I'm sure that this is my imagination. "Hello? Is anyone there?" I ask. Andrea will be honking her horn soon. I should get out of here and not look back. I should ignore my curiosity and the unexplainable urge to step closer to the figure with measured footing, crunching and grinding on the broken concrete beneath my rubber-soled shoes. Outside, Andrea's lights flicker on and off for the final countdown.

Ten.

"Hello?"

The moon has lifted higher into the evening sky.

Nine.

"Is anyone there?"

Eight.

It turns the vacant room into a shade of cool blue, illuminating the peculiar figure who is covered from head to toe.

Seven.

In a long coat.

Six.

With the hood pulled up.

Five.

I haven't seen the coat lady in years.

Four.

Not since I left Becca.

Three.

Erma said that she was a figment of my imagination.

Two.

I said she was a ghost.

"Who are you? What do you want? Why are you following me? Answer me goddamn it!"

Andrea's horn blares outside. The sound reverberates throughout the building, summoning the voices in my head to return. *Close your eyes! Don't look back!*

I run to the window and shimmy out as fast as I can, tripping on the field grass that tangles around my legs as I race back to the car, climb in, and slam the door behind me.

"Holy shit, Danni, you look like you've seen a ghost!" Andrea says.

Jenny and Nicole hold their stomachs in a fit of laughter as Andrea shifts the car into reverse and pulls out of the parking lot.

"Oh yeah, sure, I saw a ghost," I say, rolling my eyes and laughing louder than all of them. "A ghost of Bethlehem, of course."

I dig at the scar that trails up my forearm, incessantly picking at it until a drop of blood seeps into the tiny crevice around my nail.

"You know, I never believed in that stupid legend."

Andrea laughs and fidgets with the nob on the radio, moving from one station to another.

"Besides," I say, staring into the rearview mirror to watch the red glow of taillights illuminate the coat lady standing in the broken window. "Everyone knows there's no such thing as ghosts."

I take hold of Andrea's hand and squeeze hard until she looks me directly in the eye. "Right?"

13

"**D**octor, her heart rate is increasing. She's waking up."

A voice hovers above me. In a desperate panic, I struggle to move, frightened by the sudden awareness of my surroundings, machines beeping, feet scurrying across the floor, and the voice of the same nurse who had rested her hand on my shoulder and asked me to count backward from a hundred.

"It's OK, Danielle…everything's OK."

But I don't feel OK. The pressure in my back is unbearable as I lay helpless on this rigid operating table shifting my eyes back and forth beneath my lids.

"Administering fentanyl…50 mcg."

The nurse lightly strokes my arm. "You're all right; try to relax."

But I've never been all right, and Michael didn't seem to be either when he apologized before being asked to release my hand and wait in the room down the hall. The shrill clanking of surgical instruments echoes in my ears.

"You're going to be fine, Danielle. Sweet dreams," the nurse says to reassure me before I lose consciousness.

But this isn't a sweet dream.

Not at all.

This, no doubt, is an absolute nightmare...

I am a child again, walking the streets of Bethlehem toward the old Moravian cemetery, down the road from the Whitekers' house. Snow begins to fall as I approach the wrought-iron fence that surrounds a field of tombstones where there is a group of people, men and women, dressed in long coats with their hoods pulled up and their backs turned. They huddle together, shoulder to shoulder, excitedly chattering among themselves in direct opposition with the grace and ease of the blanketing snow. My hands are red and chafed, particularly my knuckles. They could suffer frostbite this way, wrapped around the icy steel gate.

"Let me in! Let me in!" I shake the fence, pushing and pulling on the latch that clatters with each failed attempt. "Who are you? What are you doing? Why are you here?"

But they can't possibly hear my voice above their relentless babble that intensifies with the increasing precipitation. A storm is setting in. I can see it in the clouds that darken overhead. I rattle the gate, forcing metal against metal, as the steelworkers did. Only this time it's me creating the insufferable noise until I burst through and approach the group that moves closer together, shielding me from what lies before them. The west has ushered in a mighty wind, warm and angry. It tosses about my hair and raises small bumps on the surface of my skin. If only they would respond to my questions or the way that I tap on their shoulders and tug at their clothes. "Who are you? What do you want? Answer me!" I yell, desperate for their attention.

How unpredictable the weather can be, changing from a delicate snow to a driving rain in a matter of seconds. The clouds tumble and twirl above me as the group of strangers turn to acknowledge my presence and part to reveal what they so diligently hid, a small tombstone erected at the base of a black, cavernous hole. On the front is a child's scribble, written in blue crayon.

It reads one word.

"Becca."

The rain turns to crimson. It grows thicker and heavier as it sweeps across the graveyard in oscillating sheets. I rush to the stone, kneel beside it, and run my hand over her name. "She's my sister," I cry, turning to catch a glimpse of the hooded faces looking down on me. "Where is she? What happened?" They close their circle around me as blood rains down and puddles at my feet. "Tell me!" I yell, losing my footing and sliding backward into the empty muddy hole...

four feet wide...

eight feet long...

six feet deep.

I can't see anything in this bloody pit. "Tell me where she is!" I shout, scratching and clawing against the dirt walls until blood from my own fingers pours down the sides and flows into the rising pool. "She's not dead! She can't be! I promised to protect her!"

The red rain fills my mouth and seeps back into my throat until I am gasping for air. I struggle to focus on the waxy letters of Becca's name that are washing away to reveal a new name deeply etched into the tomb with the same deliberate intensity as the scars that trail my arms. Perhaps this is the Valley of the Shadow of Death that Erma spoke about when she recited prayers to Becca and me before bed. And perhaps lifetimes of hostile foes have gathered before me to kick piles of dirt into the muddy grave of the one they hate the most. Their mumbled chatter evolves into an audible chant.

Close your eyes...

Don't look back...

Close your eyes...

Don't look back...

The name on the stone is clearly revealed: RIP Daniel Hoffman Pane. I reach up toward the hooded figures, arms fully extended, hands open wide. "Help me, please!"

With shovels in hand, they gather closer around the edge, whispering and giggling as I am pulled deeper into the muddy pit by arms that wrap around my waist.

"Close your eyes," he whispers in my ear, holding me firmly against him as the red water rises around us. The rain turns clear and exposes Sergeant, who squeezes me tighter, panting the way Bandit did the day he was poisoned. With one swift shift, the blustery wind knocks down the hoods of my captors and exposes all of them.

Mom.

Becca.

Alfred.

I loved and lost them all.

In unison they lift their shovels, scooping dirt from the sides of the grave and tossing it in on top of us, slowly at first, then faster, until we are buried up to our chests in cold, damp soil. With Sergeant's foul breath upon my neck, I lower my head in the presence of my enemies because this is justice.

Long awaited.

Well deserved.

This is justice.

I wake in a heated panic, drenched in sweat that soaks through my nightgown and onto the cotton hospital sheet that covers me.

"Must have been some dream," the nurse says with a curious smile. She removes the dampened bedsheet and wipes my forehead with a cool, moist cloth. I nod, trying to distinguish the difference between reality and dreams, because I'm not sure which is which anymore. But one thing is for sure. I'm in Bethlehem again, staring at a stained glass Moravian star that dangles in the hospital room window. It appears unbalanced, as it turns and shimmers in the sunlight and I feel oddly agitated by its crookedness. "It's very pretty," the nurse says, placing her fingertips on the inside of my wrist. She looks down at her watch and concentrates on the second hand before speaking again. "Someone dropped it off for you earlier," she adds.

"Who?" I ask, running my tongue across the cracks in my lips.

"A woman," the nurse says. "I didn't get her name. She stood outside in the hallway for quite a while before asking me to hang it in your window."

The pain bearing down on my abdomen makes everything else seem unimportant. So this is the pain I've needed all my life. I clench my jaw together and rub my stomach to try and grab hold of it.

"I can give you something for that," the nurse says, reaching for a rolling cart with a stack of small paper cups on top.

"Is my husband here?"

The nurse hands me a white pill and a cup of water. "I'll check the waiting room," she replies, and glances at her watch. "What's his name?"

My head is heavy, and I struggle to sit up in this weakened state. I toss the pill on to the back of my tongue and wash it down with a mouthful of cool water that plunges into my empty stomach. My left hand is bare, and there is a pale indentation on my ring finger where a wedding band used to be.

"Michael," I say, recalling the way he begged for my forgiveness as they rolled me into the operating room. The nurse hands me a clean nightgown, places a fresh sheet on my bed, and grabs her things to go.

"I'll see if he's here, but visiting hours don't start until five."

The effects of the pill will soon set in. The pain will be gone, and Michael did something terrible that I can't remember. "Nurse!" I call out.

Outside the doorway, the nurse turns and pauses.

"The woman who brought the star." I speak as loudly as the medicine will allow. "Do you remember what she looked like?" My eyelids grow heavy waiting for her response as she thinks for a moment before answering.

"Yes," she says, suddenly distracted by a doctor who approaches her to discuss a patient's chart. The star revolves in the window and casts an array of color across the hospital walls. The pain has subsided, and my eyes are getting heavy as the sun dips behind the building next door. The setting rays dart against the glass star that spins faster in the still air. I am drowsy when the nurse answers. The spectacle of color that swirls around me creates a dizzying vortex that forces my eyes shut.

Maybe Michael will be here when I wake. Maybe he'll tell me why he wants my forgiveness, why disturbing visions of Becca keep flashing in my mind, and why I'm here again, in the heart of Bethlehem, when I vowed never to return.

I can't stay awake much longer, and I can barely stomach the nauseating light show that, even through closed eyes, casts shadows that circle the room and spin out of control, reckless and untamed, embodying all that is Bethlehem. In defiance of its symbolism, I turn onto my side, away from the whirling star. I won't concentrate on this town and its tragedies or what the nurse tells me next as she nonchalantly staggers me with an answer I could never have expected.

Not in my wildest of dreams.

14

With the support of Suzanne and Doc, I left Bethlehem with Andrea a few weeks after graduating high school to attend college in Los Angeles where we could enjoy white beaches, sunny skies, and a refreshing mix of interesting new people. I had hoped that it would have all that Bethlehem lacked and everything that I desired.

Intrigue.

Opportunity.

And Alfred.

The fantasy of us being together had played out a thousand times or more in my mind as I searched for him in every store and on every street corner. But it has been four years since I moved to California, and my optimism of spotting his distinct face among the city crowds has diminished to an unlikely possibility. It's difficult to picture Alfred, a full-grown man, yet I still get excited each time I try. He is the part of Bethlehem that I never wanted to let go.

College graduation is a few weeks away, and I'll be returning to the East Coast where I've accepted a journalism internship with the *New York Times*. Doc has agreed to meet me in the city to help search for an apartment outside of Manhattan.

"Why don't you come home first for a couple of weeks?" he asked when I spoke with him on the phone yesterday. "I'll have someone fill in for me at the office so we can spend some time together and catch up. Besides, Suzanne has done a lot with the house, and she'd love for you to see it."

Doc tries harder than anyone to get close to me, which is why it's so difficult to disappoint him.

"I'd love to, really, but I have so much to do and I..." He cut me off before I had the chance to finish.

"You don't have to explain anything, kid. I understand. We'll do it another time."

"Definitely," I said. "I promise."

Doc grew up in Bethlehem with two loving parents who suffered through the Great Depression. They taught him tolerance, acceptance, and patience. But more importantly, they taught him unconditional love, how to give it and how to receive it. Unfortunately for him, I can't do either, and I can't seem to suppress the restless anticipation of returning to the Northeast.

It stormed late this afternoon. Sheets of water swept across the campus and cleared the city streets. The brief deluge pounded against the beach, creating a firm footing for my daily run.

I step out onto the sand, pull my hair back into a ponytail, and stretch out the backs of my legs. Along the shoreline, spectators have gathered to watch the arc of magnificent color forming in the darkening sky. It extends out over the horizon, far beyond where the human eye can see. The brilliance won't last long. It never does. Nature won't allow it. Such splendor is produced in limited doses.

Like Becca and Alfred.

As I struggle to set my pace, small piles of sand kick up behind me. It will take several minutes for my feet and lungs to find their rhythm. But when they do, I will meld into a peaceful existence where the aching in my lungs surpasses the aching in my heart. Only minutes have passed, and the spectrum of color is already beginning to dissipate as onlookers retreat from the sudden surge of waves that come barreling into the coast.

Finally, I have my breath.

Slow and steady.

One foot after the other.

Left.

Right.

Left.

Right.

Nothing feels better than this, except for the salty mist that cools my skin when it explodes off the breaking whitecaps. Up ahead, one spectator remains, a man, peering out over the ocean, undaunted by the fierce surf. He doesn't seem to mind the rushing waves that soak him from the waist down as they repeatedly slam into his long, slender legs. And he doesn't seem to mind that the rainbow has vanished and left behind nothing more than the subtle glow of the setting sun. My pace increases with a steady cadence.

I breathe in.

And out.

In.

And out.

Drawing nearer to him with each step.

There's something intriguing about the way that he moves, and I find myself staring at the willowy young man who opens his arms to the strong current of wind that rushes in from the sea. He kicks his bare feet into the foamy water, gazes out from beneath a loosely fitted baseball cap, and allows the last few rays of sun to rest upon his skin.

The air is dense tonight, unusually so. I didn't feel it a moment ago when each breath brought with it a sense of invigoration. But I feel it now, constricting my lungs as I approach the young man who frolics in the waves. It appears that his profile hasn't changed much in the years that have passed, nor has his brilliance. Perhaps the rainbow was just a momentary reprieve from the unstable weather and my labored breathing is merely an indicator of the storm that will come again. Or perhaps it's my palpitating heart that has me breathing so hard. But more than likely, it's the overwhelming longing for the boy I could never have.

Alfred is even more beautiful than I remember. Like a finely cultivated wine, the exquisiteness of his adolescence pales in comparison to the striking individual he is today. It's easy to admire his dainty features and chiseled cheekbones that prominently stand out beneath his milky skin. And it's easy to notice that he is more casual than he was under the rigid commands of Sergeant and more colorful in rolled up jeans and a yellow T-shirt that waves and flutters in the ocean wind. Every morning, I've jogged this beach dreaming of this opportunity. But not once at sundown.

Of course this is when he would come.

Of course.

I stop, take off my sneakers, and pull the rubber band from my hair so that it cascades down my back the way Alfred liked it. Two young girls pass before him, pointing and staring at his extraordinary appearance. You might think they saw a ghost, the way their eyes widen as they cover their mouths and gasp.

But there are no ghosts here.

We left them behind.

In Bethlehem.

The sand is soft and cool on the soles of my feet as I walk along the surf's edge, bathing in the same body of water as Alfred. It's not just me. Even the temperature of the ocean rises in his presence as the wind pushes against my back like a giddy schoolgirl, shoving me toward him, flirtatiously flipping my hair from side to side as seagulls swoop down to devour what Alfred has tossed into the air. How exciting to watch the gulls pluck his offering from the sky in midflight. I'm not sure which I find more stimulating: his effortless grace, or the scent of wildflowers and aftershave that wafts off his skin as I walk up behind him and place my hands over his eyes.

"Guess who?"

Alfred never was one to respond without a moment of calm deliberation. Seconds pass, five, maybe ten, before he speaks.

"It was kind of solemn," he says, quoting Huck Finn, "drifting down the big, still river, laying on our backs looking up at the stars, and we didn't ever feel like talking loud." He places his hands over mine. It's no surprise that, in spite of the chill in the air, his skin generates instant warmth.

"And it warn't often that we laughed," I say, continuing Huck's words that Alfred highlighted in his book, "only a little kind of low chuckle."

"I'd know that voice anywhere," he says before turning, "so this is either a cruel joke or a wonderful surprise." He slides my hands down and turns to face me. The varying shades of blue that light up the sky turn his pink eyes into a myriad of dazzling purple specks. Alfred is twenty-five years old, tall and lean, and as soft-spoken today as he was then, if not more so.

"Danni? Is it really you?" He steps back and scans me from head to toe.

"It's really me," I say, nodding

"Wow, look at you. You're all grown up."

"Yeah," I laugh. "You, too."

Alfred moves closer to me. "So what are you doing here?"

"I'm going to school at the university. I'll be graduating in a couple of weeks."

"You mean you've been here for four years?"

"Yes," I say, poking my finger into his chest. "And hoping to run into you every day."

"Unbelievable," he says, grabbing my hands.

"Well, here I am."

Alfred closes his mouth, clenches his teeth together, and waits the way he did beneath the maple tree on the night I last saw him when he was thirteen years old. But the years and distance have given him a confidence he didn't possess in his youth. He could have never looked me in the eye the way he does now.

"And here I am," I say, glancing away to catch my breath. The intensity in his eyes hasn't changed, nor has the feeling in my knees when he stares at me. "You know, the rumor back home was that you went to some military academy and enlisted in the army. But I never really bought it. I knew how much you wanted to come to California."

Alfred rolls his eyes and squeezes my hands.

"You knew me better than anyone," he says. "Probably still do."

"So what happened?" I ask, struggling to concentrate on his words rather than his touch. "Where did you go that night? How did you get here?"

I could look at him forever. The way he bites his bottom lip before answering, the way his eyes squint when he says my name, and the way his cheeks flush when we touch.

"The day you left," he says, "was one of the worst days of my life. I had to get the hell out of there, and I knew I'd have to kill him if he tried to stop me. So I shot him and ran until my legs gave out." His blank expression makes it difficult to tell if he is happy or sad. "I stayed in hostels all across the country and met some awesome people who accepted me, no questions asked. I guess you can say it restored my faith in humanity. Once I got here, I stayed with a friend of my mother."

"So Mrs. Garrity knew you were here all along?"

Alfred nods.

"And she still hasn't left that son of a bitch? Why does she stay with him?" I ask.

Alfred shrugs his shoulders. "I really don't care anymore. What about you?" he asks, changing the subject. "How have you been?"

I want to tell him how I've thought about him every day and how it really doesn't matter if he feels the same way as long as we're together. "I'm good, Alfred. I still can't believe I found you. You look great."

Alfred stares out over the ocean. "Still trying to figure some things out, but I love it here, always have." He sweeps his hand across my forehead and through my hair. "You're as beautiful as ever, Danni."

Until this very moment, I had forgotten how it felt to be exhilarated by a sudden burst of heat on my face.

"You're blushing," he says, lifting the corner of his mouth to a slanted smile that is as imperfect as he is... and as appealing. He allows the strands to sift slowly through his fingers. "It's been so long since I've seen you, and yet it feels like we've never been apart. Crazy right?"

It's hard for me to look at Alfred without remembering that day in the basement. But it's even harder not to throw my arms around him and embrace him the way I've always yearned to.

"No, Alfred, it's not crazy at all."

Over his shoulder I see that the ocean is receding with the evening tide. I suppose it could be the salt air creating the moistness between our palms, but in all likelihood it's the same infatuation intensified by the shift in Alfred's self-assurance. I've spent years trying to figure out how such a perfect combination of male and female could collide into one and how my feelings for him could deepen rather than fade with the passing years. He places his hand on my chin and guides my eyes back to his.

"You OK?" he asks.

"I'm fine, really. A little nervous, I guess."

"Me, too," he says, pulling me back from the restless sea. "Come with me." Alfred leads me to a blanket that he has spread out and secured with large shells. "Stay for a while," he says. "It's my favorite time of day, and we have so much to catch up on."

It will be dark soon, and the sun will set into the place where the sea meets the sky. Alfred sits down, removes his hat, and exposes his delicate skin to the gentlest rays of the day. His hair is much less conservative than it was in his pubescent years, long enough to blow in the wind. He runs his fingers through his platinum locks and tucks them behind his ears. The sight of him stirs up so many childhood memories: Becca's big hugs and the sound of her screams on the day I left. But most of all, seeing Alfred brings back memories of the boy who made such a lasting impression on me in just a few short years of my life.

"I'd love to," I say, sitting down on the blanket beside him, close enough to brush my legs against his. He loved me once. In some small way. Perhaps there's a corner of his heart that still belongs to me.

Alfred picks up a shell and tosses it between both hands. "What are you doing after you graduate?" he asks.

"I accepted an internship at the *New York Times* for the summer," I say, digging my heels into the velvety sand.

"So you're headed to the Big Apple," he says, holding the shell to his ear. "I've never been, but I'm definitely gonna get there one day."

I nudge my elbow into his. "Well, maybe you could visit me sometime, and I'll show you around."

He sets the shell in his lap and traces it with his fingers. "That'd be great."

The light of the moon has replaced the evening sun and Alfred's skin shines brighter in the luminous beams.

"Alfred?"

"Yeah?"

"With everything that happened the way that it did, I never got the chance to apologize for—"

Alfred shakes his head.

"Don't," he says, wrapping his arm around my shoulder and pulling me to him with the strength of a man.

"But it was all my fault. I should have never—"

He presses his hand over my mouth and moves closer. His skin is flawless, more perfect up close than at a distance.

"Sshh, no regrets, OK?" He leans in toward me until we are face to face, where I've always wanted to be. Eyes and lips only inches apart. I nod as a tingling between my legs begins in anticipation of his lips on mine.

And in this very moment, Alfred comes to me.

His mouth.

His tongue.

His breath, which rapidly increases when he draws my chest to his. I never expected this.

Not here.

Not now, on the beach, where an occasional passerby could easily see. But there's no stopping what is meant to be, and there's no turning away from Alfred, who lies down on top of me and pulls the blanket over us.

The closeness of his body makes it difficult to determine whether it's his heart or mine that is pounding so hard. But I am certain, by his quivering lips, that he is the one trembling. Alfred's hair falls down over his eyes as he kisses me again and unzips his pants. I've always dreamed of this and how perfect it would be. He pulls down my shorts and places his hand between my thighs to part them. With both hands, I brush my fingers through his hair, holding it off his face because I want to watch Alfred when I let him in so that I'll know if this is real. With his lips against mine, he drives his tongue deep into my mouth and reaches down to fondle himself, stroking and pulling on the area of his body that isn't responding.

To his touch, or mine.

The moon shifts higher in the sky as Alfred struggles to perform, exhausting every position and every ounce of strength until, fatigued and frustrated, he stops, sits beside me, draws his knees to his chest, and buries his head into his folded arms.

"I can't, Danni," he says. His voice cracks as he chokes back the tears. "I just can't."

I don't know which is brighter, the moon or the top of Alfred's silvery head that bobs up and down with every sob-filled breath.

"Who am I kidding?" he says, rubbing his eyes on the sleeve of his shirt. "This isn't gonna work. I'm sorry.

It's my fault. I never should have started this." A stream of clear mucus leaks out from Alfred's nose. He turns to me, slides his baseball cap onto his head, and pulls it down low on his ears. "If you hate me," he says, swiping his hand beneath his nose, "I'll understand."

In an effort to soothe the feminine boy who has emerged, I rest my hand on Alfred's back and move it in a circular motion the way Mom used to do when I scraped my knee or bit my tongue.

This is the Alfred that I know.

Timid and fragile.

Frightened and insecure.

Lightning flashes in the distance as a band of dark clouds moves over the moon, followed by a low, subtle rumble.

"I could never hate you, Alfred," I say, leaning against his slender frame to rest my head on his shoulder. The storm is moving closer. I can tell by the decreasing number of seconds between the lightning and thunder. Alfred and I gaze out over the ocean and count in unison as the sky lights up again.

"One thousand one, one thousand two, one thousand three."

Alfred takes hold of my hand and, like a tightly knit fabric, intertwines his fingers in mine as the clouds crackle and boom.

"Danni?"

"Yeah?"

"I'm sorry."

"You don't have to apologize, Alfred. I understand."

"No, you don't," he says. "You can't possibly understand. No one can."

Alfred is right. I don't understand. Or maybe I just don't want to.

"I care for you a lot," he says. "I always have." If it weren't for a sudden crash of lightning, I couldn't see how red and swollen Alfred's eyes are as he turns to me. "I need you to know that."

"I do, Alfred," I say, sensing his need for reassurance. "Really, I do."

He nods and sniffs. "I mean, in all the years we've been apart, I've never felt this close to anyone." With his hand still in mine, he strokes my thumb with his. "We have something pretty special, ya know?"

"Yeah, I know."

"Danni?"

"Yeah?"

"I want to tell you something that I've never told anyone." Alfred releases my hand, rubs his palms together, cups them over his mouth, and blows into them. The storm is imminent, brightening the night into day with each thunderous crash. "The thing is," he says, clearing his throat, "I'm not like other guys. I'm different..."

Before Alfred can finish his sentence, Andrea comes running toward me, waving her hands in the air. "Danni!" She is breathless by the time she reaches me. "I've been looking all over for you," she says. "Suzanne called. You need to call her; it's an emergency. Something about Doc."

I jump to my feet and wipe the sand off the back of my legs. "What do you mean? What happened? Is something wrong?"

"I don't know—that's all she said. Come on, you have to go!"

Andrea runs back toward campus without acknowledging the beautiful young man on the blanket behind me. I peer out over the ocean, into the dark abyss. A sick feeling shoots from the pit of my stomach into my throat as Alfred stands and shakes the blanket into the wind.

"You should go," he says, wrapping it around my shoulders as the sky opens up to a steady downpour of rain. I nod, force my wet feet back into my sneakers, and raise my voice above the menacing storm.

"Alfred, if you need to tell me something, tell me now! Please! It has to be now!"

He closes his eyes and lifts his face to the purity of the driving rain. "Go home, Danni," he says, spreading his arms out by his side as he did earlier when I first spotted him by the ocean. "Your family needs you."

It's the most callous thing he could say to a girl who never really had one.

"That's it, Alfred?" I yell. "That's all you have to say? When will I see you again?"

Alfred's shirt flutters against his thin frame.

"Answer me, goddamn it!"

As the waves pick up with the turbulent storm, he turns away, forcing me from the only boy I've ever loved.

The surf rolls and tumbles, crashing against the shoreline with an eerie resemblance to the steel I left behind.

I walk.

The mighty sea roars like a ferocious lion marking its territory, forcing unwelcome intruders back to their homeland with intimidation.

I jog.

With an uncomfortable moistness between my legs and a broken heart from what Alfred couldn't finish...

I run.

15

D r. Tom died last week after his morning cup of coffee when he suffered a massive heart attack and dropped to the floor as Suzanne prepared his breakfast (two eggs over easy with a slice of whole wheat toast), the same breakfast she had prepared for him for the past twenty-two years at precisely 7:00 a.m. right after handing him the daily newspaper and a freshly brewed cup of decaf (black with two sugars). Paramedics spent over an hour trying to resuscitate him, and Suzanne spent over an hour begging them not to stop.

I took the first flight home, arriving in Bethlehem within twenty-four hours of the time that Dr. Tom was pronounced dead at the house on Market Street. Suzanne's friends rallied around her, bringing food, tidying the house, and helping with the funeral arrangements. They didn't leave her alone, not for a minute.

For five days and five nights, they stayed with Suzanne as she slowly withdrew into a place so far deep inside of herself that she became practically unrecognizable. Diminished and depleted. Reduced to nothing more than a helpless, fragile child. They bathed her, dressed her, fed her, and constantly reassured her that she would be all right. But she wasn't all right, even on the day after the funeral when she managed to convince everyone otherwise by showering, dressing, and cooking a big breakfast, makeup on, hair done. Her friends reveled in her newfound strength and energy, and I breathed a sigh of relief seeing her act like her old self again. But I should have known better as she joyfully flitted about the kitchen rambling on about some big sale at her favorite department store that she wanted to go to alone because she really needed to get out of the house to think. I should have known better, and I should have insisted I go with her because she wasn't all right.

Not at all.

I could feel it, straight through to my bones.

This is why I decide to search for her this evening when she doesn't come home. She isn't difficult to find. Her car is the only one left in the parking lot. A steel-blue Mercedes with tinted windows and a license plate that reads "DOCSGRL." I pull up alongside the car, turn off the engine, and approach the driver's side window.

"Suzanne?" I peer in while gently knocking on the glass. "Suzanne...are you in there?"

I examine the front seat closely, keys in the ignition, coffee in the cup holder, and Suzanne's designer handbag on the passenger side. But there is no sign of Suzanne in the driver's seat of her Mercedes, just a white envelope with my name on it, boldly written in black ink. I move to the back window, cup my hands around my face, and press against the glass, feeling the warmth of my own breath reflecting back onto my skin as I notice a large bundled up blanket in the backseat. I study every inch that wraps around the obvious curves of what lies beneath it.

Head.

Shoulders.

Hips.

Legs.

All covered completely.

Except for the limp, blue hand that dangles over the edge of the seat above an empty pill bottle. The same familiar hand that took me away from the Garritys' house so long ago, saved me from Sergeant, tore me away from Becca, and kept me from Alfred. I never loved her or forgave her, and she knew it. If I slam my fists against my ears, I can momentarily disrupt the dissonance of rising voices that begin with the bright blue lights of a security truck that approaches and stops before me. The lights dance and swirl around a man who steps out from the truck.

"Excuse me, Miss, is everything OK?"

I can barely hear him over the screams. *Close your eyes! Don't look back! Close your eyes! Don't look back!* The security guard kneels down, reaches his arms out, and helps me to my feet.

"Are you all right?" he asks.

I dust off my knees and giggle at the same loaded question I asked Suzanne earlier today when she walked out the front door carrying a handbag filled with lethal amounts of painkillers casually slung over her shoulder. With the voices still screaming in my head, I answer him the exact same way she answered me, with a wink, a smile, and a low, steady voice teeming with resolve: "Yeah, I'm gonna be."

It doesn't take long to get things wrapped up at the Whitekers. Dr. Tom left everything to Suzanne in his will and her to him. But in the tragic event of both their deaths, everything goes to me, including the house on Market Street in the heart of historic Bethlehem, blocks from the Nisky Hill Cemetery where they were buried side by side, the way they had been for the past thirty years, since they met in college and vowed their love for each other 'til death do they part. Suzanne wouldn't allow anything to come between her and her beloved, not even their own mortality, which is why she swallowed every last pill in the concoction of painkillers, muscle relaxers, and antianxiety meds that she had accumulated. She knew exactly what she was doing and exactly what she wanted. As tragically as it ended, theirs was a true love story...or so she wanted everyone to believe.

I hardly feel worthy of all they left me, having harbored such resentment toward them all these years. Maybe that's why I still haven't opened the letter that Suzanne left me in the front seat of her Mercedes. What could she possibly have to say to a child who never wanted what she offered? I must have stared at the sealed envelope for an hour or more this morning before finally tearing it open. A faint trace of tangerine colored lipstick was smeared across the inner flap where Suzanne had licked the glue strip moments before ending her own life. I marveled at the way she prepared herself that day, impeccably dressed and groomed, and I wondered what went through her mind as she chose her outfit, her nail polish, and her lip color. The letter inside was not nearly in the same condition as the crisp white envelope that concealed it. Like Suzanne, the crumpled piece of paper was beautifully masked. Smudges and smears covered the page where Suzanne had written, erased, and written again.

> My Darling Danni,
> It doesn't seem enough to say that I'm sorry. You deserve so much more. You always did.
> With eternal love,
> Suzanne

At the bottom of the page was the name and address of someone Suzanne contacted before she ended her life. Someone who lives on the other side of town. Someone who still makes me want to take a blade to the soft flesh on the inside of my wrist.

Amy Hoffman.

My mother.

That was it.

Nothing more.

Suzanne left my life as quickly as she entered. Like a ferocious wind, she swooped me up, tossed me about, and dropped me back down. Leave it to her to open up a wound that I've fought so hard to heal. Seventeen years have passed since I last saw Mom. She never called. She never wrote. I didn't exist.

To hell with Amy Hoffman. I stuff the letter deep into my suitcase, pack my car, and head down Market Street. The sun is setting over Bethlehem as night creeps into every corner and hovers low on the streets. The air is exceptionally muggy for spring and unusually quiet with the slow demise of the failing steel plant. Most say that it will be the end of an era the day the doors close. But for me, it will be the end of a nightmare, the end of the pounding, the end of the screeching. I roll the windows down in my car to capture the delectable aura of a fallen town. I waited a long time for the sins of this city to take root and choke the life out of it. It was a slow kill but well worth the wait.

It is dark now, except for a few dim lights from the plant that linger in the black sky. Perhaps I notice, more than anyone, the stillness that rests here. But in this town even the calm causes me angst, and every mile reminds me of a lifetime I'd rather forget. I press my foot harder on the gas as the ghosts of this town breathe down my neck, acknowledging my presence in a city I never wanted to call home. The interstate isn't far away, and I would have made it out without so much as a second thought if it weren't for the red light on the corner of Market and Main. I would have kept on going and never looked back.

But the light is red.

And the streets are empty.

I tap my fingers on the steering wheel and stare at the red iridescent circle that dangles in stark contrast against the night. I press in the cigarette lighter, open the glove compartment, and rummage through a heap of clutter, gum wrappers, paper napkins, a lint brush, and the leather journal that Doc gave me on my sixteenth birthday. Except for a few pages, it is blank. I hold it upside down and shake until a flattened cigarette butt falls out from the written sheets. I place it between my lips, light up, and draw in until ashes dangle from the tip and fall scattered onto my lap. The stale smoke burns my lungs as it did the first time I inhaled it, just minutes after Eric Seton gave me what I wanted in the backseat of his Mustang.

The light is still red.

Obnoxiously so.

It's defiance is merely another example of how this contemptuous town scoffs at me, pushing me out while holding me back, daring me to face what I'd rather run from. How presumptuous of Suzanne to dredge up my mother in her final hour. Amy Hoffman is my business, not hers, yet I can't deny the temptation of turning left instead of right, in the opposite direction of the interstate, toward Amy's house. When the light changes, I will have to make the decision of whether to press up or push down on the turn signal arm that will lead me into the future or drag me back to the past. Once again, I fill my lungs with the toxic comfort of nicotine. I want to pound on Amy's door and kick and holler until I force her to acknowledge what she left behind. I want to wrap my arms around her, rest my cheek against hers, and breathe in her motherly scent that I've never forgotten. But most of all, I want to tell her about Becca, how I tried my best to care for her but failed and how I'll find her and make it up to her if it's the last thing I do.

Doc was disappointed when he called me last month after contacting Mrs. Rogers at my request.

"Becca doesn't live with the Garritys anymore, Danni," he said. "No one knows where she is. She ran away years ago. No one has heard from her since."

The light shifts to green. I toss the cigarette out onto the street and watch it roll and smolder along the macadam. Maybe Becca reached her breaking point as Alfred did the night he shot Sergeant to escape the relentless cruelty of a man who would never accept him. I shouldn't have yelled at Alfred that night on the beach. Maybe it was his way of setting me free from the hopes and expectations of something that could never be. I'd like to think that, in some way, I did the same for him. But Becca is another story, a part of me I can't let go. She is missing, and Mom is on the other side of town. I push up on the turn signal, plagued by the voice that incessantly berates me. *Close your eyes! Don't look back! Close your eyes! Don't look back!*

"Stop it!" I yell, conceding to a presence I'm not sure exists. I pull into the intersection and turn in the direction of the highway. I've waited years to see my mother again and spent countless nights wondering where she was. Cars rush past as I merge into traffic, recklessly speeding out of Bethlehem. A steady stream of wind rushes through the window and flips open the journal to the pages I wrote when I was sixteen in the dark hours of the night but never had the courage to read. They flap and flutter, mocking every written word. As the sounds of the road drown out the voice of the uninvited visitor in my head, I hurl it out the window, turn on the radio, and crank up the volume. In an odd turn of events, perhaps Amy Hoffman is waiting for me tonight.

The sweet thought of karma brings an unexpected smile to my face.

It's her turn, goddamn it.

She can wait.

16

NEW YORK CITY, 1993

"It's a fresh start," I told Andrea when she called to find out how I was doing. "New job, new city, new life. God knows I could use it." I was still trying to convince myself that I made the right decision.

"Of course you did the right thing. Opportunity knocked, and you answered. Besides, I hear the city is crawling with hot single men, so I'll have to visit sometime real soon!" Andrea laughed. As always, she looked at the glass half-full and ignored the mess of circumstances that is my life. Her enthusiasm is a trait that I can find irritating one day and refreshing the next.

"Trust me," I said, "guys are the last thing on my mind right now, but I'd love for you to visit anytime."

"You bet!" she said, ending our conversation to run to an audition. Andrea stayed in Los Angeles after graduation and took a job as a waitress in a local pub to pursue an acting career. We promised to talk at least once a week and to never lose touch with each other, regardless of our hectic schedules or the three thousand miles that separate us. It's been over a month since I left Bethlehem to intern at the *Times,* and I've managed to find comfort in a job with endless tasks that leave little time to think of anything or anyone else.

The phone rings and wakes me from the few hours of sleep I caught resting on my laptop.

"Hello?"

"Hey, Danni. It's Doug. Sorry to wake you. I need you to cover a story downtown."

Doug is the intern director at the *Times.* He's been there for years, hates his job, and lets everyone know it. I rub my eyes to focus on the time in the upper corner of my computer screen: 5:43 a.m.

"Uh…OK…where and when?"

"The corner of 7th and W 46th. A girl was beaten and stabbed in a back alley. I needed you there like an hour ago, so make it quick." He hangs up without saying another word.

I push the curtains aside and take a moment to admire the brilliance of the moon before it fades into the morning. If it weren't for its white splendor, my mind would be clear of the past, clear of Alfred.

I arrive downtown at the break of dawn to cover the story of an unidentified young girl who was raped, slashed, and left for dead in a back alley. Police officers rope off the alley with bold yellow tape as crowds of curious onlookers gather.

"Were there any eyewitnesses?" I ask of the officer on duty at the horrendous crime scene that left a seventeen-year-old lying in a pool of blood, fighting for her life. The officer shakes his head.

"No one has come forward," he says, rubbing the back of his neck. "It's no surprise, though. The public doesn't typically rush to the aid of every hooker who gets assaulted. It's far too common in these parts. She'd be dead if it weren't for the delivery boy who found her. He's a real hero."

As the crowd thickens, the delivery boy Chen Wu speaks with cops and reporters, describing in detail how he happened upon the girl's battered body while taking a shortcut to his next stop. He reacted quickly, flagging down police officers who came to her rescue. I watch as Chen uses his hands to describe what his broken English cannot: about a young girl, new to the streets, viciously stabbed until barely recognizable. He knows the streets well, and had recently seen her hanging out by the corner store, shoddily dressed, hiding behind a mound of tangled hair, selling herself cheap for a meal or a bottle.

But this story won't make headlines. They want something more tragic to tug at the heartstrings, like a Christian student from the Midwest who had come to the Big Apple to help feed the homeless before leaving the country on missionary work. Now that would be a story worth talking about. Battered whores are a dime a dozen, barely newsworthy; the public could care less. But I think differently when I follow the ambulance to the hospital emergency room and notice the discreet sobs of a stout black woman, adorned in bold African print, pacing back and forth in the center of the waiting room, ringing her hands and shaking her head. *She cares*, I think to myself as I approach her and notice how her hand trembles when wiping the tears from her saddened eyes.

"Excuse me, ma'am. I'm with the *New York Times*."

She stops and wipes her nose with a brightly colored handkerchief.

"I'm sorry, I see that you're very upset, but I was wondering if I could get a statement? Just a couple of words, perhaps about the victim if you know her."

She lifts her shawl up over her shoulders and wraps it tightly in front. "She's a good girl, she is. Not deserving of any of dis," she says, waving the handkerchief in the air. "And dats all I have to say about dat."

I jot down her statement, look up, and she's gone. The ink on my notepad has barely dried when Doug calls with my next assignment.

The Evangelical Church is only blocks away. I take a seat in the last pew and listen to Reverend Michael Pane, who called the *Times* and requested a reporter to cover the story of a vigil being held at his church to pray for a critically injured young boy. The story is uplifting and moving, but it's the man who delivers the story that takes my breath away. I place my hands in prayer position and listen as he delivers his afternoon sermon on temptation, of all things: how to recognize it and how to resist it. Not since Alfred has someone intrigued me so. Each of his features is as alluring as the next.

His hair.

His eyes.

His skin.

All varying shades of brown that exude the great outdoors and radiate the warm tones of the sun that Alfred's fragile skin so intensely rejected. There isn't one thing about Reverend Pane that isn't masculine. He is everything that Alfred was not or could not be, no matter how hard he tried. Reverend Pane's manhood comes with ease. It is obvious and palpable. I can feel it from where I am seated as he catches my eye while commanding the undivided attention of his entire congregation. Maybe it's his confident stride or the way his chest and shoulders ripple beneath his shirt with every bold declaration. The attraction is immediate and undeniable. I shift in my seat to suppress the pulsating sensation between my legs. Erma once said that an impure thought is as bad as the actual deed if you allow yourself to dwell on it too much.

"It's a sin to have lust in your heart," Erma said as she sat across from me at the kitchen table, teaching me about the birds and the bees, and trying to explain the difference between lust and love. "It'll get you into trouble if you let it," she said. "Lust is a powerful thing, but it's only temporary." She leaned back in her chair and flicked her cigarette ashes into the sink. "Love, on the other hand," she continued, "is forever."

She rested her arms on the table and leaned her body toward me. Her aged breasts heaved up over her bra and protruded out through the bright pink blouse that had come unbuttoned during her afternoon nap. She spoke in a voice that cracked and rumbled from years of nicotine as she placed her knobby hand, adorned with fingernails painted the same shade of orange as her hair, on mine. "Love takes time," she said, reeking with the potent combination of cigarettes, whiskey, and dime-store perfume. "But it's well worth the wait." She raised her penciled brows and winked her eyes that wrinkled and creased with the thick blue paste she smeared across her lids every morning. "You remember that, darlin'," she said.

And I did. I didn't understand it at the time. But I remembered it all the same. Word for word. I remembered it every night when I heard Sergeant breathlessly telling Mrs. Garrity how much he loved her as their bed pounded against the other side of my bedroom wall. I remembered it when Eric Seaton forced himself inside of me in spite of how many times I flinched from the pain. And I remembered it with the few boys since who professed their love for me in the backseat of their car, beneath the bleachers of the football stadium, or amid the high sea grass that grew on the dunes of the California beaches. Their love took no time at all and left as quickly as it came, just as Erma said it would. It seems I still have a lot to learn about lust and love, and the vast difference between the two. I bow my head and cross my legs.

"Forgive me, Father, for I have sinned," I say quietly to myself, because I can tell by the churning in my stomach and the tingling in my groin that Reverend Michael Pane is a temptation that will be difficult to resist. Not since Alfred has anyone dared me to dream.

It was difficult losing Alfred the way that I did, but how can I lose something that I never really had? And how, I wonder, as I doodle "Mrs. Reverend Michael Pane" on the cover of the church program, can I ever get what I really want?

Even if I don't deserve it.

Cupid is a son of a bitch. He sneaks up unexpectedly, draws back his arrow and...*wham!*...stabs you right in the heart. He doesn't care what is going on in your life. He doesn't want to hear about your fears or concerns. He is on a mission, one heart at a time. He lights the fire, throws in some kindling and a couple of dry logs, and blows on it for a while until it's a raging inferno burning out of control, and then he leaves as quickly as he came. That's it. He doesn't give a shit what happens from there. He gives no warnings and offers no guarantees.

It was the sting of that arrow that brought Michael and I together within the sanctity of his church walls when I dropped by his office unannounced the very next day. I could tell by the expression on his face that my visit was a pleasant surprise and that Cupid had us both exactly where he wanted us, no matter what the price.

"Come in, Miss Hoffman. Have a seat." Reverend Pane hangs up the phone and motions for me to enter his office, where he is seated behind a desk that is piled high with stacks of papers.

"You look busy, Reverend. I can come back another time."

"No, no, come in, I insist," he says, standing to greet me with a soft, steady handshake. He guides me into his office and closes the door. "It's a pleasure to see you again. What can I do for you?"

It's unusual for me to be at a loss for words, but I have come to learn that honesty isn't always the best policy. I can't possibly tell him that I can't stop thinking about him and that I feel like everything in my life, every heartache and every mistake, has somehow led me right here, to him. I can't tell him that I came to be near him, to bathe in the exhilarating aura that emanates from his very existence.

"I'd like to become a member, Reverend," I say, lying to him as much as myself while noticing the way his molasses-colored eyes smile on their own.

"Please, call me Michael," he says. He leans against the edge of the desk and folds his arms. From across the room, I can feel his masculine energy, a unique combination of strength, confidence, and tenderness.

"We'd be honored to have you, Danni. Why don't you tell me a little bit about yourself and your family."

I didn't prepare for his questions, especially this one.

"Family?" I ask, hoping he won't sense my visceral reaction to the mere word. "I…I don't have a family." Erma said that successful relationships are built on truths, not lies. My answers are a little of both. "My parents," I continue, "are recently deceased."

He softens his eyes and steps away from his desk. "And siblings," I lie, disregarding Erma's advice, "I don't have any."

Michael takes a seat beside me. He doesn't know that he's only getting a version of the truth. He doesn't know that I never knew my father, that my mother didn't love me enough to stay, or that I abandoned my little sister after hundreds of pinky swears that we would always be together. And I didn't know, until this very moment, as Reverend Michael Pane places his hand on top of mine and wraps his fingers gently around the curves of my hand, that my sorrow, no matter how unintentional or how misguided, could bring him close enough for me to notice the subtle shades of russet in his ebony hair.

"I'm sorry," he says, shaking his head. "It must be very difficult for you. I offer grief counseling, Danni, if you're ever interested."

I smile, and he brushes his thumb across the top of my hand. *He'll know soon enough,* I think to myself, pleasuring in his touch and the slight cleft that forms in the middle of his chin when he speaks, *that I'm interested in everything he has to offer.*

And so much more.

17

I am lying on my back when I wake to the fluorescent glare of ceiling lights and a woman standing beside me, dressed in white with a stethoscope hanging around her neck.

"Hello, Danni, how are you feeling?" She jots a few things down on a clipboard and makes some adjustments to the machine next to my bed that continually beeps.

My words feel thick and slurred from hours of drug-induced sleep. "What happened? Why am I here?" I ask.

"You're recovering from an accident," she says, covering me with a thin white blanket. "Considering the circumstances, your memory loss is perfectly normal. It will return, slowly but surely, and you're going to be just fine."

The glass star in the window has stopped spinning. Its presence generates a restless agitation as I recall what the nurse told me earlier.

"Did you say that a woman brought me that star?" I ask.

She nods. "She wanted me to hang it for you," she says, while adjusting the pillow beneath my head.

"Did you get her name?" I ask.

"I'm afraid not—she didn't give me a chance to."

Her lack of information causes my body heat to rise, creating an uncomfortable dampness on the surface of my skin.

"Do you remember what she looked like?"

The nurse is slow to respond, clicking the tip of her ballpoint pen as she contemplates her answer. "That's the strange part," she says, forcing her brows together at the top of her nose. "I couldn't really tell."

"What do you mean?"

"Well," she continues, "she was dressed rather odd for this time of year, in a long coat with the hood pulled way up over her head. Seemed to me that she didn't want anyone to know who she was or what she looked like." Her shoulders shrug with uncertainty. "She was here one minute and gone the next."

"Like a ghost?" I blurt out, sounding as silly now as I did in Erma's kitchen.

The nurse chuckles. "I see someone's still feeling the effects of the pain pills."

"She's followed me for years," I say, eager for someone to believe me.

"Who?" the nurse asks, placing the television remote on my lap.

"The woman," I say. "In the coat. She's a ghost."

The nurse squints her eyes and taps her index finger against her chin. "Hmmm, a gift-giving ghost," she says with a wink. "I have to get myself one of those." She pats my arm. "No, she was definitely not a ghost. The woman who dropped off the gift was most certainly real," she says, still chuckling. "She probably didn't stay because she didn't want to disturb you. Now you try and get some rest, I'll be back in a bit."

The glass star dangles from the ceiling, leaning to one side where a pane is missing.

"I don't need any more goddamn rest; I need to see my husband."

The nurse gathers her things and places the pen behind her ear. "I'm sure he'll be here soon. Why don't you get some shut-eye while you wait."

"I need answers!" I say in a panic as disturbing images flash through my mind...

the woods...

the fall...

and Becca...

over and over again...

Becca.

I wrap my hands around the bed rails and squeeze until the cold steel stings my palms the way it did the day they took Mom away. "I want to see my husband!" I yell, shaking the rails like I'm five again. "I need to see him! Now!"

But the nurse isn't fazed by my sudden outburst or the way that I scream out Michael's name. "Michael!" She places her things down and removes a syringe from her cart drawer. "Michael!" Over her shoulder, the star begins to spin as she inserts the needle into the tube connected to my wrist.

"No, please, I don't want to go to sleep! I want to talk to my husband! Please! I need to know what happened!" Thrashing about in my bed generates a pain that stabs through my abdomen into my lower back as bits and pieces of my memory begin to fall into place. "Where's Becca?" I yell out to an empty room. "What happened to my sister?"

It doesn't take long for the drugs to overpower my muscles and force me to concede to a mightier strength that slips the steel from my grip as it did when the men in white pulled me from Mom's gurney and rolled her out the door. My eyes close, drawn together like the unbreakable force of a positive to a negative. But rest is the last thing I need as my past collides with my present.

Something is terribly wrong.

Something tragic.

And the coat lady is real.

The nurse said so herself.

She isn't a ghost.

She's fucking real.

I was six years old when Erma found me sitting on her bathroom floor, tucked between the tub and the toilet. I felt safe there. It was the one place in Erma's house that reminded me of Mom and the way I used to wait for her in a steam-filled room while she showered, toweled off, and doused her skin with sweet-smelling perfume. With a cigarette dangling from Erma's lips, she reached down, grabbed me by the arms, and lifted me to my feet.

"No one ever got anywhere feeling sorry for themselves," she said, pulling me out into the hallway. She stumbled a bit, belched out loud the way she taught us not to, and coughed hard until something shot up into her mouth. She pulled a tissue from her cleavage and swiped it across her lips to discard the foul secretion. "Time heals the hurtin'," she said. "It'll heal yours too, you'll see." Erma held her arms out against the walls to steady herself and hummed the ant song all the way up the hall before staggering into the kitchen.

But here I am, thirty-two years later, and I'm still waiting for the healing to set in. I'm cold and dampened with sweat from a restless sleep. It takes me a moment to focus as I wake to an unexpected visitor who introduces herself as Dr. Janet, a psychiatrist who works on the fifth floor.

"Your doctor arranged for me to come," she says, sitting tall and rigid in the guest chair that has been placed in the corner of the hospital room. "I won't stay long. You've been through a lot, and I wouldn't want you to overdo."

"It's a little too late for that," I say, noticing my blood-ied skin beneath the leather straps that have been placed around my wrists and secured to the bed rails.

"How are you feeling?" she asks.

"Couldn't be better," I say, tugging at the restraints. "Are these really necessary?"

"They're for your own safety," she says, staring at the fully exposed scars that trail up and down my arms.

"So my doctor sent you?" I ask.

She nods and removes a pad and pen from her briefcase.

"Does this mean he thinks I'm crazy?" I shake my head to toss the hair from my eyes and drag my tongue over the cracks in my lips.

"He thinks, perhaps, you could benefit from some professional help. Do you think you need help, Danni?" she asks.

"I guess you can start by helping me get these re-straints off. There a little excessive, don't you think?"

"I'm afraid I can't do that—liability issues, you un-derstand," she says, and nods her head in confirmation. "Your doctor expressed concern about your well-being. Have you been experiencing symptoms of depression or anxiety?"

"Always."

"Which one?"

"They're pretty much a package deal, aren't they?"

"So you suffer with both?"

"I guess."

"For how long?"

"As long as I can remember."

"Any thoughts of suicide?"

"Sure, why not?"

"Because you're a young woman with a lot to live for. Tell me about yourself, Danni."

"What do you want to know?"

"Right now, anything you'd like to share would be useful."

Beneath the doctor's chair, there are hundreds of grooves scratched into the linoleum floor from those who have sat there before her, restless with worry over a sick loved one. I can sense their presence, every one of them, as though in their angst they each left a small part of themselves behind.

"I can help you, Danni," she says.

"Maybe I don't want your help."

Dr. Janet appears to be in her midfifties, conservatively dressed in a classic black tweed suit. She has olive-colored skin and black wavy hair that is streaked with silvery white strands that match her outfit. I can tell she was beautiful once.

"Defiance will only block your progress. Shall we proceed?" she asks, and she begins without waiting for my response. "Tell me a little bit about yourself."

My body aches, and for the first time I notice the scrapes and bruises from the accident that brought me here. Each wound jogs a small fragment of memory that is vague and distorted. "I'm thirty-seven, married for twelve years, and work at the *Times*," I say, conceding to her request.

"Sounds like a good life," she says.

"It should be."

"It isn't?"

"It's complicated."

"Fair enough. Tell me about your childhood."

"There's not much to tell," I say, drawing my knees into my chest, the way I used to on Alfred's bed.

"There's always something to tell," she says, jotting something down on her notepad.

"Let's just say it was extremely unconventional and dysfunctional."

"In what way?"

I'm growing weary of her questions and roll my eyes to exhibit my impatience. "In every way, OK? Are we done yet?"

"I'd like more information: where you grew up, parents, siblings."

"I don't want to talk about that."

Dr. Janet pauses. "All right." Again, she jots something down. "Tell me, then, what would you like to talk about?"

"I'd like to talk to a nurse about getting these fucking straps off my wrists."

The doctor sets the notepad down on the table beside her, walks to my bedside, and releases the straps.

"Only for a couple of minutes," she says, and she returns to her seat. "Do you have any idea why your doctor thinks you would benefit from my help, Danni?" she asks.

I shake out my hands and hug my knees.

"I don't know," I answer, swirling my finger in circles beside my head as Erma did when she warned me not to talk about the coat lady. "He obviously thinks I'm nuts."

Dr. Janet sighs and places a pair of reading glasses at the tip of her nose. "I never did like that term. Mental illness is a disease like any other and should be treated as such."

"Call it what you want." The wind has picked up outside, forcing a deluge of autumn leaves from their trees. They swirl about in a gusty onslaught and rustle up against the hospital window.

"Tell me, do you ever hear voices in your head?"

She peers up at me over her glasses. "You hear voices, Danni?"

"Jesus Christ, don't look at me like that. It's just a question."

Dr. Janet pushes her glasses up. "There's no judgment here, Danni. Each patient I treat has a unique situation, and I've treated many who complain of hearing voices as well." She picks up her notepad, flips over to a clean sheet, and begins writing with a pen that has "Best Mom" engraved on the side. The pain medicine has worn off, and a driving ache is growing in the hollows of my abdomen where a child should be.

"You must be good at it," I say.

"Good at what?" she asks.

I look up at the glass star that dangles in the window, taunting me with its baffling presence. "Being a mom. I bet you know exactly what to say and do."

Dr. Janet forces down the corners of her mouth and shrugs her shoulders. "Not always. I do the best that I can. But believe me, I've made mistakes along the way. Too many to count. All parents do."

The muscles in my arms tense and quiver as I hug my knees tighter, embracing them the way Michael embraced me at the threshold of the operating room doors when he begged me to forgive him.

"Tell me, Danni, if you had your life to live over again, is there anything you would change?"

I bury my head in my arms, detecting a foul odor on my own body. "Yep," I answer.

"What would you change?"

"Just about everything."

"Everything?"

I nod.

"Starting with what?" she asks.

I rock back and forth, thinking about my life, my relationships, and my failures that have far exceeded my successes. My hair has clumped together in long dirty strands that stick to the sides of my face. Alfred wouldn't think I'm beautiful now.

Not like this.

"Starting with the day I was born," I say.

The doctor crosses her legs and begins writing. The sound of pen against paper is amplified in this stark hospital room, and I cover my ears to the menacing noise of her meaningless observations. But nothing can shield me from the landslide of images that begin rushing through my mind as my memory returns like a gruesome slideshow.

"I did something horrible," I say, twirling a clump of hair around my finger until it snaps off at its roots, "Oh my God, I did something unforgiveable."

Dr. Janet looks up from her notepad.

"It's what happened over the past six months that brought me here." I lean forward, determined for her to hear every word.

"Where I went. Who I met. And what I did."

18

It's getting late and I should be home instead of here at work. Michael is probably wondering where I am. We haven't spoken since our argument last night when all he wanted was to be intimate with his wife. And I wouldn't have it.

"Stop it, Michael! Just stop it! Don't you get it? I can't get pregnant! So just stop trying and stop praying because your miracle isn't going to happen!"

I threw the covers off and ran downstairs. I didn't want him to touch me. The thought of trying, yet again, turned my stomach. He never came for me last night. I slept on the sofa, got up early, and came to work. It was the first time in all our years of marriage that we slept in separate rooms, something we said we would never do. I should go home, apologize, and tell him that I'm trying as hard as I can to make this work. I should tell him how blessed I am to have him in my life and how sorry I am for being so much less than the woman that he deserves. Instead I remain in front of my computer, taking on more work than I can handle so that my thoughts are louder than the voices and my tasks are substantial enough to quell my overwhelming sense of inadequacy that stems from a past that won't let me go.

The office is hectic as usual today. The sounds of phones ringing, papers shuffling, and fingers rhythmically tapping on keyboards creates a soothing hum. I would get more done if it weren't for the double picture frame at the edge of my desk that distracts me. On one side, there's a picture of Michael and me on our wedding day. Hidden beneath it, where no one can see, is a black-and-white picture of Becca and me, the only one I have, taken at a dime-store photo booth on Main Street a few days before we moved in with the Garritys. The other side of the frame is empty, where a child should be. The bottom of the frame is engraved with the word "Family," something I will never have and something Michael will always want.

Maybe it's better this way. Maybe I would go crazy like Mom did.

Or maybe I already have.

Suddenly, a warm rush of fluid leaks out from between my legs into my underwear, soaking them through. I hurry to the restroom, pull down my pants, and am, once again, reminded of my failure as a woman. How unfortunate it is that what we want most in life is sometimes the one thing we can't have. Michael fights hard for what he wants, remains optimistic, and never gives up. It's what drew me to him years ago, a strength that I miserably lack. But lately it seems that the trait that attracted me to him is the very thing that is tearing us apart because I can't have his child: not now, not ever, no matter how many goddamned prayers he says.

I clean up, return to my desk, and check my phone. No calls. No messages. I pour a cup of coffee and join my coworkers, who have gathered in front of the television to watch a news correspondent's live coverage of a breaking story in Bethlehem, Pennsylvania.

"A man was found yesterday brutally murdered in his home. Police say that it is by far the most gruesome case they have seen and the first in the history of this charming town."

I move closer to the television, wrap my hands around my steaming coffee mug, and draw it close to feel the warmth against my chest. The correspondent is standing in front of a home petitioned off with bright yellow tape that is all too familiar. She continues. "Police are still on the scene of this horrific murder that they say happened yesterday, during the early morning hours. Investigators have determined that this was not a case of forced entry and are asking for your help in gathering any information that may lead to the attacker. As of now, the victim's wife is being held in custody for further questioning, and police are in the process of gathering information from friends and neighbors."

I turn up the volume and carefully watch and listen. "Everyone here remains in disbelief, saying that the victim, Sergeant Garrity, was an upstanding and respectable member of the community. If you have any information, please contact your local police department. For Channel 89 News, I'm Kimberly Braddock, reporting live from 8th Street in Bethlehem."

It must be the explosive sound of the ceramic coffee mug crashing against the tile floor that jolts me back to reality as several coworkers gather around me.

"Are you all right? You look faint," one says, taking me by the arm and guiding me to the closest chair. "Quick, get her a glass of water."

As I stare out the window, the city fades to gray with a layer of clouds that extinguish the sun like a wet blanket thrown on a kindling fire. In the distance, a flock of geese heads west, away from the city, luring me back to the place I once called home. For years, I've allowed my past to stand before me, like a rocky mountain too treacherous to climb. But there's an unfamiliar tranquillity that is setting in, like the calm before the storm.

"I'm fine, I'm fine," I say, convincing them as much as myself. "Too much caffeine, not enough sleep," I add. "Not a very good combination, I'm afraid."

I return to my desk, put my jacket on, shut down my computer, and stare at the "family" picture frame. I think about Michael, Mom, Becca, and Alfred. The voices return, plaguing me with a continuous barrage. *Close your eyes! Don't look back! Close your eyes! Don't look back!*

There is a sixth sense in all of us. Some use it wisely, while others disregard it as insignificant, certainly not worthy of our time or attention. What a mistake I've made ignoring it. I should have told Mrs. Rogers about the evil that dwelled in the Garrity house, about Sergeant and what went on in his bedroom every night. I should have told someone about the way he violently desecrated Alfred simply because he was different. I should have knelt down beside Alfred in the basement, held him, and told him how brave and beautiful I thought he was and how sorry I was for leading Sergeant to him. I should have grabbed Becca outside of the supermarket and run away with her, far away, so no one could ever find us. And I should have told Michael everything about my past, my hurts, my regrets, and Becca.

As I exit the building, I check my phone. No calls. No messages. Perhaps I've lost him, too. I get in my car, start the engine, and head home to Michael. I hope that he's there, that he'll listen, and that he'll forgive me for what I am about to do.

It takes me an hour to pack my things. I carry my suitcase into the living room, pour myself a glass of wine, and wait in silence, for Michael. From where I sit, I can see the church directly across the street, still lit up at this late hour. The large stained glass window above the entrance boasts a myriad of colors, and I am reminded of how many times Michael and I sat beneath it, hand in hand, praying for a miracle. The truth is, I never prayed. Not once. I left that up to him. Instead, I spent the time counting pews, ceiling beams, and the number of small square tiles in the exquisitely designed mosaic cross that hangs above the pulpit. One thousand five hundred and twenty-six, to be exact. I never once asked God for a miracle. I knew then, as I know now, that I didn't deserve one. I did, however, beg him not to punish Michael for my mistakes.

But God wasn't listening to me, because it's been ten long years of high hopes and grave disappointments, of missed periods and bloodied underwear. The church slowly dims as the outdoor security lights switch on and shoot sharp beams of white light through the room. He'll be home soon. And I'll have to look him in the eye and find the right words to tell him that I'm leaving. I close my eyes and listen closely, noticing how one sense becomes keener when another is suppressed. Outside an occasional car passes, a siren sounds in the distance, and Michael's shoes tap and scrape against the macadam as he crosses the street. He climbs the steps, fumbles for his keys, and opens the door to join me in the darkness. The church lights shine through the window and onto his face as he pauses, looks at me, the suitcase, and me again. He shuts the door behind him, puts his keys on the table, and sits down beside me, taking my hand in his. He is warm and gentle. His voice calm and compassionate.

"Talk to me," he says. So with a lump in my throat and a second glass of wine, I take him back to Bethlehem, telling him what I should have told him years ago: about Mom, Becca, and the Garrity house. I share everything with him. Except Alfred. When I finish, I rest my head on his shoulder and nestle into the warm nook at the base of his neck. He pulls me close, wraps his arm around me like a safe blanket, and traces the large scar on my forearm with his index finger.

"Everything's gonna be OK," he says, kissing my forehead.

I would have been aggravated by his statement had I not finished the third glass of wine. But even Michael's unwavering optimism is tolerable in this inebriated state.

"Let's go to bed," he says. "We'll talk more in the morning."

He places one arm around my waist, the other beneath my legs, and lifts me up off the sofa to carry me into the bedroom where the flickering flame of a single candle burns brightly on the nightstand. It's been over a month since Michael and I made love, but there's something about tonight that feels necessary. He sets me down on the edge of the bed, removes my shoes one by one, and pulls my sweater up over my head. The bulge in his pants presses against my stomach as he reaches around, unhooks my bra, and softly kisses my neck. I've never wanted him as much as I do now.

"Make love to me, Michael," I whisper, guiding his head to my chest, delighting in his appetite as he fills his mouth with the temptations of flesh he preaches against.

For a moment, I wonder if God approves of how his messenger takes me the way he does, with an unbridled aggression, kissing me with force and determination, slipping his tongue deep into my mouth as though satisfying a craving that, for far too long, has been suppressed. He slides my pants down over my hips, past my thighs, and drops them to the floor before lifting me up onto the bed. He pulls off his shirt and exposes his broad, chiseled chest that creates an aching between my legs, an overwhelming sensation that heightens me to a level of arousal that I haven't felt in years. A chill covers my body as he climbs onto the bed beside me, looks me in the eye, and slowly runs his hand down the side of my neck, over my shoulder, and onto my arm.

"God, you're beautiful," he whispers, hovering his lips just above mine as he lightly caresses my stomach and trails the tips of his fingers down over my navel to the top of my pubic bone where he stops. "Promise me something," he says, his fingers lingering at the edge of my lace-trimmed panties. I would promise him anything right now, knowing full well that promises are something I never could keep. I nod as Michael's eyes drift downward over the subtle curves of my body. His voice is low and breathless with excitement. "Promise me that you want this as much as I do. For all the right reasons."

The subtle grin on my face is both a gesture of agreement and a response to the tingling between my legs that aches for his touch.

"I promise," I say, parting my legs to receive him. He leans closer, barely touching his mouth to mine, and slides his fingers down beneath my lace, touching and fondling the spot that throbs with anticipation. I turn to him, spread my legs wider, and allow his fingers to fully enter. "Don't stop," I whisper.

He kisses me, responding to my request. "Come on, baby," he says, giving me exactly what I asked for, not stopping until I shake with pleasure. It's easy to lose myself in him tonight. The enticing scent of his skin forces me to surrender to his insatiable desire as much as my own. In the glow of candlelight, Michael glistens with sweat as he climbs on top of me to take what he has to have. He opens my legs with his and strokes my inner thighs with his erect penis, searching, poking, and prodding before entering. He pulls out completely before crashing into me again. I wrap my legs around him, savoring every inch that fills me up with intense satisfaction.

"Get on top of me," he says, pulling me into position, entering me again while grabbing my buttocks to lift me up and slam me down onto him. We move slowly at first, gradually increasing to a quick, steady rhythm that forces me to climax again. For the first time in years, we make love for hours, merely for the pleasure of it, with no thought of the outcome. Erma would have called it lust, pure and simple, the kind she spoke against.

"Lust is exciting all right," she said, puckering her wrinkled lips around the butt end of a cigarette to inhale the very toxins that made her cough and wheeze with every breath. "It'll knock you off your feet and leave you beggin' for more." She blew a ring of smoke up into the air. "The problem is that it's temporary, leaving as quickly as it came with a path of destruction behind it a mile wide." Erma spoke as though from experience. "Now love, on the other hand," she continued, squinting her eyes in the cloud of smoke that billowed around her head, "takes a little longer but lasts forever." Simultaneously she nodded and winked as she drew back one side of her mouth and sucked in a short burst of air through her teeth to create a quick noise that suggested she knew exactly what she was talking about.

The sun will be rising soon. Michael finishes and rolls off me, panting from exhaustion. He holds my hand and closes his eyes, but I have something to tell him before he drifts off to sleep, something urgent.

"I'm leaving," I say, turning to rest my head on his pillow. "I'm going back to Bethlehem for a while. To find Becca."

Michael's cool disposition shines through in moments like this. "I see," he says, squeezing my hand while offering a comforting grin the way he did the day we first met. If Erma were here, I would tell her what I have learned about lust and love. I would tell her that somehow, in some way, I think I've found both.

The interstate is still. I need this time to think, and I welcome the inherent calm that comes with the mundane hum of the highway. I left Michael an hour ago. With a broad stance, he stood by the door, arms hanging in front of him with one hand cupped in the other.

"Have you thought this through?" he asked, lifting his chin above the cross that adorns his neck as a bold display of his principles and morality, "Have you weighed all your options?"

I pushed down on my suitcase to zip it. "Options, Michael? Really? After everything I confided in you last night, you're asking me if I've weighed all my options?"

Michael rested his hands on my shoulders. "I don't want you making any hasty decisions that could have a negative impact on our lives. We're trying to start a family, Danni," he said. "I believe it's God's will, and the stress of this trip could hinder that. It's not worth it." Michael pulled me close, sheltering me in a way that, for the first time, felt smothering. "Why not postpone your trip for a while so that we can pray on this? I'm leading a group discussion this week on sins of the past, childhood traumas, etc. You could join us; I think it will be very helpful. Besides, have you considered the possibility that you may not find what you're looking for? If you give it some time, I think you'll see that this isn't good for either one of us. Sometimes it's simply better to leave well enough alone."

I pushed against his chest, creating space to breath. "I'm not a child, Michael, or one of your overly impressionable parishioners who would drink the juice if you asked them to. So don't treat me like one." I picked up my suitcase and stepped around him to open the door. "I don't want to argue, but I'll be the only one deciding when my life is 'well enough.'"

The rims of Michael's eyes reddened with the frustration of his failed efforts. "So how long will you be gone?" he asked with a stoic expression that fell like a curtain over his face. It was a question I didn't have an answer for. Michael doesn't understand regret and how living with a lifetime of it can be debilitating. He doesn't understand that in spite of how hard you try, you can't run from your past because sooner or later it catches up with you, knocks you down, and ruins your life like a terminal cancer. But more importantly, he doesn't understand that I'm doing this as much for him as I am for myself.

"I love you," I said. He nodded as I left him in the doorway, rushed out to my car, rested my head on the steering wheel, and turned the radio on to my favorite station. "Good morning, New York!" the DJ announced. "It's gonna be a great day!"

The white dashed lines in the road rapidly passed beneath my car as the golden sun rose above the buildings in a bold declaration of a new day. Maybe the DJ knew what he was talking about, because for the first time ever, I head toward the pain instead of away from it, toward the immeasurable hurt and the tormenting memories, toward the beginning of the rest of my life.

19

The Whitekers' house hasn't changed much in the years that I've been gone. Suzanne's friends did as they promised and took good care of it, renting it out only to those who value its history. But the history of this town has never been something that I could appreciate. It seems every corner is lurking with unpleasant memories, especially the steel plant, which is being converted into a casino in a desperate attempt to rejuvenate this once prosperous city. So the plant will be alive again, like a menacing giant rising from the dead. But the ringing of a million slots can't diminish the resonance of grating metal or all that went on in the Garrity house.

The hotel on Main Street is like a beacon in the heart of the city, standing well above the other buildings with the words "Hotel Bethlehem" lit up in bold red block letters. Like other buildings in this historic city, it is believed to be haunted by ghosts. As I enter, a young woman is standing behind the front desk. I walk toward her and set my bags down on the floor beside me. She offers me a polite smile.

"Welcome," she says. "How can I help you?"

"I'd like a room, please. Overlooking Main Street if possible."

"Would you prefer a king or two doubles?" she asks.

In the lobby, a large flat screen television is mounted high on the wall for dining guests. A small group of people, including hotel staff, have gathered around to watch a news update on the story of Sergeant's murder that has reached out beyond city limits. Philadelphia correspondents are using the word "barbaric" to describe the crime, and New York is referring to the murderer at large as simply a "monster."

"Either would be fine, thank you," I say, placing a credit card on the counter. An older gentleman, finely dressed in vintage bellhop attire, approaches me wheeling a luggage cart behind him absently as he focuses on the news update. He nods to greet me. "Good day," he says, placing my bags on the cart while keeping his eyes glued to the news. "What a shame," he utters, shaking his head in disbelief. "He was a good man. I knew him for many years."

But no one knew Sergeant like those who lived within his four walls. It seems he had this entire town fooled. The woman hands me back my credit card.

"Mrs. Daniel Hoffman Pane," she says. "How long will you be staying with us?"

"Not a day longer than I need to," I say, inadvertently verbalizing my thoughts.

"I see," she responds with a smile that grows stiff and forced as though suddenly sensing my contempt for this town. "Enjoy your stay."

Room 932 is hot and the television is on, tuned into the same news station that was on in the lobby. I check the thermostat, adjust the switch from heat to air conditioning, and wait with my hand held over the vent for a cool rush of air. According to the news, Mrs. Garrity was released yesterday but told not to leave town. I watch the live coverage as she exits the police station: old, haggard, and frighteningly thin, with long white hair that hangs down the back of her wretched housecoat, still stained and soiled with the blood of her husband who she claims to have found slain in the center of their basement floor. She holds her hands over her eyes to shield herself from the glaring cameras as she makes her way to the old pickup truck in front of the building. But it's the sight of her bright red lips that sends a chill up my spine.

My heart aches for Sarah, the beautiful, young Southern girl who allowed such a worthless soul to diminish her very existence. It could very well have been she who repeatedly stabbed Sergeant hundreds of times with a weapon that pierced and gored through his flesh until his body was unrecognizable. Police are still trying to determine a motive, asking why anyone would want to commit such a heinous crime on such a decent citizen. But I know the motive. Hatred. Nothing more, nothing less. There are several people who loathed him as much as I did, and rightfully so. There was intense hostility in the hands of the killer who relentlessly slashed Sergeant until every body part was punctured. He was massacred in the middle of the basement floor and left in a pool of blood that seeped far out into the crevices at the base of every wall. How fitting that Sergeant's final breath was taken in the precise place where he sadistically violated Alfred. I can still smell the stench of urine, feces, and semen that filled the air that day, and I hope that Sergeant choked on the same foul odor while his pitiful life flashed before his eyes. Poor Alfred, caught up in such dysfunction, plagued by the socially unacceptable disorder of albinism and trapped in the body of a gender he never could identify with. If, by chance, he came back to finish what he started years ago, I wouldn't blame him. Sergeant deserved what he got. All of it.

I'm tired, and hot air continues to surge into the room like a sauna. I open the window, allowing the thick, oppressive heat to spill out over Main Street, where townspeople shop and dine nine stories below. From where I stand, I can see the old bookstore across the street where several people enter and exit. I watch from my room, stripping down to a camisole beneath my clothes as I fan myself with the hotel brochure. The heat in this room is as unnerving as is the energy that exists here, strange and sinister, alarmingly so. A young man dressed in baggy jeans and red T-shirt exits the bookstore with a skateboard in his hand. He drops the board to the ground, places one foot on top, and pushes off with the other, weaving in and out of shoppers, avoiding obstacles along the sidewalk. I watch as he rolls down the street, gaining speed with every push, past the ice cream store, the bagel shop, and the woman sitting on a park bench in a long brown hooded coat. If it wasn't for the bars on the window, I would have fallen from the shocking sight of her.

I haven't seen the coat lady in years. But I see her now. Staring up at me. Returning my gaze from beneath her hood. She is sitting on the edge of the seat, rocking back and forth, looking up at me as though she knew I was here. But I'll be damned if I let her get away this time. This isn't my mind playing tricks on me, and I'm not crazy.

Room 932 is too stuffy, and the television is too fucking loud.

I run out of the room and push the down button on the wall by the elevator. The sound of quiet classical music floats through the halls while I wait for the elevator to reach the ninth floor, stopping on every floor on the way up. The doors open and I enter to discover every floor button illuminated. My heart palpitates, flopping around in my chest like a fish pulled from the water and thrown onto a dry deck. The coat lady is near, and there is no one waiting on the eighth floor, or the seventh, or sixth. On each floor, the doors open to a vacant hallway.

The lobby, however, is bustling with guests enjoying a local jazz band that comes alive for the dinner hour. The television flashes images of the top story in the news, where crews have gathered outside the Garrity house reporting round-the-clock coverage of the gruesome crime scene. Outside, dodging people on the sidewalk as the skateboarder did, I head toward the woman who has haunted me my entire life. I want to confront her, woman to woman, because I'm not a frightened child anymore. I am breathless when I reach the bench. My side aches, and she is gone.

"Excuse me," I say to a young man sitting on the end of the bench fidgeting with his cell phone. "There was a woman here a moment ago, wearing a long brown, hooded coat. Did you see her? Did you see where she went?"

He briefly looks up, annoyed by the distraction. "No," he answers.

"But you had to see her," I say, still winded. "She was sitting right here, right next to you!"

He shakes his head and shrugs his shoulders, disinterested. "I didn't see anybody," he mutters, concentrating on an incoming text message.

"Please!" I beg. "Think really hard. She was wearing a long brown coat with the hood pulled up." I slam the palm of my hand down next to him at the exact location on the bench. "She was sitting right here! You saw her, right? Tell me you saw her! She's not a ghost! She's real, right? She's real!"

"I don't know what you're talking about lady," he says, springing to his feet. "You're fucking crazy!" It takes only seconds for him to disappear down Main Street. Nothing comes easy for me in this town as I frantically search in and out of stores until I end up right where I started, in front of the hotel where, inside, the band is still playing and the guests are still watching the local news. The bell-hop, standing by the entrance, removes his jacket and wraps it around my bare shoulders.

"You must be cold, Miss," he says, leading me inside. "Can I help you? Are you all right?"

"Thank you," I say, startled by how I fled the building, wearing nothing more than a thin undergarment from my waist up. "I'm fine."

I return to my room, remove Suzanne's letter from my suitcase and lie down on the bed. The air conditioning must have kicked on because the room is suddenly cold and the faint, musty smell of this old hotel is making my stomach turn. It must be in the walls or beneath the floorboards, the stale stench that seems to permeate every niche. Maybe it's the odorous breath of the ghosts that townspeople claim reside here. But it's not just the unpleasant smell that is so troubling. There's something more about this room that is unsettling, from the drastic changes in room temperature to the lamp that flickers by the bedside as I open the crumpled letter that I haven't looked at in fifteen years. A flood of emotions runs through me as I unfold the piece of paper and read again the last words that Suzanne had for me, including the name and address of Amy Hoffman.

I'm thirty-seven, and the thought of her still makes me ache. In the past, I would have taken a sharp object to the insides of my arms or pinched at my flesh until welts erupted like small volcanos on the surface of my skin. But old habits die hard, and cuts heal faster on the outside than they do on the inside, so I decide to face the woman who deserted me to see for myself if she's really crazy because I want to know once and for all why she left.

For the sake of Becca and my marriage, I need to know why.

At 697 Old Pond Road is a white single-wide mobile home with blue shutters that sits on a tiny lot. There is a patch of grass in the front yard that is well maintained and a small gnome with a red hat that is situated at the base of a dogwood tree in full bloom. I pull up next to an old blue Volkswagen parked out front with a black steering wheel cover and an air freshener that hangs from the rearview mirror. I take a moment to notice the vanilla scent, grasping onto anything, regardless of its significance, that will give me a glimpse into her life. Stacks of newspapers are piled by Amy's door, bundled and tied beneath a glass Moravian star that dangles from

the center of the porch top. A gust of spring air sweeps across the yard, through the tree leaves, and up the porch steps. This house is far from perfect, but it doesn't look like the home of a crazy person, and in a moment of hesitation I consider the possibility that I'm too late, that Amy no longer lives here. Perhaps she's in an institution again, tormented by guilt over what she did to her own flesh and blood. Or maybe she has left this earth and is serving her penance in purgatory where she struggles each day to find her way back to a maker who doesn't deem her worthy. Worse yet, maybe she fled this town and is living happily somewhere far away where thoughts of Becca and me never enter her mind. What a disappointment it would be to miss the opportunity to tell her what a coward she is and how, in spite of her absence, I have made something of myself because I never needed her anyway. I pull my sleeves down to hide my scars and knock on the door. A dog barks and someone shuffles about on the other side.

A woman answers.

Ordinary looking.

Short, brown hair, streaked with gray.

Blue eyes.

Around my size.

Tan sweater, blue jeans, and white sneakers.

A perfect stranger.

She stands in the doorway, smiling.

"Can I help you?" she asks.

Through tinted sunglasses, I scan her from head to toe, searching for something recognizable, something to love or to hate.

"Can I help you?" she asks again, and waits for me to answer. I bend down to pet the small dog that rushes out to greet me.

"Uh…yes," I say, glancing over her shoulder to peer into her home for a taste of her. The television is tuned into the local news station, and there is a vase of wild daisies on the coffee table. Her house appears far too neat and orderly for someone so unstable, and I am agitated by her normalcy. "I'm sorry…are…you…Ms. Hoffman… Ms. Amy Hoffman?"

She lifts the dog to her chest. "Yes, I am. What can I do for you?"

This is the moment I've imagined since the day she left. I slide my sunglasses up onto my head and wait for her to react to her daughter's eyes. The dog wags his tail and licks her chin as she throws her hand up to a neighbor taking out their garbage. She doesn't recognize her own daughter, and I'm interrupting her day. It's obvious by the way she glances back at the television. I wonder if she can see the scars that peek out beneath my sleeve as I hand her Suzanne's letter and the faded photo-booth picture of Becca and me. She stares at the photo for some time before taking a step back.

"Come in, Danielle," she says, acknowledging her past. "Have a seat."

She walks to the kitchen, returns with two glasses of water, rearranges the vase of daisies on the coffee table, and sits down in the chair across from me. "It's a beautiful day," she says, petting her dog with the same hands that bandaged my knees, checked my forehead for fever, and clapped for me when I did somersaults across the living room floor.

"Yes, it's unusually warm for this time of year," I say, conceding to the small talk. "I hear they're predicting a record-high summer."

"Not too hot, I hope," she says, cradling the dog's small face in her hands. "This little guy gets overheated so easily." She runs her hand along his spine and back up against the grain of his hair the way Erma said not to.

"I understand that you spoke with my adopted mother before she died."

Amy strokes the dog, forcing his hair in the opposite direction until he jumps from her lap and curls up beneath the coffee table.

"She put your address in the letter she left behind," I continue, treading lightly with a woman whose mental stability is still in question.

"Is there something I can do for you, Danielle?" she asks, fidgeting with the daisies and the stack of magazines perfectly arranged beside them. The nerve of her to utter those words. I slide my hand down the front of my neck to relax the sudden constriction on my windpipe, like a noose gripping and squeezing the breath out of me, preventing me from answering the woman

I have waited a lifetime to confront. Amy stares at the television where a reporter is covering the latest details of Sergeant's murder.

"It's awful, what happened to that man," she says, reaching for the daisies. "He must have suffered horribly." She removes the daisies one by one before placing them back into the vase. "But sometimes bad things happen to good people," she says, shaking her head while immersed in the news that seems to be of more importance than the daughter she hasn't seen in over thirty years. "And vice versa, I suppose."

She shuts off the television and moves to the edge of her seat, aging in the mere moments that I've been here. I could use a cigarette right now or a drink of something that would stop my teeth from tapping against one another while I struggle to decipher whether hers is the face of lunacy or crushing guilt.

"I always knew you'd come looking for answers, Danielle, if you're as curious a woman as you were a young girl."

If I had the guts, I'd lift my sleeves and reveal my scars so that she would understand the pain she's caused. If I could make her suffer for even a moment, it would be worth it. Somewhere on the inside it would feel good, like scratching a persistent itch that I could never find. And if I could muster up the courage, I would ask her if I had done something wrong that made her hate me or not love me enough to stay.

"His name was Johnny," she says, resting her eyes in the space between us where her memories live. The noose tightens around my neck as she begins to pull the chair out beneath me. It appears the past has filled her up completely and she's about to overflow. If I could stop time, I'd do it now, before Amy's cup runneth over with her story, our story, because I'm suddenly not sure I'm ready for it. Concentration intensifies the lines around her eyes as she begins again. "His name was Johnny," she says, as though she has rehearsed it a thousand times, preparing for this very moment when she would explain to me how, at the age of fifteen, she got involved with the wrong boy.

My father.

"Johnny was seventeen when he moved in across the street with his parents and his twin brother, Bobby. He caught my eye the moment I saw him. It wasn't his looks as much as his confidence that I noticed first, the way he held himself and spoke above everyone like what he had to say was more important. He was everything I wasn't and everything Bobby wanted to be. When Johnny wanted something, he got it, no matter what. Bobby, on the other hand, was different. He didn't talk much and kept his head down most of the time to hide a facial deformity he was born with."

It's difficult to read the expressions on Amy's face that change from joy to sorrow to anger. She moves the magazines about an inch to the right and back again.

"Bobby followed Johnny everywhere," she says, "like a shadow. Their mother insisted they stay together. Johnny resented it and acted out in any way he could, getting himself kicked out of three schools before we met." Amy rotates the vase in a round groove that has been permanently etched into the tabletop. "My parents told me he was trouble. They didn't want me to have anything to do with him, but I didn't care. He was exciting, and I wanted to be with him, but the closer I got, the more frustrated Bobby became. He didn't like sharing. I couldn't even touch Johnny without Bobby stomping his feet or pounding his fists against his thighs. Johnny hated him for that and for being nothing more than a distorted mirror image of himself, so he made a game out of provoking him. He would kiss me in front of him just to see his reaction. One night, the three of us were playing truth or dare in the shed behind Johnny's house. Johnny told Bobby to stand in the corner while he dared me to do something I had never done before." Amy rubs her hands together until her palms turn red. "I shouldn't have done it," she says. "But I loved him and thought if I made him happy, he'd love me back."

Amy's eyes dim with her darkening tale. I once told Becca that she had the same beautiful blue eyes as our mother and that one day she would be able to look into them and see for herself that I was telling the truth. But I lied. There's no beauty here. In the wake of shame and bitterness, it disappeared, possibly stolen but ultimately surrendered.

"It was the first of many nights the three of us spent in that old shed," she continues. "I did what Johnny dared me to do every time, even though I knew it was wrong. But when I told him I skipped a period, everything changed. He got angry and wouldn't touch me anymore. A week later, on his eighteenth birthday, he joined the military and was gone. Bobby blamed me for making his brother go away and promised to do something horrible if I told anyone what went on in that shed."

Amy walks to the window. It may be instinct to study her like I do, and I wonder if she can sense the innate need of her offspring. If I held my hand to hers, side by side, time would make the only difference. The sixteen years between us have made her veins more prominent. Each bulging vessel trails up her arm and disappears beneath her sleeve. If cut, she would bleed out quickly with little time for intervention.

"I was terrified," she says, peering outside. "So I kept quiet about all of it and prayed that Johnny would miss me enough to come back." She leans her forehead against the window and tilts her head to gaze down the road before continuing with the story of my life, how I came to be—nothing but a twisted game of truth or dare.

"What about your parents?" I ask.

"They were killed in a car accident before I even started to show. They never knew I was pregnant," she says and crosses her arms as I probe further.

"And Johnny's parents?"

"Bobby wouldn't allow me near them," she says. "I was on my own, and you were born on the bathroom floor after nine hours of hard labor. You were like a miracle, a part of Johnny and me. I knew that if he saw you, he'd come back to stay."

In the awkward silence that occurs between her sentences, I begin sifting through my thoughts. I vowed to hate her forever. But as my mother begins to sway, clearly shaken, unsteady and traumatized, I decide that regardless of the past, should she lose her footing and fall, I'll catch her.

"It took four years for Johnny to show up," she continues. "He asked to see you. We talked for a while, and he held you for the first time." Amy scratches her arms and her face until pink streaks cover both. "We went downtown the night he returned. Bobby came too, and we took turns drinking from the bottle he brought. Johnny held you while we walked along Main Street. For the first time, we were a family, like I always wanted." She runs her fingers through her hair. "It was so cold that night," she says, repetitively rocking from one foot to the other while describing how Johnny's breath billowed into the air when he insisted they play truth or dare, like old times. "Bobby went first," she says. "He took the dare and snuck into the old hotel on Main Street, stole a key from the housekeeping cart, and got us into a room on the ninth floor."

In a matter of minutes, Amy's appearance fades into a dark place from our past. "Room 932." The corners of her mouth bend downward, and the lines between her brows deepen and settle into an accustomed frown. "Johnny ordered Bobby to stand outside the door and keep watch while the two of us entered." She raises her chin and takes a deep breath to propel her into the rest of our story. "You were a good girl, Danielle. You didn't cry once, just sat in the corner playing with your doll."

Amy's hands shake as she describes the way Johnny put her on the bed, removed her clothes, and demanded she help him relieve the stress that had built up inside of him while he was away. "I thought he loved me," she says, raking her hand through her hair until it tangles and weaves between each finger. "The room started spinning, the lights went out, and the door opened and slammed shut. You yelled out, but he wouldn't let me up until he finished." She draws the curtains closed and sits back down. "When the lights came back on," she says, drawing her knees to her bosom, "Johnny was standing by the light switch on the other side of the room with you in his arms, and Bobby was kneeling over me with his pants around his ankles, crying and slapping himself between the legs."

Amy tugs at her eyebrows, plucking out one hair at a time. "Johnny made him do it," she says, finishing the story of how Bobby punished himself for his wrong deed, twisting and pulling at his inflamed genitals as he climbed off the bed, shuffled over to the window, opened it, and without hesitation, leaped out, headfirst, before Johnny or Amy ever had a chance to react. He fell from the ninth floor, flat on his back, in the middle of Main Street with his pants still tangled at his feet.

"Can you hear that?" she asks.

"Here what?"

Amy moves from her brows to her hair, ripping out enough each time to make her cringe. "Bobby died that day," she says. "And Johnny left me again, pregnant with Becca."

Such a tragic story deserves compassion, a tender touch or warm embrace. If I were ten, I would wrap myself around her, confident that my love would be enough to make her forget. But ten came and went without her, and love dissolved into a bitter resentment that makes it difficult to talk rather than yell.

"Is Bobby Becca's father?" I ask. "Is that why you left? Was it Becca's deformity that scared you away? Where did you go? We needed you! Becca needed you!"

Amy shifts in her seat, yields to an incessant quiver, and rearranges the daisies in the vase on the coffee table. "I heard Johnny moved down south," she continues. "Married some girl who had a child of her own. He never cared about me. He was no good just like my parents told me. But no sin goes unpunished, and if it does, or if you just get tired of waiting, there's nothing wrong with helping it along a little, ya know?"

Amy steps lightly to the window and peeks out through the drawn curtains.

"Is that it?" I ask, rising to my feet with anger. "That's all you have to say?"

"He's coming for me," she says.

"Who's coming for you? What are you talking about?"

She holds the tip of her index finger to her lips. "Ssshhh, we can't let him hear us." Outside, a yellow finch perches on the dogwood and a small child rides her tricycle on the driveway next door. "Over there," she says, "behind the tree. He thinks I can't see him."

"There's no one there, Amy," I say, losing my patience. "Can you answer my questions?"

"He can't fool me," she says. "I know he's there. He wants revenge."

"Who wants revenge?" I ask. She begins chattering to herself, lost in a world that no one can be part of. "No sin goes unpunished," she whispers.

I grab her shoulders. "Look at me goddamn it! After all these years, that's all you have to say to me?"

Amy shrinks down and covers her head with her hands. "Who are you?" she asks. "What do you want? Let me go. I have to hide before he finds me. He knows what I did."

With her dog at her heels, I watch Amy, a mere shadow of the mother I remember, scamper around the living room before squatting down behind the sofa.

"What did you do, Amy? Tell me what you did!"

The dog barks as she disappears from sight, disregarding my existence the way she has for more than thirty years. Without looking back, I walk toward the door, slide my sunglasses down over my eyes, and vow to accept the obvious.

Amy Hoffman is crazy.

Maybe loving my father is what drove her there or the humiliation of Becca, from conception to birth. I step out onto Amy's porch, beneath the glass star, and close the door to part of me I have to leave behind. As I turn off of Old Pond Road, I pull the vanilla air freshener that I bought last week off my visor, toss it out onto the street, and watch it in my rearview mirror, flipping and turning in the rush of air behind my car. When I was five years old, I promised myself that I would be nothing like her. It's a promise I intend to keep.

There's a memorial for Sergeant being held today at St. Joseph's church downtown. There won't be a burial until the coroner completes the autopsy. Friends and neighbors have gathered in the church to pay their respects and to listen to Father Russo, who stands before the pulpit leading the congregation in prayer and delivering a heartfelt eulogy for Sergeant Garrity, a dedicated member of the church who seldom missed a Sunday mass.

I didn't want to come here today, but I had to, for the chance to see Alfred. I scan the crowd searching for his distinct complexion, but I wouldn't be surprised if he didn't attend. I'm sure Sergeant is someone Alfred would rather forget.

The church is filled. It's fascinating how Sergeant managed to fool everyone into thinking he was a decent soul, including Father Russo, who continues to praise Sergeant's commendable volunteer work within the parish. I am sitting in the last pew, bowing my head as Father Russo prays for Sergeant, that he will live eternally in peace. But I know better, and I am sickened by the sight of so many tears wasted on such a despicable human being. If only they knew, they would damn him to hell, as I do. Mrs. Garrity is seated in the front row, dressed in black, staring down at the ground, dry-eyed. I've never felt as close to her as I feel at this very moment knowing that she is, perhaps, the only other person in this room who is silently celebrating his demise.

Sitting next to Mrs. Garrity is a woman, tall and thin, poised and refined, flawlessly groomed and beautifully dressed in a chic black-fitted dress and matching hat with a mesh veil that covers her face. She gently tosses her long platinum hair to one side as she leans closer to Mrs. Garrity and whispers in her ear. There is something oddly familiar about the way she moves, something I can't put my finger on. I watch her closely, admiring her style, captivated by her grace. The roar of the organ resonates off the walls, filling the air with a thunderous echo as Father Russo concludes the memorial and asks everyone to go in peace.

I exit first, return to my car, and wait and watch from a distance as mourners pour out from the church doors. Several news networks are here, continuing to cover the first murder of its kind in this quiet community. Correspondents and cameramen scurry to question those who have attended before hurrying over to Mrs. Garrity, who is now departing the church with her head hung low, covering her face with one hand and grasping on to the splendid woman in black with the other. They holler out questions while poking microphones in her face, hoping to get a response from the only one who, according to police, has been named a person of interest in the ongoing investigation.

I certainly would not recognize her in any other situation. A lifetime has passed since I saw her last in front of the supermarket, worn and weary, with Becca. But she is much older now, haggard and gaunt, with long gray hair. Her face is ashen and deeply etched with countless lines of anguish. She leans against the long, lean woman, who escorts her to a black limousine parked out front. Mrs. Garrity climbs into the car while the elegant woman shoos away reporters. The woman turns in my direction, gathers her silken hair with both hands, and pulls it to one side, cascading it over her right shoulder. Her presence is stunning, and I find myself, once again, in awe of her, studying her every move, troubled and perplexed by her familiarity. She leans down, places one foot in the car, and slowly lifts her veil…

exposing her face…

beautifully unique…

flawlessly smooth…

strikingly white.

I was twenty-two years old when I last saw Alfred. I left him on the California sand with tears in his eyes, dangling on the edge of who he was and who he needed to become. I wanted him more than anything that night, enough for the both of us, or so I hoped. But no amount of desire could have made him mine. Only now do I truly understand the beautiful boy I fell in love with as I witness him for the first time, fully transformed into the woman Mother Nature had intended.

Poor Alfred. How difficult it must have been for him. But adversity can sometimes prove to be our greatest gift if we use it wisely, as a reason to stand rather than an excuse to fall, as an incentive to succeed instead of a pardon to fail. It seems that Alfred rose above his troubled childhood and learned, above all odds, to love and accept himself.

Alfred enters the limousine next to Mrs. Garrity. He reaches into a small handbag, removes a black tube of lipstick, and glides it over his lips numerous times until his mouth boldly stands out like fresh blood on newly fallen snow. As they pull away, I think back to my days at the Garrity house and the nights I spent alone with him in his bedroom sharing secrets and dreaming about the future.

I loved him once.

Puppy love, some would say, yet all these years later my heart still sinks into my stomach at the mere sight of him.

I had hoped he would be here.

Because I have to talk to him.

About Becca.
About us.
And where we go from here.

The Hotel Bethlehem. Room 932. So much about this room makes perfect sense now. The chaos. The tragedy. The suicide. It seems my family tree is deeply rooted in toxic soil. I could stop this craziness right now, return home to Michael and take shelter in his love and support. I could put an end to all of this and leave Becca in the past where she has dwelled in a dormant state for decades, with flaxen curls and hope-filled eyes. I lay down, close my eyes, and envision all that Amy told me about what happened within these four walls with a father I never knew and an uncle I never knew existed. It's a small room with one window, six feet high, four feet wide. Bobby dove headfirst out of it while my mother lay on the bed screaming and while I fought against the firm clutch of my father's arms to get to her. It is a small, disappointing glimpse into my father's life. Amy never said if he was dead or alive, and I never asked.

The phone rings loud in room 932.

"Hello?" I answer and prepare for what I expect to be the front desk asking if I would like a wake-up call in the morning. The voice on the other end is sweet and pleasant.

"Hello, Danni."

I recognize it immediately and sit up on the edge of the bed in anticipation of his next words.

"I hope I'm not bothering you."

"Of course not," I say, pressing the receiver against my ear to draw him closer.

"If it isn't a good time..." he says.

I reach for my handbag on the end of the bed and remove a fresh pack of cigarettes.

"Of course it's a good time, I've been wanting to talk to you. How did you know I was here?"

"It's a small town—word travels fast. How have you been?"

I squeeze the phone between my shoulder and ear to light up. "I'm doing well. Not crazy about being back in Bethlehem, but other than that, I'm pretty good." I've never smoked as much as I have over the past couple of days, replacing meals with cigarettes. "And you?" I ask.

"I'm good. So much has happened," he says. "Can we meet?"

I drop my cigarette butt into a half-filled soda can, pull out another, and hold it, unlit, between my trembling fingers.

"I'd like that. When?"

"Tomorrow, around noon? I can come there if that's all right."

I nod to myself before answering. "Sure, I'll see you then."

With the phone still pressed against my ear, I listen as he takes a deep breath and releases it with a sigh. "Wait!" I blurt out before he hangs up.

"Yes?"

"Uh…when I see you tomorrow, how should I address you?"

He laughs and responds in a voice that hasn't changed much from the soft-spoken adolescent boy he was. "Alexa," she says with a self-assurance that Alfred never had. "My name is Alexa."

The temperature in the room has switched again. It is suddenly hot, disturbingly so. Maybe Bobby's unsettled spirit is here, crying out to me in an effort to divulge his version of what happened that night. Or, quite possibly, it's my own body temperature rising in response to the overwhelming feelings for Alfred that surge through me as they did so long ago.

Back then.

When I was ten.

"I want to show you something, Danni," Alfred says, grabbing my hand and pulling me out the kitchen door. He leads me around to the backyard, where he abruptly stops before the shed. There's an excitement in Alfred's eyes that I've only seen late at night in his bedroom when he speaks of getting out of this town. He pulls his baseball cap down low and peers out from beneath the brim with eyes that grow wide with enthusiasm. "Shut your eyes," he whispers, taking my hands in his and blindly leading me someplace I have never been before, someplace behind the shed, behind the wall of arborvitaes that line the yard. The steel plant has been unusually quiet since I've gotten to know Alfred better. And I've been unusually happy. Even Becca has noticed.

"Why are you thmiling tho much?" she said to me this morning as we were getting dressed.

"I'm excited about our trip to the zoo," I lied.

"Me too!" she said, bursting with joy. It wasn't really a lie. I was excited about going to the zoo. But I was more excited about Alfred.

Alfred stands behind me and places his thin hands over my eyes. The sun is warm on my face as I wait to see what makes him so jubilant.

"Are you ready?" he asks.

I impatiently nod.

"OK, you can look," he says, removing his hands to reveal a large open field bursting with color, more color than I have ever seen in my entire life. Bright, bold, explosions of yellow that reach for the sky. Alfred leads me out into the middle of his sanctuary where hundreds of sunflowers stand taller than my arms can reach.

"Wow," I say, in awe of something my eyes have never witnessed before. "Did you do this, Alfred?" I ask, looking up at the brilliant yellow that starkly touches the clear blue sky. Two geese fly overhead, side by side, silently passing over Alfred's hidden treasure.

One male.

One female.

Mates forever.

Perhaps, they too are amazed at the field of flowers as they gaze down upon such vibrancy. Alfred nods, reaches into his pocket, pulls out a handful of fresh seeds, and scatters them on the rich soil below. I marvel at Alfred's creation and how he stands before me invigorated, charged up with an energy and passion that I yearn for. No one has ever made me feel the way he does, so I do something unexpected, something wonderful. I lean in close to Alfred, closer than I've ever been before, and I kiss him, right then and there in the blossoming sea of yellow before I lose my nerve.

It's my first kiss.

And from the look on Alfred's face, I think it's his first kiss, too.

"This is the most beautiful thing I've ever seen Alfred!" I say. "Thank you for showing me."

Alfred's cheeks burst into red as he reaches down to hold my hand. I can't help but feel a little bit guilty for lying the way that I did, because it isn't the most beautiful thing that I've ever seen.

Not by a long shot.

The most beautiful thing I've ever seen…

no doubt…

is Alfred.

At 9:01 a.m. there's a soft knock on the door of room 932. Alexa Garrity is more casual today than she was yesterday and much more colorful, wearing white jeans and a red sweater that hugs her lean figure and small breasts.

"Alexa," I say, trying hard not to search for Alfred. "Please come in."

Alexa enters the room beneath the wide-brimmed hat that has replaced the baseball caps Alfred wore to protect his fragile skin from the scorching sun. As she moves, her ponytail shimmers and bounces off her back. Seeing Alfred this way is oddly intriguing. It should be no surprise that I am as awestruck now as I was then.

"It's good to see you, Danni," she says, placing her hat on the bed before taking a seat beside it. She crosses her legs and folds her hands in her lap.

She is perfect.

From head to toe.

As stunning a woman as she was a young man.

I pour a cup of coffee and hand it to her. "Cream and sugar?"

"Black is fine, thanks," she says, batting her snowy lashes over the pink eyes I got lost in as a young girl.

A lifetime has passed, and yet I still feel giddy. I expected more of myself in this situation, more calm, more composure.

"Please, sit down," she says softly, motioning for me to have a seat next to her. It's hard to determine whether it's the caffeine that is making my heart palpitate or the way she studies me as I walk toward her. It's been years since I sat next to Alfred on his bed in the Garrity house. We talked for hours in the dark while Sergeant menacingly roamed the halls, and yet it feels like yesterday as feelings come flooding back.

"Danni," she says, "I know it's a shock to see me like this. I wanted to tell you years ago, but something inside always stopped me." Alexa sets her coffee, untouched, on the end table. "More than anyone else," she says, gazing into the steaming black liquid, "I wanted you to know." But seeing her like this isn't nearly as shocking as the emotions that have surfaced again, igniting my senses like no time has passed at all.

"You're beautiful, Alfred," I say, tucking my hair behind my ears and drawing my knees to my chest like a child. "I mean…Alexa…you're really beautiful."

It was all I wanted to say. And from the look on Alexa's face, it was all she wanted to hear. There's something divine about being the only one on earth who could possibly recognize the sorrow of Alfred's past overshadowed by the exuberance of Alexa's present. She reaches out to stroke my hair, passing her fingertips along the side of my face and down my neck until they gently rest on the curve of my shoulder.

And I fall again.

Head over heels.

In spite of Alfred's transformation.

"Thank you for coming," I say, hugging my knees tighter to shelter myself from the overwhelming stimulus.

If Alexa blinks, the tears that are pooling up in her eyes will fall. "What is it, Alexa? Are you OK?"

"We've been through a lot, that's all," she says, widening her eyes to dry them.

"Uh, ya think?" I say, and I laugh to lighten the mood.

"Yeah," she smiles, nudging her shoulder against mine. "I think. So what brings you back to Bethlehem? I know you despise this town as much as I do. Is it what happened to Sergeant?"

Her hand slides over my shoulder and down my arm, and folds firmly around my palm. I hope she doesn't notice the way I respond to her touch or the lengthy pause before I reply, but it was always difficult concentrating with Alfred so close. Today is no different.

"That's one reason. But there are others," I say, recalling the day I led Sergeant to him, to her. "When I saw you last, on the beach, you didn't give me a chance to apologize for…"

Alexa squeezes my hand. "Danni…listen to me," she says. "You don't need to apologize for anything. Sergeant was an evil son of a bitch who hurt a lot of good people and managed to get away with it." She pulls a tube of lipstick from her pocket and glides it across her lips. "Until now." Alexa rubs her lips together, using her ring finger to smooth the paste evenly over her mouth.

"Any idea who could have done it?" I ask, allowing my journalist instincts to kick in. "I heard it was barbaric."

Alexa nods. "He would have been lucky to die when I shot him years ago," she says. "But I think that time has a way of giving people exactly what they deserve. Don't you?"

There has always been a special place in my heart for Alfred. I kept it tucked away as one of the few good memories of my childhood that still remains vital and alive. He was innocent then. In some way, I had expected him again, unaffected by time and circumstance. But this isn't Alfred. This is Alexa.

"Let's not waste any more time talking about him," she says. "Besides, I should be the one apologizing for what happened on the beach. I was confused and should have never…"

I quickly cup my hand over her mouth. "No regrets, remember?"

She removes my hand and holds it in hers. "Right. So where have you been for fifteen years?"

"Well, let's see," I say, feeling suddenly self-conscious under Alexa's intoxicating gaze. On my best day, I could never be as striking. "I'm a journalist at the *Times,* which I find rewarding most of the time, but I'd be lying if I said that being bombarded with bad news on a daily basis doesn't occasionally get me down." I watch Alexa's hand gently caressing mine. "These days, more than occasionally, unfortunately." I had hoped that the years would shelter me from my wants and desires, but it becomes apparent that no amount of time can bestow such refuge. "And believe it or not, I'm married!" I throw my hands up in the air. "Surprise!"

"Why would I be surprised?" she asks. "I always knew you'd make someone a beautiful bride...it's just that..."

"It's just that what?"

"Nothing," she says. "It doesn't matter anymore. I'm happy for you, Danni. He's a lucky guy."

I close my eyes to picture Alfred the way he was the last time I saw him on the California sand, still a man. "Alexa?" I whisper, the way I used to in the middle of the night.

"Yes?"

"Are you happy?" I ask, wanting her answer to be yes as much as I want it to be no because I wanted to be the one to make Alfred happy. More than anything, I wanted it to be me.

She smiles broad enough for me to notice the single tooth that still protrudes slightly farther than the others. There is so much about Alexa that is different from Alfred, but some things have remained exactly the same. Like the way she leans toward me when she speaks as though I'm the only one in the world special enough to hear what she has to say. Or the way she asks me a question and then curiously raises one platinum brow while eagerly awaiting my answer. Her adoration is as peculiar today as it was the day Alfred first entered my bedroom, brushed my hair, and probed into the part of me I thought I hid so well. It was like I had finally connected with a soul that hurt as much as mine did.

"Sure, I'm happy," she says. "I live a good life in LA. I'm a florist, one of the most successful in town."

And yet there's something about her answer that leaves me unconvinced.

"And you know what?" she adds. "Of all the flowers I work with, I still have a favorite." She reaches into her pocket, removes a handful of seeds, and places them in the palm of my hand.

"Sunflowers!" I say, laughing for the first time since I came back to this ghastly town. "I guess there are some things that will never change."

Alexa laughs too, louder and harder than Alfred ever did, straight from somewhere deep inside that makes her hold her stomach, in spite of Sergeant's horrific death or because of it, I'm not sure which. She lifts her coffee to her crimson mouth and returns it to the table without spilling a drop. Surely, a killer's hands wouldn't be so sturdy, but even the most gentle person can be pushed beyond his or her limits to a point of unbridled insanity. Maybe her injustices got to be too much for her and she snapped.

I'd love her anyway.

Alexa leans against me. "So what about you, Danni?" she asks. "Are you happy?"

She smells sweet and clean, like a mix of lavender and vanilla on a spring day, and I want to tell her that right now, in this very moment, I am happy for the first time in a long time. But this is too complicated, and I long for Alfred. Now more than ever.

"I'm a work in progress," I answer, shrugging my shoulders.

"Sometimes I wish things could have been different," she says, wrapping her arm around my waist. I don't want her embrace to excite me the way that it does.

"Me too," I say, turning to acknowledge her wants as much as my own.

And her lips meet mine.

Unexpectedly.

Right here.

Right now.

Woman to woman.

Soft and gentle.

With a tender passion that has emanated from Alfred since he was a boy, more natural and more meaningful than any kiss he could have offered as a man. So this is who he is, who he longed to be. I feel his presence now more than ever as Alexa draws my chest to hers and touches her tongue to mine. It's exhilarating, to say the least: the sensation of our breasts pressed together. I'm not sure which of us is breathing heavier. Maybe, as our mouths part, she is delighting in the taste of my lingering lips as I am in hers. Alexa's eyes twitch beneath her flawless, pallid lids. I want to know what she's thinking at this very moment—more importantly, what she's feeling. Perhaps her pounding heart is an indication. Sometimes it's the quiet moments that speak the loudest. The thoughts unspoken, the words unsaid. It was all we needed and all we could have.

Alexa opens her eyes, gathers her things, and walks to the door. "Take care of yourself," she says, adjusting her hat on the top of her head. "And don't lose touch."

"I won't."

"Promise?"

Using my finger, I make an *X* over my heart. "Promise."

She opens the door and turns to go.

"Alexa, wait," I say. "I need to find Becca. Do you know where she could be?"

"She ran away years ago, Danni," she says, applying a fresh stain of red to her lips. "No one heard from her again. I'm sorry, that's all I know."

The arrow over the elevator lights up and the doors open. Alexa checks her appearance in a hallway mirror, steps into the elevator, and waves good-bye.

But this isn't good-bye.

Not by a long shot.

After what just happened, it couldn't possibly be.

"Danni, what a wonderful surprise." Standing in the doorway of her office, Mrs. Rogers looks as classic as I remember, with honey-colored hair swept up off her neck and a printed linen dress that cinches at the waist and flows softly to her knees. She has aged gracefully with the passing years. The lines around her eyes and mouth have spawned a finer, more seasoned version of her younger self.

"Please come in," she says, appearing delighted with my request to meet with her. Her embrace feels as genuine and safe today as it did on the day she left us at the Garrity house. More than anything, I wanted her to take us with her, to call us her own. I thought if I squeezed her hand tight enough or held her waist long enough she wouldn't let us go. I was wrong.

"Let me take a good look at you," she says, holding me at arm's length and scanning me from top to bottom. "Well, it's no surprise," she says, her eyes smiling before her lips, "You're absolutely beautiful. Please have a seat. Can I offer you anything? A cup of tea maybe?"

"Yes, thank you."

"So tell me how you've been," she inquires, handing me a tea bag and a cup of steaming water.

"Good," I lie. "I'm in town for a while, taking care of some business, so I thought I'd get in touch with some old acquaintances."

The smile falls from her face. "I suppose you heard about Sergeant Garrity," she says. The mention of his name creates a sensation on the back of my neck, like tiny, leggy insects crawling by the hundreds through my scalp.

"Yes, I did."

"People can't stop talking about it," she adds. "There's no telling who could have done it."

I'm grateful for the way her eyes avoid mine because I can't lie straight to her face and I won't tell her that I know exactly who could have done it and why.

"No telling," I say, and out of habit, I smile the way I grew accustomed to smiling in her presence when meeting prospective parents for the very first time.

"So what can I do for you, Danni?" she asks, bobbing her tea bag up and down. "I'd like to think this is just a visit, but I have a feeling that there's more to it."

Mrs. Rogers is as sweet and composed today as she was the day she took me away from Becca. I should hate her for what she did, but it was her unfortunate job to clean up Mom's mess, so I can't blame her for that.

"I have to find my sister, Mrs. Rogers," I say. "I would appreciate any help you could offer."

She coughs, suddenly choking on nothing more than her own saliva as she lifts the tea bag from the water and places it on a napkin next to her cup.

"I see," she says, sipping the hot tea. She removes her eyeglasses, sets them down beside the napkin, and sighs the way Mrs. Garrity did before she went to bed at night, like she had something on her shoulders far too heavy to carry for even a minute longer. "Where do I start?" she asks.

It could be a draft that is creating the sudden chill in the room, but more than likely it's my nerves reacting to her question. It's the same question I've asked every therapist I've ever seen: so complex and yet so simple. I sit down on the edge of a small wooden chair placed directly in front of her desk and wrap my hands firmly around the cup of hot tea. If the water were boiling, I'd take a big gulp so that I could suffer the scalding liquid on my tongue and throat. The pain would offer respite from what is about to come as I answer her the only way I know how.

"At the beginning, Mrs. Rogers. Please, at the beginning."

"Remember me?" Becca asked. On this day, about six years ago, a flashy young woman, beautiful in spite of her tawdry appearance, walked into her office and closed the door behind her. "Remember me?"

Mrs. Rogers looked up from her work to acknowledge the woman standing before her in a tightly fitted red dress and an excessive amount of jewelry that jingled with her every move.

"Excuse me?"

"I asked you a question," she said, approaching Mrs. Rogers's desk. She placed both hands on its surface and leaned in close enough to emit the potent perfume that saturated her skin.

Mrs. Rogers closed the folder in front of her and pushed it to the side. "Can I help you with something?"

"I said, do you remember me?" The woman brushed aside the curls that framed her face and tossed a small photo onto Mrs. Rogers's desk, a tattered black-and-white picture of two little girls taken long ago in a dime-store photo booth. It would be impossible for Mrs. Rogers to forget the girls: one as exquisite as the morning sun, the other not, shamefully hiding behind a mask of tresses. Mrs. Rogers studied the woman before her, petite and fair with stunning blue eyes and a handful of freckles scattered across the bridge of her nose that made her appear more youthful than she was. But it was her mouth that Mrs. Rogers studied the most, her beautiful mouth: full pink lips tainted only by a thin faint scar that extended from her upper lip to the bottom of her nose.

"Becca?"

The woman looked away.

"I can't believe it's you," Mrs. Rogers said. "It's been so long. Please have a seat."

Becca's nostrils expanded with each breath. "I want to know who my mother is," she demanded.

"Becca, please sit down. I'd like to hear how you've been."

Becca slammed her palms on the desk. "Tell me who she is, goddamn it!"

"I'm afraid I can't do that. All information on birth parents is strictly confidential. That's not to say that you can't get the information that you're looking for from other sources."

Becca paced across the room, lit a cigarette, and blew a stream of smoke into the air. "I look a little different than the freak you remember, huh? How do you sleep at night knowing what you did?"

"It was a difficult case," Mrs. Rogers responded. "I did what I thought was best."

"Difficult? It was a difficult case? Is that all you have to say? Tell me, Mrs. Rogers, do you have any idea what went on in the Garrity house?" Becca's eyes widened. "Do you know what that son of a bitch did to me?"

"What are you talking about?" Mrs. Rogers asked. "Please, have a seat so we can discuss this."

"Discuss this?" Becca seethed. "Are you kidding me? What exactly would you like to discuss Mrs. Rogers: the way you left me in a house with a fucking monster?" Becca wrapped her arms around herself and sharpened her gaze. "Or would you like to talk about how it feels to have a penis shoved so far down your throat that you either vomit or pass out? Why don't we discuss the way the man you left me with would hold me down on the bed and force himself inside of me until my sheets were soaked in blood. Or how, late at night, after screwing his wife, he would sneak into my bed, still smelling of her, press himself against me, and pant like a fucking dog until he ejaculated all over my back." Becca dropped her cigarette to the floor and pressed it into the linoleum with the toe of her stiletto. "No, Mrs. Rogers, I don't want to discuss anything with you. I came here to find out who my mother is."

"Dear God," Mrs. Rogers said, rubbing her hand across her forehead. "I...I don't understand. The Garritys were thoroughly screened like every other family. Their reputation in the community was impeccable. I don't know how that could have happened."

"Don't tell me you didn't know!" Becca said, stabbing her finger into Mrs. Rogers's chest. "It's your fucking job to know! But you aren't very good at your job are you?" She lit another cigarette, held it firmly between her index and middle finger, and waved it in the air as she spoke. "Not then. Not now," she said, sweetening her voice before ejecting the venom that would satisfy her craving for revenge. "I mean, how could you be good at anything with all that's on your mind? Like your marriage, for instance." She placed her hand on Mrs. Rogers's shoulder. "Poor thing, being married to a man like your husband is never easy for a woman like you," she said, running her fingers up Mrs. Rogers's neckline to the diamond stud in her ear. "I wonder who he fucked before he bought you these?"

"I know what you're trying to do, Becca, but it's not going to work," Mrs. Rogers said, walking to the door. "I'd like you to leave."

Becca tossed back her hair. "Surely after all these years you're not still fooling yourself into thinking that you have a good marriage, are you? Tell me, Mrs. Rogers, how does it feel to be married to a man who has to go elsewhere to be satisfied? How many women do you think your darling Bill has had over the years? Ten? Twenty? Or have you stopped counting? You can't blame him, you know. That's what happens when a woman doesn't know how to please her man."

Mrs. Rogers pushed open the door. "Get out."

"I should be thanking you," Becca said. "After all, it's women like you who keep women like me in business." She removed a man's gold watch from her wrist and handed it to Mrs. Rogers. "Can you do me a favor and give this back to your husband? He left it on the nightstand last night. The engraving is touching."

Mrs. Rogers snatched the watch from Becca's hand and turned it over.

> Happy Anniversary Bill.
> All My Love,
> Linda.

"Get out!" she screamed, hurling the watch across the room.

"Oh, one more thing," Becca said, raising a pleasing brow. "Tell Bill I won't be able to make that business trip next week, I have some personal business to tend to. By the way, thanks for all your help with finding my mother. I really appreciate it."

Mrs. Rogers looks up from her cup of tea.

"I never heard from her again, Danni," she says.

The rain has paused and the spring sun streams through a break in the clouds. As I stare out the window, I am reminded of what the season represents: new life, new hope, new beginnings, what I had hoped would be the outcome of this trip.

"I have to find her, Mrs. Rogers. Do you have any idea where she could be?"

"Not everyone can be saved, Danni," she says, walking to the door. "I learned that the hard way. Becca's not the innocent little girl you remember. I have to live with the mistakes I've made for the rest of my life. Why don't you go home to your husband and leave the past behind you?"

"I tried that already. I'm going to find her with or without your help."

She shakes her head and hands me the business card of Ms. Adebola Akingbade, a counselor at a local girls' crisis center.

"Rumor has it, Becca moved out to Las Vegas," she says. "If anyone would know more, it would be Adebola. I hope you find what you're looking for, Danni. For your sake, I'd like a happy ending to this story."

As I exit Mrs. Roger's office, a robin lands on the branch of a cherry tree that lines the street. He hops up several branches onto a half-built nest, where he diligently works, using mud and twigs to build a strong, sturdy foundation that will be able to withstand the summer storms that are certain to come. Several times he flies away and returns with more twigs, strategically entwining each one into a sound structure. I think about what Mrs. Rogers told me about Becca and how she suggested that I leave town and go home to my husband. The wind kicks up and blows several twigs from the nest onto the ground as the sun disappears again behind a mass of clouds. A cool breeze rushes over my skin. Maybe she's right. Maybe I should go home, throw my arms around Michael, and embrace the future, regardless of the past, because what I stand to gain isn't worth what I stand to lose.

The sky rumbles, followed by a shower of rain that forces the robin from his nest. He will wait for the storm to pass before continuing on, trusting his innate instincts to guide him: one very distinct difference between animals and humans. I hum the ant song out loud in an attempt to drown out the voice that returns, plaguing me with an incessant banter. *Close your eyes! Don't look back! Close your eyes! Don't look back!* I once knew Becca better than I knew myself. I won't go home until I find her, in spite of Mrs. Rogers's advice and the voice that screams out warning me not to.

"Attention passengers...we are now boarding aisles one to ten for Flight #1244 to Las Vegas, Nevada."

I place a small blue pill on the back of my tongue, force it down with a sip of lukewarm coffee, and check my ticket one last time...

Flight #1244...

Philadelphia to Las Vegas...

Seat 13C.

It's been almost three weeks since I started my trip and several days since I spoke with Ms. Adebola Akingbade, an elderly African woman who moved to the States many years ago, dedicating her life to young girls in crisis. I spent an entire afternoon with Bola, as she is known among girls on the street who recognize and respect her for her lifelong commitment to helping them improve their lives. I found her on the front porch of a modest row home on the southside of Bethlehem. She sat in an old wicker rocking chair beneath a hand-carved wooden sign that read "She Met Honor," the African meaning of her name, Adebola. She explained to me her cause and described the years of abuse she suffered as a child in Africa: molested and raped by her father, uncle, and cousins; treated as nothing more than an object; and given less value than the animals they raised for food. Bola was a rather large woman, dressed in a boldly printed blouse and wrap skirt from her native land of Nigeria. She had long, gray braids that hung out of an elaborate red cloth creatively tied and twisted around the top of her head. Her skin was the color of dark cocoa, lined with wisdom that she wore proudly, like badges of honor.

There was something familiar about Bola, something I tried to put my finger on as I listened to her speak in a low voice, still thick with her native tongue, that resounded through the air like the steady beat of a tribal drum. Her dim black eyes had witnessed far more evil than I could even imagine, and I wondered, as I studied and visually traced every detail of her face, which of her lines resulted from smiles and which ones from tears. *It's no wonder she relates so well to troubled girls*, I thought.

Yet in spite of it all, Bola exuded peace, humbled by grown women who come back years later to thank her and by young girls who still come knocking on her door in the middle of the night with nothing more than a shirt on their back and a glimmer of hope in their heart, desperately searching for help and guidance. She had much to be proud of: accomplishments and success stories of young girls, too many to mention.

"But dere are some girls dat keep me up at night," she said in a dialect almost too strong to translate. "Dose dat slipped through my fingers like fine sand." Bola's rocking chair creaked and slowed to a halt. "As Becca did," she said. "I knew your sister well."

I board the plane, place my carry-on in the overhead compartment, take a seat, and close my eyes. It's early morning. A wave of nausea induces a cold sweat and a hardy swallow that forces a rush of vomit back into my stomach as I recall what Bola told me about Sergeant and Becca. I clench my teeth together, but there's no stopping my gut from hurling its contents into the small bag that I pull from the seat in front of me. Sergeant molested Becca until the age of fourteen, when he dropped her off in the middle of the night with a dollar in her pocket, nowhere to go, and no one to turn to. He told her to never return, that she was nothing more than illegitimate trash. It was Bola who found her weeks later, rummaging through a garbage can behind a Thai restaurant downtown, just blocks from her house, dirty and painfully thin. Bola told me about the young girl who crouched down behind a dumpster when she saw the strange African woman approaching her. Bola sat down beside her in the midst of the trash, reached into a large sack that draped over her shoulder, and pulled out a piece of homemade cornbread wrapped in cellophane. She held it out to the girl, who snatched it, ripped it open, and devoured every last morsel with a twisted mouth that was unlike anything Bola had seen since she left her native land.

"What's your name, child?" she asked the girl, whose brilliant blue eyes made her heart swell with empathy. Bola opened a thermos of cool tea, placed it in the young teen's soiled hands, and embraced them with hers. The girl guzzled it down before looking up at the dark woman who hovered over her like a warm, safe shelter.

"Becca, ma'am. My name ith Becca."

Bola smiled and wrapped her arm around Becca's shoulders.

"Well, child, dis must be my lucky day. Where I'm from, da name Becca means "prophet," one who is gifted with extraordinary insight. I had a feeling when I woke dis morning dat today was going to be extra special, and now I know why."

Becca's head hung low. "I don't have any gifth ma'am," she said with regret. "But thank you all the thame for the bread."

Bola placed her finger beneath Becca's chin and lifted it to look directly into her eyes. "I live down da street, Becca. I would be more than honored if you would have lunch with me." She stood and held out her hand. "Dat is, if you don't have any other plans, of course."

Becca, tired and weary from weeks on the streets, managed a crooked smile as Bola helped her to her feet and guided her back to her house, where she offered her a soft chair while preparing lunch. As Bola moved about the kitchen, she spoke of her homeland's cultures and beliefs, filling the air with the soothing rhythm of her deep voice that lulled Becca into a contented slumber. "You're safe here, child," she said, satisfied by the poetic cadence of Becca's breath. "Sleep well."

We're next in line for takeoff. The sounds of the engines grow from an easy hum to a deafening roar as the pilot accelerates down the runway. I close my eyes and think about how Michael and I made love for hours the night before I left, with no expectations and no inhibitions. In those moments, I thought nothing could feel more natural or more exciting. I thought it was enough to deny the love I harbor for Alfred. But Alexa changed all that with her soft lips and the way she caressed my back while exploring my mouth with her tongue. The nose of the plane tips up, catches air, and lifts into the sky. I open the book I brought for the flight, turn to the first chapter, and read the words that meant so much to Alfred. In all these years, I never read *Huck Finn*, but I know the story well, the way Alfred recited each line, breathing in the first words like the very oxygen he needed to survive: "And so when I couldn't stand it no longer I lit out. I got into my old rags and my sugar-hogshead again, and was free and satisfied."

Over the loud speaker, the captain makes an announcement. "Ladies and gentlemen, for safety reasons, we ask that you remain seated and keep your seat belts fastened as we may be experiencing some heavy turbulence due to inclement weather patterns. Flight attendants will delay food and beverage service until further notice. Thank you."

It's a five-hour flight to Vegas, where I will search for Becca, better known as Rebecca Rose to her affluent clients who, according to Bola, consist of high-powered businessmen and politicians who are willing to pay her price. With Alfred's sweet voice in my head, Alexa's soft lips on my mind, and Rebecca Rose heavy on my shoulders, I lean back and close my eyes. The medicine will soon take effect, and I'll be able to rest, regardless of the turbulence that violently shakes the plane and the turbulence that most certainly awaits me in the city known for sin.

"Flight attendants, please prepare for landing." Looking at my watch, I am shocked by the time, relieved that I slept the entire flight, and grateful for the hours of reprieve from my own obsessive thoughts. I lift the tray in front of me, return my seat to the upright position, and think about my conversation with Ms. Akingbade. Becca stayed with Bola, who promised not to contact the Garritys or child services, recognizing the signs of abuse that Becca demonstrated: from the look in her eyes of fear, betrayal, and dejection, to the way her entire body jumped and tensed with nothing more than a simple touch. Bola had seen it all before, as well as the symptoms that Becca exhibited soon after her arrival: morning sickness, breast tenderness, and frequent urination. A drugstore test confirmed what Bola suspected.

Becca was pregnant.

About six weeks.

With Sergeant's child.

No wonder he disposed of her. Her changing figure would have to be addressed and would cause far too much detriment to his community image. Becca begged him not to desert her, professing her love and commitment to him. Bola described how Becca cried for weeks over the man she claimed was the only one who had ever loved or needed her.

"There is a powerful bond between an abuser and a victim dat is extremely difficult to understand and even more difficult to break. You have to realize the dynamics of such a relationship and the emotional ties dat develop with such an imbalance of power. Dat poor child based all of her self-worth on him, what he told her, how he treated her, good one minute, bad da next, rewarding her, den punishing her. It's a vicious cycle. She wanted nothing more dan for someone to love and accept her, so she tried in every way to earn his love by pleasing him, in spite of how much he hurt her. Abusers are masters of manipulation dat prey on the naive and innocent. He was all dat she had." Bola shook her head. "A tragedy, dat's what it is, a God-awful tragedy."

"Did she ever mention me?" I asked.

Bola fidgeted with her dress and cleared her throat. "I'm sorry, Danni. Until today, I didn't even know dat you existed."

There was a pressure in my chest, a heavy weight pressing into it, forcing the breath from my lungs as Bola continued her story about Becca, who insisted on having the baby, refusing to destroy an innocent life regardless of the circumstances.

"She knew what she had to do," Bola said. So in the summer of 1991, with the help of a midwife, Becca gave birth to a baby boy (six pounds, eight ounces) in the second floor bedroom of Bola's row home as the adoptive parents anxiously waited downstairs. Becca held her son for a short time, cradled him in her arms, inhaled the sweet scent of his forehead, and kissed his perfectly formed lips. He was the most beautiful thing she had ever seen, from the top of his small round head to the tips of his tiny toes, perfect in every way...unlike her. Becca traced every curve of him with her finger, marveling at how something so right could come from something so wrong, and carefully examining the small, distinct birthmark to the left of his navel. She placed her finger on the dark brown, uniquely shaped mark.

"It lookth like a dolphin leaping from the ocean," she laughed, wiping the tears from her eyes as he wrapped his tiny hand around her finger and held on tighter than anyone had ever held Becca before.

"It's time, child," Bola said.

Becca kissed her son and rested her cheek against his as she sang softly in his ear:

> *Juth what makth that little old ant...*
> *Think he can move that rubber tree plant...*
> *Anyone knowth an ant...can't...*
> *move a rubber tree plant.*

She struggled to finish.

> *Cauth he'th got...high hopeth...*
> *He'th got...high hopeth...*
> *He'th got...high apple pie in the sky hopeth...*
> *Tho anytime you're feelin' low...*
> *Thtead of letting' go...*
> *Jutht remember that ant...*

Becca pulled her finger from his grip and gently poked his stomach.

Oopth, there goeth another rubber tree...
Oopth, there goeth another rubber tree...
Oopth, there goeth another rubber tree plant.

She held her son to her chest and rocked him before lifting him up to Bola. "Take him, Bola!" she screamed. "I never want to thee him again! Ever!"

Becca turned away, held her hands over her face, and curled up into the same fetal position as her newborn son. She cried for hours that day for everyone who had ever left her. Through the window, the evening sky turned from a deep shade of blue to a somber black as she gazed at her reflection, tugging on her curls and lifting her hands to her grotesque mouth, pressing and squeezing her upper lip together to visualize how a normal mouth would look. Harder and harder she rubbed and twisted the flesh that had caused so much heartache and suffering. She couldn't blame any of them for leaving her. Who could love such an embarrassment? From her nightstand, she picked up a hand-painted ceramic vase and read out loud the words that were neatly carved into the bottom:

To my beautiful Becca...
Love, Bola

Becca looked again at her disfigured reflection in the window and watched as she drew her arm back and lunged it forward, hurling the vase through the air, into the glass. "Liar!" she screamed, listening to the thumping of Bola's feet rushing toward her room. "I'll never be beautiful! Never!"

I exit the plane, head to the ladies' room, and throw a couple of quarters into a slot machine conveniently located at the entrance. It chimes and dings as cherries and gold nuggets spin around, stopping one cherry short of a win.

Becca is thirty-one years old...

a grown woman...

a complete stranger.

I roll up my sleeves, splash some cool water on my face, and dab it dry with a paper towel. A young girl exits a stall, washes her hands in the sink beside me, and stares at the scars that cover my forearms. If she were my child, I would tell her that I had made a lot of mistakes. If she were my child, I would tell her that Erma was wrong. I would tell her that pain on the outside doesn't stop pain on the inside from hurting. But she's not my child. I killed mine when I was sixteen years old.

Baggage claim is swarming with people. I grab my bag from the belt and walk outside where buses, limousines, and cabs line the street. "Taxi!"

A driver gets out of a cab parked in front of me, scratches the top of his head, and tightens his lips to secure the cigarette that dangles from the corner of his mouth. "Where to?" he asks, squinting his eyes in the menthol smoke that rolls up in front of him.

"I need a hotel room on the main strip," I say, putting confidence in a man who emits the same barroom odors as his car.

"Not a problem," he says and drops the cigarette to the ground to stomp it out.

It's a short ride to where I will be staying. The hotel grounds are adorned with palm trees and a pool that overlooks the Strip. The room is modern, the temperature is just right, and the lights don't flicker as they did in room 932. I sit on the edge of the bed and rub my fingers along the scars that trail up and down my forearms. The longest begins on my left wrist and ends at the crease of my elbow. At the age of sixteen, I thought that the acute pain of a safety pin ripping at my flesh would relieve the guilt I felt for letting Becca go. I did nothing that night in front of the supermarket as Sergeant drove away with her, caressing and stroking her hair as he passed. I hated myself. But that night I think I hated her more for never leaving my thoughts. I was sixteen, goddamn it. I didn't want to worry about her anymore.

So on that night, I didn't. As my friends and I drank cheap beer behind the movie theater, I didn't think of her at all. I laughed harder and drank more until my body tingled and throbbed, consumed with sensation instead of thoughts. Letting go of her felt good. And so did Eric Seton in his car on our way back from the movie theater when he parked in a vacant lot at the steel plant. He didn't say much before he turned off the car, leaned over, rubbed his left hand up and down my thigh, and kissed me, forcing his tongue deep into my mouth as his breath grew heavy with excitement. I closed my eyes, still spinning from the alcohol, and enjoyed the subtle pulsing that began between my legs as I kissed him harder, opened my legs and leaned into his hand with the anticipation of his touch. He unzipped my jeans, slid his hand down to the irritating throb that yearned for him and kissed my neck, sucking my skin between his teeth while inserting his finger into me. It was something I hadn't felt before, something unexpected and stimulating. He pulled me closer, moving his finger in and out of me, slowly at first, than faster until my entire body shook. The smell of stale beer filled the car as he climbed on top of me, pushed my seat back, and lifted my sweater to fully uncover my breasts, grabbing and squeezing as the weight of his body held me against the seat until I could barely move.

"Eric," I said as he dropped his head to my chest, "I've never done this before. I'm scared. What if it hurts?"

He yanked my jeans down and unzipped his pants to expose his erect penis. "Ssshhhhh, it's supposed to hurt a little the first time," he said, climbing on top of me.

"But I don't think I'm ready."

"Trust me," he moaned, forcing my legs apart with his while holding my hands up over my head. "You're ready. You've been asking for it all night."

I could have fought him, I suppose, but he was right. I allowed it to go this far. What kind of girl would I be if I didn't finish? And with one forceful thrust, he took my virginity in the front seat of his Mustang as I yelled out with the sharp pain of him ripping through my last ounce of innocence. Through the window, I stared up into the star-filled sky and concentrated on the clanking noises of the steel plant that echoed through the night air as I screamed Erma's happy song in my head. But none of it would drown out the revolting grunting in my ear that continued on with the steady motion of Eric's hips. I rubbed the cut on my forearm against the seat until I couldn't feel him anymore, just the gnawing sting of an open wound. Eric groaned and the car rocked faster until coming to an abrupt halt. He climbed off of me, zipped his pants, started the car, and drove home in silence while I adjusted my sweater and shimmied back into my jeans. We never spoke another word to each other. And no one ever knew what happened that night. It's something I'd rather forget.

But the scar on my arm is a constant reminder. Eric Seton knew what he wanted. With no regard for me, he looked me in the eye and took it on the same night that I looked Becca in the eye and betrayed her. I wondered, as he shoved himself deep inside of me, if Eric could smell the foul stench of my detestable soul as he dominated and conquered nothing more than a weaker version of himself. I deserved what I got that night for trying to forget her.

I pull my sleeves down, open the phone book, and flip through the yellow pages to the Las Vegas gentlemen's clubs. There are many, but one club stands out more than the rest, listed as the largest, most famous club in the country. I jot down the address on a piece of paper. It's midafternoon, and according to Erma's famous words, "There's no time like the present." No matter how hard I tried, I never forgot about Becca.

I don't know how long it will take me to find her.

But I won't stop until I do.

Becca left Bola's house soon after the birth of her son. Late one night, she packed her bags and climbed out her bedroom window and down the large oak tree that grew next to Bola's house. She thumbed a ride to New York City with a couple of girls from the streets who convinced her that life would be easier there: more people, more opportunities. She left behind nothing more than her pillow, still damp with tears. Almost two years had passed when Bola received a call in the middle of the night from a Manhattan emergency room where Becca had been admitted after a Chinatown delivery boy found her in a dark alley, curled up by the side of a building, badly beaten and left for dead. It was a tattered business card in Becca's wallet that led emergency personnel to Bola, who rushed to her side. Her body was pummeled, barely recognizable, and covered with slashes and welts that swelled into shades of black and blue. Bola stayed with Becca, who remained in intensive care for months, undergoing numerous surgeries to repair the massive injuries suffered at the hands of her attacker. She sat by Becca's side as she recovered and gradually recalled the details of the night she was accosted while working the streets of Times Square.

She was approached from behind as she stood next to the magazine stand where she had started every working night in a red miniskirt, with a mouthful of fruit-flavored gum and a soda can filled with cheap vodka to numb her senses. The first trick of the night was always the worst. Becca bent down, picked up a smooth white rock that stood out in a sea of gray, and rubbed her thumb over the level surface. She had one rule: never look a customer in the eye. It was a tactic she had discovered as a child when Sergeant entered her room for the first time on the night that Danni left with a pocket full of candy and a new game to play. At the age of five, a tickle game sounded like fun to Becca, but the way Sergeant tickled her felt wrong. She had never been touched there before and had never experienced a feeling as pleasurable or shameful. So she took the candy and the tickling, and looked away, focusing on anything but him, accepting the physical sensation while denying the sin, just as she did on the streets with every trick she turned. Becca wrapped her hand around the stone, concentrated on its strength and durability, and waited for the man who inched closer behind her to make his move.

"How much?" he asked, standing close enough for her to feel him on the back of her neck.

"Fifty," she answered, and she squeezed the stone tighter because it seemed that no matter how many times she said it, it never got easier.

"For how long?"

"A half hour."

"You're charging fifty bucks with a fucking face like that?"

Her lower lip quivered. "That'th the prithe—take it or leave it."

Becca finished the last of the vodka, shoved the empty can into her bag, and waited for his response.

"Why would I pay for something I've already had for free?" he said, breathing out the odorous combination of whiskey and cigars before breathing in her youthful scent as he pressed the bulge in his pants against her buttocks. "Remember me, baby girl?"

"What are you doing here? Leave me alone," Becca said, hiding beneath her dangling locks as she stumbled over her heels to get away from the man she feared the most. The city streets

weren't dense enough for Becca to lose Sergeant in the crowd. He followed closely behind, adjusting his pants where the swelling had erupted between his legs.

"How about a little favor for old time's sake? Huh? You owe me that much, for adopting a fuckin' freak like you."

With one hand he reached out, grabbed her by the hair, pulled her into a side alley, and yanked her to the ground. "Don't run away from me, you little whore," he grumbled, pinning her down beneath him as he forced her hands above her head and held a knife inches from her mouth. The moon was high and full, shining like a spotlight on the city beneath it. Sergeant leaned over her and slowly ran his tongue up the side of her face. "This doesn't have to be so hard—you used to like it remember?"

Becca kicked and screamed in the dark shadows of the alley as hundreds of people walked the streets only feet away. "Pleathe don't hurt me," she cried. "Get off me!"

He pressed the blade into the corners of her mouth until the razor-sharp edge pierced her flesh. "You were my favorite, ya know," he said, sliding the knife across her mouth until Becca screamed out in distress, addressing him with the respect he demanded.

"Stop it, sir! Please!"

But he didn't stop, and no one heard her cries for help as he tore off her skirt and pressed her bare buttocks into the coarse pavement with the weight of his body, driving his pelvis into hers, deeply embedding hundreds of small gray stones into her fair teenage flesh. The sounds of the city echoed in the alley as she gazed up into the night sky, yelling out in pain with every thrust and punch until all she could feel was the perfect white stone dropping from her grip and the warmth of her own blood flowing from her skin as he sliced through her with no effort and no remorse.

That's all she remembered of that night. She never turned Sergeant in, and she never found a reason to believe that there was anything less than evil in the world, regardless of what Bola told her one afternoon, after months in the hospital, as she stood before her holding a mirror while doctors slowly unraveled the bandages from Becca's face.

"There's a whole lotta good dat can come from something bad if you just open your eyes, child," Bola said as doctors exposed Becca's beautifully transformed face. Becca didn't recognize the young woman in the mirror. She lifted her hands to her flawless face and ran her fingers over her full lips and perky nose. This was the woman she was supposed to be. Tears washed over the single scar that ran from the bottom of her nose to the top of her lip, the only reminder of what she once was.

Bola pulled a tissue from her pocket. "You're perfect child," she said, dabbing Becca's tears. "Like a rose in full bloom."

Becca held the mirror closer to stare at the woman who would put an end to the pathetic little girl that deserved nothing and settled for anything. She buried Becca that day—somewhere deep inside she buried the little girl no one wanted and damned everyone who had abandoned her. For the first time in her life, she was beautiful. There was a difference in her stride when she exited the hospital. She held her head high, shoulders back, and swayed her hips to command attention.

"Come home with me, child," Bola pleaded. "Make a better life for yourself."

Becca turned toward the sun, pulled her hair back off her face, and tied it back into a ponytail.

"Home?" she shrugged. "Never had one."

Her eyes no longer gleamed with the innocence and virtue of the young girl Bola once knew. A single cloud moved over the sun, and the wind shifted in the opposite direction as Becca disappeared onto a crowded city street.

"Good-bye, child," Bola said, holding her palms together at her chest. "May God shelter you from the storms." Bola knew that she had lost her that day. A single goose flew overhead, honking and squawking as though frantically searching for his flock. Bola wrapped a shawl around her shoulders and watched the goose fly by, heading in Becca's direction.

She wondered if he was lost, too.

As Becca was.

Undoubtedly and undeniably.

Lost.

20

It's a hot day in Las Vegas. Sunny. Ninety-five degrees. I'm sitting in a rental car across the street from the Sapphire Club, the most exclusive gentlemen's club in town. In front of the building, a digital marquee repeatedly flashes the dancers' names. I've read every one a hundred times, but one stands out above the rest, appearing last on the screen in large, bold letters: their featured dancer, Rebecca Rose.

It's my first time in a strip club. Michael would be appalled if he knew. He would tell me that it's not the place for a reverend's wife. But the truth is, I never fit that mold anyway. Not then. Not now.

The club is dimly lit with purple lights that line the perimeter of the floor and cast a violet hue on the white cocktail tables that fill the room. The music is thumping, and several girls are socializing with clients as strobe lights flash in the middle of the stage on a young brunette who barely looks legal. She is spinning around a smooth steel pole in a black-fringed thong and nothing else. I take a seat in back, light a cigarette, and order a drink while the room fills with men of varying ages. Many come alone. Others enter in groups, some with wives or girl-friends. A middle-aged announcer steps out from behind the curtain, and the music fades. He walks to the center of the floor with a microphone in one hand and a hand-kerchief in the other, wearing stonewashed jeans, snake-skin cowboy boots, and a tightly fitted crossbones T-shirt that accentuates his bulging biceps and the extra weight he carries around his middle. The diamond on his little finger sparkles under the spotlight as he wipes the sweat that drips down from beneath a poorly fitted toupee.

"Are you ready to have some fun?" he asks, provoking the crowd, which explodes into applause. He holds the microphone out over the audience. "I said, *are you ready to have some fun!*" The crowd roars and whistles. "I'd like to thank you all for coming out tonight," he says. "As you know, the Sapphire Club is known for bringing you the hottest, sexiest, most beautiful women in the world!" In the corner of the room, a group of young men wearing fraternity jackets raise their bottles, clash them together, and race to see who can chug the quickest. "And tonight is no different," the announcer continues. The boys lift their fists in a congratulatory declaration of the winner, who slams his empty bottle down on the table, places a long-stemmed rose between his teeth, and staggers to the foot of the stage.

The announcer clears his throat and signals for the lights to dim. "Gentlemen," he says, "and ladies, of course. You are in for a treat! The Sapphire Club proudly brings to the stage the girl you've all been waiting for, the girl dreams are made of: the one, the only, Rebecca Rose!"

The lights go out and he exits. For a moment, the room is as pitch-black as it was in the Garritys closet the day that Mrs. Garrity wrongfully punished me for stealing her new tube of lipstick. For hours I waited in the small, dark space, anxious and frightened by what was to come. As I do now. But I'm not ten years old anymore, so I won't close my eyes and bury my head in my lap or pinch and twist at the soft flesh above my pubic bone until the physical pain exceeds the emotional.

I move to the edge of my seat as a new song fills the room, a sultry tune that grows louder with the glow of a red spotlight that pierces the darkness. It shines down center stage, highlighting a petite silhouette. The crowd thickens, and bodyguards surround the stage where some have gathered with wads of cash in one hand, red roses in the other. From the back of the room I watch the dancer saunter across the stage in a sheer dress that clings to her firm breasts. A cascade of curls flows down her back and rests on the curve above her buttocks. She leans down to accept a rose from an aroused fan who has come to watch her take her clothes off. According to the sign out front, he won't leave disappointed. They never do.

She places the flower between her teeth, purses her lips and blows a kiss to the audience as the music escalates into a salacious roar that thunders through the room. It would be easier to leave right now, before this goes any further, because maybe Mrs. Rogers and Bola were wrong about everything...maybe it isn't Becca dancing beneath the spotlight. I move closer, squeezing through the swarm of admirers until I can see her clearly. She squats down, unzips her dress, and allows a young man from the audience to remove it, enticing the crowd that chants her name as she takes to the pole, wraps her bare body around it, and hoists herself up, spinning and twirling while dozens of red roses hurl through the air and land on the floor beneath her.

It's getting stuffy in here. A dense cloud of cigarette smoke lingers in the room of patrons who are getting what they want from Rebecca Rose as she satisfies their appetite like fresh meat thrown to a pack of ravenous wolves. One man reaches into his pocket, pulls out a roll of cash, and tosses it to the stage. "Marry me, baby!" he yells, holding up his drink. He stumbles and falls back into his seat as Rebecca finishes her set, gathers her money, and pauses for a moment to bask in the adoration of her fans. She is as beautiful as Bola said: her nose, her mouth, and her eyes that sparkle like jewels in the stage lights the way they did when we played in the summer sun. The crowd is still cheering as she walks offstage. There's no doubt her performance was everything they expected. And there's no doubt that I finally found Becca.

Behind the building, several dancers have gathered by the rear entrance. I pull into the lot, roll my window down, and listen to them joke about the horny frat boys at table one. A car honks in the distance, followed by a screech, a thud, and a couple of people yelling obscenities. It all sounds the same: Las Vegas, New York. A city is a city, except for Bethlehem. The noises there were different, especially when the plant was in full operation and the sound of silence rang out between the crashing and banging. But I wasn't the only one disturbed by the gruesome noises. Nature itself seemed altered by the disruption. Even the crickets heard it on those muggy summer nights when Becca and I lay in bed with the window open, nightgowns stuck to our skin, listening for their sweet songs. Not once did they muster up enough nerve to chirp in the midst of such chaos. They didn't have the guts to make a noise. But neither did I the night that Sergeant entered our room, knelt down beside the bed, and spoke to Becca in a pleasing voice that I hadn't heard him use before.

"Hey baby girl…are you awake?"

I pretended to sleep while keeping one eye slightly lifted.

"Yeth, thir."

"We have to use our secret voices," he said, "so we don't wake everyone up, OK?"

"OK," Becca whispered.

Sergeant rested his hand on her shoulder. "I had to work late, honey, so we didn't get a chance to play that game I promised we'd play."

Becca rubbed her eyes. "That's OK."

"No, it's not OK," he said in her ear. "A promise is a promise." Sergeant slid his hand beneath the blanket onto her stomach. "But we can play now."

Becca nodded.

"And if you win," he said. "You'll get a prize, OK?"

"OK." Becca squeezed her eyes shut and rested her arms by her sides.

"Ready?" Sergeant asked.

"Mmmhmm," she said.

Sergeant began rubbing his hand in small circles on Becca's stomach while reaching into his pants with the other. Becca's eyes twitched beneath the surface of her lids while a thin stream of saliva dribbled out the corner of her mouth, down the side of her face, and onto her pillow.

"You're good at this," he said.

"I am?" she whispered.

"Better than anyone I've ever played with before."

Becca smiled and squeezed her eyes tighter together. I didn't understand the game Sergeant was playing or why his hand moved faster in his pants while he rubbed Becca's stomach, continually sweeping over her chest and pelvic region. I wanted to tell him to stop. Actually, I wanted to scream it, but Becca was smiling and she played the game well. She didn't move. Not once. Nothing distracted her. Not even the sound of Sergeant's racing breath or the steady motion of his body shaking next to the bed. The game didn't last long.

"You win," he said, removing his hand from his pants.

"Do I get a prize now?" Becca asked, pulling her nightgown down.

"Tomorrow, baby," Sergeant said and wiped his hand on his shirt. "You'll get a prize tomorrow."

Sergeant left the room and Becca pulled the covers up to her chin. "I won a prithe," she whispered to herself before drifting off to sleep.

I slipped out of bed and locked the bedroom door because I didn't want Sergeant playing that game with Becca again. Not tonight. Not ever. I pinched and twisted the soft flesh on my inner thighs. I hated Sergeant, maybe not as much as Alfred did, but I hated him all the same. I wanted Becca to hate him, too. She didn't need Sergeant's kind words or his stupid prizes. And I didn't need another reason to wish him dead.

The dancers are still chatting by the rear door when Rebecca Rose walks out to join them. The showgirl is gone, along with the heavy makeup she wore on stage. This look is much more becoming: loose curls, jeans, and a sweatshirt. She cracks her gum and jokes with the girls as she walks to her car.

"See ya tomorrow night!" she yells, jingling her keys in her hand.

I've rehearsed this moment for years, and yet I'm still unprepared. I get out of my car and call her name the way I did when we were kids. "Becca!" After all this time, it still sounds the same.

She stops, swings her head around, and squints her eyes in the light of the moon. "Becca, it's me, Danni."

Across the lot, several girls hop into a small black convertible and speed off, waving and calling out to her as they pass. "Bye, Reba! Ciao!"

Becca points her keys at a shiny, red Jaguar until the yellow lights on the sides illuminate. She opens the door and tosses her handbag onto the passenger seat before getting behind the wheel. "You've got the wrong person," she says.

I step closer. "Please don't leave Becca."

She tosses her hair back and spits her gum out the window. "I said you've got the wrong person!" She puts a key in the ignition and starts the engine.

"I won't let you go," I say, rushing to the front of the car. "Not again." As she presses the gas pedal on the idling vehicle, bursts of hot air shoot out and sting my skin. "I know you hate me, Becca. And you have every reason to!"

She pounds her fists on the steering wheel and the horn blares above the noise of the city. "I'm not Becca!" she screams, stepping on the gas until the engine accelerates into an insidious roar that takes me back to Bethlehem...

to an incident I had forgotten…
or suppressed…
until now…

I kissed Alfred on the lips that late summer day in the middle of a sunflower field where he took me after dinner while Mrs. Garrity stacked her white dishes and while Becca went with Sergeant to get her prize, her favorite chocolate candy, the kind she got when he allowed her to dig deep into his pants pockets for them, one at a time. Sergeant never offered Alfred and I candy, but Becca was younger and deserved it more so I tried not to let it bother me too much. The kiss with Alfred only lasted a second, but I'll never forget it and I'll never know if Alfred liked it or not because he didn't say a word. But his face turned awfully red and he held my hand longer than he had ever held it before. Maybe I would have kissed him again if it weren't for the startling sound of Sergeant's truck engine revving up in the driveway. Alfred released my hand and ran when he heard it, got on his bike and disappeared down 8th Street. Mrs. Garrity scrambled around the kitchen, and I walked over to the end of the driveway, placed my fingers in my ears to ward off the offensive noise of the truck, and watched as Sergeant sat in the driver's seat with his face contorting. He closed his eyes, opened his mouth, and leaned back in his seat, shaking and quivering the way he had the night before by our bed. I stepped up to the side of the truck to have a closer look. He never saw me standing there. But Becca did. She smiled at me as she sat close by Sergeant's side, reaching deep into his pocket for her chocolate. The engine roared as Sergeant's legs stiffened and pressed the gas pedal to the floor while Becca reached farther into his pocket, delightfully digging until they both got what they wanted.

I was too young to understand what I witnessed that day, and I never thought about it again, until now, as I gaze through the windshield into Becca's troubled eyes and cringe in response to the earsplitting noise of the accelerating engine and the thought of what ghastly actions Sergeant performed on her after I left. She yanks the keys from the ignition, gets out of the car, and stands before me, face to face, sister to sister.

"What do you want?" she asks, shifting her eyes to avoid mine.

"I know this is hard," I say, trying to earn an ounce of trust I don't deserve. "I'm not going to pretend that I know how you're feeling right now because I don't. I just want to talk to you."

Her words fire from her mouth, short and direct. "How did you find me?"

"I spoke with Mrs. Rogers. She told me all that she knew and said I should contact Bola."

Becca shakes her head, staring off into the passing traffic. "You've got to be kidding me," she mutters, rubbing her hand across the back of her neck. As she talks, I can almost hear Becca's childhood lisp, and I am reminded of how many nights I sat next to her practicing her speech as she struggled to annunciate her words with a mouth that wouldn't allow it.

"They told me everything, Becca."

"Well, you wasted your time because they don't know anything about me," she says, folding her arms across her chest. "No one does."

"They told me that I might find you here," I say, carefully choosing my words. "And they told me about Sergeant. I'm so sorry."

"How dare you," she says, raising her voice. "It takes a lot of nerve to show up after all these years and act like you give a shit. Did your fairy-tale life not turn out the way you wanted, so you decided to make yourself feel better by visiting your pathetic little sister?"

A cold sweat emerges on the surface of my skin. I'd know exactly what to say if I were ten again. I'd wrap my arms around her and tell her that everything is going to be all right because we're together. I'd tell her that we can get through anything as long as we have each other.

"I don't blame you for wanting nothing to do with me, and you have every right to be upset. I was just hoping that…"

"My name isn't Becca," she interrupts, dropping her gaze downward as she leans back against the car. She could be five again, the way she looks, kicking pebbles by her feet and secretly wishing the world away.

"I'm so glad I found you," I say, pressing my hands against my thighs to steady them. "It's been so long."

"Exactly," she says, nodding her head. "It's been too long. What's the point?"

My chest stings from the dry desert air that rushes into my lungs as I try to catch a single deep breath before continuing. "I know it's not enough to say I'm sorry for everything, but I am."

"Sorry?" she asks, looking me in the eyes for the first time. "For what?"

"For leaving you without saying good-bye and for making you trust me the way Mom made me trust her. But most of all," I say, wringing my hands, "I'm sorry for what Sergeant did. I should have protected you." The apologies spill out of me, one after another.

"I don't know what you're talking about," she says, steadying her bottom lip between her teeth.

"Bola told me." Tears pool up in the base of her eyes. "And she told me about your son." Becca blinks, and tears stream down her cheeks, dangling for a moment from her chin before dropping to the ground. "If I could turn back time, I would change everything, Becca."

"Stop it!" she shouts, covering her ears. "I'm not Becca!" She wipes her eyes with her sleeve and brushes back the curls that stick to her dampened face.

"I should have told Mrs. Rogers what went on in that house," I say. "I hate myself for not saying anything."

Becca narrows her eyes and tilts her head. "You mean you knew?" she asks, stepping toward me, shifting her position to offensive, standing taller and more rigid than she did a moment ago. "You fucking knew?"

"I saw things," I say, shrinking in Becca's shadow. "Things that I knew were wrong." Her contempt for me couldn't possibly match my own.

She places her hands on her hips, sticks her chest out, and smiles the way she did on stage when she cunningly lured customers to her, like insects into a spider's web. "So that's it," she says, circling me with the audacity of a street-learned hustler.

"What do you mean?"

"You feel guilty. You didn't come here for me at all." She is only inches away, inundating me with the scent of her profession: smoke, alcohol, and designer perfume. "Is your conscience getting the best of you, big sister?" Becca's pupils swell into black, bottomless wells as she pulls a cigarette from her cleavage and holds it, unlit, between her fingers. "Is this the part where I'm supposed to throw my arms around you, tell you that I forgive you, and invite you over to my place for coffee so that we can reminisce about the good old days?" Using the cigarette as a pointer, she slowly traces the curves of my face, from my forehead to my chin, before placing it between her plump, glossed lips. "You always were the prettier one," she says, and she lights it with a shiny gold lighter, distinctly engraved with one long-stemmed rose. She draws in a mouthful of smoke and releases it into the early morning air. "Not anymore," she says, stepping back. "Listen, I'm gonna save you some trouble. You don't need to feel guilty anymore because I'm doing just fine, so no hard feelings. As a matter of fact," she says, running one hand along the side of her luxury vehicle, "I could say you did me a favor." She reaches into her car and pulls out a roll of money from the glove compartment. "Here," she says, tossing the cash at my feet before getting into her car. "For your flight home."

"Wait, Becca, don't go!" I slap my palms against the window as she starts the engine. "You don't have to live like this. You deserve better!" With the glow of the Vegas Strip lighting up her face, I can see the freckles that embodied an innocence that no longer exists. She shifts the car into drive.

"Becca is dead," she says and speeds off, firing gravel at my legs like a fully loaded pellet gun.

Mrs. Rogers warned me of this. She said that nothing could prepare me for the woman Becca had become. Rebecca Rose is alive and well. Friends call her Reba. Clients call her the best they've ever had, a real pro, willing to do anything for the right price. Out front, the bouncer promises that he will give Reba my message: the name and number of the hotel where I will be staying for a while because I don't believe what she said.

Becca is alive.

I'll prove it to her one way or another.

If I have to die trying.

"Michael, it's me."

"Hey," he says in a tone deepened by sleep.

"How are you?" I ask.

"Fine."

"And the church?"

"Good." He yawns. "Danni, it's four o'clock in the morning. What's going on?"

"I needed to hear your voice."

"Where are you?"

"Las Vegas."

"What?" he asks, raising his voice to match his surprise. "What the hell are doing in Las Vegas?"

"She's here Michael...I found her."

"What's she doing out there? Did you talk to her?"

"Yes."

"So how'd it go?"

"Not too well, I'm afraid."

"So what are you gonna do?" he asks.

"Help her, of course."

"How? Does she even want your help?" Through the phone I hear the bed squeak the way it does when Michael rolls over or quickly sits up. "Well? Does she?" I can't answer his question, and the urgency for a reply generates tension that I haven't felt from him before. "You can't save someone who doesn't want to be saved. You've been gone over a month; you have responsibilities here. What about me? What about the church? How long am I supposed to make excuses for a wife who just up and left? How do you think your absence makes me look?"

Michael spends hours, weeks, and months helping members of his church deal with problems. He's a friend and mentor with extraordinary patience, a quality I can love or hate.

"It makes you look real, Michael, like a real person with real problems, instead of a fucking saint!"

"I want to know when you're coming home," he demands.

"I'm not sure. I won't leave her again. I'm sorry if you don't understand. She needs me."

"I understand completely. Priorities, I mean." He sighs and clicks the television on to the early morning news.

"I thought you would support me through this," I say, speaking over the meteorologist's cheery forecast. "Not punish me for doing something I believe is right."

Michael fluffs his pillow with his fist and collapses back onto it. "I have supported you. For years I've stood on the sidelines of your past. It hasn't been easy, and it's affected what we could have, what we should have." He takes a deep breath and exhales slowly into the receiver.

"I thought you were OK with this," I say.

"I'm not OK with knowing that this marriage falls somewhere at the bottom of your list."

"That's not true."

"Then why am I here and you're there? I'm beginning to think that this isn't just about your sister anymore, Danielle. If you put half as much energy into your present as you do your past, we'd have a family by now."

For years, I convinced myself that Michael only instilled guilt as a tactful tool to keep parishioners on the straight and narrow so that one day they could be pleasingly judged by their Maker. "So you do blame me," I say. "All that talk over the years about God blessing us with a child when the time is right meant nothing?"

"How can God bless someone who isn't willing to receive it?"

"That's not fair and you know it."

"By the way," he says, changing the subject. "Who's Alexa?" His question catches me off guard. I never said anything about Alfred to Michael. I couldn't.

"Alexa?"

"She sent you flowers and called twice trying to reach you. She said she was a good friend of yours and would like to see you while she's in town. I don't believe you've ever mentioned her."

"I'm sure I must have at some point over the years. She was a friend of mine growing up in Bethlehem. She must have heard about Sergeant's death."

I won't tell him that I can't get Alexa off my mind and that somehow, in this very moment, I feel her absence more than his.

"One more piece to the unsolved puzzle that is your life, Danielle."

"What's that supposed to mean?"

"I'm sure you can figure it out. I'm tired and I have to get up in a couple of hours so I'm gonna go."

Michael can't see the phone shaking in my hand as he ends the call without another word. With the lights off, I can't see it either. Maybe I can fool myself into thinking

I'm OK, but loneliness has a way of creeping up in the dark. It won't be long before the sun peeks over the horizon and a new day begins. It's been several hours since Becca left me in the parking lot staring at her taillights as they disappeared down the highway. There was nothing I could do or say to get her to stay.

I would try to sleep if it weren't for the sudden pounding on the door that grows louder by the second, developing into a raucous beat that shakes the walls with every strike. I turn on the light, rub my eyes, and focus on the chain lock that rattles and clanks against the door. On the other side, someone is ferociously rapping like my heart within my chest. With one eye open, I walk to the door and peer out the peephole at a woman whose image is drastically distorted by the beveled edges of the tiny glass. In a glance, I wouldn't recognize her straight black hair, bronzed skin, or deep purple lips. But once again, it's her eyes that give her away, conveying such clarity in the midst of ambiguity. I unlock the door and allow her to enter.

Like a raging bull released from his pen, she tramps through the room, hurling remarks and comments in a furious fit that I am unable to process. The dress she is wearing matches her synthetic locks and clings so tightly to her body that it occasionally hikes up to expose the bottom curves of her buttocks. In a flurry of cursing, she takes a seat, rips off her wig, tosses it to the floor, and shakes out her long blond curls. She pulls a bottle of whiskey from her handbag, swallows nearly half, and slams it down on the table beside her. At this very moment, I can see our mother in her, the way her skin puckers between her brows in the same way that Amy frowned with despair the day she was born. If it were a compliment, I would tell her how much she reminds me of her. But it was Amy who started us on this track so long ago. I wouldn't wish her despicable traits on anyone, least of all Becca.

"Do you know what you did?" Becca asks, lifting an accusatory brow. She takes another mouthful of whiskey and tears the fake eyelash strips from her lids. "Do you have any idea what you fucking did?" she hollers, wiping and smearing the black tears that stream down her cheeks. "All I ever wanted was to forget," she explains, lifting the bottle to her mouth again. "I built a life here. I have customers who'll pay anything to spend time with me." Her eyes settle on the bottle in front of her. "They don't care where I'm from or what I used to look like. They want me as I am, right here, right now. No questions asked." She raises the bottle. "I'm not cheap either," she laughs. "As long as they get what they pay for, they keep coming back." She kicks off her heels. "Then you show up out of nowhere, on some sort of rescue mission, expecting some fucking happy, long-time-no-see reunion. Well, big sister, you can't help me. You've done nothing but hurt me my entire life." She rises to her feet and stumbles toward me, close enough for me to taste the whiskey on her breath. "And that's exactly what you managed to do again. But this time is different." She leans against me until my back presses into the door. "This time I can't let you get away with it!"

"I've made a lot of mistakes, Becca, but all I've ever wanted is what's best for you."

Becca staggers to the center of the room. "You've ruined me!" she says, lifting her bottle into the air. "So here's to you, Danni. A toast, to the best goddamned sister a girl could ever have." She trips, falls back onto the bed, and soaks her dress with the remainder of whiskey that spills from the bottle. Staring up at the ceiling, she chuckles the way Amy did when she talked about my father and the horrific night at the Bethlehem hotel where his brother dove from the ninth-floor window.

"I took a gig at the Motel 8 tonight," Becca says. "The fucking Motel 8!"

She struggles to a seated position, pulls a tissue from the nightstand, and wipes it across her face, removing the thick coat of makeup that conceals all that is Becca, from the chocolate colored freckles that sprinkle over her fair-skinned nose to the pink scar that trails down beneath it. Right before my eyes, she transforms into the girl I once knew.

"A bunch of frat boys from the club tonight wanted to show their friend a good time for his birthday," she says, staring down at the makeup-stained cloth. "I took the gig." Her lower lip begins to quiver. "It's been years since I've done anything like that." She lifts her head and peers out through a curtain of flaxen curls. "I'm Rebecca Rose, goddamn it! I have a name in this town!

Some of the most prestigious men in the world pay to be with me." She pulls up the strap of her dress that slips off her shoulder. "I sleep in five-star hotels and dine in fine restaurants! I don't waste my time on young boys who wanna throw back a shitload of beer and get off while their buddy gets a hard on over his first lap dance!"

If she'd allow it, I'd wrap myself around her to keep her from falling apart the way I would have done with Mom when I was five years old had the men in white given me the chance.

Using the edge of the bedpost as support, Becca lifts herself to her feet. "But I did tonight! Because of you!" Her knees buckle in the hysteria that builds behind the stream of erupting tears. "Because you brought it all back, everything I worked so hard to forget!" She drops to her knees, covers her face with both hands, and sobs. "I did something horrible tonight, Danni. Oh God, I did something unimaginable!" Her eyes narrow. "And it's all your fault! I hate you! More than ever, I fucking hate you!"

A hush falls over the room as Becca recounts the incidents of the night, describing in graphic detail everything that happened. In my worst nightmare, I couldn't have imagined such a calamity, so tragic, wretched, and vile. In these darkest hours, the voice returns, prodding and poking at my sanity. *Close your eyes! Don't look back! Close your eyes! Don't look back!* So with Becca screaming in front of me and the voice screaming within, I drop to the floor and listen as my sister relives the most horrific night of her life.

❧

"I didn't want to go home to an empty house, so I turned around, went back to the club, and talked with some of the girls for a while in the back room." Becca leans back against the bed, folds her legs together Indian-style, and rests her chin against the palm of her hand to stop her teeth from knocking against one another.

"We were joking about some of the customers," she continues, "when Rocco, the club manager, came in and asked if any of us would be interested in making some extra cash after hours." The freckles on Becca's face are less prominent when backed by the shades of red that flush her cheeks—Erma would say, like chocolate sprinkles on strawberry ice cream instead of vanilla.

"I took the gig because I wanted to get my mind off everything," she says, and she runs her hand through her curls to twist around her finger. "I got to the motel around midnight," she adds. "Like they wanted."

The sky has lightened enough to offer a hint of orange creeping into the horizon. This is one of Alfred's favorite times of the day and, by far, my worst. The night is gentler and more discreet, much better at keeping the secrets that daylight reveals and much better at hiding the circles under Becca's eyes as she describes how a young frat brother opened the door and escorted her into a small motel room that reeked of marijuana, stale beer, and cheap aftershave. It was nothing she hadn't seen before: a bunch of college kids hanging out, looking for a good time for their friend's birthday. She danced for them while they passed around a pipe and drank to the birthday boy. It was a one-hour dancing gig, nothing more. It was what she had agreed on, and most of the time things went as planned.

"Some of the guys were getting a little rowdy," she continues, "joking about the birthday boy still being a virgin, when one of them grabbed the kid, forced him into a chair, and duct-taped his hands and feet together so he couldn't move." Becca's lower jaw slams against the top, trapping her tongue in between. "He seemed OK with it," she adds, barely flinching at the blood that oozes from the dangling flap of flesh. "They chanted his name and took turns funneling beer into his mouth."

Watching Becca, it's difficult to tell if it's the rapid flow of blood-infused saliva or the repulsion of her story that is quickly draining the color from her cheeks.

"His name ith Jake," she says, returning to the speech impediment she endured as a child as she describes the fair-skinned boy she danced for. "And he'th beautiful," she whispers. A river of black tears runs down her face, muddying the crimson streaks before them.

Becca coughs, choking on the bitter taste of her words as she describes the way she danced and provoked him the way a girl of her profession does. "I was there to dance," she insists. "That's it. I wanted to get my mind off things for a while and show him a good time, ya know? I didn't want it to go any further than that." She rubs her face across her sleeve. "He'th just a kid. A beautiful, innocent kid," she says, crying over how he blushed and turned away when the boys tugged and pulled at her clothing until her naked body touched his. "Jake was shy," she says. "And polite." Becca places her hands over her heart. "He called me Miss Rose."

The music thumped louder as his friends cut the duct tape off his hands and feet, and urged him to make a move, calling him a faggot if he didn't. "That's when the room started spinning," she says, holding her head in her hands. "There must have been something in my drink because I couldn't think straight. But I know that he didn't want to do it," Becca says, recalling his moist palms that reluctantly pulled her down on the bed beside him under the pressure of his peers. "And then he kissed me," she says, closing her eyes the way that Jake did when he rested his quivering, inexperienced lips on hers. "Soft and gentle." Becca's eyes never looked as blue as they do right now, framed in smudged black liner. Or as shattered. "I tried to leave," she insists. "But the room was spinning and they surrounded the bed, chanting his name until Jake unzipped his pants and climbed on top of me."

Before my eyes, Becca reverts back to the insecure child she once was, struggling to pronounce her words. "I didn't want it to happen, Danni. I thwear. No matter how much they were paying me. I'm not like that! He'th a kid!"

There's a part of Becca that never grew up. I can tell by the way that she's looking at me, seeking my approval while trying to convince me of her true intentions—the way she did at the age of five, just weeks before I left the Garritys, when she woke up early one morning cold, wet, and reeking of urine. I lifted the covers to a large yellow stain that had soaked through the sheets into the mattress. Becca had never wet the bed before. I cleaned her up, washed the sheets in the tub, and dried them for almost two hours with a blow dryer so Sergeant and Mrs. Garrity wouldn't find out. "I'm thorry, Danni," Becca had said, apologizing for doing something she knew would get us into trouble. She pushed her glasses up high on her nose and wiped the saliva that leaked down from the side of her mouth with the sleeve of her shirt, "I won't do it again, I promith."

But Becca did do it again, the very next night and every night after that. I didn't know why, she didn't know herself, but she begged me not to tell Sergeant, who threatened never to take her to the candy store again if she ever misbehaved.

Becca gets up from the floor and walks to the window. Staring out into the early morning, she lifts her hand to the glass and traces the outline of her reflection with her index finger. She crosses her arms in front of her, wraps them tightly around her chest, and briskly rubs up and down to ward off the chill that consumes her as she continues describing how the frat boys drew in closer, hovering over them like vultures until Jake did exactly what they wanted. With his eyes still closed, he pulled his semi-erect penis from his boxers and forced himself inside of her, shaking the bed beneath her with every thrust until collapsing from relief and exhaustion. They cheered his success as he climbed off her, zipped his pants, and gathered Becca's clothes from the floor for her to dress.

"I tried not to look at him," she says. "I just wanted to get the hell out of there. But like a perfect gentleman, he escorted me to the door and apologized. Can you believe that? He apologized to me!"

I wait for her to finish.

"And that's when I saw it," she continues, wrapping her arms tighter around herself to keep from falling apart. "On his stomach. The birthmark, like a dolphin leaping from the ocean." Becca screams out to a Maker who turned his back on her long ago. "Oh God, what have I done?" She rushes toward me. "You did this!" she screams. "This is your fault! You should have never come here! You ruined everything!"

"I'm sorry, Becca," I say and step in front of her to absorb her wrath. "I want to help you."

"Do you know what you've done?" she asks, stabbing her finger into my chest as spit begins to foam up in the corners of her mouth. "He's my son!" she screams, painfully spewing out each word, like fragments of broken glass. "Jake ith my son!" A flushing heat rises up from my neck as she pushes past me and opens the door. "What do I do now?" she sobs, hitting her chest with closed fists. "How do I live with this?" Becca wipes her tears and allows the fire in her gut to ignite the words that burn off her tongue.

"I didn't want to hate you, Danni!" she says with blood still dripping from her mouth. "But you'll pay for this! I promise, you'll fucking pay for all of it!"

21

"**M**ay I speak with the reverend, please?"

"This is Reverend Pane. May I ask who's calling?"

"My name is Rebecca Rose."

"How can I help you, Miss Rose?"

"I'd like to make an appointment to speak with you."

"Sure, what is it regarding?"

She pauses on the other end of the phone.

"Hello? Miss? Are you still there?"

"I'm still here."

"What would you like to discuss?"

"Sins."

"Well, you've come to the right place. Can you be more specific?"

"Sins of the flesh, Reverend," she says. "Lust, desire, promiscuity: I dabble in all of them. You get the picture."

Michael hesitates, stunned but intrigued by her candor. "Yes, of course. You can come in anytime, preferably after a service." There could be tears or laughter behind her exhalation that follows—Michael isn't sure which. "Miss Rose, is this about repentance? Are you seeking forgiveness?"

"I'll see you soon, Reverend," she replies, wiping her eyes as she prepares to reach an all-new low because she's not seeking forgiveness at all.

What Rebecca Rose is seeking...

is revenge.

The scent of her perfume wafting up the church aisle catches his attention as the last parishioner exits. Michael looks up from the podium while gathering notes from his evening service.

"Can I help you?" he asks, closing his Bible.

"I wouldn't have come if I didn't think so," she says, strutting toward him. Only a dead man wouldn't notice the curves of her white dress or the scooped neckline that reveals the top of her cleavage. It's been well over a month since Danni left, since he's felt the warmth of her body beside him at night or pleasured in the sensation of her skin against his.

"What can I do for you?" he asks, reminded of Romans 8:7 ("For the mind that is set on the flesh is hostile to God, for it does not submit to God's law; indeed, it cannot."). He repeats the verse twice to himself before she answers.

"I'm Rebecca Rose," she says, stopping before him, "and I…"

"Welcome, welcome," Michael interrupts, extending a hand out to hers as he steps down from the pulpit to meet her eye to eye. "I'm Reverend Pane, Reverend Michael Pane. Is this your first time here?"

She smiles and nods, firmly holding his hand with an assuredness that matches her appearance. He's never seen her before. He's sure of it. He would have remembered. With all the beautiful women in the city, she stands out in a way that's difficult to put his finger on.

"Your message tonight was inspiring," she says, giving his hand a subtle squeeze before releasing it to fluff the Dior scent from her hair. "Unlike any others I've listened to. You have a real gift, Reverend Pane."

"Thank you. It's been a calling of mine for as long as I can remember. So you're the woman I spoke with on the phone," he says, trying not to stare at the way her skin glistens under the bright church lights or the way her eyes sparkle and shimmer like sun kissed pools of cool blue water.

"It's nice to meet you face to face," she says, setting her handbag down in the front pew before taking a seat beside it. "I don't mean to be rude, Reverend, but these heels weren't made for comfort."

"Not at all," Michael says. "Please, make yourself comfortable." He coughs, bothered by the way his heart begins to race in her presence. "So on the phone you said you wanted to discuss sin."

Rebecca crosses one bare leg over the other and slips her foot from her shoe. "You think it was a man who designed the first high heel, Reverend?" she asks, lifting a corner of her mouth to a half smile while massaging her feet. The man in him notices the pink polish on her toes and the matching gloss that moistens her lips, but the Reverend searches deeper than the flesh.

Michael nods. "Actually it was," he says, conceding to her diversion. "Only you'll be surprised to know that high heels were first designed for men, European aristocrats in the 1600s. They were a status symbol then, worn by the elite, the nonworkers." He rubs his chin and squints his eyes as though channeling his memory. "I believe it wasn't until the 1630s that women, trying to appropriate masculine power, began wearing them."

Rebecca switches legs to remove her other shoe. "That was a rhetorical question, Reverend," she laughs. "But I'm curious as to how someone like you would know that."

Michael crosses his arms and leans against the pew. "Don't ask me," he says. "I have a wealth of useless information up here." He taps his forefinger against his head and laughs for the first time since Danni left. He raises his brow, "I suppose growing up with three sisters might have something to do with my knowledge of shoes."

It's easy for Rebecca to see why Danni married him. He's handsome and witty, with a heart of gold that's easy to read. Attributes that, on any other day, would be considered a strength instead of a weakness. But it's what Rebecca Rose preys on.

"So you come from a big family," she says, sliding her dress slightly above her knees to reveal the dark space that exists between them. "I suppose your sisters are as beautiful as you are handsome."

Michael clears his throat. "They're lovely women... and thank you."

"As is your wife, I'm sure."

"Beautiful as well," he says and rakes his fingers through his hair.

"She's a lucky girl," Rebecca says, probing on. "She must enjoy your sermons even more than the rest of us. I'll bet she doesn't miss one." She looks around the church. "I'd love to meet her."

Michael loosens the tie around his neck. "Actually, she's out of town for a while."

"That's too bad."

Michael nods.

"Well you must have children running around here somewhere, right?" she asks and playfully peeks beneath the pews.

"Unfortunately no, not yet," he says, amused. "But I'm sure you didn't come here to discuss my family matters, Miss Rose."

"Do you believe in hell, Reverend?" Rebecca asks, abruptly changing the subject while moving her gentle massage from her feet to her calves.

"I'm asked that question often," he says, stepping away from the pew with his back to her. He puts one hand in his pocket and rubs the back of his neck with the other. "But no matter how many times I answer, it's still difficult. I pray that all souls find their way to Jesus, accept and acknowledge Him as the Son of God, and therefore one day enter into the kingdom of heaven."

Rebecca pulls her mane of golden curls up off her shoulders and ties the bundle into a lose knot at the nape of her neck. She waits for Michael to turn before pulling her bare legs up to sit Indian-style on the pew. If Michael moves to stand in front of her, he'll be able to see the thin strip of white lace between her legs and she'll have him exactly where she wants him. If he doesn't, if he walks away, his willpower is strong and his commitment to Danni stronger.

"And those who don't?" she asks, looking noticeably more subdued than when she arrived. "What about the sinners who never find God? Or those who give in to temptation and act on something they know they shouldn't. Where do they go, Reverend?"

Michael swallows hard and turns away. "We all sin, Miss Rose," he says walking to his podium. "The body is weak, but the mind and soul can be far stronger with the guidance of Jesus Christ. Is that why you're here tonight? Do you need to be forgiven?" He picks up his Bible and holds it against his chest. "I can pray with you," he says, looking up at the cross that hangs above him. "If that's what you're looking for."

Rebecca pulls her knees to her chest to further expose the lacy gap between her thighs. "What about you, Reverend?" she asks, luring him to her. "Do you sin?"

With his back still to her, Michael closes his eyes, once again reciting Romans 8:7 while trying to ignore the images of her warm, bare skin against the cool, wooden pew. "Miss Rose, I'd like to help you," he says, ignoring her question. "If you would just tell me what you want."

"It must be such an arduous task," she says. "And please, call me Rebecca."

"What do you mean?"

"Your calling. Always doing for others. Certainly you feel the need to be selfish every once in a while. To do something you wouldn't normally do simply because you have needs and wants like the rest of us."

Michael's heart elevates to the growing discomfort of an aching groin. Never before has the stillness of the church brought such torment. "As I said," he answers, squeezing his eyes shut. "We all sin. What's important is that we learn and grow from our mistakes." Michael grips the binding of his Bible until his knuckles turn white. "Life is a journey, Rebecca, with countless tests and learning experiences along the way. If we live through Christ, we will be led home to eternal life."

In the silence of the church, it's easy to hear Michael's quickening breath.

"Have you ever given in to temptation, Michael?" Rebecca calls him by name in a voice that is sweet and sultry, the way her clients prefer. "Because you wanted something so bad?" Michael tenses as his aching grows to an uncontrollable erection. "Have you ever acted on something"—she continues, matching her breath to his—"just for the fuck of it?"

The church bells ring. It's 6:00 p.m., and the lights dim to an automatic timer. She's played this game before. Many times. Only this time it's personal.

"What do you want from me?" Michael asks, placing his Bible down in front of him.

"The question is, Michael, what do you want from me?" Rebecca parts her knees to entice him with the very temptation he speaks against. Michael lifts a cloth from his podium, covers the sacred book, and turns to her, growing harder with each step that brings him closer to her offering.

"Like candy from a baby," she whispers, pleased by the growing bulge in his pants. Rebecca pulls the neckline of her dress down and shakes her hair loose until her tousled curls spill over her exposed breasts.

"I can't do this," Michael says, standing before her.

"You need this as much as I do," she says, lifting his hands to her breasts.

Michael bows his head. "Why are you doing this? Why did you come here?"

Rebecca doesn't answer, enticing him by the growing desire that mounts in the seconds of silence that follow.

Michael slides his hands to her waist, grabs her curves firmly with both hands, and squeezes to fill his palms with the soft flesh of a woman. "Is this what you came here for?" he asks, lifting her onto him. "Is this what you want?" He wraps her legs around him and grinds his stomach against her lace that has dampened by an equal yearning. "You need this as much as I do, don't you?" Michael says, unzipping his pants while leaning to brush his tongue over her hardened nipples. "Talk to me," he says and presses his rigid penis into the thin strip of material that separates his flesh from hers, taunting her with his masculinity before pushing around the lace to enter.

"I need you, Michael," Rebecca moans, being pulled down onto him.

"Show me," Michael says, panting with pleasure, "I want to feel you cum." Rebecca clasps her hands behind his neck to savor her first orgasm before being bent over the chestnut pew where countless parishioners have sat to listen to the reverend preach the gospel.

"Fuck me, baby," she cries out, loud enough to echo through the righteous walls of the church, because Danni deserves this.

Michael lifts her dress, exposes her bare buttocks, and caves into his appetite of the flesh.

"I'm cuming," he says, releasing into her months of frustration and deprivation. Michael steps back, lowers her dress, and wipes the sweat from his forehead. "You can't come back here," he says, zipping his pants while staring out into his once sacred space. "I mean it." Rebecca slides into her heels and throws her handbag over her shoulder. "Relax, Reverend."

"No one can ever find out about this," Michael says, catching his breath. "Do you understand me?"

"I said relax." Rebecca straightens the tie around Michael's neck and delivers a kiss to his cheek that leaves a red stain. "It's like you said, Reverend—we all sin." She hands him a shiny black card with her number etched into a pink embossed rose. "Some of us just hide it better than others." Rebecca tosses back her hair and exits as she arrived, smiling despite the lump that swells in her throat. She got what she came for, and Michael got what he needed.

One good sinner deserves another.

Amen.

22

O n the outskirts of Las Vegas, where the desert sand meets the Strip, there is a seldom-seen plant called the ghost flower. Spending most of its life underground, it grows in quiet obscurity, surfacing only when conditions are favorable to bloom. Since it does not require sunlight to survive, the flower, when it appears, is a ghastly, unnatural white. The ghostly translucency of the pale blooming flower makes it rare, unusual, and fascinating.

"When I promised to keep in touch, I meant it," Alexa says, stepping from her car into the open desert field where I asked her to meet me. "I made my first trip to the Big Apple hoping you could show me around." She bends to pick a white flower growing in the field. "For you," she says, speaking in the sweet, delicate voice that enchanted me as a child.

"It's beautiful," I say. "Thank you."

"I briefly spoke with your husband on the phone," she adds. "I hope you don't mind."

"Not at all. I'm flattered that you made the trip."

Alexa appears different than when I saw her in Bethlehem, softer and more relaxed. Maybe it's the easy expression on her face or the long cotton sundress that floats over her lean, white body in the desert wind. She leans against the car, presses her hands into her pockets the way Alfred used to, and drops her head to hide from the last rays of sun that tint her delicate cheeks to match the faded red tinge on her lips. As the sun slips behind the mountain peaks, I am reminded of all that is Alfred and how the years apart have only managed to bring us closer together. Never would I have expected to find such comfort in his unique transformation.

"You changed your hair," I say, noticing the way Alexa's newly bobbed tresses sway back and forth over her shoulders when she moves. "It becomes you." I smile to the old familiar feeling of butterflies in my stomach. "I'm glad you came, Alfred...I mean, Alexa." I throw my hand over my mouth and shake my head. "I'm sorry."

"Don't be," she laughs. "Old habits die hard. So what are you doing here? Sin City isn't exactly the kind of place for a reverend's wife."

"You're right about that," I say, wondering if she senses my longing for her. "Becca's here, Alexa. At least she was here. It's a long story."

Alexa nods. "I hope you find her and that the two of you can work it out. How long are you staying?" she asks, tilting her head in question.

"As long as it takes, I guess."

"What about your husband? You must be eager to get home to him." Alexa kicks off her sandals and brushes her bare feet across the desert sand.

"To be honest, my life is kind of a mess right now."

"I'm sorry to hear that, Danni. How so?" she asks, straightening her face as though her entire future rests on my answer.

I take a deep breath. When I asked Alexa to meet me here, I spent all night deciding what to wear. I chose a coral blouse that would accentuate what's left of my summer tan and bring out the auburn tones in my hair. I planned how I would act and what I would say, hoping that my words and body language would reveal enough but not too much because there's a fine line between getting a reaction and showing desperation.

"Marriage isn't as easy as I thought it would be. Michael is a good man, but I don't think he's ever really understood me. Maybe I've never understood him either. All I know is that he deserves the kind of wife who will devote her life to him and the church. Someone who can give him the children he's always wanted. As much as I've tried, I've never been able to give him either."

"But you love him, right?" Alexa asks, nervously shaking her leg. She looks away to wait for my response.

"I'll never be able to give him what he wants, Alexa."

"If you love him, it'll all work out," she says, shifting her eyes to mine. "Love conquers all, doesn't it?"

I watch as Alexa's pupils expand to embrace the soft radiance of evening and am reminded of how her most exquisite moments come with no effort at all.

"I'm still trying to figure that one out," I say, throwing my hands up. "Look at me. I traveled thousands of miles for a sister who wants nothing to do with me and now, instead of going home to a husband who loves me, I'm here in the middle of a desert field getting breathless over my childhood crush." In nervous anticipation of her response, I tuck my hair behind my ears and laugh. "Crazy, right?"

Alexa's irritation is evident by the tone of her voice, not the volume. "Childhood crush? Is that what this is?"

"I don't know what this is, Alexa. I've been trying to figure it out my whole life."

"If you love your husband, Danni," she says, emphasizing the word *love*, "he should be all that matters and you should go back before it's too late. It's that simple." Alexa pushes her back off the car, steps toward me, and grabs my shoulders. "Do you love him? Yes or no. It's a simple question."

"I need more time to think about things, that's all."

"That doesn't answer my question," she says. "And you've had twenty years to think."

The scent of her skin washes over me, invigorating my senses with the combination of a subtle masculine musk and the sweet floral bloom of a desert flower.

"Why are you here, Danni?" she asks, pulling me closer to where I've always wanted to be, where I can bask in her warmth as I did on the nights we lay side by side on Alfred's bed. "And what's making you stay?" As expected, she's more beautiful this close, more delicate, more intriguing, and more difficult to resist. "If you love your husband, say it, but if you don't..." Alexa rests her lips on mine, breathing into me the passion she's suppressed since she was an adolescent boy, softening her voice to a sensual whisper. "I've thought about you every day since I was thirteen years old," she says.

Turning away from Alfred was something I could never do. With Alexa, it's no different, perhaps harder. With one hand pressed firmly into the curve of my back, she lifts my shirt with the other and runs her fingers up and down my stomach. "Have you thought about me?" she asks, stopping where my bra begins. "Have you dreamed of this as I have?" Alexa's hair spills down over her face as she caresses the smooth skin between my breasts. "Tell me what you want," she says, holding me closer. Alexa's skin moistens with excitement in the dry desert air, and I kiss her, the way I kissed Alfred behind the Garrity house amid the towering sunflowers, only longer, holding less back than ever before and knowing that a kiss will never be enough. Michael was right. This trip isn't just about my sister.

"I can't do this, Alexa," I say. "I'm sorry. I want to more than anything, but it's not right."

She pulls her hand back and steps away. "Goddamn it, Danni. If you love your husband, say it!" She gets back into her car. "But if not, then you're nothing but a fucking coward and I never want to see you again!"

When Alfred shot Sergeant, he yelled so loud that the neighborhood dogs howled in the distance. It was like he had to scream on the outside to cover the anguish he felt on the inside. I would have done anything to take his pain away. Anything at all. Alexa's tires rip into the sand as she races out of the desert field. But there are no dogs here to respond.

There's only me.

And the silent blooms of the ghost flower.

23

The Big Apple is warmer and mustier than when I left months ago. There's a damp, stale odor that seeps through the car windows to welcome me home. I had hoped to return with good news, but everything went horribly wrong. The girls at the club said that Becca left town unexpectedly, with no explanation. They weren't sure whether or not she'd ever be coming back. But I waited anyway, for her and for Alexa, anticipating another chance that never came. Just ahead, the steeple of the Evangelical Church reaches toward the sky, standing out amid the other buildings that surround it. In proclamation of the noon hour, the bell in the church tower chimes out a resounding hymn. With the exception of a few regulars, the parking lot is empty. Across the street is the house that Michael and I have lived in for nearly fifteen years. By now, there should be a wreath on the front door, a planter on the stoop, and children running in and out. I should, after all this time, happily call it home. But it looks as stark and lonely today as it ever has, perhaps more so.

Several people exit the church through large double doors, marking the completion of the late morning service. I enter the historic cathedral and take a seat in the last pew. An array of color dances over the cross that hangs above the pulpit as the sun shines through the stained glass windows that poignantly depict the Stations of the Cross. The last time I attended church was for Sergeant's memorial service. I didn't say a single prayer that day as the congregation folded their hands, bowed their heads, and prayed that Sergeant would rest in peace. If there is a God, he will see to it that he doesn't. According to the news, police have ruled out Mrs. Garrity as a suspect and the murder is still under investigation. Sergeant never made a will, so his assets, which consisted of nothing more than a few hundred dollars and the run-down house on 8th Street automatically went to Mrs. Garrity, But rumor has it that Mrs. Garrity happened upon something one afternoon as she cleaned out that old house, something that the cheap bastard never wanted her to find: large sums of money in the form of cold, hard cash, neatly rolled and stuffed inside the stacks of empty paint cans that were piled against the basement walls. I place my hands in prayer position in honor of Sarah Garrity, that she may find a way to enjoy the bittersweet fruits of his labor, and for Becca and Sergeant's son Jake, that he may never discover the rotten roots from which he came.

The aisle of the church seems longer than it did on the day of my wedding, when the desire to hear the words "Mr. and Mrs. Reverend Michael Pane" drew me to the altar where Michael waited for me in front of a church full of applauding parishioners. But I could hear a pin drop in here today as I walk the halls that lead to his office. He'll be happy to see me and to hear what I have to tell him, that I'm home to stay for better or for worse, from this day forward, 'til death do us part.

On any other day, I would swing open the door and throw my arms around him, but the sound of angry whispers stops me inches away from his office. It's unlike Michael to get so heated in his place of worship. As long as I've known him, few things have ever caused him outrage. I move closer and jump at the startling slam of the rear office door that exits to the back parking lot, where a car starts and races off. Michael is pacing on the other side of the door, mumbling something to himself that I can't make out. I lift my fist, take a deep breath, and lightly knock. He races to the door, grabs the knob, and jerks it open.

"What now?" he snaps. His eyes widen and the color of his face fades to an alarming pallor. "Danielle!" he says, leaning past me to search the empty corridor. "You're home." He puts his arm around my shoulder, jerks me toward him, and releases me.

"Wow, don't act so excited to see me," I say.

He shoves his hands into his pockets and shrugs his shoulders. "I wasn't expecting you, that's all."

"Who were you expecting then?" I ask, tousling his hair the way I used to when it was fun to kid around. "It's good to be home; I missed you."

"Yeah, I missed you, too," he says, and he combs his hair down with his fingers while staring at the floor.

I slip my jacket off my shoulders and place it on the chair in front of Michael's desk, where papers and folders are piled high. The bookshelf needs dusting, and the floor needs waxing. "Looks like you could use a little help in here," I say, straightening out a pile on his desk.

"I'll take care of it," he says, shaking his leg the way Alfred did on the day his teacher phoned Sergeant to question Alfred's absence from school.

"You don't seem too happy to see me," I say. "I guess I expected you to be more surprised...in a good way, ya know? What's wrong?"

Michael is clearly troubled, and his leg won't stop trembling. "Nothing," he says in a voice that quivers as rapidly as his leg. I should throw my arms around him until the shaking stops because I owe him that much, but Michael has never needed comforting before and I've never been any good at helping someone on the verge of a breakdown. I suppose nothing has changed after all. No matter how much time passes, there's always something, no matter how big or how small, that brings me back.

To Bethlehem.

Mrs. Hopkins called early that evening, after Wednesday night's chicken potpie dinner, as those goddamned metal cars screeched along the tracks of the steel plant, like nails dragging slowly across a chalkboard. Maybe it was the insufferable sounds of the plant that suddenly made me feel sick to my stomach, or maybe it was the way that Sergeant didn't say a word as he listened to Alfred's teacher.

"Hello, Mr. Garrity. It's Mrs. Hopkins. I'm sorry to bother you. I'm calling about Alfred." Sergeant's face gleamed with intensity as he listened. "He wasn't in school today, and I was wondering if everything is all right. As you know, we have a very strict attendance policy here, and it's not like Alfred to miss class without a phone call from home."

Mrs. Hopkins's voice was loud and clear on the other end of the phone. From where I stood, I could hear every word if I held my breath and listened real hard. But poor Alfred didn't hear a thing from the far corner of the living room where he sat with his platinum head buried deep into the final chapters of *Huck Finn*. The tips of Sergeant's ears grew red as he targeted Alfred, and my stomach flipped a couple of times until something thick and lumpy shot up into the back of my throat. Sarah's chicken potpie was tasty most of the time, but on nights when Sergeant got home early, it seemed unusually dry which made it harder to swallow and impossible to digest.

"Thank you, Mrs. Hopkins," Sergeant said, holding the phone between his ear and his shoulder while unbuckling his belt with both hands. "I'll get to the bottom of this."

He slid the belt out from his pants and snapped it several times, startling Alfred, who dropped his book and jumped to attention. "I can assure you, it won't happen again."

Sergeant hung up the phone and concentrated on Alfred, who stood before him with his head lowered and his legs trembling like a newborn fawn. Alfred's lily-white face reddened as the second hand ticked past the early evening hour. Without a word in his defense, Alfred grabbed the kitchen chair and dragged it out from beneath the table. It must have been something pretty bad to make Alfred skip school knowing what the consequences of his actions would be. I wondered if it was that bully again, picking on him, calling him a snow-white faggot.

I sat on the sofa and pretended to be interested in the evening news, pretending not to hear Sergeant positioning himself on the chair as Alfred's pants dropped to the floor and pretending not to hear the sharp slaps of the leather belt across Alfred's bare bottom. But I heard it all, the strikes and the restrained whimpers. I don't know how many times Sergeant whipped Alfred that night—I lost count after ten, when Erma's ant song grew so loud in my head that I couldn't hear the swift, crisp snaps of leather on his smooth skin anymore. But he must have hit him a lot because Alfred flinched and took long deep breaths when Sergeant made him sit on the end of the sofa to take the rest of his punishment.

"You're a soldier, boy. Act like one," he said, demanding that Alfred sit perfectly erect for the rest of the night, hands folded on his lap, looking directly at the clock on the wall until it was time for bed: no talking, no reading, no watching television, and absolutely no sleeping. From the corner of my eye, I watched Alfred do as he was told. His bloodshot eyes focused on the second hand before him that echoed through the room with a pounding cadence. Blotches covered his milky skin, and the outline of Sergeant's hand welted up on his forearm. It lasted for hours but was gone in plenty of time for school the next morning. Sergeant was real smart about where he left any lasting marks, and I was real smart about making sure that Becca and I followed all of his rules so that he would never have to use that belt on us.

Michael's office phone rings. "You have the wrong number," he says and hangs up. He looks tired, thin, and frustrated by the phone that rings again. "Damn kids," he says as he picks it up and slams it back down. "They really need to find something more productive to do with their time, like attending a service or two." Irritation deepens the furrow between his eyes. "Or they could burn up some of that youthful energy volunteering around here. An idle mind is the devil's playground," he says, pacing.

"There's a million things I could have them do to keep them off a fast track to nowhere.

"They're kids, Michael," I say. "Is everything all right? You're not yourself. You seem rather tense."

"You caught me a little off guard," he says, yanking the phone cord from the wall with one hand. "Everyone's allowed to have a bad day once in a while, aren't they?" He shuffles through a stack of papers on his desk. "If anyone should know that, it's you, right?" he says, glancing up from his work with one stern eyebrow raised higher than the other.

"Yeah, of course. I just expected a different homecoming, that's all."

"Homecoming?" Michael scrolls through a message on his cell. "Is that what you call this?" he says, replying with a quick text. "You disappear for months and now show up out of the blue, and you expected a different homecoming?" He sets the volume on his phone to vibrate and puts it in his pocket. "This was your choice," he says. "You did this."

"Look, Michael, I don't want to argue. I missed you."

He rests his forehead in the palm of his hand. "I can't do this now, Danielle. I have a lot of work to finish." Outside, a car screeches to a halt, a door slams shut, and footsteps tap across the parking lot, up the stairs, and onto the small porch that leads to his office. Michael's phone hums and vibrates in his pocket as he wraps my jacket around my shoulders and leads me by the small of my back to the hall door. "We'll talk later over dinner, around eight. I promise."

"Michael, what the hell is going on? I've never seen you act like this before."

"Don't worry about it," he says, startled by the sudden rapping on the door.

"Are you expecting someone?" I ask. A fist slams against the wooden frame and the knob jiggles.

"Trust me, I'll take care of it," he says, escorting me out.

"What do you mean you'll take care of it? You'll take care of what?"

A band of perspiration has formed on Michael's forehead. A drop of sweat trickles down his temple and onto his cheek. "Michael, you're scaring me. Tell me what's going on!" He wipes his face with his sleeve.

"Don't read anything into this, Danielle, really. Just go home." Michael's head snaps back as chimes ring out in the bell tower and a woman screams out his name.

"Michael! I know you're in there! Open the door, baby!"

He wipes his palms against his pants as a sudden rush of red rises up from his neck to his cheeks and spills into the whites of his eyes. His breathing has accelerated, and I can sense the overwhelming pulse of his blood surging through dilated vessels as she strikes the door again, alternating between open-palmed slaps and the dull heavy thuds of closed fists.

"I don't like being ignored, Michael!" she yells. The door jolts and a loose hinge clanks against the frame. "Do you hear me? I'm not the type of girl who will be ignored!"

If this is a bad dream, I want to wake up now before my rapid heart creates an insufferable pain that shoots from my gut into my chest. And if this is real, I want to have the courage to open the door and face the woman who's screaming out my husband's name.

"What the hell is she talking about?" I ask, straining to speak past the obtrusive lump that has formed in my throat. "Please tell me this isn't what it seems."

Michael shoves his hands into his pockets, drops his head, and exhales until his chest caves inward. I never saw him broken before, surrendering the dignity and manhood he's spent a lifetime earning. I want to grab him and shake him into the man I married, the man I love and respect, the man who would prove to me that this is all a big mistake.

"Let me in, you son of a bitch!" she yells, releasing a series of kicks against the bottom of the door. "You think you can just push me away like that? You owe me, you bastard! Now open the door, or I'll make sure your precious wife hears all about what you did while she was gone."

Perhaps now more than ever I should listen to the voice in my head that has returned, squawking like a mother goose who instinctively protects her young from the dangers of hostile predators. *Close your eyes! Don't look back! Close your eyes! Don't look back!* I press my hands against my ears.

"My God, Michael, what did you do?" I ask as the door bumps with a continuous barrage of strikes.

"Open the fucking door!" she screams.

Michael shakes his head, walks to the door, and places his hand on the knob. "I made a horrible mistake, Danielle," he says, and he turns the handle. The pounding has stopped, and the silence gives way to the woman's labored breath, which seeps through the cracks around the door. Tears pool up in Michael's lower lids. "I messed up, and there's nothing I can do about it. I went against everything I believe in and everything I stand for. In my weakness, I've forsaken God and betrayed you. I'm supposed to be better than this." He rips the crucifix from his neck and tosses it to the floor. "I won't ask you to forgive me. I don't deserve it. I just want you to know how sorry I am." With trembling hands, he wipes his eyes and opens the door.

And so it goes, the fine art of betrayal, masterful and subtly deviant in its ability to destroy as it takes root and manifests into a terminal cancer. As Michael turns away from a wife he deceived and a God he defied, I think about how life can change in an instant and force you down a bumpy road. My chest is heavy and my throat narrows, limiting my airflow. I've felt pain before. When they rolled Mom away, I cried so hard that my lungs felt like they would explode. When I searched for solace in the front seat of Eric Seton's Mustang beneath the fiery blast furnaces, I burned and bled for days after. And when Suzanne ordered Dr. Cressman to remove the innocent embryo that grew inside of me, the scraping and suctioning felt like a dull knife sawing through my lower back. But as Michael opens the door and she stands before me...

face to face...

I realize that, until now...

until this very moment...

I've never really felt pain at all.

The church floor is cold against my cheek, ingrained with the scuffs and scratches of over a century of footsteps. The hemlock planks are even more primitive from this angle, where the nail holes of our ancestors are visible. I should have felt something when my body collapsed and slammed into the ancient wood. But as Michael lifts my head to his lap, I still feel nothing.

"You fainted," he says, raising me to a seated position while holding a cup of water to my lips. "Take a sip." Michael brushes the hair from my face. "I'm not going to try and justify what I did or give you any sorry excuses," he says. "I was lonely and I fucked up, and now I have to live with the consequences." His lips are still quivering and thick; white spit has collected in the corners of his mouth. "You should have never left, Danielle. You know I don't like to be alone."

The calendar on Michael's desk reads September 30. Twenty-eight years ago Becca and I sat across from each other, Indian-style, on the floor of our bedroom at the Garritys twin on 8th Street. It was an autumn day much like this, crisp and clear. From the open window, a light breeze still carried the sweet smell of honeysuckles and the melodic sounds of a cricket's wings. I ripped out the last match from a pack I took from the Garritys' kitchen drawer and swiped it against the flint strip until a bright flame erupted from the tip. With one hand cupped around the flame, I lit two candles on top of a Hostess Twinkie and placed it on a small plate between us. I shook the match, savored the aroma of the small puff of smoke that wafted through the air, and held my hands out to Becca, who positioned her small palms on mine. Every year I allowed Becca to make the very first birthday wish.

But that year was different.

She insisted.

So I obliged.

"Birthday candle burning bright, grant me what I wish to-night." Before closing my eyes, I looked at Becca, who stared up at me, wide-eyed, raising both eyebrows above her glasses and smiling as though waiting for something wonderful to happen. I shut my eyes, squeezed her hands, and took a deep breath. *I wish for a mommy and daddy...a real mommy and daddy...the kind who will read bedtime stories and make us eat spinach...it's the only wish I want...and I'll never ask for anything ever again.* It's ridiculous to think

that a birthday wish could really come true, but not long after the Whitekers came for me and left Becca behind kicking and screaming. Over the years, I've often wondered what Becca wished for that night. Maybe a doll or a hamster. I know she didn't wish for a mommy and daddy. I told her not to.

It takes me a few minutes to get to my feet.

"I don't need your help," I say, pulling my arm from Michael's grip. "Where is she?"

"I don't know," he says. "She left as soon as she saw you. Danielle, please sit down. You don't look so good."

"Where did she go?" I ask, stepping out the door to an empty parking lot. "Tell me where I can find her."

"I don't know, I swear. I don't know anything about her. She came here a couple of months ago asking for my help. She was troubled and thought that joining the church could save her. I never saw her before that."

My hands are tingling, and the saliva in my mouth is thickening on the back of my tongue. "Do you have any idea what you've done?" I ask, shaking my hands.

"It was one time, Danielle. I need you to know that. And yes, I hate myself for what I did, but I needed you and you weren't there. I didn't mean for this to happen."

It may be the cool air flowing from the air conditioner vent that is causing my skin to crawl, but most likely it's the flock of geese that have landed in the parking lot with a symphony of chatter.

"You say that like it was a fucking accident that couldn't be helped," I say, grabbing my keys. "I have to find her."

Michael takes hold of my arm. "Please don't," he pleads. "You don't know anything about this girl. She could be dangerous. Besides, this is my mess to clean up."

In the animal kingdom, the male goose searches and carefully chooses his mate, the one with whom he will share his journey, the one he will stand by for the rest of his life.

"That's where you're wrong, Michael," I say, looking past him to the geese that honk and lift their wings to flight. "I know a lot about that girl…it's you I don't know anything about." I take a cigarette from my bag, place it between my lips, and light up, something Michael would never approve of. "And by the way," I say, exhaling a cloud of smoke into his once virtuous office, "she's not a mess, you son of a bitch." The birds take to the sky in a *V* formation that points me to her.

"She's my sister."

24

BETHLEHEM, PENNSYLVANIA,
SEPTEMBER, 2008

The water below would feel like concrete if I hurled myself into it from this height. Perhaps I would lose consciousness when my body dropped from the ledge and tumbled through the air like a rag doll before colliding into the cold, dense surface. I'll admit it's not the first time I've thought about it, and from the look in Becca's eyes, I can tell it's not the first time she's thought of it either.

I knew I'd find her here, on top of the hill-to-hill bridge that runs through the heart of Bethlehem. It must be the unnerving essence of this city that repeatedly draws us back. As children, jumping off the bridge seemed like a viable option to all of us.

"The river can lead us away from here," Alfred once said, pointing to the water below. "It can take us someplace new and exciting." He leaned his scrawny chest over the rail of the bridge and watched the water flow by beneath him as Becca and I stood mesmerized by the mere possibility. "If we had a raft like Huck we could go anywhere," he said. His pink eyes widened beneath the brim of his baseball cap.

"Anywhere?" Becca asked.

"Yep," he answered.

Becca wiped her mouth and pushed the curls from her freckled face. "Could we go to Dithney World to thee Mickey Mouthe?" she asked.

"Yep," Alfred answered, bending farther over the ledge.

"Did you hear that, Danni?" Becca asked, tugging on my arm. "If we had a raft, we could go thee Mickey Mouthe! Can we get a raft, Danni? Huh? Can we? Can we?" Becca's curls bounced and bobbed as she jumped up and down. I smiled and stood closer to the ledge, closer to Alfred. He wouldn't say it if it weren't true. The wind gusted and blew several leaves from the trees. They danced on the sweeping breeze until resting gently on the river.

"Goddamn lucky leaves," Alfred said as the three of us stood and watched them sail away to a place unknown, a better place. It seemed so simple. Becca reached into her pocket, pulled something out, and held it in her grip.

"Thith is my favorite thtone," she said, opening her hand to reveal the smooth white rock. Her curls dangled and swayed as she reached out over the ledge and tossed it into the wind. "It's going to Dithney World," she said, watching it fall rapidly from the bridge. It took only seconds for the stone to plummet and sink into the water. "Where's my thtone?" Becca asked, waiting for it to resurface. "Where'd it go, Danni?" She stood on her tiptoes and leaned farther over the edge. "Why didn't it sail away with the leaves?"

"Stones don't float, Becca," I said, patting her shoulder.

"Well, I want it back!" she yelled, leaning over until the top half of her body outweighed the bottom. In an instant, Becca slipped over the edge, before I could scream out her name or wrap my arms around her. I would have lost her that day if it weren't for a rusty old rod protruding out from the side of the bridge that snagged her pant leg. It caught her just in time for me to reach over and pull her to safety.

"Don't you ever do that again, Becca," I said, grabbing her shoulders with both hands to look her dead in the eye. "Do you hear me?"

She nodded, swiped the back of her hand across her tear-filled eyes, and squeezed her bottom lip to stop it from trembling. "I'm thorry," she whispered.

"What if I couldn't save you?" I yelled. "What then? I can't always be here to save you!"

Becca stares out over the same ledge where she almost lost her life nearly thirty years ago. "You should have let me fall," she says, looking as innocent and helpless today as she did then. "I told you I'd get you back for what you did in Vegas," she says, leaning against the rail. "I told you." She pulls a rubber band from her hair and tosses it to the wind to watch it freefall into the water below.

"Please don't stand so close to the edge, Becca."

She shakes her head and unleashes a mound of curls that fall along her face and down her back. "What are you doing here, anyway?" she asks. "It's not your job to save me, Danni. Not then, not now. You said it yourself, remember? So if this newfound sisterhood is coming from a place of obligation, don't bother. I'm letting you off the hook."

The sun is deepening in color as the evening hour approaches. Orange rays stream through Becca's shimmering locks and light up her eyes the way they did on days when we played hopscotch until the last beams of sun dimmed into the night like a fire's final embers. Becca closes her eyes, arches her back, and reaches for the heel of her pump. With one hand, she slips it off her bare foot and tosses it over the rail. It splashes into the river and disappears for a moment before bobbing to the surface.

"I understand why you did it," I say, watching Becca do the same with the other shoe before unbuttoning her blouse and sliding it over each shoulder, seductively exposing her arms and bare breasts the way Rebecca Rose did on stage for an audience of hungry onlookers. "Did you hear me?" I ask, taking a few steps closer. "I understand why you seduced Michael." The words stick in the back of my mouth—hard to swallow, like the spoonfuls of sugar that Erma gave us to stop our hiccups. Back then I washed the sugar down with water, choking on the dry granules until they melted in my mouth. This I'll have to choke down with nothing more than a heaping dose of pride. Becca removes her shirt and holds it open to flap and flutter in the current of wind before sacrificing it to the freedom of the rushing water.

"Sergeant was an evil man," she mumbles, tilting her head from side to side with the shifting wind. Trails of blackened tears run down her neck, onto her naked breasts. "He did horrible things to me," she says. "I cried, but he wouldn't stop." Her blouse lands on top of the water and rides a drift out of town. "Getting pregnant was the only thing that ended it," she says. "That baby saved my life." She steps closer to the metal railing, presses her bare stomach against the cool steel, and leans over until her curls swing loosely above the fifty-foot drop.

"Jake was the best thing I ever did," she says, succumbing to an onslaught of irrepressible sobbing. "Regardless of how he came to be, it was like something right came from something so wrong." She spreads her arms out in the open space. "That'th why I had to let him go," she says, lifting her arms like geese preparing for flight. "So that he would never know. So that he would have a chance at a better life. It was my way of returning the favor." She straightens her arms so she can soar. "But none of that matters now because I ruined him anyway." After every sentence, Becca sucks in a burst of air. "I robbed him of his innocence and got paid to do it," she cries, swallowing hard before the wretched memory of that night forces her stomach to contract and expel a yellowish-brown fluid. "All I ever wanted was to protect him."

"It's my fault, Becca," I say, reaching for her. "None of this would have happened if I had left you alone."

Becca rips her arm away. "I can't live with thith, Danni! Let me go!" Her toes lift from the ground, shifting the bulk of her weight over the rail.

"Becca, you're all that I have," I say, grabbing her waist and pressing into the soft tissue that surrounds her navel until my nails pierce her flesh and release a trickle of blood that to my fingertips is eerily warm and familiar. "Please don't, I can't hold on much longer!" The bridge is empty for this time of day, unusually so. If it weren't for the sound of a car horn that blares in the distance, I would think the city was deserted, that we were the only two left. Becca's face deepens to purple as blood courses through the vein that bulges up along the side of her neck, supplying the very sustenance she needs to fire off her next words.

"I'm pregnant," she says, altering her sharp tone so that each word is soft and smooth enough to slip through my ears. "With Jake's or Michael's baby."

I've often heard that a rush of adrenaline can generate superhuman strength. But as Becca kicks her legs up over the rail, I feel nothing. As her bare torso scrapes down the side of the jagged concrete bridge, I feel numb.

No added strength.

No extra might, as she slides through my fingers.

Her waist.

Her legs.

Her feet.

I saved Becca once, on this very bridge, but as I watch her fall, her golden curls tangling around her limbs that plummet and flail through the air, it becomes painfully obvious that letting her go then may have saved all of us a hell of a lot more now.

25

Dr. Janet moved me here, to room 5B, after I screamed so loud the patients down the hall complained. We're not allowed to have sharp objects on the fifth floor, and the orderly keeps our nails trimmed short so that skin gouging is impossible. No knives, no forks, no spoons. Nothing to take the pain away or make the voices stop. For now, I eat with my bare hands. No strings of any kind are permitted. No shoelaces, no cords, no dental floss, and absolutely no glass star dangling in the window. Dr. Janet sets her pen down on her clipboard and removes her glasses.

"I know that it's painful for you to relive all of this, Danni, but it's crucial for your recovery."

"I tried to stop her," I say, rubbing my wrists where the thick leather straps have left an annoying irritation. "I held on as long as I could. I didn't want her to fall, regardless of what she did with my husband. You believe me, right?"

Dr. Janet stands and brushes her hands over her pantsuit to straighten the wrinkles. "Do you remember anything after that, Danni?" she asks.

"Bits and pieces," I say, noticing the clumps of hair scattered across my lap. "Trees, lots of them, and a storm, the kind that Erma taught us about. There's a difference, ya know."

"A difference?" she asks, gathering her things to end our session. "A difference in what?"

"In storms. The kind you play outside in and the kind you take shelter from."

Dr. Janet raises an eyebrow and hands me a small blue pill with a cup of water. "Are you speaking literally or metaphorically?" she asks.

I gather the hair into a large clump, toss it to the floor, and watch it tumble to safety beneath a rolling chest of drab white drawers that match the grotesquely yellowed walls.

No print. No design.

If insanity had a color, this would be it.

"Danni, we've been meeting for weeks and you've made tremendous progress, but I believe you're blocking something, perhaps from your childhood." She grabs my forearms, holds them out in front of me, and points to the trails of scar tissue that map my life. "Whatever it is," she says, squeezing my arms with a frustration she hasn't exhibited before, "caused this."

"I've told you all that I remember," I say, yanking back my arms while flinching to a pain that shoots through my abdomen like an alarm, alerting me of my empty womb. I wish they had taken it all, every female organ that has failed me.

"Where's Becca? Is she all right? Is her baby OK?"

"Her doctors will let us know when you can see her, but right now you need to focus on yourself. I'm trying to help you, Danni."

"Is this what you call help?" I ask, tugging on the leather straps attached to the bed rails.

"Precautionary measures, that's all," she says, tilting her head to one side and then the other until her neck cracks loud enough for me to hear. "I think it's time that you see something." She opens the closet and removes a cardboard box. On the fifth floor, boxes are sealed shut with small pieces of duct tape that are much too short to engineer an effective noose. "This is for you," she says, handing me the box that has a familiar name printed on the side in permanent black marker. "It's hospital policy that all personal items of the deceased be left to the closest family member."

Dr. Janet's voice becomes soft and muffled, fading into some sort of parallel existence that briefly shields me from the initial blow as I stare at the name on the side of the box. "I'm sorry, Danni," she says. "Amy Hoffman was a patient of mine, on and off the fifth floor for many years. She returned about a month ago with one of her worst bouts of mania ever."

I always wondered how I would react on this day. I suppose somewhere deep inside I knew that eventually the news would come. I just wasn't sure how it would feel, like a bag of bricks to the stomach or a ten-ton cross lifted off my back. As usual, the mention of her name sparks a visceral reaction, shocking and painful, like plunging into an electrically charged pool of water.

"Yeah, well, I'm not interested in any of her things," I say, pushing the box back. "She never wanted anything to do with me or my sister anyway."

Dr. Janet lifts her head, slow and thoughtful. "Shortly after she arrived last month," she says, "one of the nurses found her, lifeless, curled up in the corner of the room clutching an old photograph." She places the worn-out picture in my hand. "It was one of several snapshots she carried with her at all times." As hard as I try, I am unable to resist the natural impulse to coil my fist around the tattered photo.

"So how'd she die anyway?" I ask, searching for the courage to look.

Dr. Janet leans against the side of the bed. "Her doctor couldn't pinpoint a cause." She lifts her fingers to form quotes in the air. "Complications," she says, and folds her arms across her chest. "Broken hearts lead to broken spirits, Danni. I'm afraid modern science doesn't recognize either as terminal."

I bear down on the picture until my knuckles are mottled in red-and-white blotches. "So I guess you expect me to be upset, right? After all, she was my mother, so you're waiting for me to show some sort of emotion, like crying or sulking or something?"

In moments like this, Dr. Janet's expertise shines through. She is quiet when she needs to be. And still.

"Well, don't hold your breath, Doctor. It's really not a big deal," I add, using Dr. Janet as a sounding board to convince myself. "I barely even knew her, so I won't miss her and I could care less about some stupid picture she carried around."

Fueled by denial, I lift my fingers to the faded image that my mother held when she took her last breath. In spite of its condition, I can see it well: Becca and me playing hopscotch in front of the Garritys house. My hair is unkempt, longer than I remember, and my pants are much too short for my adolescent limbs. Becca is standing on one foot hopping onto block number two. She is smiling, probably laughing. But there was nothing funny about foster care, or the Garrity house, so I'm not.

"Where did she get this?" I ask as the voices begin to murmur, secretly chattering as the geese did on the day they took her away. "Tell me where she got this from!"

Dr. Janet pulls a pen from behind her ear and stabs the top of the box. "She took many pictures of you and your sister over the years," she says, and she drags the tip of the pen through the cardboard, ripping apart each piece of tape until the flaps spring open. "She was closer than you think Danni, but how she managed to stay so close and go undetected is still a mystery to me." She tucks the pen behind her ear and, with one swift move, dumps the contents of the box into my lap. "I have a lot of questions about Amy Hoffman," she says, poking through the items for clues, "most of which will remain unanswered, I suppose."

I should tell Dr. Janet that the voices are back. I should press my hands over my ears and scream their words louder than they do. *Close your eyes! Don't look back! Close your eyes! Don't look back!* And I should tell her that the brown-hooded coat lying in my lap has triggered an emotional landslide that a little blue pill can't stop.

Dr. Janet lifts the coat up by the shoulders. "She was wearing this when she died," she says. "There's a name written on the tag inside. Does the name Garrity mean anything to you?"

She points to the frayed label where the ink print, barely legible, has blurred to purple. On the fifth floor, it's important to keep calm because any emotion, no matter what the catalyst, can be interpreted as crazy.

"No, nothing," I lie. Dr. Janet draws both lips inward, squints her eyes, and nods, an expression of disbelief that I've come to recognize.

"I believe that something traumatic happened to Amy years ago," she says. "But no matter how hard I tried, I could never get her to speak of it. I wouldn't be surprised if her tragedy somehow ties to you."

I steady my hands on the coat, squeeze until the coarse fabric fills both hands, and fight to contain the significance of the Garrity name.

"Don't be afraid to confront your past, Danni. It may be the only thing that can save you."

"But what about Becca?" I ask, trying to distract myself from the onslaught of stimuli that have triggered the voices to erupt in force. *Close your eyes! Don't look back! Close your eyes! Don't look back!*

"Please, I need to see my sister."

"It was a bad fall, Danni. She's being closely monitored. I can assure you that they're doing everything they can for both her and her unborn child. I want you to concentrate on your health right now. You'll see her soon." Dr. Janet tucks the wrist restraints up under the bed. "I'll let the nurses know you won't be needing these any longer. Oh, one more thing," she says before exiting. "I have a group therapy session scheduled for tomorrow morning. I'd like you to come."

I nod, as much to dismiss her as to acknowledge her request. Erma didn't believe me when I told her about the coat lady. I wasn't sure I believed myself. I lift the weathered cloth to my cheek.

"It was Mom," I whisper, embracing the cloak she hid beneath to watch Becca and me from a distance. Evening is approaching. I wrap Mom's coat around my shoulders and settle into the night. Slipping my arms into the sleeves, as she would have. Pressing my hands into the pockets, as she did. I hated her. Or so I thought. But for every ounce of hate, there was an equal longing, a thirst unquenched, a hunger unfed. The weight of the garment envelops me like a warm hug, and in some strange way I find myself feeling closer to her in death than I ever did in life. The woman I visited not long ago was Amy Hoffman, but the spirit of this coat is Mom. I'm not sure which is more surprising, her gentle scent that seems to waft from the woven fibers or the discovery of my old journal buried in the bottom of the right pocket. It's baffling how Amy could have found it and how, after all these years, the leather has aged well, the pages barely worn, barely yellowed. For all that it reminded me of and for all that it contained, I never wanted to see it again.

I run my fingers across the tan, velvety cover, up the spine, and down the smooth golden edges of precisely stacked parchment. I was sixteen when I wrote my only entry, the night I gave myself to Eric Seton in front of the fiery furnaces. It seemed the voices screamed louder than ever that night, demanding to be heard. So I wrote for hours in the dark, releasing everything they said. Everything. No matter how shameful or wicked. I wrap Mom's coat around me tighter, open the journal, and turn to page one. It was a tragedy that went down in history that the people of Bethlehem would never forget. I never remembered it. Or read about it. Because I lived it. I just never had the courage to admit it.

Until now.

Bethlehem Hotel, 1975, Room 932…
"Don't be such a pussy! Just fuck her and get it over with!"

I pretend not to hear the man who turns
red when he yells.

I crouch down in the corner of the room.

Behind the table.

Me and my doll, Cindy.

He is a bad man.

Everything inside tells me so.

He reaches for me.

"Come here, baby girl."

I wrap my Cindy doll in a blanket, lay her
on my shoulder, and act like I don't notice
him lurking over me.

Mom is on the bed.

Naked.

Breathing heavy.

"It's all right," the man says. "I'm your
daddy."

The man has short brown hair, shaved up
the sides, flat on top, and a neatly ironed
shirt that matches the color of his tan,
creased pants. He kept his clothes on
when he ordered Mom to undress and get
on the bed. I rocked Cindy to sleep to the
rhythm of the bedsprings. When he was
done, he pulled up his pants as quickly
as he dropped them. He didn't wrinkle
at all, and he made sure to wipe off the
thick, white fluid that dripped from his
penis onto his shiny black shoes.

"Go ahead and fuck her, Bobby! Now's your chance! Don't blow it!"

Cindy starts to cry.

I hold her.

The way Mom holds me.

I'm four years old.

I won't look at him.

Or the man he calls Bobby.

"It'th not right, Johnny," Bobby says, struggling to speak normally from a disfigured mouth that forces him not to. The bad man clasps his hands behind his back, lifts his head, and pushes his chest and chin out.

"From now on you will refer to me as Sergeant! Got that, soldier? Now grow some balls and do what I say!"

He places his hands beneath my arms and lifts me to his waist. "Come here, baby girl. Daddy's got you."

Cindy cries louder.

He doesn't care that she's frightened or that the gold ring on his finger is pressing into the fragile skin on the underside of my arm. He wraps my legs around him and pulls me closer.

Our stomachs touch.

And I smell a nauseating blend of sweat and aftershave radiating off his skin.

The lights go off.

"Mommy!"

He presses his lips to my ear.

"Ssshhhh."

His breath is hot.

And the room is black.

I tangle my fingers in Cindy's hair and listen for Mom.

"It's OK, Danni," she says. "Everything's going to be all right."

He pulls me closer.

Holds me tighter.

"Mommy!"

Feet shuffle across the carpet, quick and heavy.

"Do it now, Bobby! She's fucking waiting for it!"

A belt is unbuckled.

And a zipper pulls quickly through its teeth.

Mom takes a deep breath, and the bed squeaks from the added weight.

The headboard knocks against the wall.

Pounding into a steady tempo.

"Harder!" he yells.

Cindy cries louder, and I pull her hair until it snaps off at the roots.

Grunting, groaning.

Mom stifles her screams, fighting to keep her lips together more than her legs.

Breathing, panting.
The man wraps his arms around me and watches in the light that filters through the curtain from the street lamps outside.
"That's it, soldier! Let her have it!"
He slides his hand along my spine.
Down the small of my back.
Into my pants.
I'm four years old.
I take a deep breath.
And hold my lips together tight.
Like Mom.
He slips his hand beneath my favorite underwear, purple with pink hearts, and runs his fingers over my bare buttocks.
Another deep breath.
Mom grabs the bedpost and squeezes until her knuckles turn white. A tear rolls down from the corner of her eye, and a glass of water on the bedside table tips over and crashes to the floor. The bad man pushes his hand farther down my pants and stops at the soft spot between my legs.
He's not my daddy.
I don't have one.
Never did.
I take another breath and hold it.

Mom's legs are forced farther apart. "Danni, close your eyes!" she demands, "Don't look back!"

He brushes his warm, wet lips across the side of my face. "Close your eyes. Don't look back," he mimics.

His fingers are warm, too.

He rubs until I'm sore.

Groaning like the man on top of Mom.

Parting his fingers to spread me open.

Entering a place I didn't know existed.

I'd close my eyes if I could.

Like Mom told me to do.

But my eyes grow wide with the pain that shoots through me, burning, stabbing, and throbbing.

One final groan for them.

One last breath for us.

The lights come on, and Mom quivers on the bed as Bobby rolls off, removes his brown hooded coat, and covers her with it. With his pants still around his ankles, he shuffles to the window, opens it, and without hesitation, dives from the ninth floor, headfirst, screaming louder than the sirens that follow.

Louder than the steel.

Mom stands, wraps the coat around her,
and pulls the hood up over her head. She
looks nothing like the Mom I knew.
I close my eyes before she looks at me.
So she won't know what I saw.
Or what I did.
It was wrong.
All of it.
I'm only four years old.
But I know it.

It's never quiet on the fifth floor. No one here sleeps. Across the hall, a small bald-headed man yells out the time every five minutes and an anorexic girl hides behind her door, sneaking in hours of jumping jacks from the night-shift nurses. By morning she'll have racked up thousands, more than enough to cover the calorie count of breakfast and lunch put together. From my room, I can hear her breathing pattern, two jacks on every breath in, two jacks out. She'll jump about three hundred times before the little man's next time proclamation.

"Four fifty!"

And I'll read the journal entry again.

"Four fifty-five!"

And again.

Until the story sinks in and the voices stop for good.

"Five o'clock!" he shouts as the clock ticks to the number five in declaration of my revolting and shameful revelation. I pull the coat hood up over my head, the way my mother did all those years, and flip through the remaining empty journal sheets, stopping at the last page where a bloodied pane of stained glass has been tucked into the binding to mark Mom's only entry.

> He begged, he screamed, he tried to run,
> and so began his setting sun.
> Gored his flesh with raptured ease,
> Satan's soldier to his knees.

Amy chose her weapon carefully, from the Moravian star that hung above her door, razor-sharp and symbolic of where she lived and died. Using her weapon as a pen, she wrote in the blood of the man she loved and murdered.

Sergeant John Garrity.

My father.

"Hi, it's me, Danni.

"Please don't say anything.

"Just listen.

"Something terrible has happened.

"I don't know where to begin except to say that I'm scared and I need you, now more than ever.

"I have to ask you something.

"If you say no, I'll understand.

"Can you come back?

"Please?

"I need you here.

"In Bethlehem."

"Danni, I'm sorry to wake you, but it's urgent."

For a moment I convince myself I'm dreaming, that the nurse tapping on my shoulder doesn't really exist. If I could, I would stay in this safe place forever where life is manageable. It's unfortunate that my body will soon wake and catch up to my mind, reuniting both my physical and mental states. The two are difficult enough, but when the emotional state joins in, it can be devastating. And like every other morning of my life, I'll have to figure out how to handle today without dwelling on yesterday or anticipating tomorrow.

"Danni, Dr. Janet asked me to wake you," the nurse says. "It's regarding your sister, Becca. You can see her now."

The sound of her name is like a flaming bullet that shoots through my abdomen, entering below my navel and ricocheting through my vacant uterus before exiting out my lower back.

"Now?" I ask, jolting up to a seated position, uncertain I heard correctly.

"Yes, now. She's in intensive care; we need to hurry. I'm afraid we don't have much time."

With the nurse's assistance, I stagger from bed into the wheelchair parked beside it.

"What do you mean we don't have much time?" I ask, embracing the warmth of Mom's coat around me. The nurse leads me out into the hallway where patients are lined up for their morning shower wearing hospital socks and green gowns that open up the back. She stops in front of an elevator and presses an illuminated button to the second floor. The doors open, she wheels me in, and the two of us listen to the soft music that escorts us to the intensive care unit.

"Your sister suffered massive injuries from the fall," she says before the doors part. "They managed to keep her alive long enough to give her baby a fighting chance."

Soft music shouldn't be allowed in the elevator going to the second floor where bad news comes as fast and loud as the onslaught of monitors and respirators. Each bed is filled with an elderly patient, well on in years. Except for one, where Becca lies. The nurse rolls me up to her bed. "They're taking the baby today, Danni," she says. "You'll have to say your good-byes." She draws the curtain closed around Becca's bed. "I'll leave you alone."

If it weren't for a few remaining scratches, she would be flawless, appearing more like a sleeping child than a dying woman. I place her hand in mine, palm to palm, the way we did for birthday wishes.

"How did we get here, Becca?" I ask, stroking her soft, blond curls. "How did everything go so wrong?" With the back of my hand, I caress the freckled curves of her face. "Like chocolate sprinkles on a vanilla ice cream cone," I say, unable to force a smile. "It shouldn't be like this. You deserved a happy ending." I squeeze her hand.

"Can you hear me, Becca?" I squeeze again. "I'm here—can you hear me?" Her hand is cool and unresponsive. I close my eyes to picture the way she was when she was five, the way I've held her in my heart all these years. I can see her clearly.

"Danni?" she asks, gazing up at me with her soulful eyes. "Can you thing me the ant song?" She jumps up and down, tugging on my shirt for a reply. "Pretty pleathe, with a cherry on top?" She is happy and breathless with excitement.

"Sure, Becca," I answer, kneeling down to her level. "I'll do anything for you." Becca throws her arms around my neck and kisses my cheek. Her breath is warm and smells like sugar. "Anything."

I open my eyes to the subtle movement of Becca's bulging abdomen. Laying my palms on her stomach brings a gentle kick from the child living inside, a child Jake or Michael could never accept. Either would be ruined. The shame alone would destroy them. How worthy is a reverend who succumbs to the very temptations he preaches against? And how reprehensible is a young man who impregnates his own mother. The baby kicks again. At a time like this, nothing else could make me smile. Becca said she wanted revenge. But nothing could be further from the truth. This isn't revenge at all.

"You wanna know something?" I say, speaking over the methodical whoosh of the ventilator so her unborn child can hear. "Your mommy and I used to make the best mud pies ever. We'd pat the mud down in a bowl just like this." I tap my hand on Becca's stomach. "Then we'd flip it over and sprinkle sand on top like a fine sugar coating. We didn't care how messy it was or how dirty we got. We'd play for hours sometimes, until the sun set and the mud dried hard on our skin." I rest my head on my sister's fertile womb and wrap my arms around both of them. "One day, I'll teach you how to make mud pies, too," I say, watching Becca's chest rise and fall with each push from the bedside machine.

Michael often preached about how God giveth and he taketh away, like there was some sort of justifiable balance to His divine plan. It infuriated me that he made it sound so logical, because in my lifetime, He taketh so much more than he gave.

"Excuse me," a nurse says, peeking her head through the parted curtains. "I'm sorry, but it's time."

"Just one more minute. Please."

The nurse nods, busies herself with another patient, and pretends not to notice me climbing into bed next to Becca. I lay my head beside her, the way we did for bedtime stories.

"I found Mom, Becca," I say, opening Amy's coat to let Becca in. "Just like I said I would." Her appearance, as angelic as the day she was born, masks all the years in between. "She loved us and she would have stayed if things hadn't gone so wrong. I know she would have." The curtain waves and the nurse clears her throat. "I would have stayed too, Becca," I say, hoping she'll hear me. "I need you to know that I never meant to leave you." I look at Becca, mentally tracing every feature so that I'll never forget. If life came with a rulebook, older sisters would die first. If Erma were here, she'd tell me that everything happens for a reason and that good can come from bad if you let it. So in honor of Erma and my little sister,

I sing.

Just what makes that little ole' ant…

In Becca's final hour.

Think he can move that rubber tree plant…

As the clock on the wall ticks into a new day.

Anyone knows an ant…can't…move a rubber tree plant…

Because I need my sister to know.

But he's got high hopes…he's got high hopes…

That I'm here.

He's got high apple pie in the sky hopes...

Finally.

So anytime you're feelin' low...'stead of lettin' go...just remember that ant...

Physically, mentally, and emotionally.

Oops, there goes another rubber tree...oops, there goes another rubber tree...

Thanks to Becca and the miracle growing inside of her.

Oops, there goes another rubber tree plant.

I'm actually here.

Dr. Janet's meeting room is at the end of the hall. I've never believed in therapy, but on the fifth floor it's protocol, one of many unpleasantries, like cavity searches, cold showers, and in my case, identifying the deceased body of my next of kin. There were only minutes between the time of Becca's death and her child's birth.

Minutes.

I wondered if they used the same ink on both cer-
tificates, and I wondered how I would ever be the mother Becca would have been. Becca's daughter was born
at 6:32 a.m. as the sun was rising on Bethlehem. The
city was stunning, and the star on the mountain shone
brighter than ever before. I named her Rose, and I held
her for as long as I was allowed. When I returned to my
room, I brushed my teeth, combed my hair, and put on
fresh clothes for the first time since I arrived.

Dr. Janet waves me into the room where chairs have
been bolted to the floor in a circle, eight to be exact,
with the doctor being the beginning and ending point.
The third chair is empty between a woman who won't
stop giggling and an older gentleman who keeps pulling
up his socks.

"Welcome, Danni," Dr. Janet says, pointing to the vacant seat. "Please, sit down. I'm glad you decided to join
us."

"Thank you."

The walls and woodwork in the therapy room are
painted lavender like an endless field of lilacs. If this
were yesterday, it would have annoyed the hell out of
me that on the fifth floor color is intentionally limited
to this room, as though to promote sanity here and nowhere else. But this is a new day.

"I'm happy to be here."

Dr. Janet raises her eyebrows and looks to the others in
the room. "Everyone, this is Danni. Please welcome her."

I sit to a flurry of welcomes and nods.

"So how are you feeling this morning?" she asks in a way that indicates she knows the answer already.

"Better, thanks. A little anxious, I guess," I answer, thinking of how, in spite of everything, Becca entrusted me with her child, naming me sole guardian in a will that she made the day before the accident, as though she planned it all. She never named the birth father. In a twisted way, Becca gave me something that I always wanted but could never have. I fan my face with a tissue to cool the sudden heat that rushes up behind it.

"It's amazing what a day can bring," I say.

Dr. Janet signals a patient to begin the group introduction. "Well, we're here to support you in any way we can."

"Yes, of course," I say, responding to the curious stares with a forced, flat smile.

"I know you had a difficult night, Danni, but if you have anything you'd like to share, this would be a good time."

I tear the tissue in half and then in half again, ripping it into small pieces while gathering enough courage to get this off my chest. "Actually, I do have something I'd like to say."

It's my turn.

All eyes rest on me as I look up from the shredded tissue scattered across my lap.

It's my turn to tell the others in the room about myself.

I hesitate.

Clear my throat.

Swallow hard.

And begin...

"My name is Danielle Hoffman Pane.

"I was born here, in the small industrial town of Bethlehem, Pennsylvania.

"Not far from the old steel plant.

"I never had a father.

"And my mother went crazy.

"Oh...

"One more thing...

"I'm a murderer."

Dr. Janet's pen dances across her notepad. One could hear a pin drop in the silence that follows.

So I laugh.

Just a little.

Enough to end the silence and make the woman beside me start giggling again.

"How's that for sharing, Doctor?"

"You've had many tragic losses in your life, Danni. None of which are your fault. It's very common for misplaced guilt to stem from a dysfunctional and abusive childhood."

Dr. Janet knew what she was doing when she chose this lavender room. Maybe it's the serene pastel hue causing this unexplainable bliss that allows me to let down my walls.

"I appreciate your analysis, Doctor, but there's no clinical explanation you can give me that will change the way I feel. It's just something I have to live with, that's all."

Dr. Janet crosses her arms. "There's a fine line between what you have to live with and what you choose to live with, Danni."

On the fifth floor, it's common to experience a wide range of emotions, laughing one minute and crying the next, but there is a heightened sensation surging through me. Something I've seldom experienced before.

"You're right," I say, delighted by an overwhelming anticipation that has my heart racing. "Life is about choices, and I've made many that I regret. But things are going to be different now. I'm leaving here with a little girl who, because of me, will never know her mother. I don't know how I'll ever make that up to her, but I choose to spend the rest of my life trying. And because of that, I feel more alive than ever, like I have a second chance to be there, for Becca."

"Everyone needs a purpose in life, Danni. It sounds like you've found one."

It's late autumn in Bethlehem. Even the steel bars on the fifth floor windows can't stop the intensity of the seasoned sun. It blankets the lilac walls and illuminates all that is white.

"Maybe you're right, Dr. Janet," I say, noticing the brilliance of a familiar face that appears in the lavender door window. "Or maybe I've found two."

With feelings like this, I should have known she was near. Her beauty is palpable, second only to her mystique.

Dr. Janet glances back and forth between us. "Do you know her?" she asks as I smile and stand to see her clearly. But I won't answer. Alexa is my secret. She belongs to me. Silently, I form words with my lips, a technique that Alfred and I mastered in the Garrity house.

"You came," I mouth from across the room. Staring into Alexa's eyes has never lost its magic, comforting and thrilling at the same time. "Will you wait for me?" I ask.

She tilts her head the way Alfred did when he waited at the base of the Whitekers' maple tree. I would have followed him anywhere that night.

Without a moment of hesitation, Alexa responds.

"This time, forever."

26

THE GARRITY HOUSE, OCTOBER, 2008, THIRTY-SEVEN YEARS OLD

"I t's the first stop on the road to the rest of our lives," Alexa says, sliding the key into the doorknob. As promised, she stayed in Bethlehem until Dr. Janet discharged me from the hospital. The nurse placed Amy's box in my lap and baby Rose in my arms, and wheeled us out to the curb where Alexa stood in front of her car. She handed me two sunflowers, one for each of us, then drove straight here, to the Garritys' vacant twin on 8th Street.

"Are you sure you want to do this?" I ask, holding baby Rose snug against my chest.

Alexa brushes her hand through my hair, separating my auburn strands with her pale fingers. She takes a deep breath and pulls the brim of her baseball cap down low on her platinum brow. I can see Alfred today in everything she does. In spite of how hard she's tried to leave him behind, he's still here, chin up, chest out, shoulders back, stomach in, the way he was taught. She turns the key and opens the door.

"I've never been more sure about anything in my life," she says, tightening her jawbone until it waves beneath her milky skin.

Alexa didn't say a word on our drive here. Somewhere in the silence that can be awkward between two people, we found comfort. Alexa wraps her hand around mine, and we enter.

"Are you scared?" I ask, flinching as the screen door slams shut behind us.

Alexa hesitates for a moment in the doorway. I pretend not to notice her bottom lip quivering or the whites of her eyes turning as pink as the center.

"Nope," she says, squeezing my hand with a strength young Alfred never possessed. "Are you?"

I lift baby Rose and touch my lips to her forehead.

"No," I answer. "Not anymore."

Alexa walks to the kitchen and removes a can of lighter fluid and a pack of matches from the cabinet, precisely where Sergeant left them. There's a four-leaf clover on the box of Sergeant's "lucky" matches that he once used to light the cigar that would "burn the faggot" out of Alfred. I heard his flesh sizzle beneath the ash that day and watched the bottom of his foot turn from red to white before Sergeant allowed him to put ice on it. I never saw flesh bubble up like that before, but I noted the suffering it caused for weeks to follow.

Enough, I thought, to make the voices in my head go away forever. But as I've come to learn, nothing but the cold hard truth will shut them up for good.

Alexa douses the sofa and curtains with the flammable liquid, squirting it up and down the steps that lead to the bedrooms. If Becca were here, she would want this, too.

"There's not going to be anything left," Alexa says, standing before the basement door, holding the can out in front of her as Alfred held the gun to Sergeant. She shoots the last of the fluid at the door to saturate it completely, then takes us outside, swipes a "lucky" match across the flint strip, and tosses it into the living room before pulling the door closed.

"It's over," she says, leading us to a safe spot on the sidewalk. Side by side we watch the curtains ignite into brilliant flames that contrast the sapphire sky and heat up the autumn night. Or maybe it's Alexa again, standing so near that makes me this warm. This safe.

"We can be together now, Danni," she says. Her voice is soft and reassuring, hovering somewhere between a man and a woman. "We can go anywhere and start over, where no one knows about us, or any of this. Somehow we can make it work. I know we can."

As Alexa's car idles on the street behind us, the Garrity house bursts into flames and sirens sound in the distance. I look at baby Rose, asleep in my arms, perfect from head to toe, deserving of a life her mother never had. Alexa reaches into her pocket, pulls out a handful of sunflower seeds, and holds them out as an offering. "So what do you think?" she asks, grinning with one corner of her mouth lifted slightly higher than the other. "We don't have much time, Danni." Her eyes deepen to red with the infusion of the orange blaze.

"But where will we go?" I ask.

Alexa shrugs her shoulders long and hard the way Alfred used to, taking a moment to reflect before answering.

"Wherever this goddamned city wind takes us," she says, half laughing.

Overhead, a flock of snow geese blanket the sky like a fluffy white cloud, directed and guided by a changing current. When I was ten years old, I fell in love with Alfred. I trusted him. So much has changed. And yet nothing at all.

Ours is not a typical love story.

Never has been.

Never will be.

Some will call it a sin.

But love is love, right?

How could anything bad come of that?

I stare into Alexa's eyes and watch the reflection of the sun dip into the horizon.

"You're safe now," I say, removing her hat to expose her skin to the gentle dusk. Her hair spills down and frames her face like a fresh white canvas.

"Danni?"

"Yeah?"

"I have to tell you something."

I cover her mouth with my hand and allow the tears I've held back for years to finally fall.

"I love you, too," I say, lifting my fingers from her lips. Alexa smiles with one tooth protruding slightly out from the others.

Perfectly imperfect.

Still.

I toss Amy's box into the inferno and race Alexa to the car, crying and laughing at the same time. With sirens screaming toward us and embers of our past wafting high above the city of steel...

we drive...

we cry...

and we let it fucking burn.

THE END

ABOUT THE AUTHOR

 Sharon Lee Villone is a proud mother of two children and has lived in the Lehigh Valley for twenty-five years. After working as a private business owner, aerobics instructor, and columnist, she took a position at the Hotel Bethlehem. There, she learned quite a bit about the history of the city—including the rise and fall of one of the world's largest steel plants and the paranormal activity said to haunt Bethlehem to this day.

Villone's debut novel, Harness the Storm, is inspired by the essence and soul of the "steel city," as well as a whirlwind of emotional turmoil the author has faced in her own life.

Made in the USA
Middletown, DE
30 April 2017